Joseph Telushkin
and Allen Estrin

HEAVEN'S WITNESS

The Toby Press

First Edition 2004

The Toby Press LLC
POB 8531, New Milford, CT. 06676-8531, USA
& POB 2455, London WIA 5WY, England
www.tobypress.com

ISBN I 59264 090 7, *hardcover*

A CIP catalogue record for this title is
available from the British Library

Typeset in Garamond by Jerusalem Typesetting

Printed and bound in the United States
by Thomson-Shore Inc., Michigan

For Ron Temkin, the most generous of friends, and a man of unending kindness—Joseph Telushkin

For Susan, who makes everything possible—Allen Estrin

Contents

He has dug a pit and hollowed it
and then fell into the ditch which he made.
His mischief will return upon his own head,
and on his own skull
his violence will come down.

Psalm 7:16–17

Prologue

San Fernando Valley, 1970

She had a simple plan—isolate Daddy from Pudding Face, get the answer she needed, and then split.

At 2:30, she saw her chance. Her mother had gone to the back of the house to do laundry, leaving Daddy alone in the kitchen with his *Daily News*. She pulled a carton of orange juice from the fridge, poured herself a small glass and watched him carefully. His glasses were perched on the tip of his nose, his face pushed against the stock market tables in the business section. In a casual voice, she asked if she could meet her friends after rehearsal. Without even glancing up, he inquired where this rendezvous would occur.

"A place called Hamburger Heaven," she said between sips.

"Hamburger Heaven? Never heard of it. Where is it?"

"It's... you know... around here. They have great fries."

"Uh huh," he nodded, his attention focused on the paper.

And then from behind her. "Hamburger Heaven. Isn't that in Malibu?" It was her mother's voice—that nasal whine that drove her crazy. *What the hell is she doing here? She'll ruin everything.*

Her father snapped back the newspaper, reversing the crease.

"Why do you want to go to Malibu?" her mother pressed.

13

"A few friends are meeting there later. That's all."

"Which friends?"

"Friends. A few friends. I just told you that." She turned back to her father. "How are your stocks doing, Daddy?"

"And how are you planning to get there?" her mother asked, as she reached under the sink for some fabric softener.

"I was going to drive. Daddy's not working today, so—"

"Sounds okay to me," her father answered, his face back in the paper. "Just be careful, Sweetie."

"Thanks, Daddy!"

"Bill, I don't think she should be on those winding canyon roads at night. She just got her license six months ago."

"But Daddy just said I could," she protested, her voice louder than she intended.

Her father looked up from the paper, his brow furrowed with second thoughts. "Mom has a point, Pip."

"I know how to drive. I can be careful on winding roads."

"If it was during the day, honey," her mother said, "it would be different. But it's just too dangerous at night. Not just the roads, the people out there too."

"Too dangerous?" she said, shouting now. "Everything I ever want to do is too dangerous. Why don't you keep me locked up in this house? Then you'd never have to worry."

Her mother paled. The fabric softener slipped out of her hands and dropped onto her foot. She glared over at her husband as she bent down to pick it up.

"Now, Pip," her father cautioned. "I don't like to hear you talking to your mother that way."

Her younger brother Peter came in, holding a basketball under his arm. "What's everybody shouting about?"

"Go back outside," her mother snapped.

"Geez, what did I do?"

"You heard your mother." Peter rolled his eyes and did an about face. "I think the best plan," her father resumed, his tone patient, his approach logical, "is for you to come home after the rehearsal. As it is, it won't end till almost eight. Then, once you get home, you can

14

stay up talking to your friends as late as you want—burn up that new phone line we got you."

"But every single person who means anything to me is going to be there, and I'm going to be left out. How do you expect me to belong to any group, to keep any friends? Do anything? How?"

She could see her dad waver. *Maybe, just maybe*, she thought. But then she saw him look at Pudding Face.

"Just come home," he finally said.

She wanted to scream.

"Pip," her father said. "Come on, now."

She looked up at her mother's soft features, the pudgy little nose, the flat cheeks. This was all her fault.

"I'm just worried about your safety, honey," her mother said in a low voice, trying to underplay her small victory.

She stood in place, chewing on her thumb. The skin around her nail was already bloodied from her picking.

"Now that that's settled," her mother announced, "should I make a parfait for dessert tonight?"

Instead of answering, she tore the final piece of flesh from her thumb, and ran out of the room.

*

As soon as the rehearsal wrapped, she ran to the bank of pay phones that stood against the east wall of the school lobby. She dropped change into the slot, and prayed that her father would answer. He did. "The rehearsal is running very late, Daddy. Mr. Childs threw an absolute fit over the clambake number, and insists we rehearse it until we get it right. We have less than a month till opening night."

"I understand, sweetie. Good luck, and just be *very* careful on your way home." She had a sense that he knew she was telling a lie, a white lie. He wanted her to see her friends; he just didn't want to put up with Mommy's whining. Who could blame him?

She hung up the phone and hurried to the family car, a brown Pontiac Grand Am. It was an embarrassment. Daddy had wanted a Firebird, but you-know-who had nixed that idea, insisting that it was "not practical, too expensive," and "we'll look silly driving around in a sports car." If it had been up to her mother, she wouldn't even have gotten her own phone: "You'll stay up all hours talking, and sleep through your first five classes."

She turned onto Topanga Canyon and drove west toward the ocean. The road snaked its way up and over the Santa Monica mountains. She handled every curve with ease, rock music from her favorite FM station keeping her company as she drove. Nearing the restaurant, she reminded herself that as long as she got home at not-too-crazy an hour, everything would be fine. She pulled into the parking lot, checked her face in the mirror; thank God she had her father's high cheekbones. She puckered her lips and applied a coat of her favorite gloss—Midnight Moon.

Santana's "Black Magic Woman" was still resonating inside her head as she stepped into the restaurant. Her friends—Linda, Julie and Melissa—had already been there half an hour. For a change, Hamburger Heaven was more empty than full, a few couples scattered about, four or five solo diners here and there, and, near her friends, a clean-shaven man in a plain white short sleeve shirt. Mid-twenties with dense dark hair cut in a Marine buzz, muscled forearms to match, he nervously stirred his coffee with his spoon, creating a scratching sound every time the stainless steel struck the porcelain. Beverly took no notice of him, but he did of her. Staring into his cup, he could hear every word of the conversation two booths away.

"The star has arrived," Linda announced.

"How was the rehearsal?" Julie asked.

"Great," she said, as she slipped off her light summer windbreaker and eased into her friends' booth.

Linda dabbed a French fry in a puddle of ketchup, and held it up like a matchstick. "So, is it true, Babs?" Her friends called her Babs in honor of Barbra Streisand. Her dad called her Pip. Only her mother ever called her by her real name. "Did Larry Keeton ask you to homecoming?"

They all looked at her.

She nodded.

"What did he say?" Melissa probed.

"What do you mean 'what did he say'?" she answered, knowing full well what Melissa meant.

"Come on, give," Julie pleaded between slurps of her strawberry shake.

Linda, Julie and Melissa were her best friends. Although all four girls attended Madison High in Woodland Hills, they loved to travel "over the hill" to Malibu. Only sixteen miles away as the crow flies, this was the home of the Beach Boys and Hollywood movie stars, a world of promise and romance—so near, yet so far away.

"Well, we talked for awhile about last year's English class—he really liked *Franny and Zooey*."

"That's a good sign," Julie noted.

"And then, right in the middle of the conversation, he said, 'Are you going to homecoming with anyone?' I didn't want to say no, like, no one had asked me. So I sort of changed the subject, but then he said, 'Would you like to go with me?' and I said 'Okay.'"

"Was your heart pounding?" asked Julie.

"No." she answered, as if the question was stupid. And then added, "Yes," with a rippling giggle that was immediately taken up by the other girls.

"What else did he say?" Julie asked.

"Not much. Pretty soon his dad told him to get off the phone and that was it."

"I can't believe this!" Linda cried out. "Now we all have dates, and school hasn't even started yet."

"He's cute, isn't he?" she asked.

"Very," Melissa confirmed. "But he's more than cute. He's so serious."

"I wonder if he's a good kisser," Linda said.

"They say the quiet ones are," Julie smiled and winked. "You know, all that pent-up passion. And he does have nice lips."

"Guys!" she protested, her face quickly assuming a ruddy glow.

For the next hour they talked about what they would wear to the dance, rehashed the latest summer rerun of *The Mod Squad*, and gossiped about teachers, especially Mr. Petersen, the trig teacher they were scheduled to have next year, who, the word was, had terrible breath. Yes, she had finally "arrived." She wasn't just looking in anymore; she was in the middle of everything. More than that, she sensed that other girls were starting to envy her. Envy *her*. Well, why not? She had popular friends, she had won the lead in the school play, and now she was going to the homecoming dance with a boy she really liked.

"Oh my God, I've got to go," she said with alarm as she looked at her watch.

"It's only 10:15," Julie said. "Don't be a deadbeat. There's no school for another—"

"I'm not even supposed to be here. My mom's probably calling the police right now."

She stood up and pulled her windbreaker on, catching her long blonde hair in the collar. In one smooth motion, she lifted her hand behind her neck, grabbed her hair like a cord of rope and lifted it free, so that it fell over the outside of her jacket.

"I'll see you guys," she said, slapping her share of the bill down on the table.

They toasted her with their half-empty milk shakes.

"You won't forget us when you become a star, will you?" Linda teased.

She dipped her head and shook her hair with the melodramatic gestures of a silent movie star. "Of course not, my darlings."

Laughing, she swept past the cashier and out into the cool ocean air.

Later that night, much later, her parents received a telephone call. From a man. He didn't give his name, but he said he had a message for them. From their daughter. He gave them the message and abruptly hung up. And then nothing. For thirty-two years.

Sunday

Los Angeles, California, 2002
Sunday, 9:40 P.M.

I t was a joke in Jordan Geller's family that the first word he ever spoke was not "Mama" or "Papa" or even "bottle," but "why?" "Why don't the clouds fall? Why do we have a shadow? Why are people mean?"

Of course, as he got older the questions grew more sophisticated. Why does a baseball curve? Why do girls take so long to get ready? Why did God make mosquitoes? Why is there so much evil in the world?

Why? Why? Why?

Although he was now twenty-eight and only three months away from becoming the youngest graduate ever certified by the prestigious Dittmyer Institute of Psychoanalysis, the "why" word still consumed him, at times even paralyzed him. As in, why was he standing in front of this door? Why had he accepted Harry Stanton's invitation to go to this party? And why and what the hell was he feeling so nervous about?

A few times on the way over he had almost made a U-turn

and headed back to his apartment and his books and professional journals. God knows, he had plenty of reading to do, not to mention writing up the last three days of sessions. But he stayed the course and followed the directions—left on Amalfi, right on Toulon—that the irrepressible Stanton had given him.

Why?

He had run into Stanton two days earlier at Borders Bookstore, and the portly emergency room doctor had immediately invited him to the party. Jordan had made his usual excuses: he had too much work to catch up on, he wasn't in the mood. Stanton responded by bringing his thumb and forefinger into virtual touching distance in front of Jordan's face.

"You're about this close to becoming a certifiable hermit. They're going to do a musical about your life, 'Phantom of the Book Store.'"

"I like bookstores, Harry."

"And so do I. But you don't go anywhere besides this place, your office, your apartment and Stan's Grill."

"I've been seen at Trader Joe's."

Stanton's brown eyes bore down on him. "Jordan, it's been over a year. Time to get on with things. You'd tell that to one of your patients, right? And you know Carrie would tell you that too, if she could. So why can't you tell it to yourself?"

He scribbled down directions, and stuffed them in Jordan's pocket. "Be there or beware."

Now, standing in front of the elegant Spanish Mission style house, straightening the hem of his dark blue sports coat, he wished he could just look up at the heavens and ask Carrie flat out what she would have wanted. Stanton had been so sure of Carrie's wishes, but Jordan was not. Intensely possessive and highly jealous—aspects of her personality Stanton had never seen—Carrie loved to soliloquize about how each person had one destined love, and how lucky she and Jordan had been to find each other so young. A lovely belief, Jordan thought, if both partners made it into their eighties, but a hell of a depressing belief when one's destined partner died at twenty-seven, a victim of a drunken driver speeding down Westwood Boulevard. Nor did it help matters that they had had a bitter fight minutes before she was killed.

He squared his broad shoulders and smoothed his hand over his hair. It was a wasted gesture; he kept his thick hair cropped so short that a windstorm couldn't have blown it out of place. *It's only a party*, he thought. Still he hesitated. *Elinor would be happy if she knew I was here; progress, she'd call it. Though Carrie would see it as betrayal.* "*You're so ready to forget me?*" "*Yes, he's ready,*" Elinor now responded in her frank way. "*It may be sad for you, but Jordan must be allowed to continue his life without your interference.*"

The two women, his fiancé and his mentor, Elinor Fischer, one dead, one living, debated the issue in his head as if they were standing right next to him. He tried to banish them both with a deep exhale and fix his eyes on the doorbell. Just as he reached for it, his pager started to vibrate. He checked the number and sighed; second call within twenty minutes, and from the one person more likely than himself to be alone this Sunday night. Now he had to go in. He needed to use the phone. He had left his "cell" in his car.

A woman opened the door. She was almost as tall as Jordan. Trim, dark-skinned, with jet black hair and almond eyes, she greeted him with a self-assured "Hello." Behind her, Jordan could see that the living room was crowded with people.

"Come on in," she smiled. "I'm Donna Sanders."

He stepped inside and extended a hand. "Jordan Geller."

"*Doctor* Jordan Geller," Harry Stanton proclaimed, stepping into the hallway, his meaty hand gripping a plastic glass full of pink liquid. "Don't be so modest."

"Hello, Harry, or should I say *Doctor* Stanton."

"We were roommates in med school," Stanton explained to Donna, who nodded with a smile. "He could have been a brain surgeon, a neurosurgeon. Anything he wanted. Instead he becomes a shrink. I tell him there's no money in it, but he doesn't listen. But just being a psychiatrist isn't enough for him. He wants to be an analyst, too. So, now he's at Dittmyer, Elinor Fischer's fair-haired boy. Ever heard of Elinor Fischer? Scary woman."

"If you know Harry," Jordan said to Donna, "then you know

that, unless he's talking about one his favorite diseases, he doesn't know what he's talking about half the time"

"She's not scary?"

"She's brilliant and charming. Just like you."

Stanton pinched his friend's cheek. "I love this guy. He's so cute."

"What's in the punch, Harry?" Jordan asked, laughing.

"Join the party and find out."

"I have to use the phone first," Jordan answered, gesturing to his pager.

"I would try the one in the kitchen," Donna said.

"Thanks."

As the woman returned to her guests, Stanton raised his eyes in exasperation. "You think maybe you want to come in for a minute before you start making calls."

"It's a patient, Harry," he said, holding up his pager. "What do you want me to do, pretend I didn't hear it?"

Harry tapped Jordan's watch. "Okay, but I want a time limit. Like five minutes. I know you."

Jordan weaved his way through the living room into the kitchen. Three women were standing by the dishwasher in the corner, talking. He lifted the phone and punched in the numbers.

"I've been trying to reach you all night," the male voice on the other end began accusingly. "Where are you?"

"Well, Simon, at the moment I'm at a party."

"Perfect, I'm in agony, and you're partying."

"What are you in agony about?"

"Take your pick. My mother, my father, my sister, the goddamn head of my department."

"I need you to please be a little more specific."

"I can't do that, Dr. Geller. Everything stinks. That's as specific as I can be."

Jordan paused a minute. "Are you alone?"

"No, I'm not alone. Cindy Crawford's in the next room panting for me.... Of course I'm alone. *Jesus!*"

Jordan almost burst out laughing. Simon was a high maintenance patient, but at least he was entertaining.

"I know how tough weekends can be for you, Simon."

"You don't know anything, party boy," Simon answered.

Yeah, I'm a real party animal. You should only know, my friend.

"If you start getting abusive, I'm going to hang up."

"Wait, wait." He heard a catch in his patient's voice. "Don't do that to me. I need to talk to you. You're my doctor. I need help. This is an emergency."

Simon Cox's weekend special—"I need help. This is an emergency." If Jordan's favorite word was "why" Simon's was "help"; he was a man with no minor problems. The youngest child of a sickly mother, a workaholic father who disdained vulnerability in his only son, and a conniving older sister, Simon had long since learned that the only way to get attention was through some big dramatic gesture. And not surprisingly, any slight, like a threat to hang up, could trigger a panic attack.

"Okay, Simon," Jordan said soothingly, "I'm here. Now what's bothering you?"

"It's my sister, my fucking sister. She was bugging me about my not calling Dad more often. So I told her exactly what I felt. If he's so desperate to hear my voice, he can call me; I'm not putting out for him anymore. So now she's going to tell him what I said, the tattletale."

Jordan stared over at the three women standing by the dishwasher. Would any of them believe that the man to whom he was speaking was not fourteen but thirty-four, and an assistant professor of American History at UCLA? An impressive attainment, Jordan knew, only it didn't diminish by one iota Simon's fear and anxiety about his parents or his sister. When it came to his family, to any relationships, Simon Cox was fourteen on a good day.

"Simon, it's late now, and I can't stay on long. So I'm going to give you a suggestion. Call your father early tomorrow morning and just have a chat. But call early, before your sister calls him."

"But I can't talk to him."

"Talk to him about the weather."

"This is L.A. The weather is always the same."

"Then talk to him about something else, just as long as it's neutral. What about movies?"

"He never goes."

"There must be something he likes to talk about."

"Real estate."

"Fine. So tell him you're trying to decide between a fixed rate mortgage and a variable, and what does he think? All you need to do is speak to him for a few minutes without getting into a fight. Then, you and I will talk about your conversation and what's going on with your sister at tomorrow's session."

"Alright... I'll try." Suddenly, Simon's voice brightened. "Hey, I've got an idea. I could come to your party. Maybe you could introduce me to someone there, or we could talk some more."

Jordan smiled; he had to give the guy credit. "I can't do that. It wouldn't exactly be professional."

"Yeah, I guess not. Listen, am I bugging you too much, doctor?"

"You're bugging yourself too much, Simon. And you deserve better. We'll talk about it tomorrow."

Jordan hung up the phone and turned back toward the kitchen. The three women hadn't budged. They were still deeply engrossed in whatever they were discussing—men, Jordan guessed, judging by the intensity of their expressions. Suddenly, dealing with a roomful of people, all of whom, except for Stanton, were strangers to him, seemed overwhelming. Becoming so addicted to the role of Dr. Advice or Mr. Fix-it made it, ironically, a strain to meet people on level ground socially. Particularly when you hadn't had to do so for four years. Particularly when your heart was still involved with a woman who happened to be dead. He'd stay for an hour; that was what he had promised his friend. Only when he came out of the kitchen he learned that Stanton had big plans for him. "She likes you."

"Who likes me?"

"Donna Sanders, the woman who let you in. You impressed her."

"Harry, she met me for one minute. What impressed her, the way I asked to use the phone?"

Stanton threw his hands up. "Listen, Jordan, she's very attractive, will you at least concede that?"

He looked over at the woman, standing in the middle of a group, talking. Slender, self-assured in her gestures, and with those exotic eyes he'd noticed immediately. *Yeah, I'll concede that.*

"And she's smart," Stanton went on as Jordan continued his inspection, then let his eyes briefly wander over the other women in the room. "She's one of the top administrators at Cedars. When you walked away, she was asking me about you. Said you have presence."

"What does that mean?"

"I suppose it's an offhand way of saying that you're not terribly handsome, but you've got charm or something."

"Thanks." Stanton was on a crusade, and he wasn't going to stop till Jordan at least gave him some commitment. "Okay, Harry, you win, give me her phone number."

"*Her phone number?* She's ten feet from you."

Jordan thought of the sheer effort it took to meet someone new. "I don't think so," he finally said. "Not tonight."

"This makes no sense. You spend your whole working day trying to convince neurotics to stop torturing themselves, then, spend your whole night torturing yourself. She's a real person over there, and a nice one, I know her."

"So why don't you go out with her?"

Stanton pointed to his more than ample gut. "I'm afraid I've got too much presence for her."

"Look, Harry, I'm sor—"

"This is not about me, Jordan."

"Harry—"

"What do you have waiting for you at home—the latest issue of *Psychoanalytic Review?* I hear they just published a groundbreaking piece on Oedipal complexes among early twentieth century Viennese insurance salesmen."

Despite himself, Jordan laughed. "I'm sorry, Harry. I appreciate what you want to do, I'm just not ready."

"I understand completely."

"Thanks. You're a good friend."

"Better than you realize." Stanton raised his large hands and gave three loud claps. "Ladies and Gentlemen," he announced in a booming voice that quickly quieted the noisy room. "What's a party without some entertainment? And we have with us tonight a man who can make you do things you never thought you would."

Jordan swung his head around toward his friend. *He wouldn't. Yes, he would; this was Stanton.* He glanced frantically at the front door. But Stanton had boxed him in against the couch.

"Harry, don't do this," he urged in a stage whisper.

"What tricks do you do, big boy?" a heckler called out, pointing his glass at the emergency room physician.

Stanton stared the drunk down. "I cut body parts out of people who get cirrhosis of the liver." He turned back to the party. "As I was starting to say, I have the pleasure of introducing one of the great psychiatric practitioners of hypnosis in America today, the mesmerizing Dr. Jordan Geller."

You diabolical bastard. Five years earlier, while in med school, Jordan had become fascinated with hypnosis after watching a gall bladder surgery performed without anesthesia on a hypnotized patient. He had taken thirty hours of hypnosis training and, for a few months, hypnotized anyone who set foot in his and Stanton's apartment. While he never participated in any attempts to hypnotize someone in lieu of anesthesia, his skills were much in demand at med school parties; once, just a couple of months before he had met Carrie, he had even hypnotized six people simultaneously.

But Jordan hadn't hypnotized anyone in over three years. He couldn't just get up now and start doing it. He was about to make his excuses, when he saw Donna Sanders inspecting him, an appraising look on her face. And then he noticed another woman; mid-twenties, with dense ribbons of copper hair surrounding inquisitive green eyes. Her skin was clear, pearl-colored; from a distance it looked flawless. *Where were you hiding?* Jordan wondered.

Stanton crocked a finger at Jordan. "Herr Dr. Geller," he intoned in a heavy German accent, "your patients avait you."

Jordan's mind raced back to those med school parties, trying to reconstruct exactly what he used to do. He started toward the group, silently cursing Stanton as he stepped. When he reached the center of the room, he cleared his throat; then tried to speak with far more confidence than he felt.

"I want everybody to stand up and extend your palms in front of you, so that they are facing each other."

Most of the crowd greeted his request with nervous laughter. A few guests went on talking as if they hadn't heard him at all; another group retreated to the kitchen. But about a dozen people gathered round, including, he noted with satisfaction, both Donna and the redhead.

"The hypnosis technique is very simple and totally harmless," he began, making brief eye contact with each of his potential "subjects."

"In a moment, I'm going to count backward from three to one, and when I reach one, your eyes will close and you will find yourselves feeling very powerful magnets on the palms of each of your hands. These magnets will feel so powerful that they will quickly draw your palms together. This will start to happen as I count backward from three to one. Three," Jordan said, his voice loud and deliberate. "Two... one."

The volunteers all closed their eyes, and a few palms started gravitating toward each other. Jordan stood in front of Donna; her fingers were still far apart. "As your palms move nearer and nearer to each other," he told her, "you're feeling the magnetic attraction growing stronger and stronger." He spoke with firm assurance but her hands were not moving at all. Jordan quickly surveyed the rest of the group; about half were experiencing some movement. Except for the redhead; her palms were already touching.

He took up a position in front of her. Close up, he could see a light spray of freckles across her forehead and cheeks. "As your hands touch," he said, "you will feel your fingers start to lock around each other." Seconds later, her hands were gripping each other. "Just focus for the next minute on your fingers closing down, tightening," he told her. As she did so, he went over to the other participants, tapped them on their shoulders, and whispered to them that they could open their eyes and sit down. Three or four others were good candidates, but he was out of practice. No way he'd do multiple hypnosis tonight.

He returned to the redhead. "Your fingers and hands now feel as if they were fused, as if they were sculpted from a single piece of wood. In a moment, I am going to count to three, and when I do, I am going to ask you to try and pull your hands apart, and you will find that the harder you try to pull them apart, the more they will remain locked together. One—you feel as if your hands were sculpted from a single piece of wood. Two—the harder you try and pull them apart, the more they will remain locked together. Three—try and pull your hands apart."

The woman's brows tightened, and she started pulling, but her hands didn't respond. Jordan let her try a few times, until her fingers began to turn purple from the exertion.

He observed with some satisfaction that the group that had retreated to the kitchen had filed back into the living room.

"Stop straining yourself," Jordan said in a soothing tone. "You're feeling very calm now. In a moment, I'll run my hands over your arms and fingers, and everywhere I touch will become very relaxed, and no longer fused from a single piece of wood. So that when I tell you to try and pull your hands apart, you will find that you can do so effortlessly."

Jordan lightly traced his hands down her arms; then told her to release her hands. She did so easily. A few people applauded. Jordan instructed her to open her eyes.

She came out laughing. "Wow," she said, then repeated it. "Was I hypnotized?"

Jordan nodded.

"How do you know?"

"Put your hands together now and pull them apart."

She did so.

"Now you can pull your hands apart instantly. But a moment ago you couldn't because you were hypnotized into believing that your hands were made of one piece of wood."

"What else can you do?" a man's voice called out.

Jordan looked at the woman. He remembered enough from his earlier study of hypnosis to recognize her as a deep trance subject, one of the ten percent or so of people who could quickly go into the deepest sort of hypnotic trances.

"Would you like to go under again?" Jordan asked.

"I don't want to start running around the room like a dog, barking."

Everyone laughed, but Jordan looked straight into her green eyes. "I would never do that. "

"What do you want to do?" she asked.

"I want to relax you, then relax your mind. Maybe I'll suggest that you forget how to count."

Again she laughed, a musical trill that made him smile. "No way."

"Are you willing to try?"

She thought for a second, then nodded.

"By the way," Jordan said, "I should know your name."

"Robin Norris," the woman answered, and extended a hand. Her grip was firm, but the skin was soft. It had been a long time since just touching a woman's hand had seemed so exciting. Suddenly, the hypnosis mattered a lot to him.

"Robin," he said, "first thing, why don't you make yourself comfortable?"

He brought her over to a padded armchair. She sat down and he told her to just let her hands fall to her sides. Within the next few minutes, he gave her suggestions that relaxed her entire body. She slumped slightly in the chair, her eyelids so heavy she couldn't open them. "Now," he continued, "just as we have relaxed your body, I want to relax your mind. I am going to tap your forehead, and tell you to count backward from one hundred. But your mind will quickly relax the numbers right out of your head, and they will disappear like a vapor from your mind."

The front door pushed open. A man with a lion's mane of gray hair pulled back into a ponytail stepped inside. Glancing up,

Jordan guessed he was in his early fifties, maybe older; he waited a beat, expecting the new guest to sit down, but the man remained standing by the door.

Jordan turned back to his slowly breathing subject, and tapped her lightly on the forehead.

"One hundred," Robin now said very slowly.

"The numbers are just disappearing from your mind," Jordan said.

"Ninety-nine... ninety-eight..." Her voice sounded drugged. "Ninety-sev..." she began, but never finished.

Jordan let her sit quietly a moment, then restored the numbers to her memory. "In a moment, I am going to bring you out of hypnosis. And when you come out, you will feel calm, confident, relaxed and fully aware. But I am going to give you one post-hypnotic suggestion. You will forget that your name is Robin Norris. That name will seem totally unfamiliar to you. Your name is Myra Apple. But if at any time I snap my finger and say to you 'sleep now,' you will immediately go back into a comfortable hypnotic trance."

He quickly brought Robin out.

She opened her eyes and stretched her back, like a person waking from a long nap.

"So how did it feel?" Jordan asked.

"Great," Robin answered. She yawned. "Feel like I slept for hours. It's strange, though, I think I remember everything."

Jordan nodded. "It's a misconception that people forget what happens when they're under hypnosis."

"What do you remember?" a woman called out.

"The way I couldn't open my eyes. I was sure I was going to be able to, but then I really couldn't. And the way I forgot how to count backward."

"Count backward now," Jordan instructed. "Starting from a hundred."

"Walter," she said to the gray haired man who had walked in. "When did you get here?"

"We're all waiting for you to count backward, angel," the man said with the precise diction of an English stage actor.

She quickly rattled off the numbers, "One hundred, ninety-nine, ninety-eight, ninety-seven…"

"Very good," Walter congratulated.

"You ought to try this, Walter. It's fascinating."

"Some other time." Walter turned to the other guests. "I hate to spoil everyone's fun, but I'm afraid I must take this lovely lady home. Robin?"

Robin stared at him.

"Robin, you knew I was coming at eleven."

Her face retained its puzzled look. The room had suddenly become center court at Wimbledon, heads swiveling back and forth between the Englishman and the redhead.

"What's your name?" Jordan asked her.

She was silent a minute, as if her mind was straining for the answer. "Myra Apple," she finally said.

Walter looked at Jordan. "I'd very much love to play along, but I really do have to get… Miss Apple home. She has a long day of fittings and rehearsals tomorrow."

"Walter, come on, I'm not the least bit tired."

"Robin, really now…"

"And why are you calling me Robin? Who's Robin?"

"Quite impressive," Walter said to Jordan. He turned to Robin. "I wish you took direction from me as well as you take it from this gentleman." And then again, back to Jordan. "But it's late. I really think you should end this immediately."

"Who's Robin?" Robin asked again.

"Myra," Jordan said to her. "Please sit down in that chair." As soon as she was seated, he snapped his finger at her and commanded, "Sleep now." Immediately, her eyes closed and her head slumped forward.

"In a moment, I will bring you out of hypnosis. You will remember everything that has happened this evening. You will remember that your name is Robin Norris, and that under hypnosis, I told you to forget that name and to think your name was Myra Apple." He counted to five, and instructed her to open her eyes.

"What's your name?" Jordan asked her.

Robin waited a moment before responding. "Myra Apple, of course."

"Bloody hell," Walter shouted.

"Walter, Walter," Robin said. "I was joking. It's me, Robin." Then, with a theatrical flourish. "I've come back to you, my darling."

Walter's lips tightened into a thin smile. "That's the best news I've heard since I walked in here." He came over beside Robin. "Can we please go now?"

A minute later, she waved a hurried goodbye at Jordan, mouthed a thank you, and followed her director out the door.

Almost immediately, Harry Stanton drew up alongside him. "You still have the touch, old buddy. Donna was impressed."

Jordan looked over at him. "Donna?"

"Hello? You still here? Remember, Donna? Cedars Sinai?"

"Sure."

"You want her number?"

"Whose number?"

Stanton blew out audibly. "Donna's."

Jordan's eyes were still focused on the now closed door. "What can you tell me about Robin Norris?"

Monday

Monday, 2:15 A.M.

*H*e pulled the car up alongside the small adobe guesthouse, let out a deep breath; then glanced at the dashboard clock. It was past two. He'd been up since seven that morning, but didn't feel the least bit tired. Good thing. He still had one final task to carry out.

He walked into his bedroom, pulled out a small, purple, velvet jewelry pouch from the pocket of his pants and emptied the contents onto his dresser: two rings, one silver with a small turquoise stone and one gold with a little Egyptian design, two gold pierced earrings in the shape of shamrocks, and a beaded necklace which looked homemade. He rolled them around in his palm. *My little girl*, he mused. *Finally, safe. Where no one can hurt her again.*

He carefully returned the jewels to the pouch, and rested the bag on the night table. He'd put them in the safe later. He stripped off his clothes and stuffed them in a laundry basket.

For the next ten minutes, he luxuriated in a hot shower, scrubbing himself, going over his body with the wash cloth two and three times. Although his mind was calm, his heart was still beating quickly. *This one went so quietly. Barely said a word. He had to tell her to speak up. Once she realized what was happening, she just went into shock. The shock of final recognition. Still, he tried to make her understand. But she just couldn't. It didn't matter, though. He knew what was best for her, what was best for all of his girls.*

He shut off the shower, pulled on his burgundy robe and stepped into the kitchen. He took a skillet from the cabinet and placed it on the gas stove. Breakfast after midnight; that was always a special treat. With his hands still feeling electrified, he turned the knob and watched the pilot light flare. The flames spun in a circle around the burner. He reached into the fridge and pulled out some eggs and ham. He placed the meat on the cutting board and chopped off a large slab.

After he finished, he returned to his car. He kept his windows down, the fresh, moist air blowing hard against his face. Almost 3 A.M. now, the streets quiet, as if he were the only one alive in a city of millions. He wished he could fully relax, but he couldn't. His lips began twitching again, those damned lips. It was always like this when he went out on his missions. Only then. He hated it. There was a leaking, cracking sound coming from inside his mouth, inside his teeth. As if mosquitoes and moths were being caught there and burned alive. At a closed gas station, he spotted a pay phone. He slipped in fifty cents, squinted down at the paper in his hand and punched in the numbers.

"Monica?" an anxious male voice asked on the other end of the line.

"No, but I have a message from her." He sucked on the tips of his fingers, trying to close those damn lips.

"Who is this?"

"I asked Monica if she had anything she wanted me to tell you." Zap!

"Who is this?" the man demanded. He could hear a woman's voice in the background. "Keith, is it her?"

"Are you Monica's father?" he asked.

"That's right, I am. Now, who am I speaking to?"

"You didn't protect her."

Zeet!

What's that noise?

"You didn't do your job. So, I had to."

"Who is this?"

"Monica's friend."

"I don't recognize your voice."

"Of course you don't. How could you?"

"Listen, I'm running out of patience. Where is my daughter?"

"Do you want to hear Monica's message or not?"

The zapping, zeeting sound was louder now. He couldn't stop it.

"Keith, what's going on?" he heard the woman ask fearfully in the background.

"Yes, I want to hear her message."

"She said she loves you. I'm sure you were expecting more. Me, too. But even that was hard to get. Sorry."

"Who the hell are you?"

"She was shy. I liked that about her."

"I'm hanging up and calling the police."

"It's better this way. She'll always stay pure. Someday you'll understand. Monica does."

"Is this some kind of a sick joke? Because if it's—"

"I would never joke about something like this."

"Please, listen, if you know where my daughter is, tell me right now and I won't say anything to anybody. I'll forget about this call. I promise you."

His lips fluttered and his neck muscles became taut. "Why are you so worried about Monica now? Letting her run around at all hours. Where were you, when she needed you? No, you left it up to me."

"What? What are you talking about?"

"I'm not talking anymore."

"Don't hang up!"

But there was nothing more to say.

Monday, 6 A.M.

For the third time in the last ten days, Lieutenant Ben Lemoski woke up in the middle of the night worrying about money. Two hours and a bag of Oreo cookies later, he was still worrying. Everything boiled down to two possibilities—make more money or bring down the house nut. Neither scenario seemed likely. As a seventeen-year veteran in the LAPD homicide division, the last ten in the West Valley Division, his salary had peaked. As the father of three daughters, one of whom would be going to college in eighteen months, his expenses had not.

The phone rang. He grabbed it on the first ring.

"Lemoski."

Before the person on the other end even spoke a word, Lemoski knew it was bad news. The phone doesn't ring at six in the morning in the home of a homicide detective to bring good news. More than likely, somebody's universe had ended the night before.

"You're up."

"What's going on, Jimmy?" Lemoski asked impatiently.

The man on the other end cleared his throat. "We got a body. Female Caucasian. Fresh."

"Where?"

"Eagle Canyon."

"Who found her?"

"Someone taking a dawn hike with his dog. Loo, we've got a report of a parent getting one of those calls."

Lemoski muttered an expletive to himself. "When?"

"Around 2 A.M."

"I'm on my way."

"I'll call your car with exact directions."

Lemoski returned the receiver to its cradle. He wasn't worrying about money anymore.

Monday, 6:10 A.M.

The neophyte psychiatrist pulled himself out of bed, his mind already racing. The sun of a new day usually made everything seem brighter, but this morning his mood was dark. His head throbbed with a hangover not from booze—he hadn't touched a drop—but anxiety. What if word were to get out? Get back to Elinor and the others at the Institute. He'd be a laughing stock. And for what? A feeling, a moment of attraction? Yes, he wanted to see her again. But that would never happen. Not now.

He hadn't felt this way when he finally got to bed last night. Then, his spirits were high, buoyed by the encounter. She had jolted him with her fresh smile, the soft press of her hand. And he liked the feeling. But as he lay in bed, sleep not coming, doubts began to gnaw at his new optimism.

By the morning, the high spirits had totally vanished. He wondered at his behavior, ashamed of it now, ashamed because he knew he had done something he shouldn't have. Something wrong. Stupid, even. But, still, he couldn't deny that he had enjoyed the experience. Having that power. Commanding attention. Inspiring awe. How many other people could do what he had done?

He dragged himself into the bathroom. A swim and the two egg, hash browns special at Stan's would buck him up. Get him back on track. Maybe things weren't so grim after all. He had a full calendar of patients to occupy his mind. And then tonight, there was the Dittmyer Fundraiser. *Come on, snap out of it. No way word of this is going to get out. Who'd tell anyway?* So, he had nothing to worry about. All he had to do was bury his fear. Bury it deep. He had done it before.

Monday, 6:30 A.M.

Detective Jimmy Lee greeted Lemoski with a paper cup filled with rapidly cooling black coffee.

"You've got to see this one to believe it." It was a short walk through wet grass to the crime scene. "A real Van Gogh, this guy."

Lemoski took a sip of the liquid and stared at the victim.

A young woman, no more than eighteen or nineteen, hung from a tree. Her arms, almost translucently pale, extended up and away from her body. Leather straps, attached to each wrist and to a thick branch above, held her in place. Her ankles were bound together with duct tape. She wore a long white lace dress—it could have been a wedding dress. And strapped to her back were a pair of white angel wings, the sort you might buy a little girl for her Halloween costume.

But this angel wasn't smiling. Instead, her eyes bulged out. And around her neck, like a necklace, a purple pattern of bruises.

Lemoski turned his gaze heavenward. "God Almighty," he prayed, "please help me catch this bastard."

Monday, 9 A.M.

alter Amicke turned the key and entered the small house Robin Norris had rented on Greenfield Street in Westwood. In what had become almost a daily ritual, he was carrying bagels and Starbucks coffee. "Robin, where are you?" he said.

"I'll be out in a few minutes," she called from the bathroom.

"Your fitting's in less than an hour."

"I know, I know."

He sat down on the maroon-colored living room couch and picked up the remote control from the glass coffee table. "And don't forget, I want you at rehearsal at 2:45." He took a sip from his latte, and flicked on the television.

A few minutes later, Robin stepped into the living room, toweling her mass of red hair with a fierce rubbing motion.

"Did you hear what I said about the rehearsal?" Walter questioned, his eyes on the TV screen.

"2:45."

"Sharp," he emphasized. "That doesn't mean 3:00. The situation's serious, Robin. Very serious."

Robin turned her attention to the TV. Yearbook pictures of two local high school girls, both recent murder victims, filled the screen. Now, the news anchor reported, the police had discovered a third body, also a high school girl. The name of the newest victim had not yet been released, and wouldn't be until her family had been notified. All three teenagers had been killed within the last few months, the latest victim within the last twenty-four hours, according to police sources. Sweet faces, Robin thought of the two pictures on the screen. They could have been sisters. The news anchor, her face fraught with melodramatic anguish, went on to say that police now believed a new serial killer was loose in the area.

"Walter, turn it off," Robin said, feeling herself sinking into a funk. "That's the last thing I need to hear in the morning."

Walter pressed the mute button and handed Robin her drink. Suddenly, she felt lightheaded, dizzy, as if there wasn't enough air in the room or in her lungs. *Damn it, damn it! It's happening again!* Sucking in a breath, she sat down, clutching at her double latte for dear life. She took a sip—as much as she could manage through the quarter-inch gap in the plastic top—and felt herself starting to calm.

"Jesus, you're not getting sick, I hope." Walter said, staring at her. "That's all I need."

"I'm fine. That news report upset me, that's all. Put on anything. The Weather Channel. Just not this."

"Put it on yourself," he said, scraping the last corner of cream cheese from the serving-sized container.

The elixir of caffeine continued to work its magic. Robin started to feel like herself again, confident enough to venture forth into a subject area that had been occupying her mind for the last twelve hours.

"I've been thinking about what happened last night. Who knows, maybe Jordan Geller can help me with this problem I'm having with my throat? Make me forget about it like he made me forget my name."

"Who's Jordan Geller?" Walter asked as he took a much-anticipated bite of his bagel. Lost in the enjoyment of this culinary pleasure, it took a few seconds before the name registered. "You're joking, I hope."

"I'm perfectly serious."

Walter scowled and took another large bite, leaving a sample of cheese on the right corner of his mouth. "Why would you waste your time seeing some wanker who does party tricks," he said as he dabbed himself clean with a napkin.

"You don't know he's a wanker," she responded forcefully, punching the last word, Walter's favorite English slang put down.

"You're right. That shrink who made you beat a chair with a foam bat, she was a wanker. This guy's worse. He's a mind-fucker."

Robin sighed deeply but said nothing.

"He's a performer, that's all."

The phone near Walter rang, but he ignored it. "What sort of real shrink goes around making people forget their name? Trust me, this guy is bad news."

He finally scooped up the phone on the third ring.

"She's right here, Adrian," Robin heard him saying. "Hang on." He turned toward her, his palm covering the phone's speaker. "Speaking of bad news..."

"Oh God," Robin whispered. "I don't want to talk to her now."

"You never want to talk to her," he whispered back, and handed her the receiver.

"Hi, mom."

"It would be nice, honey, if I called your house and the phone was picked up for once by a man who was actually attracted to women."

Robin rolled her eyes and waited for her mother to fill the silence.

"Did you see the report on the news about this serial killer?"

Here we go, Robin moaned to herself. "Yeah, Walter and I just saw something about it. It's terrible."

"He calls the parents afterward. Did you hear that? I want you to be careful. I don't want to be getting such a call."

"Yes, yes. It's hideous."

"Don't get in any cars with strange men."

"Don't you know? All men are strange." From the corner of her eye, she watched Walter licking cream cheese off his fingers.

"Don't make jokes, Robin. It's not a joke to the parents of these poor girls."

"You're right."

"Sweetie, that's not even why I called. I'm very worried about this swallowing problem of yours. It scares me."

Why did I tell her anything at all about this? I should never have told her I was only eating soup. I should never tell her anything. I have to learn that. Never tell her anything.

"I really can't talk now. I'm late for a fitting."

"I'm leaving today for that retreat in the Rockies. Weren't you planning on saying good-bye?"

"Of course, I was… Good-bye."

"There are no phones there, Robin. It won't be easy to reach me."

"I hope I'll survive."

"Robin, I think you should drop out of the show."

An airless silence followed.

"Nothing's worth risking your health," Adrian continued.

"I am fine. I'm having a slight—"

"You are not fine. There's something very wrong going on. You can't eat solid food. You can barely sing, and until you find out the cause, I don't think you should be taking any risks. Think of me, if not of yourself. I've already lost your father."

"Enough, mom."

"What if you pass out in the middle of a performance, or if you open your mouth and can't sing?"

"I am not going to pass out," she said, carefully enunciating each word.

That got Walter's attention. He looked up.

"There'll be other shows. Of course, if you'd just go back to school—"

"Stop it!" The telephone was stuck to her palm as if it had been glued on.

"All I'm saying is that you should save yourself for something more important."

"*More important?* There's nothing more important to me."

"Honey, nobody cares about the Westwood Civic Light Opera."

"I'll be sure to share that with Walter."

"It's not worth risking your health. I told your father—"

She held the phone out at arm's length. She could hear Adrian's voice cracking through the little holes in the receiver.

No wonder I can't catch a breath. She's choking me. Choking me. Telling me what to do and when. What a curse that I'm back in Los Angeles. Why couldn't they have staged this show in Nome, Alaska, for God's sake? Any place away from her. Robin brought the phone back to her mouth. And then, in one long burst: "I'm hanging up now. Have a great time on the retreat and thanks for the encouragement." She banged the hand piece into its cradle.

"What's dear old Adrian on about now?" Walter asked as the phone started ringing again.

"Don't answer it," Robin commanded.

"You don't seem to have the most amicable relationship with your mother," Walter added in the best tradition of British understatement.

"Never have… Never will."

The answering machine picked up after the fourth ring. Robin could hear the distant echo of her mother's voice, and she could just make out the words: "Darling, don't be upset with me. I only want what's best for you. Robin, I know you're there, pick up the phone. Please, Robin…. please, please…."

Monday, 11:50 A.M.

The sun edged past the tops of the canyon pines. The light, unhindered by cloud cover, was harsh, and given what it illuminated, almost cruel. The scene of the crime, dream-like in the morning mist five hours ago, now appeared all too real. Lemoski put on his sunglasses to screen the glare. It wasn't even midday and all he wanted to do was take a nap. Another cup of black coffee—it would be his fourth of the morning—would have to substitute. Diving into a murder investigation usually gave him a rush of energy. Time to saddle up and get the bad guy. That was his job, his *raison d'etre*, and he liked it. But this murder gave him no such charge. In fact, it only depressed him. Maybe because the killer had obviously taken so much pleasure in his crime; maybe because he knew how difficult it would be to solve. And maybe because he was getting older and it didn't seem to him that good was gaining any ground in the battle against evil.

Just ten minutes ago, he had ordered the young woman's body to be taken down from the tree and sent to the morgue at the West Valley Station. The hunt for forensic evidence—prints, fibers, DNA and so on—would continue for the rest of the day and beyond. He had commissioned a small army of cops to surround the murder site to keep out the media. The news of the killing had already been broadcast on TV, but he didn't want to take the chance of some aggressive photographer or mini cam operator getting a shot at any gruesome pictures. He considered a murder scene a sacred place, and he was a real stickler—some said obsessive—that it not be violated. Bad enough, he thought, that the forensic team, the police photographers and detectives, had to tramp through it. They were essential. News hounds were not.

He had already spoken to the chief and the mayor by phone. They delivered all the usual clichés: promised their full support, asked if there were any leads and insisted on daily updates. He said all the right things in return. All parties understood the exchange was more style than substance, but nobody knew another way to play the game. Being a lieutenant in charge of a high-profile murder investigation—and the profile of this one was growing more prominent by the hour—was as much about being a politician and a diplomat as it was about being crime-solver.

Monica Johnson's parents had also called. They, of course, had seen the news reports and were in a state of panic. Lemoski had not talked to them directly. Jimmy Lee had. As much as the lieutenant felt for them, there was nothing he could say to assuage their anxiety. The autopsy had to be performed before the body could be released for identification purposes.

The Johnsons, he knew, would have a very bad day and a worse night. After that, he didn't want to guess how they'd feel.

Monday, 1:45 P.M.

P at Haman, secretary at the Dittmyer Institute for Psychoanalysis, stepped into Jordan's office. She was carrying a large red Macintosh apple.

"It's not from me," she said in response to Jordan's bemused expression. "There's a woman outside who wants to see you."

Jordan's look of puzzlement grew. "A patient?"

"Nobody I've ever seen here. But she says she met you, and this apple might remind you who she is."

Jordan drummed his fingers on his desk. "Did she say anything else?"

"She seems like a playful type."

Ten years manning the front desk of the institute had been its own special kind of education for the secretary. She didn't have any medical degrees, but her intuitive judgment of people was as good as anyone's in the office. "Said she'd be disappointed if the apple didn't do the trick, but if it didn't, I should tell you her name."

"Good, we're making progress."

"Myra Apple," Pat chuckled. "Is that really her name, or is she putting me on?"

Jordan's eyes quickly scanned his daily calendar. "Send Ms. Apple right in."

And then she was there. He had taken it for granted that they would never meet again because he wasn't going to initiate the contact. The one thing he hadn't counted on was that she would.

He tried to play it cool, but failed. He felt his cheeks reddening; he just hoped she didn't notice. "So what do I call you, Myra or Robin?"

She laughed; it was an engaging, infectious laugh. Jordan had liked it when he first heard it last night; he liked it even more today. "I called someone I knew at the party to ask about you. She told me you were a hotshot analyst, super busy. I figured I'd better find some creative way to get in."

"So is this call social or business?"

"Social or business?" Robin mused aloud. "If that means, do I want to go into analysis, I don't think so."

Exactly the answer he wanted. "I'm happy to hear that."

Robin's dark red brows drew together. "Why should that make you happy? Isn't that how you make your living?"

Jordan fidgeted. "I suppose I mean," he finally said, "that ninety percent of the people with whom I deal are either in analysis, have been in analysis, are going into analysis, or are analysts. So it's a nice break in my routine for someone to walk in who has no desire to be in any of those categories."

He paused, trying to assess her reaction. "So what can I do for you, Ms. Apple?"

"Do you do hypnosis here?"

Jordan shook his head. "If I ever tried to hypnotize a patient I was treating, Elinor Fischer—she's the director—would have my head. We're pretty orthodox at Dittmyer. No funny stuff. And most analysts today definitely regard hypnosis as funny stuff."

"Because?"

"They think it's too directive, that the only worthwhile things are what come out of the patients without any outside suggestions."

"So hypnosis is"—she struggled to remember Walter's earlier words—"Just a party trick?"

"Not exactly. A few years back, when I was a med student, I took some hypnosis workshops, and the truth is, I think it does have some limited, but powerful applications. Who knows, when I'm practicing on my own, not just as a resident, I might play around with it again." He paused. "Robin, why are you asking? I hope you haven't been experiencing any unpleasant aftereffects from last night."

"Not at all. As a matter of fact, it amazed me the way I couldn't open my eyes or count backward. Is such a response unusual?"

"The intensity of your reaction was a little uncommon, but, no, it's not all that rare. In hypnosis literature, people like you are called 'deep trance subjects,' the type who can go under quickly and very deeply."

"And who would therefore be very receptive to suggestions while in such a state?"

"Possibly."

"Can I ask you a question as a doctor?"

He held up a palm like a stop sign. "I don't think I have any openings for patients right now, if that's what you mean."

He was searching for words. He didn't want to sound cold, but of one thing he was sure: he did not want to become this woman's doctor. Becoming her doctor didn't mean the beginning of a relationship, but the end of one. Doctors had to wait at least two years after treatment before they could initiate any personal contact with an ex-patient. This was not just a medical school suggestion, but California law. And if it sounded silly for dentists, it did make sense for shrinks. A lot of patients go gaga for their psychiatrists. It was an occupational hazard. Who are you going to fall in love with, if not the person to whom you reveal your innermost thoughts and secrets? And Jordan knew just how he interested he would be in learning Robin Norris' innermost thoughts and secrets—just not as her analyst.

"If you want, I can put you in touch with some very competent psychiatrists I know."

"I just want to ask you something about hypnosis."

By this point, Jordan was back behind his desk, Robin seated in a comfortably padded leather chair opposite him.

"Ask away."

"Of all the things you did last night, doctor—"

"Call me Jordan."

She smiled. "Good. Of all the things you did last night, Jordan, the one that most amazed me was making me forget my name."

Jordan chuckled. "I remembered that from the old days. It blows people's minds. Like your friend's, I suspect."

"Walter could have done without that, I'm sure. But that's not what I want to know."

"Go on."

"If you can make me forget my name, something I've known and lived with my whole life, could you hypnotize me to forget something that's been a part of me for a much shorter time?"

"Maybe, maybe not. Your question is too theoretical. I can't give you a blanket response."

"I want you to know that I'm willing to pay."

"Money is not the issue."

"Really, I'm not looking for bargains or favors."

"Listen," Jordan answered. "If, in fact, I were to end up hypnotizing you again, I'll do it as a friend, as a favor. Hypnosis is just not something I do professionally."

"I understand."

"Okay, so now tell me why you want me to hypnotize you, and start from the end."

Six weeks ago, she told Jordan, she had moved to Los Angeles from New York to play the part of Julie in the Westwood Civic Light Opera production of *Carousel*. Within days of her arrival, actually the first day of rehearsal, her throat had started to give her problems. She felt like something was trapped in her esophagus. Short of breath, she couldn't sing in full voice, and had difficulty swallowing. One day at rehearsal, during a lunch break, she choked on a piece of chicken. One of the stagehands performed the Heimlich maneuver; otherwise, she very well might have died. After this incident, she went to a throat specialist who did a battery of tests, none of which showed anything unusual.

She then went to see a psychologist, a woman. They met three times in three days. During the third session, the psychologist came to the conclusion that Robin had been abused by her father, and that the pressure of starring in a new production in a strange city had released the repressed memories. Handing Robin a blue foam rubber baseball bat, she instructed her to whack a chair three times a day while yelling, "I hate you, daddy! I hate you for what you did to me."

"I said 'no thank you' and left," she concluded. "I have my share of hang ups, but being abused by my father is not one of them."

"So, you've been to see a medical doctor, a psychologist and now you want to try hypnosis."

"I would never have thought of it until last night. As I said, the way you made me forget my name, I thought maybe you could make me forget this throat thing. It's playing hell with my singing voice. My show opens in two weeks... I'm desperate."

Jordan tapped his pen on his desktop. "You've never had problems with swallowing or breathing before. No asthma..."

"Nothing. I'd remember."

"Are there any terrible memories, any frightening things you remember happening in your life?"

"My dad's death."

"I'm sorry. I can understand why the therapist's suggestion was so hurtful. How old were you?"

"Fourteen. He died of cancer."

Jordan shook his head in sympathy. He thought for a moment about his own father's death seven years previously, the victim of a sudden stroke.

"Any other very painful memories?"

"Like what?"

"Have you ever been sexually coerced?"

"You mean raped?"

"Forced to do something sexually you didn't want to do."

Robin shook her head vigorously. "I've had some persistent dates. But nothing I couldn't handle."

Jordan could think of a hundred more questions he should ask. But that would be taking him down the slippery slope toward therapy.

"I haven't eaten a piece of solid food in weeks without having to chew it into mush, and I haven't sung full voice now for six days. I just want to be normal again. To take a bite out of something without it becoming a whole big deal."

"Could all this be just an extremely intense form of stage fright? Sounds like this play is a big opportunity for you."

"I know what stage fright feels like; this isn't it. If it's some big phobia, I'll deal with it, but after the show. I need help now. Today."

He considered her words for a moment; then, shook his head. "Robin, I'm sorry, I just can't do it."

"You did it last night."

"Last night was for fun. This is where I work. As I said, this is not something we do here."

She stood up suddenly. "Maybe you're right. Maybe this was a stupid idea. Sorry." She turned and started toward the door.

Let her walk out. Just let her go.

"Robin, I have no idea if this would even help at all."

She turned around. "And if it doesn't, I'll be in the same shape I'm in now."

True enough. What's the down side? You know very well what the downside is.

Then, against his better judgment, he finally spoke.

"Okay, but you understand, if I do this, I'm not doing this as Dr. Jordan Geller, psychiatrist. It's Jordan Geller, amateur hypnotist. Is that acceptable?"

Robin nodded. "Gifted amateur hypnotist," she added.

"Is that acceptable?"

"Let's go for it."

He liked the way she said that—her spunk. And her confidence in him was touching. It gave *him* confidence, more, in fact, given what she was asking him to do, than he had any rational reason to have.

"Just give me one minute."

Jordan stepped outside and quickly walked over to Pat Haman's desk. "Please don't put any calls through to my office until I tell you."

Pat raised an eyebrow. "Whatever you say, but she didn't fill out any paperwork. We don't even have an address to send a bill."

"No bills, Pat. This is personal, not business. I'd just prefer not to be disturbed."

Pat shrugged. "Whatever you say, doctor."

Back inside, Jordan directed Robin to the leather chair in front of his desk. "Remember," he said, "all hypnosis is self-hypnosis. You're not going to do or say anything you don't want. All that is going to happen is that we'll let your unconscious express whatever it wants to express without any suggestions from me."

He told Robin to rest her arms at her side, pick out an imaginary spot on the ceiling overhead, and focus all her attention on it. Then he directed her to take a deep breath and fill up her lungs completely, all the time keeping her eyes focused on the imaginary spot.

The goofy psychologist who had her whack the chair might have been wrongheaded in her methods and conclusions, but she had probably been right in at least one respect: coming to Los Angeles, maybe starring in this play, had probably stirred up some buried memory which, unable to present itself cognitively, was presenting itself symptomatically. He would take her back to the source of the trauma, bring it to the surface and expose it to light. Clarity would enhance the power of suggestion. He liked the plan. It was quick and simple. It might even work.

Within two minutes, Jordan had brought Robin into a deep trance, more profound, he could see, than the night before. "Focus on your breathing," he told her. "We're going to go deeper now, much deeper. Then, in just a few moments, I am going to count to ten, and when I reach the number ten, you will find yourself back in time, to an event that is somehow associated with the swallowing problem you're now having. You will find yourself reliving this point in time; you will remember everything and will be able to describe all that is happening. And all these recollections and realizations will come as soon as you hear the number ten and I tap your forehead."

Jordan noted with satisfaction that Robin's breathing had remained steady, free of any signs of stress. "One," he said, beginning the regression, "your mind is now going backward from today. Two, you are spinning back further and further to whatever it was that is now causing you to have trouble swallowing and singing. Three, your mind is going back to that event." More quickly now, he counted four, five, six, seven, eight and nine, each time offering additional suggestions.

Finally, he said, "At the next number, you will be fully back in time, back to whatever is responsible for your fear. As soon as I say the next number, I will tap your forehead, and you will be able to describe everything that is happening. Ten."

He tapped her forehead. "Are you indoors or out?"

Robin said nothing. Ridges of worry formed on her forehead. She began to shake her head ever so slightly to the left and right, but still said nothing.

"Are you indoors or outside?" Jordan repeated.

"Outside," she finally said, her voice barely higher than a whisper.

"Daytime or nighttime?

"It's night."

"Are you alone or with someone?"

"Alone." She shifted in her chair as if she wanted to bolt, and the next words came out strangled: "*But he's coming back.*"

"Who's coming back?"

"I don't know. He told me to call him John."

"He *told* you to call him John?"

"Yes."

"But you're not sure that's his real name?"

"I asked him that and he slapped me." Robin's face went white.

"Remember, you are totally safe in this room," Jordan said, anxious to calm her, and himself as well. "All that's going on is that you're describing things that happened a long time ago, but they're not happening any more. You are totally safe, no matter how frightening some of these things might seem when you remember them. Do you understand what I'm saying?"

Robin nodded.

"Okay, let's go on. When did you meet him, this guy who calls himself John?"

She took a long breath. "My car broke down on Topanga Canyon."

"What time was it?"

"10:20, maybe later, it might have been 10:30. I kept hoping a police car would pass. But nothing did."

"No police car, you mean?"

"Almost no cars. They just drove right by."

Jordan made a quick calculation, *if she was driving a car, her father must already have been long dead.* "Did you call your mom?"

Again, Robin seemed on the verge of breaking down. A passing fire engine siren was competing with her now shaky voice. Jordan placed his ear just inches from Robin's mouth. "I was afraid to get out of the car. I didn't see any phones around. Also, I knew my mom and dad would kill me." *My mom and dad*: Jordan wondered at the words. "I shouldn't have even been there. I told them I wouldn't drive on Topanga Canyon at night."

Jordan struggled to process the information. Robin was in her mid-twenties. When had this happened? Maybe when she was very young, four or five, and she had suppressed the memory. No, that would be ridiculous. She was driving a car by herself. That means she had to be at least sixteen or seventeen. Even if she was too young to drive—but no, that couldn't be it; her parents seem to have given her permission. And why the references to her father; had her mother remarried? Did she call her stepfather "dad"?

"How old are you?" he asked.

"Seventeen. My birthday was last month."

All right, at least we cleared up that mystery.

"Okay, let's go on. You're in the car, it's broken down, it's late at night, and no cars are coming by. What happened next?"

"A car pulled up near me. An older guy got out."

"How old?"

"Much older than me. Maybe twenty-five, I guess. I don't know why, he looked familiar."

"From where?"

Robin shook her head mutely.

"Okay. What happened next?"

"He parked his car. Then he got out and asked me if I needed help. I said yes, and he told me to release the hood. He lifted it up and looked at the engine. He told me that something with my ignition was totally out of whack. Only he didn't say it like that. He used technical language, like he was a mechanic or something. He seemed very nice, so I got out, and we pushed the car off to the side. He told me he'd drive me to a phone if I wanted to call my parents. It felt scary there alone on the road, so I went with him."

"You're with him in the car now." Jordan said. "Tell me what's going on."

"At first, everything was okay. We talked a little; he asked me what school I went to. Then, he turned on the radio."

"A music station?" Jordan asked. If she remembered one or two of the songs being played, it would be easier to narrow down an approximate date.

"I don't know. It was a news report."

Jordan nodded. "Do you remember anything that was said?"

"It was the stuff they had been talking about the whole day. How that Manson guy raised a newspaper in court with the big headline about the President saying he was guilty."

"*Manson?*" Jordan asked.

"Yeah, Charles Manson. The guy who sent that gang to murder Sharon Tate."

Jordan sat quietly, trying to absorb this last comment. *How did Charles Manson get in here?*

"You're seventeen, right?"

"Yes."

Jordan calculated, then tried to phrase the next words in as non-challenging a manner as possible. "But the Manson murders happened more than thirty years ago?"

"What are you talking about?" Her voice took on a petulant tone. "It happened two years—"

"Robin, tell me what year it is."

She said nothing.

"Why aren't you answering?"

"You were speaking to somebody else."

"Robin, I'm speaking to you. There's no one else here."

"Who's Robin?" she asked.

Jordan felt a cool sweat on the back of his neck. He held up a hand in front of his face and blew softly against his palm.

"I'm speaking to you, Robin Norris. Do your friends call you by some other name, a nickname?"

"I don't know any Robin Norris," she said, her voice peeved.

"What is your name?"

"Beverly Casper."

Jordan knew from his own experience—he had done it just last night with Robin—how easy it was to make a deep trance subject forget her own name. But he had never read or heard of a hypnotic subject spontaneously forgetting her own name and assuming a new identity.

"Do you know what today's date is?"

"August 4th"

"And the year?"

"1970."

"And what is the date of your birth?"

"July 11, 1953."

He marked the dates down on a piece of paper, then made a pyramid with his fingers and sat quietly for a long while. He didn't come up with any brilliant thoughts. In fact, he felt rather dumb. The dumber he felt, the more anxious he got. He had no answers, no solutions, no clue. *We're down the rabbit hole*, he thought, and it seemed to him that he had no choice but to follow Robin into whatever warrens of space and time she was taking him.

"Okay," he finally said, "you're in the car, the story about Manson is on the news. Now what happens?"

"He laughed. Then he said, 'we don't want to hear anything about people who slice people with knives, do we?' And he shut the radio off."

"Go on."

"We've been driving a while now. I ask him where the telephone is. He doesn't answer. He asks me if I like him. I don't know what to say. My heart is beating so fast, I think it's going to burst. I just tell him that I'm grateful to him for helping me out."

Jordan noted that Robin had shifted from the past tense to the present. She was reliving the event.

"'Do you like me?'" he asks again. "'Am I your sort of guy?'"

"I'm trying to figure out what he wants me to say. So I tell him, 'You seem like a nice person, but I'm just going into my senior year in high school. You're a little old for me.'"

"How does he respond?" Jordan asked.

"He doesn't like that. 'You need somebody older,'" he shouts. 'How the hell do you expect me to protect you?'"

"I don't know if he expects an answer. I sit there quietly, and he starts talking, his voice softer. 'You're a young girl, I know that. But I'm exactly what you need and you're exactly what I need. You're still pure, I can tell that. Because I don't want some slut who's done everything with everybody.' He has one hand on the steering wheel, and with the other hand, he pulls his fingers through my hair. It's terrible, but I can't move. 'You haven't done a lot, have you?'

"'What do you mean?'

"'You know, with boys?'

"'No,' I tell him. 'I haven't done much with boys.' I don't know what to say. A part of me wants him to think I'm real loose. Maybe that will turn him off, and he'll just drive me down to a gas station or supermarket and kick me out of the car. But the angry way he says, 'some slut who's done everything with everybody,' I'm afraid what he might do if he thinks I'm fast."

"Can you tell me where you are now, Beverly?"

No answer.

"Try and visualize it," Jordan pressed.

Her voice became agitated. "He's turned off to a side road, a dirt road. I shout at him to turn the car around. Branches are slapping against the window. There are no houses around, just a lot of trees."

"Turn the car around!" I yell. "Let me out."

"He stops the car, and pulls my hair hard. 'Don't you ever raise your voice to me again, is that clear?' I'm sitting there shaking. 'I asked you a question. Is that clear?' He's very angry.

"I jerk my head up and down. My throat is so tight now I feel I can't breathe.

"He lets go of my hair. 'That's better,' he says. 'I'm sorry I had to yell…. You look like an angel. Anybody ever tell you that?' He rubs his fingers on my cheek. 'What's your name, angel?'

"I want to say the first name that comes to me, but no words are coming out. Finally, I say, 'Bonnie Jackson.'

"'Are you telling me the truth?' He grabs my purse. I try to yell, but it comes out hoarse. With one hand he pushes down hard on my shoulder; with the other hand, he finds my driver's license. 'Well, well. What do we have here?'

"I don't say anything. I can't believe how stupid I was to lie to him.

"He turns the light on in the car. It's dim and yellow. He stares at the photograph a long time, looking back and forth between the picture and me. He starts reading from the card, 'Eyes—brown.'" Jordan stared at her, confused yet again. Robin Norris' eyes were green, strikingly so.

"He stares at me," the hypnotized woman was now saying, "and tells me to show him my face. I feel his clammy hand on my chin, turning it. His face is a few inches from mine."

"'Your name's Beverly, right?'

"I move my head up and down.

"'Don't you know, Beverly, that you don't have to lie to me? I'm your friend. Don't you know that by now? I would do anything in the world for you. So, don't lie to me. Promise?'

"'Yes,' I say." Her voice was a whisper.

"'Good. I'm so glad you understand.' He starts to stroke my cheek again… my neck."

Robin started crying, soft repetitive sobs.

"'I'm sorry I lied,' I tell him. 'I've never met a man like you before.'

"'Damn right you haven't. Until now, you've probably just been with some pimply-faced high school boys. It's exciting to be with a real man, isn't it? I was in the Marines, did I tell you that? They only take the best… Only the best for my angel.' He smiles this big scary smile at me, showing me his teeth. I can hear them grinding.

"'Please take me home.' I'm begging him.'

"'Didn't I say I would?' He looks again at my license. 'Happy birthday, Bev. I see you just turned seventeen.' He keeps smiling and now he's making a strange, popping noise like there's something in his mouth. And he's talking faster. 'Well, now that you, or at least your license, has introduced itself to me, maybe I should tell you who I am. They call me John.'

"That's when I said that thing to him, 'Is that your real name?' As soon as I said it, I knew it was dumb. I didn't want to know his name. And he slapped me again, this time harder than before. And then he laughed, 'Don't you know, girl? You never ask a John his name.'

"I want to say something that will make him let me out, but I don't know how to speak to him. Then suddenly, I see a light. It isn't really close, but it doesn't seem too far. I push open my door and try to shout. He's all over me in a second. He yanks me back inside, and puts a hand over my mouth.

"'And I thought you were a friendly girl,' he says. 'Fooled again. No angel, just another liar and tramp, like my old girlfriend.' He puts his hand over my mouth, and with his other hand takes out handcuffs from his jacket pocket. He puts one of them on my left wrist, then attaches the other one round the steering wheel. 'I'll be back real soon,' he says. 'Just got to make sure we don't have any guests.' He pulls out a big knife. 'And we're going to stay real quiet, aren't we?'

"My throat has a dry, burning feeling, and I hear a ringing in my ears. He gets out of the car, and I manage to look out the back window. I can't see the light anymore."

Jordan shuddered, his mind a jumble. Just a half hour earlier, Robin had told him that she had no recollection of any sexual trauma. Was it possible? Had she, unbeknown to her conscious self, been attacked, likely raped, when she was seventeen?

Worse, this man didn't even sound like a rapist, he sounded like a killer. But she couldn't have been killed; she was sitting here in front of him, talking about what happened to her seven years ago. So what was going on? Was she making all this up, or had the older Robin totally disassociated herself from this experience by adopting the separate persona of Beverly Casper? That way her unconscious mind could reassure her that it was Beverly Casper, not Robin Norris, who had been raped.

And how the hell did the Manson case get into it? The Manson murders had occurred before she was born. Nothing was hanging together. Abused children, he knew, often went into disassociative states to shield themselves from the miseries being inflicted on them. But could a raped seventeen-year-old suppress something that had happened at so advanced an age?

"He's walking away," the hypnotized woman continued, "but then he turns around and sees me looking. He draws the knife across his throat and I duck down."

She grew quiet, then began again. "I'm scared, so scared. I want my daddy, I want my mommy. I'm praying, not saying any words, just asking God to help me. Help me. I will never do anything bad again. I know how wrong I was to lie to my parents and how wrong I was to go off with a strange man. I won't do it again, God, I promise."

Jordan took Robin's right hand and held it gently between his hands. "Robin," he said, then, corrected himself, "Beverly, you're in a very safe place now. Nothing bad can happen to you. You're going to be able to tell me all that happens to you so that you can understand yourself better and overcome certain fears and problems you have with swallowing and breathing. Remember, you will be able to express everything you see and feel because you are very safe here. All that you're recalling are certain very unpleasant things that may have once happened to you. But they are not happening anymore. Do you understand what I am saying?"

Robin nodded.

Jordan raised her right hand by the thumb. "I want you to let go of all the weight in your arm," he told her, "so that when I let go of your thumb, your arm will fall to your thigh like a wet, limp dishrag. When it does, you will find that you will have moved forward in time. Perhaps it will be to when this man has returned to the car, or to a later event, but it will be to something you can tell me, something that helps explain this constriction you're feeling in your throat."

He let go of her thumb, and her hand fell like a dead weight. She sat there, breathing heavily, but saying nothing.

Jordan ran his hand back and forth over his scalp, trying to remember the different techniques he had learned for stimulating recall. "In a moment," he said, "I'm going to count to five and touch your forehead and, when I do, you will be able to answer my questions."

As soon as he said "five" he lightly touched his forefinger to the top of her head.

"Tell me what's going on."

"We're near a big pit."

"A pit?"

"A big hole. Only it looks like someone dug it."

"What makes you think that?"

"Because there's a giant mound of dirt right next to it."

"Go on."

"I'm on my knees, my hands are handcuffed behind my back. He takes out a necklace from his pocket with little angel figures on it. He puts it around my neck. 'A little gift from your boyfriend,' he tells me. 'I'm your boyfriend, Bev, right?'"

In her seat, Robin nodded, tears streaming down her face.

"He's taking off his belt. 'C'mon, Bev,' he says. 'Your boyfriend wants to know how much you love him.'

"I try and look away, but he grabs my hair. 'Look at me,' he says. Then, he forces my face down."

Jordan felt nauseous; worse, he felt powerless. He desperately wanted to help this woman, but all he could do was listen.

"It's horrible. I take it in my mouth. He's so big, I'm choking. 'I know you will love me. I know you will thank me...' He's digging his fingers now into my shoulder blades. I keep trying to suck, but I'm gagging. He kicks me away. 'You fucking cunt! You've always been a cunt.'

"'Please, please,' I'm begging him.'" Her voice was high-pitched, squeaky, almost hysterical. "'Just take me home. I swear to you, I'll never tell anybody. I'll never tell. Never.'

"'Why don't you understand?!' he screams at me. 'Why don't you understand? I tried to explain, didn't I?' He's behind me now. I can hear his teeth grinding. Snapping. Clicking. In between every word. 'It's time to go home now. Just like I promised.'

"I can feel something around my neck. It's his belt. It's cutting into my skin! He's pulling it tighter.

"'Most people get old, then get sick and die. But not you. You're going at your peak.' I tense my neck muscles, but it's no use. 'Any final words before you go? Want to leave a message for your mom and dad?'

"'No, no... don't,'" Robin gasped.

"'Last chance,' he says. 'I know they'd like to hear from you.' I can barely get the words out. 'Please tell my mom and dad that I'm sorry for everything, that I love them, and I know that I'll see them someday in heaven.'"

Then, Robin started screaming. *"Air! I can't breathe!"*

Jordan, his heart thumping in his chest, took her hand in his. "Yes, you can breathe. Calm down, Beverly, it's all past. You're safe now. This man can never hurt you ever again."

There were two quick knocks at his door. Pat Haman, the office secretary, pushed it open, an expression of confusion and concern written across her brow. "I heard a scream. Is everything okay?"

"Close the door, Pat. Everything is fine," Jordan said sharply. Haman looked back at him, dubious. "Close the door."

The secretary retreated. Jordan turned back to Robin. She seemed suspended on the edge of hysteria. He had to pull her back. He instructed her to breathe deeply, to focus on the flow of air in and out of her lungs. "With every breath that you take, cool fresh air is circulating throughout your body, from the top of your head to the tip of your toes. And every time you breathe out, you find yourself expelling tension, expelling all the anxiety and horrible memories of what happened with John. So that with every breath that you take, and with every exhalation that you make, you are growing more and more relaxed."

Jordan leaned back in his chair, never taking his eyes off his patient. He watched anxiously as Robin's breathing steadied. The color returned to her pale skin as her face gradually evolved back into the characteristic expressionless hypnotic mask. One crisis had ended, but another was about to begin. In a few minutes, he'd have to bring Robin out of hypnosis. But how did he want her to come out—remembering everything she had described, or forgetting it all, every horrific detail? He knew, as he had told Robin at the party, that, with very rare exceptions, people who have been hypnotized remember everything that happened while they were under. That is, unless the hypnotist instructs them to forget.

His first instinct was to let her recall what had taken place. Why not? It was just some sort of nightmare, not even a real trauma. She was here, so nobody, no John, had murdered her. It was just some sort of fantasy, a hallucination she had constructed. Then again, this fantasy must have something to do with her gagging; this scene, after all, was where her mind regressed when he suggested she go back to the trauma that was the source of her fears. Would it be bad, therefore, for her to remember what she had told him about Beverly Casper? Maybe she grew up knowing such a person, or about such a person? But the dates, those damned specific dates, August 4, 1970, and July 11, 1953, where did they come from? Maybe it would be best to just bring her out, let her remember everything that had happened, and then they could just talk about it.

But then again, even if this stuff never happened to her, even if it was all fantasy, might it not be harmful to let it become a part of her conscious mind? He thought of his mother, a highly sensitive woman with an overly active imagination, who refused to watch violent movies because the action scenes, no matter how fantastic, would keep her up all night. But that was comic book blood and guts and this sounded shockingly real. His thoughts shifted to his father, a Holocaust survivor. He did have thoughts like this and they weren't fantastic.

Jordan felt the paralysis of indecision creeping over him. He needed a door out of this funhouse. Now. The digital clock on his desk was relentlessly pushing time into the future, and his next patient would be here any moment. Then, at what seemed like the last possible instant, the decision became clear. *He would instruct Robin to forget everything she had told him.* Before the hypnosis, she had indicated no knowledge of this incident—clearly, it wasn't part of her consciousness—so a well-phrased hypnotic suggestion would leave it in her unconscious, undisturbed. Later, if he thought it necessary for her to recall these things, he could always put her under again, and bring these recollections back. Yes, better let her forget for now. In the meantime, he would speak with Elinor. He knew what Elinor thought of hypnosis; she'd be furious. But he needed guidance here; she could advise him what to do.

In the few minutes that had elapsed, Robin had remained on the chair quite still, rhythmically breathing in and out.

"Okay," Jordan finally began. "In a very short while, I am going to count to ten, and when I reach ten you will be fully restored to the present, to today. You will recall that your name is Robin Norris, and you will have no recollection of anything that has happened since you first sat down on this chair to be hypnotized. You will have no recollection of ever having had the identity of a woman named Beverly Casper, or of ever having had a violent encounter with a man who told you his name was John.

"The reliving of this experience, even though it will not be part of your conscious memory, will, however, bring you a certain sense of peace, and a great relaxation of your problems with swallowing, gagging and singing. You will find that you will be able to eat easily and sing with full voice. Your complete return to the present will happen naturally and smoothly as I count to ten.

"*One.* You feel yourself moving away from the unpleasant scene you earlier described to me. All memory of it is fading, quickly fading from your mind. *Two…*" he went on, returning Robin to the present very gradually. He was taking no chances that at the count of ten, her eyes would open and she would start screaming as if she was being choked. "*Nine,*" he said, "and you are now fully restored to today. Your name is Robin Norris, and you are now back in the present. At the next number, your eyes will open, and you will feel calm, confident, relaxed and fully aware. *Ten.* Let your eyes open."

Robin's eyes opened slowly, and she blinked a few times.

"I thought you were going to hypnotize me."

"You were hypnotized. How do you feel?"

She raised her shoulders and stretched her arms out full length, just as she had done at the party. "Like I had a great nap." She stifled a yawn, then looked down at her watch. "Oh, my God. You must have had me under for forty minutes. What happened?"

"Let me just ask you a few questions first," Jordan said.

Robin nodded.

"Are you familiar with Topanga Canyon in Malibu and the area around it?"

"I've driven by there maybe once or twice. I wouldn't say I know it, but I have some idea where it is."

"Do you have any relatives or friends named Beverly?"

For a few seconds, she seemed to be examining some point on the wall, high above Jordan's head. "In elementary school, there was a girl who sat next to me in fifth and sixth grade named Beverly."

"Were you good friends?"

"Not really. I have some vague recollection of going to a birth-day party at her house. Who knows, maybe it was the other way around and she came to my house. Nothing more than that."

"Do you know of anything bad, any crime or something like that, that might have happened to her?"

Robin shook her head.

"Did you know—"

"Wait a second, Jordan. Are you telling me that under hypnosis I started talking to you about Beverly Wall?"

"Was that her last name?"

"Yes. This is nuts. I can't believe I started having memories about Beverly Wall."

"What about the name Casper? Did you ever know anyone with the last name Casper?"

Robin laughed. "The only Casper I know is the Friendly Ghost. I hope I wasn't talking about ghosts. This is feeling very weird. Could you please tell me what happened?"

"In a minute. I just need to ask you a few more things." Outside a bell went off. "Do you know who Charles Manson is?"

"Of course, the guy, that psycho who murdered all those people."

"Do you know the names of any of his victims?"

Robin shook her head. "It happened before I was born. He stabbed some pregnant actress, I know, but I don't know her name."

"How are you feeling now, Robin?"

"My body feels okay. But your questions are making me feel strange. I obviously was babbling about Beverly Wall, Charles Manson and somebody named John."

Somebody named John? I never asked her anything about John. "Tell me, Robin, what do you remember about John?"

"John? I don't know. The name just popped into my head. I don't remember anything about John." Robin stared him down. "Am I flipping out?"

"I certainly have no reason to think so."

A bell sounded again. Jordan looked down at his watch.

"I'm not some sort of nut, right?"

He gave a reassuring laugh. "No, Robin, I assure you you're not. I wish I could tell you more. But you know what the bell means? My next appointment is waiting outside. As it is, we've run a few minutes late, so I can't keep him any longer."

"So is that it? Are we done? Am I going to be all better now?"

"We'll just have to wait and see."

"Will you ever tell me what happened?"

"That's up to you, Robin. If you want to know, call me."

"Okay," She looked at the Macintosh apple on Jordan's desk. "Are you planning to eat it?"

"Take it, if you'd like."

"I think I will. I'm starving." She took a large bite out of the firm red apple, chewed a few times, swallowed it, and then took an even larger bite. "Mmm, it's really sweet," she said. She pulled the door open. "We'll talk again soon, mystery man."

In total violation of office protocol, Simon Cox came marching through the doorway even as Robin was leaving. "I followed your advice and called my dad. Thanks to you, I'm refinancing my house now. He says I should go with a variable. What do you think?"

Cox went on, but Jordan's gaze remained focused on the still half-opened door. Robin Norris had told him that she had not had a carefree bite of solid food in weeks. Now, effortlessly, after reliving this horrifying—what should he call it—nightmare, she was obliviously munching on an apple. *What the hell was going on?*

Monday, 3:10 P.M.

The fifteen minutes it took to get from Dittmyer to the theater seemed like five. The apple had gone down smoothly, and now she was singing—*Carousel*, the Beatles, Cole Porter—whatever popped into her head. Full voice. She wondered what the drivers at the stoplights were thinking, hearing her belt out show tunes.

Did this Jordan Geller discover something real, or did he just say some words? She didn't know, and right now she almost didn't care. *He did it, really did it.* But who was he? This "masked man," this doctor, this psychiatrist who had been a total stranger to her twenty-four hours ago? Some kind of connection had been made last night. Signals had been sent, the kind men send to women to whom they feel an attraction. This afternoon the signals were even stronger—all that stuff about not wanting her to be a patient. She hadn't understood why he was so agitated, but now that she could get some oxygen into her brain, she knew exactly what it was about. He wanted to ask her out on a date. Or at least he wanted to keep his options open. He had several medical degrees and a reputation as an up-and-comer, but she didn't sense any arrogance. As far as she could tell, he seemed genuinely kind. And genuinely cute. And, here she laughed to herself, quite mesmerizing. *But why did I say something about Charles Manson and Beverly Wall and some guy named John? And Topanga Canyon? Where is that? And why don't I recall anything from this hypnosis? I did after the hypnosis at the party.*

Enough, she thought, and her voice, as if of its own volition, snapped into a rousing rendition of "I've Got You Under My Skin." She pulled into the theater's parking lot, anxious to break the good news. She hurried through the backstage area, past the dressing rooms and the old props stacked against the walls. Then, for maybe the first time since leaving Jordan's office, she glanced at her watch. A half-hour late; Walter had made a big deal about this run through of *What's the Use of Wond'rin'*, the show's romantic ballad.

As she neared the stage, she could hear the voice of Deb White, her understudy. It took a few seconds to register that it was *Wond'rin'* pouring out of Deb's mouth.

She waited for the understudy to finish, then walked onto the stage. "Sounded pretty good to me," she forced herself to say.

Deb, a fresh-faced ingénue with shoulder-length flaxen hair parted down the middle, was frowning. "I gotta little reedy at the end, didn't I?"

"Oh, I wouldn't wor—"

"*I'll* work with you on it." Walter broke in. Deb nodded, and started away.

"Don't be late again," the director said sharply, making no effort to hide his extreme displeasure. "This is the last time I'm going to say that. Do you understand?" He didn't wait for answer. Instead, he immediately launched into the rehearsal, ripping a small strip of yellow duct tape off the stage floor. "I want you to move toward the center stage as you start the song, then end up here." He moved the tape to its new place.

"Fine," Robin answered. "The fitting went great."

Still bent over, his eyes focused on the wood planks as he spoke. "I'm glad something's going well."

"Walter, I'm sorry. I'm a few minutes late. I really think you're overreacting."

"You're right. Just because you've been giving me sub par work for weeks, and you then show up a full half-hour late for a key rehearsal—you're right, why should I be angry?"

"Is that why you staged this little exhibition with Deb?"

"Deb White has some weaknesses, but she's here on time and she can do the job. Can you?"

"Yes, I can."

"Then prove it."

Furious, Robin started back to her dressing room. *Can I do the job? Hah! I sounded great in the car, didn't I? Then again, that was the car, not a large hall.* By the time she left the dressing room, she felt like she was auditioning for the show, not rehearsing it.

When she returned to the stage, Walter was sitting in the middle row of the darkened theater. Rick Kauf and Tom Reibman, the actors playing Billy and Jigger, were ready in the wings. "Okay, Robin," Walter boomed.

As soon as she hit her first note, she knew she was okay.

What's the use of wonderin'
If he's good or or if he's bad,
Or if you like the way he wears his hat?
Oh, what's the use of wonderin'
If he's good or he's bad,
He's your fella and you love him,
That's all there is to that.

She sang with passion and pathos and nuance. For weeks, all of them, the actors, the stagehands, everyone affiliated with the production, had assumed that she had the lead because she was such a close friend of the director. Now, finally, they knew better.

Walter jogged up to the stage. He put his arm around Robin and pulled her aside. "That was fantastic. Like my old Robin. What happened?"

What was the point of telling him about the session with Jordan Geller? "I think it must have been when I heard Deb singing. I just got angry and… Walter, you're a genius. I know you did that for me."

He took her strong chin in his hands. "I'm just here to help you spread your wings, my angel."

Monday, 6 P.M.

Jordan glanced at his watch, and just managed to suppress a curse. He would have given a lot to be able to duck this party; all he really wanted to do now was check out Robin's story, particularly those very specific dates. But unlike last night's event, his attendance at this one—Dittmyer's annual fundraiser—was mandatory.

The host was Avery Conniston, a television producer who had been fabulously successful in the eighties and early nineties with a half-dozen glitzy evening soap operas. Conniston had taken a good portion of his TV fortune and plowed it into modern art, in which he soon made his second fortune. "Make trash, buy art" had become his motto. He had even confided it to an interviewer in an incautious moment. A sampling of his best pieces—a Jackson Pollock, an early David Hockney, a Jaspar Johns—could be found on the walls of his Bel Air estate. *Architectural Digest* had featured the house three times in the last nine years, a publication record.

Five years earlier, Conniston had entrusted his dangerously bulimic daughter, April, into Elinor Fischer's care. Where everyone else had failed, Fischer succeeded. Within a short time, the brilliant young woman had overcome her eating disorder. In spring she had graduated from Yale Law School, where she had been an editor on the law review. A grateful Conniston had become a major advocate of Fischer's and a generous patron of Dittmyer.

"You look quite distinguished in that tuxedo, Dr. Geller," April Conniston observed, the first person to greet Jordan as he stepped down three parquet stairs into the large living room.

At Fischer's insistence, the fundraiser was black tie only. Sports jackets were usually as formal as Los Angeles got, with two notable exceptions—the Academy Awards and the Dittmyer event.

"You're looking pretty distinguished yourself," Jordan responded. April was wearing a black silk strapless evening dress with silver lace trim. It took a model's figure to pull it off, but April had one—small, firm breasts and narrow hips.

"Thank you."

"I haven't seen you since—" Jordan stopped himself. April had been at Carrie's funeral—home from New Haven for Christmas break—a little over a year ago. He remembered her coming over to him at the cemetery, telling him how she hoped she could be there for him. "I heard you passed the bar. Congratulations."

April lifted two wine glasses off a passing platter, gave one to Jordan and raised the other.

"And I heard you made protégé. From one Elinor Fischer disciple to another, cheers."

A waiter offered Jordan a tray of *hors d'oeuvres*.

"No, thank you."

"Oh, go ahead."

"I hope this won't destroy your image of me, but I can't stand caviar."

That was true. But so was something else. Ever since Robin Norris had left his office four hours ago, his stomach had been feeling queasy. Imagining those fish eggs swimming around in his intestines made him wince.

"You've probably never had the good stuff. Try it. It's Beluga. Something like $700 a pound."

She took a cracker from the waiter and ate one bite. "Mmm. You don't know what you're missing."

"So how does it feel to be in L.A. again after three years?"

"Better than I expected. I mean it's a little odd to graduate in the middle of the year. But it's worked out. I'm with a small firm that does a lot of criminal defense work. Mafia dons, drug dealers, assorted ax murderers… charming people like that."

He wondered if she was kidding. "I thought you were more of a corporate law type."

"Maybe you don't know me as well as you think you do. You know, we should get together. Think of all the things we have to talk about, like Elinor, for instance. That should be good for our first decade at least."

Since they had first met at the fundraiser at her father's house two years earlier, April had made scant effort to disguise her crush on Jordan. Though only three years separated them, in those days, the gap seemed much wider. And in any case, there was Carrie, with whom Jordan was living and with whom he had expected to live forever. But that was two years ago, and two years at Yale had made a difference. April had always been smart and quick-witted, but now she had added self-assurance to her brief.

"I'm not sure that would be such a good idea."

God knows he was tempted. But he felt uncomfortable pursuing anything more than a light flirtation over a glass of wine because, even though April had undoubtedly been in treatment with someone in New Haven, she was Fischer's patient. And worse, he already knew a lot about her. Fischer had discussed the case of "Nancy D.," often in her Dittmyer seminars.

"People do change, Dr. Geller. Like me. It might be clinically interesting for you to find out."

At that moment, and to Jordan's immense relief, a well-built man with a smooth, unlined face that belied his middle age bounded up to them. "You want to introduce me to your friend?"

"Jordan Geller, meet Mike Fields. He's living in the guest house here."

"Just until I get on my feet. I'm going through a divorce."

"Mike is my dad's cousin," April explained, clearly irritated that she no longer had Jordan's full attention.

"Avery is trying to show me the TV business." Fields adjusted his tie. "Do you find these things as uncomfortable as I do?"

"Dr. Geller is with the Dittmyer Institute," April interjected.

"A medical man? Impressive. Hey, can I ask you a professional question?"

The peril of all doctors, especially psychiatrists: go to a party or stand in line at the grocery, for that matter, and the moment people find out your profession, they try to elicit a sixty-second diagnosis, one, ideally, that agrees with their own. Jordan really felt like saying, "office hours are nine to five," but, of course, he didn't. This was the Dittmyer Fundraiser, and this man was Avery Conniston's cousin, and Avery Conniston was the institute's foremost patron.

"Go ahead."

"Why would a happily married woman, out of the blue, pick up and leave her husband?"

"You're sure she was so happily married?"

"That's the obvious question, right? I don't know. I gave her everything. Maybe it's a cultural thing. She's from the Philippines." Fields sighed.

"How long were—"

"Mike," April broke in, "Dr. Geller's here for the party. I don't think it's fair—"

"Of course. You're right, April." He turned to Jordan. "Sorry."

"No need to apologize."

"She used to be so sweet. I think she got too Americanized."

Jordan nodded sympathetically. He wondered if Fields was Avery's first cousin—probably was if he was putting him up at the guest house—but he certainly lacked the producer's sophistication and polish. Then again, Jordan didn't know where Avery had acquired these qualities. Were they inherited or learned? If Mike Fields' lack of social grace was any indication, the latter must be true.

"You could always make an appointment with Dr. Geller." April smiled at Jordan. "I'm sure Mike would qualify for the family discount."

Fields laughed. "On what your dad is paying me? Don't get me wrong. I love Ave like a brother and I'm really grateful to him, but I gotta watch my pennies. Associate Producer sounds great, but with the cost of the divorce, I'm just getting by. Oh geez, I almost forgot what I came here for. Your dad says we better steer the guests inside and start dinner."

April squeezed Jordan's hand. "Call me sometime." Then she walked away with Fields.

A moment later, Elinor Fischer stepped over. "She's very bright. Quite attractive too, don't you think?"

Jordan couldn't help but smile.

"She's obviously quite attracted to you. And why shouldn't she be—a handsome, accomplished young man with ambition, a future."

Jordan looked over his shoulder as if she were talking to someone standing behind him.

"False modesty is quite boring," Fischer declared.

"It's just that I never thought of you as a matchmaker."

"Heaven forbid. But sometimes, my dear boy, we don't see what is right in front of us. Now why don't we join the others for dinner? Everything looks quite delicious."

But nothing, as it turned out, looked good to Jordan—not the endive salad, not the thin green beans, not even the mesquite grilled salmon with a cucumber salsa. Sitting between Avery Conniston and Fischer at a circular table, Jordan ate as little as he could without insulting his host.

Avery Conniston waited till the tiramisu was served, then tapped his crystal wine glass with a gold-plated fork. A little over five-and-a-half feet tall, finely boned, bald except for a Julius Caesar wreath of light brown hair, Conniston had spent his adult life and a good portion of his fortune erasing all traces of his lower-middle class upbringing. His perfectly manicured hands, tailor-made silk tuxedo, alligator wing-tip shoes all testified to the complete success of this project. He wanted only the best—the best art, the best house, the best masseuse, the best personal trainer, the best plastic surgeon, the best psychoanalyst.

Addressing the crowd of 150 invited guests, Conniston's eyes were alert, darting. "It is my great privilege," Conniston began, "to introduce a woman who has profoundly influenced my life, and done favors for my family and myself that can never be repaid. I know many of you have had similar experiences. If you haven't, I strongly suggest you get an appointment... if you can." He waited for the gentle laugh to subside. "A line from a rave review in *The New York Times* about her latest work, *Midlife Transformations,* sums up the role Elinor Fischer now plays in American therapy and American culture: 'From Freud to Fischer, there is none like Fischer.'"

The psychoanalyst rose from her chair. Argentinean born, her family refugees from Nazi Germany, Fischer's English was accented and formal. After thanking Conniston and the other Dittmyer patrons, she launched into a trenchant analysis of how, in an age of radio psychologists and of easy answers to complex problems, it was more important than ever to maintain the high standards of the institute. "And not only maintain, but expand. Dittmyer is an elite institution, and we don't have to apologize for that. What we do have to apologize for is that we have cures to offer, and we are capable of giving them to only a fraction of the people whose lives could be transformed and healed. But if we expand our facilities, expand our staff and thereby expand the number of people we can touch, then it is within our capacity to reach out and affect the entire fabric of this society."

"Whoa, whoa," called out Brad Markus, film producer and a frequent visitor to Fischer's office. "You're not speaking to Fort Knox, Elinor. Just how much money are you expecting us to give tonight?"

"Let me tell you a story, Brad. A man, a pretty affluent man, a film producer to be precise"—and the audience chuckled—"was at a dinner party when he started choking on a fish bone. He couldn't dislodge it, until one of the guests, a physician, walked over and extracted it. The man had almost choked to death. Now, relieved, he said to the doctor, 'How can I ever thank you? What can I give you, doctor?'

"The doctor answered, 'Just give me half of what you would have been willing to give me when that bone was still in your throat.'"

When the laughter subsided, Elinor resumed, her face now grave. "Most of you have had that fish bone in your throat or in the throats of someone dear to you. We have the ability to dislodge those fish bones from thousands of throats." She pointed to Jordan. "You have all met Dr. Jordan Geller at previous functions. He's a brilliant young clinician, one of the most incisive minds I have ever encountered. He might be the one leading us into the next generation. But he needs, and I need, and America needs, more men and women like him to take us forward. Poorly trained psychologists and psychiatrists, who encourage patients to pop pills, today dominate the mental health community in America. The future of our field must be more than Prozac and Zoloft. It must be to understand the brain, and to use that understanding to help people regain control over their lives. At Dittmyer we have the ability. All of you here in this room tonight have the means. Together, we can bring a new voice of sanity to America."

When the last standing and clapping member of the audience sat down, Jordan, as arranged, rose to thank Fischer. "It says in the Bible, 'the beginning of wisdom is the fear of God.' I once quoted that to Elinor, and she told me, 'More often, that's the beginning of neuroses.' At Dittmyer, as I am sure many of you here know, the beginning of wisdom is the fear of Elinor Fischer."

The guests nodded and laughed.

"But fear, or rather, awe, is really only a small part of my feelings for her. Love is another. I have learned more from this remarkable woman than I can ever express. To Elinor, I owe a debt that I can never repay."

"Enough about me, Jordan," Fischer chirped from her seat.

Jordan pointed at her. "You see! She can dish out the praise, but she can't take it."

The guests, Fischer included, laughed again, harder this time.

"And don't start talking about debts that people can't repay." Fischer added, building on the high spirits in the room. "That makes me nervous!"

Jordan smiled back at his mentor and then waited a moment before beginning again.

"In all seriousness, I am honored by the way Elinor has spoken of me. And I am honored that she has asked me to continue at the Institute when my residence is completed in three months. I look forward to working with and learning from her for many years to come. Thank you."

As soon as he could, and certainly earlier than Fischer would have wished, Jordan made his exit. His stomach finally seemed to be settling down and he desperately wanted to get to his favorite Borders Bookstore that would be closing in less than an hour. April Conniston accosted him at the front door. She slipped a piece of paper into his jacket pocket, gave him a quick kiss on the cheek and whispered: "Give me a call. I don't bite, unless you want me to."

Monday, 10:00 P.M.

Do you know of any books on the Manson killings?"

The young Borders' clerk—a tag identified him as Chris—laughed. "I gather you're not much of a true crime buff."

He walked Jordan over to the True Crime section and handed him a copy of *Helter Skelter*. "Bugliosi was the prosecutor in the case, knew more about it than anybody."

Uncertain of what he might find, Jordan thanked the man for his help, then headed for the store's cafe. Except for a few nibbles at the fundraiser, he barely had eaten since breakfast. He ordered a piece of cheesecake and sat down with his new book. Forty-five minutes before closing, there was no shortage of empty tables.

He opened it at the table of contents. Bugliosi had given each chapter a name, then listing the relevant dates under it. A quick inspection revealed that the trial itself had taken place between June 15 and November 19, 1970, consistent with what Robin had told him under hypnosis. *Who the hell knows? Maybe she read this book.* Still, a part of him, a big part, would have felt a lot happier had she had the dates wrong.

He tried to recall precisely what it was she had said—something about Manson having held up a newspaper at the trial with a headline saying that the president had declared him guilty. But which president? Of some university? Nah, everybody must have been saying Manson was guilty; a newspaper wouldn't headline something like that. *The President of the United States?* Hard to imagine an American president commenting on a murder trial. Then again, Manson was one of the most famous murderers in American history; 1970—who was President? Jordan knew his history, no problem: Richard Nixon.

Somehow, true crime books didn't strike him as the sort that would have scholarly apparatuses, like indexes. He made a silent prayer, turned to the back, and there it was: a detailed index. "Nixon, Richard Milhous." Jordan casually turned to the first listing, but when he read the opening words, it seemed like his heart would stop: "It was Monday, August 3, 1970," Bugliosi's account began. "I was on my way back to court from lunch, a few minutes before 2 P.M., when I was abruptly surrounded by newsmen. They were all talking at once, and it was a couple of seconds before I made out the words: 'Vince, have you heard the news? *President Nixon just said that Manson's guilty.*'"

Nixon, it appeared, had been speaking to law enforcement officials in Denver. He had been denouncing the press, one of his favorite pastimes, for glorifying criminals, when he started speaking about the Manson case: "Here is a man who was guilty, directly or indirectly, of eight murders. Yet here is a man who, as far as the coverage is concerned, appeared to be a glamorous figure."

Jordan let out an involuntary whistle. For heaven's sakes, he thought, the President was a lawyer. What a dumb thing to say! Jordan scanned the following pages. Nixon's comment had become the lead news item that day. The trial judge had issued an immediate ruling to keep the jury away from radios, televisions and newspapers. Yet sure enough, the next day, Manson, through one of his lawyers, it seemed, somehow had smuggled an *L.A. Times* into the courtroom and held up its headline, "MANSON GUILTY, NIXON DECLARES," for the jury to see. The judge had immediately cleared the jury out of the courthouse.

Jordan put the book down. It was the day after Nixon's speech that Manson had pulled that stunt in the courtroom: August 4, 1970. *Just as Robin had said.* How could she have known something like that? Robin had been born in 1977. When he questioned her after bringing her out of hypnosis, she claimed to know nothing about the Manson case, other than familiarity with his name. But Beverly Casper had known the details. Even he, no great follower of crime stories, had heard of Sharon Tate, the most famous of Manson's victims. And he also knew that Manson hadn't done the slayings himself; he had sent over some groupies to commit them. Robin hadn't known that, but Beverly had. Robin had assumed that Manson was himself the murderer. And all she knew was that he had killed some actress. She didn't know her name.

How then could she know this thing about President Nixon, the kind of detail only people alive at the time, or real students of the case, would be apt to know? And it was unlikely that even they would remember the date. But it was more than that, it was the way she mentioned it, so casually—"It was the stuff they had been talking about the whole day. How that Manson guy raised a newspaper in court with the big headline about the President saying he was guilty," as if it really was August 4, 1970, and everybody in the United States knew, of course, what had happened in court that day. That, he could believe. He remembered the coverage of the O.J. Simpson trial. When O.J. couldn't fit those gloves on, everybody knew about it. Fine, that made sense. But would people remember it in 2020? What are the chances that a woman born seven years after the O.J. trial would wander into a psychiatrist's office and, under hypnosis, recall hearing that story being broadcast on the radio?

Anything seemed possible. He turned back to the index, checked under "C" for "Casper." Maybe there was some Beverly Casper connected to the Manson story who had been murdered. His search yielded nothing. There was an entry about a Paul Caruso followed by one about Winifred Chapman. No intervening Casper.

Suddenly, the nausea returned. He leaned back in his chair and forced himself to focus on his breathing. As he monitored himself inhaling and exhaling, a strange association popped into his mind; the cross-country car trip he had taken with his parents when he was seven.

His father wanted to relocate to Southern California; his mother wanted to stay in New York, near her family and friends. Throughout the trip, Jordan suffered terrible stomach cramps. It seemed like every other rest stop, he was hanging his head over a toilet.

As the nausea retreated, he stood up, paid for the book and set out for home. Along the way, he rolled down the car windows. The moist, cool air refreshed him.

At the intersection of Wilshire and Westwood, waiting for the interminable light to change, his mind returned to that childhood odyssey. Before leaving, he recalled overhearing his parents argue about the proposed move. Finally, they agreed that "Jordan will decide," a phrase he could hear his father uttering like it was yesterday. If he liked Los Angeles, the family would move. If he didn't, they would stay in New York.

"Jordan will decide." Quintessential Frank Geller—a man who couldn't make up his mind, couldn't make a decision. And, if he had to, he'd look for someone to make it for him, even his seven-year-old son. Of course, there was a reason for this neurosis, a reason so obvious that when Elinor saw it almost immediately after Jordan started his analysis with her three years ago, he was ashamed at his own obtuseness in not having seen it himself. Franz Geller (Frank after he emigrated to the United States) had been a brilliant medical student in Budapest in 1941, top of his class. On track to be a surgeon, he was the favorite of all his professors. There was only one problem. He was Jewish. Once the war began, his sisters, Leah, one year younger, and Celia, two, begged him to take them out of the city, out of Europe. Leah saw clearly what was coming. Franz, buried in his studies, his natural arrogance inflated by his success, only expressed irritation at his siblings. Judaism meant nothing to him. He might have been a Jew by blood, but he was an atheist by choice. There was no place in his scientific world for ancient superstitions. And even if the Nazis were as bad as people said, he was confident that they wouldn't harm doctors. It made absolutely no sense to the young rationalist. Still, the sisters begged. But they were powerless when he refused to listen. Orphaned three years earlier, the two siblings had worshipped their brilliant older brother. And though thoroughly modern in belief, Franz was traditional in family. So were his sisters. If he stayed, they must.

The Nazis came, of course. And drew no distinctions between those Jews who practiced their faith and those who didn't. Nazis didn't have any trouble making decisions. They wanted all Jews dead. They arrested Franz while he was watching one of his professors perform a liver resection from the observation deck of the operating room. They arrested the professor, also a Jew. They let the patient, a Jew, die on the table. When the Nazi thugs pushed him down the stairs leading to the main entrance to the medical school, his left arm shattered in three places. He survived that, though he could never fully grip anything in his left hand again. He also survived two years in a labor camp and one in a concentration camp. He never saw his sisters again. He asked everyone he met if they had seen them, but never got an affirmative answer. They had vanished in the night.

Plagued by the guilt that he, Frank, in his hubris, was responsible for his sisters' deaths, and that he, who had been so imperious, so brilliant, but stupid, survived, and they, who had been clear-sighted and good, had died, he emerged from the flames of the Holocaust a very different man. If he didn't make any decisions, he could never again make a bad decision. He came to the United States, married another Holocaust survivor, and forgot about medicine. Doctors had to make decisions all day long. He spent the rest of his working life as a salesman—mostly wholesaling jewelry. He met and married Jordan's mother after divorcing his first wife. She was fifteen years his junior and Jordan was an unexpected, and—Jordan still had not resolved this issue—perhaps unwanted surprise.

Later, after the family completed the cross-country trip, Frank Geller took his son to see a pediatrician about those stomach woes. After relating some of the details of the journey to the kindly doctor, the pediatrician wrinkled his brow and smiled. "There's nothing wrong with you, young man. Your stomach problems are all in your head." Obvious as that diagnosis sounded now, to young Jordan it had been a startling revelation. The idea that the mind could so deeply impact the body made a profound impression on him. So profound, he chuckled to himself twenty-one years later, that he ended up becoming a psychiatrist.

When Jordan got home he popped a Sonata—he needed sleep—chasing it with a swig of Pepto Bismol. He went to his bookshelves and pulled down a book he hadn't read since junior high. Though he had lost or discarded many books over his years in high school, college and med school, this was one he always took with him; *They Call It Human Nature* by Dr. Hugo Miller, M.D.

A couple of years after the Gellers had settled in Los Angeles, Jordan's fourth grade English teacher asked everyone to read a book that focused on their future career ambition. Most of the boys read sports biographies, but Jordan read *They Call It Human Nature*, which he had found quite by chance while browsing a second-hand bookstore in Santa Monica. It confirmed everything the pediatrician had told him about the mind influencing the body, and gave a long list of startling examples from Dr. Miller's own practice. He blew some dust off the top of the book and opened it in the middle. Both pages were marked with brackets and stars highlighting the passages he had found important, a habit he still practiced today.

Of course, he knew the reason for this latest bout of nausea. Anyone who could eat at Stan's Grill four or five times a week could not, by definition, have a sensitive stomach. It was the research he had to do tomorrow morning that was sending his insides roiling. If it confirmed even a bit of what Robin Norris had told him, then he would have to confront Elinor, a prospect that would make the strongest man queasy. But there was something more, more intimidating by far than Elinor Fischer—he would have to confront every basic assumption on which he had based his life in the seven years since he had entered medical school. He couldn't help wondering if after all these years of medical and analytical training he really knew much more about the human mind than he did after he first encountered Dr. Miller's book.

Maybe he knew less. Perhaps the boundaries of the mind extended beyond the body, even beyond time. Something very powerful inside of him told him to run away from this thought. Didn't he hear what Elinor had said at the fundraiser? He was the heir apparent to her throne, the potential head of one of the most prestigious mental health institutes in the country, if not the world. Common sense, better yet, good sense, dictated that he stay on this path.

Eventually, the Pepto calmed his stomach. The Sonata did nothing, however. At 5 A.M. he was still wide awake.

Tuesday

Tuesday, 9:00 A.M.

During his undergrad years at UCLA, Jordan had minored in modern American history. He had done enough research papers to know how to work the library's collection of *L.A. Times* microfilm without difficulty. Now—it was nine in the morning, he hadn't slept more than two hours—he withdrew copies of the newspaper from August, 1970, and quickly inserted the microfilm into a reading machine. Every rational part of him was hoping he'd slog through a month of papers and find no mention of Beverly Casper. But then again, not every part of him, he was rapidly discovering, was rational.

He turned first to August 4th, just to see the infamous headline, "MANSON GUILTY, NIXON DECLARES," and read through the story carefully. He then turned to the accompanying articles detailing different reactions to the President's words. All this, for no particular reason; Nixon's speech had nothing to do with why he was there. But somehow, he found himself anxious to delay the actual search. Accurate or not, true or false, he'd know everything within a few minutes. Either prospect frightened him.

Finally, his delaying tactics finished, he skipped to the August

5th edition: If there was anything to the Beverly Casper story, it couldn't be in the August 4th paper. According to Robin's account, Beverly would have been kidnapped the night of the 4th, so the earliest mention would be the 5th. He carefully perused every headline, starting on page 1 and going straight through. Nothing.

He kept pushing ahead, determined to read through every *L.A. Times* until August 10. He didn't have to go that far. On August 6th, at the bottom of page 3, there was a Woodland Hills dateline:

FEARS MOUNT FOR MISSING TEEN

August 5, *Woodland Hills*: Police in this West San Fernando Valley town are investigating the disappearance Tuesday evening of Beverly Casper, a seventeen-year-old high school student at Madison High in Woodland Hills.

Miss Casper's parents, William and Alice Casper, reported their daughter missing about 1 A.M., Wednesday morning. According to Alice Casper, she and her husband had been nervously waiting up for their daughter, who had been due home earlier in the evening, but had called to say she would be detained. At 12:50 A.M., the Casper's phone rang. A male caller, she said, told her he had a message from Beverly. When the shocked Mrs. Casper asked to speak with her daughter, the man told her Beverly was sleeping. The caller then said a few more words, and hung up.

The bizarre nature of the call so frightened Mrs. Casper that she immediately alerted the Woodland Hills police to her daughter's disappearance.

Although general police department policy dictates postponing investigations of missing persons until a minimum of twenty-four hours have elapsed, police Lieutenant Michael Broder immediately initiated a criminal investigation into the girl's disappearance.

So far, all that is known is the following: Beverly had gone out late that afternoon to a rehearsal of a high school play due to premiere in September, at the beginning of the school year. After the rehearsal, she joined several girlfriends at Hamburger Heaven in Malibu. One of the girls, Melissa Wine, reported that she and Beverly had been there with two other friends. According to Miss Wine, Miss Casper, a senior at Madison High, left the restaurant alone shortly after 10:15 P.M. Her deserted brown Pontiac Grand Am was found by police on Topanga Canyon about 3 A.M. Wednesday.

Both the local police and the Casper family have issued an appeal to anyone having any knowledge concerning Beverly Casper's whereabouts or what happened to her on August 4th, to come forward. Police have set up 555-6150 as a police hotline.

Jordan stared at the article with unblinking eyes: Beverly Casper had existed. Beverly Casper had disappeared at age seventeen.

He dropped his head into his palms and rubbed his temples and his forehead. There might be a simple explanation, he thought. Maybe the Casper parents had left the Woodland Hills area after the tragedy and moved near to where Robin's family had lived. Maybe Robin heard the story as a child and suppressed the recollections.

There had to be some connection between the Norrises and the Caspers, he kept telling himself: Isn't that how all these stories end?

And yet, he couldn't turn away.

Nothing more on August 7th. August 8th the case reappeared:

FRIEND OF MISSING GIRL QUESTIONED

August 8, *Woodland Hills:* Lawrence Keeton, rumored boyfriend of Beverly Casper, the high school student missing since leaving Hamburger Heaven in Malibu shortly after 10 P.M. Tuesday, was brought in for questioning by police last night. On the evening of her disappearance, Casper had confided to friends that Keeton had been calling her, and had asked her out.

Police first learned of Keeton's connection to the missing girl the morning after her disappearance, and briefly questioned him at his home. However, a source inside the police department informs us, police interest in Keeton increased significantly yesterday, when the police hotline received an anonymous call informing them that Miss Casper had been seen with Mr. Keeton after leaving Hamburger Heaven.

Keeton, we have learned, denies having seen Miss Casper that evening. According to one source, he told police that he had simply asked Miss Casper out for a date, but that they were by no means a couple. After two hours of questioning, the police released Keeton in the custody of his father, local attorney Frederick Keeton.

When this reporter caught up with the Keetons outside their home., the young man angrily denied seeing Casper that evening. When asked why someone would leave a message on the hotline saying he had, Keeton didn't answer. When the question was repeated, the elder Keeton responded: "My son is in shock because of the events of the last few days. He has the highest regard for Beverly Casper, and is praying for her safe return. He is, of course, in no way involved in Miss Casper's disappearance."

Shortly thereafter the articles started growing shorter and less frequent. Jordan turned to the newspaper's index, and found three more entries for 1970. In early October, a brief item noted that Lieutenant Broder had reported the absence of any further leads in the Casper disappearance. A month later, a young woman's partially decomposed body was found in Malibu Canyon, and there was press speculation that it might be Beverly's. However, an autopsy soon identified the body as Norma Thompson, a nineteen-year-old coed from Orange County studying at Pierce College. Driven by an ever-widening net of curiosity, Jordan now checked Thompson's name in the index. He learned that her ex-boyfriend, a Franklin Jonathan Cole, was arrested two days later and charged with the murder. *Franklin Jonathan Cole*, Jordan read over again; *They call me John*. The connection was ridiculous, he realized, or was it? He found himself marking Cole's name down on a card.

A December 31st article merely mentioned Beverly's disappearance within the context of a year-end review of serious, still unsolved, crimes and disappearances in the Los Angeles area.

Jordan remained at the table, reflecting on his earlier certainty that there must be some connection between the Casper and Norris families, that Robin might have heard a thousand details about this crime when she was a child. But that still didn't make any sense. Why under hypnosis would she speak about these events as if they had happened to *her*? More important, from where could she have heard about John? Certainly, at least based on what had so far been reported in the papers, not from the Caspers.

He sought out the 1971 *L.A. Times'* index. Only one additional article concerning Beverly Casper had appeared, on February 6th. He scanned the microfilm quickly but, when he found the article, it offered no additional information. Still, it made for painful reading:

HS SENIOR FOUND DEAD; LINK TO MISSING TEEN

Feb 5, *Woodland Hills*: Lawrence Keeton, the seventeen-year-old Madison High senior questioned by police last August in the disappearance of the still-missing Beverly Casper, was found Wednesday evening in the forests of Topanga Canyon, the victim, preliminary investigation suggests, of a self-inflicted gunshot wound. Keeton's father, Woodland Hills attorney Frederick Keeton, acknowledged that the gun found near his son's body was his. The elder Keeton claims to have acquired the gun a year earlier during a rash of break-ins in this middle-class, west San Fernando Valley town.

In a statement made to this reporter subsequent to his son's death, Frederick Keeton denounced the police department for the widespread publicity generated by their questioning of his son in the aftermath of Casper's disappearance. "My son was harassed at his school. Larry would find sick notes on his locker calling him a pervert and a killer."

When this reporter confronted Lieutenant Michael Broder with Frederick Keeton's angry comments, the lieutenant expressed sadness, but no anger: "I want to convey my sorrow to the Keeton family over this unhappy occurrence."

When Broder was asked if it could be definitely assumed that Larry Keeton was in no way involved in the Casper disappearance, the lieutenant refused to comment: "The Casper case remains open. We still have no idea what happened to the girl. That is all I have to say."

What a response! After a statement like that, did anyone, aside from immediate family, show up for Larry Keeton's funeral?

If "John" was real then it wasn't only Beverly Casper whose life had ended that night. Larry Keeton had just as surely been a victim.

Tuesday, 10:32 A.M.

hat are we doing here? I don't want to be here," Claire Johnson insisted to her husband. "Let's go."

"Claire, honey, please. If Lieutenant Lemoski told us to come here, he had—"

"Monica could be waiting for us at home," Claire interrupted. "Hurry now, or we'll miss her."

Johnson forced himself to turn away from his wife. The coroner lifted the sheet from Monica Johnson's face. He pulled it back only to the chin; no need for the parents to see the neck, with its sickening purple bruises.

"She's going to CSUN," Claire told Lemoski, oblivious to the coroner, oblivious to her husband. Out of the corner of his eye, Lemoski saw tears coursing down Keith Johnson's stubbled cheeks. He could only imagine how those tears must have burned. The man's daughter was dead. She wasn't going anywhere, except six feet into the ground. The consequences of that dark fact, he knew, would oppress these two decent souls every day of their lives.

Suddenly, Claire Johnson looked down at the corpse, shaking

her head violently from side. *"That's not my Monica."* She turned away and then back again. *"It's not! It's not!"*

Keith Johnson touched his wife's elbow and guided her toward the swinging doors that led out of the morgue and into a new life of endless grief.

"You're not going to let them walk out of here, are you?" Jimmy Lee asked, catching up to Lemoski in the hallway. "We haven't questioned them yet."

"Jimmy," Lemoski said. "The woman is in total denial, and the husband is going to have his hands full just dealing with that, not to mention his own pain."

"But—"

"We'll have plenty of time to talk to them tomorrow. Now, let me just arrange to get them home."

Lee shrugged his demurral; the lieutenant had has own way of doing things.

"She's going to be a vet," Claire Johnson told Lemoski as he opened the door to the police cruiser. "She has such a special way with animals. She speaks their language, doesn't she, Keith?"

The man stared ahead, his bloodshot eyes fixed on the horizon.

Lemoski had seen many reactions to murder. He'd seen people look at their dead loved ones and laugh. He'd heard men wail like women. He had often wondered how he would react if he should have to identify someone close to him. There was no way to know, no way to prepare. Who would want to?

As the police car drove off, escorting the Johnsons back to a home whose population had just been reduced by a third, the lieutenant's mind flashed back to yesterday morning, and his worries about how he was going to pay for Kathy's college tuition. Paying tuition. It was a problem he was suddenly grateful to have.

Tuesday, 11:09 A.M.

Less than twenty-fours hours had elapsed since Robin had left his office, but to Jordan it seemed as if the rest of his life might well be divided into B.H. and A.H.—before and after the hypnosis. Of course, it was not just the hypnosis that had so excited him, but also the revelations at Borders last night and at the library this morning. And yet, at each stage along the way, he kept asking himself, "What would Elinor say?"

Now, as he entered the Institute, he found Fischer's office door half-open. He tapped lightly.

"Yes?"

"It's me, Elinor," he said—Jordan had once confided to a friend that the day Fischer asked him to call her "Elinor" he felt as if he had just been drafted from a college baseball team straight into the majors. He stepped inside. "Do you have a minute?"

Fischer glanced up without moving her head. "Is that going to be sufficient?"

Dressed in a creamy yellow suit that complemented her olive skin, Fischer spoke with patrician formality. "Sit down, Jordan." She gestured to the leather chair in front of her desk. "Somehow, I don't think you're here to tell me about how much you enjoyed the fundraiser last night."

"It came off very well, I thought," he answered, not wanting to seem overly anxious to rush the conversation along.

"You spoke very nicely, although we all could have survived without your trademark citation from the Bible. Anyway, I was a little disappointed you departed so soon after dinner. Several people asked about you, including April."

"I had some work to get done."

"I suspect that work has something to do with this impromptu consult. And from your body language, I can see that you are not in a subtle mood. You're reeking of something momentous."

Jordan returned the grin. "Am I that transparent?"

"I'm waiting, expectantly."

This was the moment Jordan had anticipated but, now that it had arrived, also dreaded. He desperately wanted Elinor's input about Robin. But to get it, he would have to tell her everything, starting with how he had met Robin at the party. And Jordan was no fool. The only question in his mind was: Would Elinor be slightly annoyed about the hypnosis or truly furious?

He tried to glide over the details preceding the hypnosis, mentioning only that he had been astonished when Stanton had made his announcement and summoned him up.

"Let me make sure I'm understanding what you're telling me," Fischer cut in. "You performed as a stage hypnotist at a party?"

"Yes, but—"

"And when this so-called friend, this Stanton, introduced you, did he honor you by telling everyone present that you were a doctor?"

Jordan nodded glumly.

"A psychiatrist, to be precise?"

Another glum nod.

Fischer's eyes hardened into two stones. "Did he mention your affiliation with Dittmyer?"

"No," said Jordan in an unintentionally loud voice.

"Then we should be grateful for small mercies" Elinor said. She stared into Jordan's eyes, and shook her head back and forth. "Jordan, I know you've come here to tell me of something that happened, something that is troubling and exciting you. And, of course, I will listen. But, my young friend, before I listen to you, what I need is for you to pay attention to me for a minute."

She paused, groping to find the right words, the words that she clearly hoped could convince him. "I meant what I said about you last night. You have all the qualities that make for a first-rate analyst and, more than that, you have leadership skills. Yet you're still so worried about impressing people. And that is self-defeating. Because the one thing I can promise you: if you go around and play hypnosis games at parties, your career will end before it begins. Would you go into analysis four times a week with someone you saw doing tricks at a party?"

Jordan felt his face getting hot. "It won't happen again."

Fischer nodded slowly. "I hope not. Now tell me what brings you in here."

Jordan started in right away, and explained about the hypnotic susceptibility test he had performed and how he had quickly identified Robin as a deep trance subject.

"Was Robin the only one whose hands were coming together?" Fischer asked.

"A few others, but her instance was the most marked."

"And why didn't you then try to hypnotize a few of the subjects simultaneously, as you said you had done at that earlier party with this Stanton person?"

"Robin seemed to have the most promise."

Fischer chuckled. "Promise of what?" She waved her hand at him. "Continue."

The whole time he was talking, Jordan tried to read his mentor's face, a disconcerting experience, since she had by now managed to strip it of all expression. An hour earlier, examining the library microfilm, Jordan had been filled with confidence; he had envisioned himself in this very office, sharing all that he had uncovered, while she sat still in her chair, imbibing his breathtaking discoveries. But the reality, personified by the Argentinean's fixed, dark brown eyes, was nothing like his fantasy.

"So," Fischer now said, "Robin was anxious, talking about how she had no desire to do analysis, how she wanted a quick solution." Jordan nodded. "Why is it that I now fear that you are going to tell me that you put this young woman into a deep hypnotic trance, instructed her that from now on food would melt in her mouth and she would sing like a nightingale? Then, you dispatched her home a changed woman, and just this morning received a call from her notifying you that she had a steak for dinner last night and will be performing a solo concert next month at the Music Center."

"That's not fair, Elinor," Jordan shot back. "I came here to tell you something serious."

Fischer's palm came down hard against the desk. "Analysis is serious, Jordan. Hypnosis is not. If this young woman's complaint is to be cured, she needs to discover on her own, aided by an analyst's insights, the *source* of her complaint. Once she makes that discovery, improvement and very likely a complete recovery will follow. But if you've learned anything here, it is that such a process doesn't happen through supposed shortcuts that end up extending the length of the road three times over. Jordan, do you know why Freud—"

For the first time in his years at the Institute, Jordan cut his mentor off. "Excuse me, but I didn't come here to discuss hypnosis with you."

Fischer's face instantly transformed back to the expressionless mask. She nodded at him to continue, her lips set in a determined line.

"Okay," Jordan began. "Your guess, if not your analysis of what happened, was right. I put Robin under again. I repeated some of the things I had done the preceding night. Within less than two minutes, she was in a deep trance. Then, I did an age regression, my intention being to take her back to the initial trauma responsible for her gagging problem."

Jordan was speaking quickly now. He summarized the high-lights of Robin's hypnosis, and then told Fischer about the Bugliosi book and what he had learned that morning at the library. "I feel shaken," he finally concluded. "Under hypnosis, Robin became amnesiac about her own identity and assumed another, what I had at first assumed to be almost a textbook example of a disassociative state. But now, it turns out that what she has told me about this other person, this Beverly Casper, doesn't seem to reflect any sort of schizophrenia at all."

"And therefore?" Fischer prodded.

"*Therefore*," Jordan was almost yelling now, his hands in the air, "Therefore, Elinor, I want to know. Could all this be true?"

"Could all what be true?"

"Everything. Reincarnation. Afterlife. All those things."

Fischer rubbed her eyes slowly, then favored Jordan with the briefest of smiles. "Jordan, my student, my friend, and one day very soon my colleague, I cannot say I am happy with what you have done. I think I understand why you acted as you did, but I am not happy."

"But—"

She lowered her right hand as if to close his mouth. "Jordan, Jordan, I give you my word, I will respond to everything you have told me. In time. But first, I want to ask you a few questions."

Suddenly, everything felt familiar and, for the first time since entering the office—and despite, or maybe because of, the tension— Jordan relaxed. Fischer had responded to him as he had responded to Robin: not with answers, but with questions. How much of his persona and his interactions with patients, he now wondered, was authentically his, and how much just a reflection of what he had observed in Elinor?

"When Robin told you that she had no interest in doing analysis, but just wanted a quick solution, what did you feel?"

"Well, I thought—"

"Not what you thought, what you felt. Describe to me what you were feeling."

"Excited," Jordan conceded.

"Because?"

Jordan said nothing.

"Is it possible," Fischer began "that you like this person and hypnosis is a way of making her dependent on you?"

The heat returned to his face.

"Very possible," Fischer resumed, "likely in fact. Indeed, this is the first time since Carrie's accident that you have come in here speaking to me about a woman with enthusiasm. And that is a good thing, Jordan. But the reason you resorted to hypnosis yesterday was out of fear that if you didn't do it, this Robin would walk right out of your office and your life. Out of your office and out of your life," Fischer repeated, softening her inflection. "Just as Carrie had done. She walked out of your house...and then a drunk driver took her out of your life." Fischer said nothing for a few moments; when she resumed her voice was firm. "Robin Norris was going to leave your office yesterday. You like this woman, but you were in a dilemma. If you had convinced her to become your patient, you would preclude any social relationship. If she left and went home, you probably wouldn't feel comfortable just calling her. And so you went for what was available to you, the one way you could keep her close to you—hypnosis, an instant, and very temporary, placebo. I assume you now realize that what you should have done is refer her to someone who could offer her lasting help."

Even as Fischer was speaking, Jordan's mind returned to that final night with Carrie. Not just to the accident, but to the fight, the fierce fight. Fischer knew most of it, but not everything; not what really mattered. Not the details that haunted him. Those he kept locked inside himself and not even Fischer could pry them out.

"For the sake of argument let's say you're right about me." Jordan answered. "Still, there's one big hole in your explanation. You haven't accounted for the remarkably accurate bits of information Robin transmitted to me about Beverly Casper."

Fischer acknowledged the challenge with a deliberate nod of her head. "Fine. If we are done for the meantime with hypnosis, I will gladly turn to reincarnation which, I suspect, is the real reason you marched in here this morning so excited. So let me tell you about a case that happened in the '50s to a Canadian psychiatrist named Rosen; like you, a man who liked working with hypnosis. One day, Dr.

Rosen puts a patient in a trance and the man starts writing on a page in a complicated, totally unfamiliar, script. When Rosen brings the patient out and shows him what he has written, the man is shocked; like the doctor, he hasn't the faintest notion of what is on the paper. So, Rosen, like you or, like me, for that matter, is curious. He shows the writing to professors at a nearby university. They are all baffled. But then one scholar of ancient languages tells him that he recognizes the writing. The language on the paper is Oscan."

"Oscan?" Jordan repeated.

"Don't feel ignorant. I had never heard of it either. It turns out that this was a language spoken over two thousand years ago in western Italy. It died out, I don't know, I think in the first century B.C., when it was replaced by Latin.

"As you can imagine, very few examples of Oscan writing have survived, the most famous being, it turns out, what is known as the 'Curse of Vibia,' a scroll the Oscans used to insert into a coffin to help the dead person on his journey to the underworld. And, lo and behold, it was this 'Curse of Vibia,' the scholar tells Rosen, that his patient had produced under hypnosis."

Fischer paused. "Need I add," she quickly resumed, "that the patient, an educated man who had attended university, had never heard of Oscan, let alone studied it, or, for that matter, any other ancient language. Extraordinary, isn't it? But what would you say to this, Jordan?"

Jordan, as Fischer had obviously anticipated, said nothing.

She continued. "This case, I believe you would admit, is even more remarkable than a hypnotized subject speaking about a disappearance that happened in this very area only thirty-two years ago. Which means that if what happened yesterday with Robin Norris suggests reincarnation to you, then think of what must have gone through Dr. Rosen's mind: a man in Toronto sets down words in a language that has been dead for more than 2,000 years; moreover, this is a language that was spoken some 5,000 miles away from where he is now residing. If you were Rosen, what would you do with this information?"

"Check again, maybe this 'Curse of Vibia' had been taught in some ancient history class the man had—"

"Bravo! I like your response. I'm happy to hear that you would not advise the good doctor to go off and publish a paper on the subject."

"And then again maybe it is reincarnation," Jordan insisted.

"Yes, a number of possibilities confronted the doctor. He certainly could have published a sensational account of what happened, how in his very own office, a man had been reborn as an Oscan, and revealed information that could only have been learned in an earlier life. Fortunately, Dr. Rosen was a cautious man. So instead, he rehypnotized the patient, and asked him if he had ever seen or heard of the language Oscan. This time, the man recalled sitting in a library while somebody next to him had opened a book to a page containing the 'Curse of Vibia.' The word 'curse' had intrigued him and, perhaps when the other person went to the bathroom, he took the book and read the page. Not surprisingly, he retained no conscious memory of having seen the page or having heard of Oscan. But the letter's images had imprinted themselves so strongly on his unconscious mind that he could reproduce them with stunning accuracy."

Fischer stopped for a moment before resuming. "Who knows, Jordan? Robin Norris could have been sitting on a bus one day, and people alongside her were speaking about this Beverly Casper case and it became part of her unconscious memory? Cryptomnesia is what we call it when people obtain knowledge through normal channels that they are later unable to recall. You learned about this in medical school, Jordan. I'm surprised at you. Why do you allow yourself to be taken in so easily?"

Jordan looked at his watch, then fidgeted with the strap. The final barb he could have happily lived without. "I've been here much longer than I intended. You've cast a whole new light on this. I want to think about it, Elinor. Thank you." He started to rise.

"One more thing," Fischer said, motioning him back into the chair. "As you can see from my knowledge of this case, I am not utterly unfamiliar with the claims made by reincarnation enthusiasts. Their arguments can be attractive, and certainly tempting." When she next spoke her voice vibrated with drama, as if she was addressing a large crowd: "We live again! We are not really responsible for our problems; they're due to events and traumas that happened lifetimes ago! Jordan, belief in reincarnation can work on a person like an addictive drug, and with the same effects. It will destroy one's critical capacities and then one's career. My most remarkable professor in medical school was Geoffrey Bolton. For a long time, Bolton was my model of everything a psychiatrist should be. And he was a great scholar as well; he had written one of the standard textbooks on psychiatric diagnostics. Then, suddenly, in some sort of mid-life crisis, just the sort of thing I analyze in my book on transformations, Bolton turned into a reincarnation enthusiast, arguing that previously ignored or misunderstood disorders were due to traumas from earlier existences. In no time, he became a joke in the psychiatric community. People stopped using his textbook, fearful that other peculiar ideas might be embedded within it. University presses stopped publishing him; from what I understand, all he has come out with over the last years are tracts about reincarnation, the sort of books published by, what do they call them, 'theosophy presses.' Need I add that he was very quickly forced out of UCLA."

Fischer pulled open a desk drawer and fished out an envelope, "And now, I learn, there's a movement afoot to expel him from the American Psychiatric Association. Look at me, Jordan, and listen to me better than you've ever listened to anything I have told you. I have seen careers destroyed by such madness. If you want to go out with this woman, find a way to do it—without bizarre treatments that will destroy you and imperil the very name of this institute. Catch yourself now, while you still have time."

Tuesday, 12:20 P.M.

Chastened, Jordan left Elinor's office, and stepped outside; he needed a walk to clear his head.

He kept reviewing the conversation. The Oscan story had shaken him, and yet, even if Robin had heard about Beverly Casper from others, what about John? She certainly hadn't heard about him listening to a conversation on a bus. Then again, who knows if this John had even existed? Could she not have combined information she had heard from others, mixing it with characters from her own life? Maybe that's why she mentioned John when she came out of hypnosis. She didn't forget him because he was someone from her life.

Before he knew it, he was back at Borders, his home away from home, browsing New Age, the only area of the store that he had never visited.

New Age, he quickly discovered, was its own world, a large section with subdivisions on angels, metaphysics, paranormal experience, spirituality, magical arts, the occult, sections called by words Jordan had barely heard of, such as "channeling," and, of course, reincarnation. He quickly located two works by Geoffrey Bolton, the first, an oversized paperback, *When Life Follows Life: The Casebook of a Past-Life Psychiatrist,* the second, a high-priced hardcover volume, *Reincarnation: The Pros, the Cons, the Evidence.*

Standing in front of the bookcase, Jordan turned to the paperback first. A quick skimming of the book revealed that Bolton had been led to reincarnation by experiences similar to what had happened between him and Robin. During his years of psychiatric practice, Bolton had occasionally used hypnosis with patients who seemed unresponsive to conventional therapy. On several occasions, he had asked them to regress to an early trauma associated with the difficulty they were now experiencing. It usually worked, and when Bolton brought them out of hypnosis, they would discuss and analyze the remembered trauma. Many times, though not always, the symptoms that had long plagued these patients, sometimes for years, would quickly recede. But then a number of patients, following his suggestion to regress to the initial source of the trauma, regressed to incidents in earlier lives. Bolton had been confounded by the recollections; he certainly didn't assume that these memories reflected objective reality. But what astounded him was not only the depth of details that casually poured out of these patient's mouths, but that after they experienced these past-life recollections and analyzed them with him, they too started to experience significant symptomatic improvement; an improvement that had been denied them when their therapy had been restricted to events that had happened in their current life. As he was reading, Jordan found himself nodding along; he pictured Robin happily devouring the apple moments after he brought her out of hypnosis.

Bolton's second volume was less accessible, more "textbooky," reminiscent in style—if not in substance—to the books Jordan remembered from medical school. Perusing a few sentences, Jordan had an image of the exiled Bolton composing this treatise to win back the esteem of his now alienated colleagues.

He turned to the book's back flap, hoping to see the doctor's photo. Unfortunately, but in keeping with the style of textbooks and scholarly works, the flap contained no picture, just a short bio identifying Bolton as a graduate of Harvard Medical School, and the former Harvey Mayerson Professor of Psychiatry at UCLA. Bolton, the bio's final sentence noted, now resided in Venice, California, where he devoted himself fulltime to reincarnation therapy and research.

As Jordan glanced through the sober manual, he tried to visualize Elinor examining the book. He shook his head. Easier to imagine Elinor sighing or letting loose with a Spanish curse and tossing the book in the wastebasket.

There was one other browser in the section, a woman in her early twenties, a caricature of the popular image of New Age devotees, with multiple rings in both ears, on almost every finger and a final one looped around her right eyebrow.

"Excuse me," Jordan said, and showed her the two books. "I was just wondering. Have you ever heard of Geoffrey Bolton?"

Her large brown eyes widened. "Geoffrey Bolton is like, like…. I don't know. He's amazing."

"You've read his books then, I gather?"

"Better. I've attended his seminars."

"On reincarnation?"

"It's incredible. He'll hypnotize four hundred of us at a time, regress us all."

"Simultaneously?" Jordan asked. "He regresses four hundred people at once?"

"It's the coolest thing," she said. "You ought to try it."

Jordan ignored the suggestion "And you had a recollection of a previous life?"

"Five," she said. "I remembered five lives." The more the woman spoke—she started her "journey" as a slave to a family of nobles in ancient Egypt—the more reasonable Fischer's assessment sounded to him. That a rare individual, one of the small minority capable of going into deep-trance states, might retain memories of a past life, particularly of a trauma—that, he was now willing to consider. But what this girl was describing, a sort of supermarket hypnosis, this made no sense at all. "And my last life was less than a century ago," the woman was concluding. "I could see myself as clearly as I see you. I was a farmer in South Carolina, picking cotton, my hands filled with little cuts."

"Does Bolton only do group regressions?"

"Oh, no, Dr. Bolton's like a real psychiatrist. He has sessions with individuals. At his clinic, down by the water. In Venice."

What the woman had told him had sounded bizarre, hypnosis by the dozen. Bolton's credentials were academically impeccable, yet that also didn't necessarily mean much. He remembered hearing about some brilliant linguist at MIT, a man with an international reputation, who had written something that served as a preface for a book denying the truth of the Holocaust. But as evil and ridiculous as that was, at least it was outside the linguist's area of expertise. Bolton, on the other hand, espoused reincarnation as a psychiatrist, apparently believing that psychiatrists who refused to do such therapy would find that a significant percentage of their patients could never be helped. Jordan was confused. Fischer's condemnation had made an impression on him, but so too did the session with Robin. And so too did the information in the Bugliosi book and in the 1970 *L.A. Times* articles. He couldn't just rely on Fischer; he had to see Bolton himself, one-on-one, and he had to take his own measure of the man.

"Oh, yeah," the young woman was now saying. "A friend of mine's been trying to see him. 'Two-year-waiting-list,' some secretary in Bolton's office told her."

"So what did your friend do?"

"Bolton's the best," the girl said, "she didn't have a choice. She put her name down. What's the hurry? If Bolton can get her to go back four thousand years—one of his patients lived seventy-one lives—a two-year wait really doesn't mean very much, does it?"

To me, it does, Jordan mused. *If this guy has something to teach me, I need to learn it now.*

Tuesday, 5 P.M.

*T*he early TV news reports.
All the local stations.
Never miss them.
How could I?
I'm the headliner, the star of the show.
"The Messenger."
I like that.
Those cute newsreaders.
Trying to be calm
But they can feel the heat.
My heat.
Turns them on.
The danger.
Sex and violence
Good for business.
Show business.
I make their ratings go up.
So, they secretly admire me.
Envy my power.

Cheer me on.
Though they'd never admit it.
Too bad I can't tell them the truth
At a news conference.
The glorious truth.
But I have to focus on the big picture.
On the personal sacrifice
On my girls.
Safe. All safe now.
Like Loni
I saved her from drowning
In all this filth.
This ugly world.
Now others are waiting.
For me.
I'm coming, my darlings.
The angel maker is coming.

Tuesday, 5:35 P.M.

Geoffrey Bolton's office was a two-story wooden frame house on Rose Avenue, a few blocks up from the Venice beach. A small sign on the front door read, "Eternal Life Center—Dr. G. Bolton." Across the street, an enterprising shoe store had hung a far larger sign, "Eternal Soles."

Jordan pressed the bell, and a buzzer sounded. He entered and looked around. Bolton might be busy, but if his office was any indication, he wasn't making a lot of money. Or if he was, he wasn't spending it on interior design: a chipped mahogany couch that needed to be recovered, a couple of generic waiting room chairs, and inexpensive wall-to-wall bookcases, all full.

A frosted glass window slid open. A frizzy-haired woman in her late forties peered out over a pair of silver framed bifocals. A nameplate on her desk identified her as Marion Tenner.

She looked from Jordan to an appointment book and back to Jordan. Her lips curved, almost into a smirk. "You are not, I assume, Barbara Simon?"

"Not in this life," Jordan answered.

Tenner groaned. Jordan could only imagine how many jokes

like that she had heard. He stepped forward and extended a hand. "Dr. Jordan Geller. And as you seem to have guessed, I don't have a great sense of humor and I don't have an appointment." He paused for a few seconds, then plunged ahead. "But it is important, urgent, that I see Dr. Bolton."

"You and the rest of the world."

"I assure you, I'm not exaggerating."

"Of course not," Tenner responded. "Unfortunately, no one has ever come in unscheduled with anything less than an emergency."

"And how many of them have been doctors?" Jordan asked.

"What sort of doctor are you?"

"A psychiatrist."

Tenner's right eyebrow arched. "From where?"

"UCLA."

"That's interesting."

"Because?"

"Because most of the people who come in here and introduce themselves as doctors have mail order degrees."

"In that case—?"

"In that case, you still can't see him today." Tenner looked back down to her appointment book and started paging ahead, a week at a time. "Now, if you're willing to come in—"

"I need something now," Jordan insisted.

"Dr. Bolton is booked straight through this evening till ten," the woman answered impatiently. Jordan glanced at his watch; it wasn't even six.

"Does he see patients that late every day?"

Tenner nodded. "Except Monday. That's his early day. Anyway, when he finishes at ten, that's it. He goes straight home."

"If I write a note to Dr. Bolton, a short note, will you take it in to him when this next patient leaves?"

Tenner sighed. "It won't do any good, but if it'll make you feel better...."

Jordan grabbed a sheet off the desk. He thought for a second and then wrote. He folded the sheet, and handed it to the secretary.

Five minutes later, a man walked out of Bolton's office and

Tenner went in. When she came out, her face was flushed. "Dr. Bolton will see you now."

"Thank you."

Geoffrey Bolton must have been pushing seventy, casually dressed in jeans and an open white shirt, with a silver beard, perfectly trimmed. Jordan had imagined a face bearing testament to a lifetime of struggle, but Bolton's countenance appeared serene.

The doctor remained in his chair, but the smile he extended to Jordan was welcoming. He peered down his bifocals and read Jordan's note aloud: "My supervisor, Elinor Fischer, sent me."

"I stretched the truth, I admit it," Jordan answered, reacting to Bolton's good-natured eye roll. "But she did talk to me about you. That much is true."

"I can only imagine the look of delight on dear Elinor's face when she learns that you came to see me."

"I hadn't thought that far ahead," Jordan said. The truth is, he could think of no reason he would ever tell Elinor about this visit.

Bolton chuckled. "The law of unintended consequences. I somehow doubt that Elinor's telling you she knew me was done with the intention of having you come here."

"You were once colleagues?"

"Elinor was one of my star students. Later, she became a friend, a very dear friend. She was also a brilliant diagnostician, very direct, and…"

Jordan waited for Bolton to finish his sentence.

"Doctor?"

Bolton's eyes refocused. "Elinor sees the world in a very straightforward manner; she doesn't like deviations. We came up against a wall. I saw a door and walked through. Elinor remained outside."

His eyes remained on Jordan but it did not take an analyst to know that his thoughts were far removed from this room. Is it just a professional conflict he's describing or a personal one as well—the sort that separates lovers as well as colleagues?

"How is she?" Bolton asked, his features softening.

"Dr. Fischer is fine. The Institute is thriving."

"I mean, how is she? Is she happy? She was always so driven."

"She's still very motivated, that's for sure. But I can't tell you how happy she is. She knows me very well, but—"

"But you don't know her.... Your note brought back memories," Bolton said. He rolled a pencil back and forth between his palms. "But I'm sure you didn't come here to talk to me about your supervisor. How can I help you?"

Jordan filled Bolton in on the session with Robin. In contrast to Fischer, Bolton was a cauldron of reactions, his bushy white brows rising and descending, his watery eyes widening at each of Robin's most dramatic revelations. "Extraordinary, extraordinary," he murmured more than a few times.

"So, does this sound like what you would categorize as an authentic past-life recall?" Jordan asked.

"First, I want to know how you feel about it. Did it seem true to you?"

"Did it seem true? Definitely! But the only thing I remember ever hearing about reincarnation is the Bridey Murphy case, how under hypnosis everything seemed so definite."

"She used old Irish words," Bolton interjected, "recalled minute personal details of her past life in Cork and Dublin; danced a complicated nineteenth-century Irish jig, even—"

"Until they discovered that the hypnotized woman had grown up in Chicago next door to a Bridey Murphy."

"Yes," Bolton conceded in a low voice, "a detail like that would seem to throw the reliability of the hypnotic regression into question."

"*Seem to*, Dr. Bolton. That's pretty mild."

"Not if the detail was fabricated. Believe me, the rationalists, desperate to destroy the belief that something survives death, will stop at nothing. Virginia Tighe, the woman who under hypnosis became Bridey Murphy, grew up in Chicago near a woman named Bridey, to whom she never spoke, and whose last name wasn't, and never had been, Murphy."

"But didn't the newspapers—"

"The newspapers," Bolton sneered. "You know what they say—'Everything you read in a newspaper is one hundred percent accurate, except for the occasional story of which you have personal knowledge.'" Bolton paused. "Okay, so I'm asking you again. Without your medical-school prejudices, and without Elinor whispering in your ear, did the regression seem true to you?"

Jordan looked away. "The emotions seemed real. Yes. The emotions definitely seemed real."

"And the violence of Robin's recollections? Did that also seem real?"

"Very much so. The truth is, I found it frightening."

Bolton's nod was empathic. His right eyebrow raised itself into a tiny arc. "I remember how shocked I felt the first time I heard a person describe being murdered."

"The *first* time?"

"It happens much more frequently than you'd think. Makes one wonder what percentage of people throughout history have come to bloody ends."

"You've also had such cases?"

"Many. But none approaching this one, with the quantity of details you were told. Like this Robin's mentioning August 4, 1970, and your then verifying the disappearance of Beverly Casper on that day. I must admit that I'm a little bit envious."

Jordan cracked a thin smile. "Beginner's luck."

Bolton pushed back on his chair. "Just a few months ago I had a case in which a woman came to me complaining that she'd been suffering for years from a series of disturbing nightmares. The nightmares themselves were not recurring, but they had a recurring theme. In each dream, she was being pursued by someone who wished to murder her, and each time, after moments of terror, she was killed."

"How?"

"That varied. Usually, she was shot, other times knifed, sometimes strangled, once she was drowned."

"And when you hypnotized and regressed her?"

"She was, like Robin, a deep trance subject. The first time I put her under, she was a five-year-old girl on a farm hiding from her grandfather in the attic.

"It soon came out that when her parents were away for the day, she had seen her grandfather, as she put it, 'lying on top of a girl who had no clothes on.' The girl, she said, looked very unhappy. My patient, the five-year-old, seeing all this, made some sort of sound. The grandfather heard it, turned around, and gave her a furious look. That's when she ran to the attic. I took her forward in time to see what happened. She became semi-hysterical, yelling, 'I hear him on the stairs! I hear him!' A minute later, the grandfather entered the room. He grabbed her and shook her like a rag doll. Then he threw her against a beam, cracking her skull."

"And when you brought her out?"

"Needless to say, she was very disturbed. As was I. I had felt the terror of this helpless five-year-old girl. Later, she told me a lot more than had come out during the hypnosis."

"I don't understand."

"It sounds odd, I know, but under hypnosis, although a person responds only to the hypnotist's questions, they are also seeing a lot of things that they don't mention simply because they are not asked about them. After the session, this woman told me that this five-year-old girl was being regularly molested by the grandfather, and that he had threatened her life if she ever told her parents what he was doing to her."

"I wonder whatever happened to the grandfather?" Jordan asked. A wild thought sped through his mind: *Whatever happened to John?*

"You mean, was he ever caught and punished?" Bolton shrugged. "No way we'll ever find out. From some of the details she gave me, I have always assumed this happened around the turn of the last century, though I don't know exactly when."

"And did this whole experience help her?"

"You mean, did she stop having nightmares?"

Jordan nodded.

"At first, her reaction wasn't so good.... For several days, she couldn't sleep; she'd lie in bed thinking about this little girl. As you can imagine, the combination of not sleeping and obsessing on this tragic past life depressed her. Quite severely, I might add."

"What did you do?"

"I had her come to my office daily. I'd put her under, give her relaxation suggestions and tell her that she'd sleep deeply that night. Then, every morning she'd call me back; she still hadn't slept. At this point, I was in a real bind. She had told me under hypnosis that she wanted to live a life without secrets.

"Makes sense," Jordan offered. "She had been forced to keep the secret of her grandfather from her parents."

"Very good, very good," Bolton said, wagging his finger approvingly at Jordan. "So I couldn't simply hypnotize her and instruct her to forget everything about this terrible past life. Doing that, pushing everything back into her subconscious would undermine her wish to lead a life without secrets, and cause her trauma to once again express itself symptomatically."

"So what did you do?"

"I instructed her, under hypnosis, to recall only those details which she felt her conscious mind could accommodate."

A very elegant solution. "And that was enough?"

"It took a while, though not really very long in fact…a few days. But yes, she started sleeping through the night, and better yet, still has not had a dream in which she was pursued or been hurt since." Bolton leaned back on his chair, and locked his hands behind his head. "You see, that's how I see my job, to provide help now, in this life. The regressions are just a useful tool to achieve that goal."

"Just as a conventional analyst would use free association or dream interpretation."

Bolton nodded, clearly pleased that Jordan had made this connection. "I don't expect you to buy into all of this right off the bat, Dr. Geller. I certainly didn't. All I ask is that you keep an open mind."

"Have you ever had a case," Jordan asked, "in which the person's current life began very soon after her past life ended?"

"You mean like your Robin?"

"Yes."

"I haven't, no. But there are cases. The most famous one took place in India in the '70s. It's all in this book."

Bolton stepped over to a shelf, and pulled down an oversized paperback. "A very young girl named Reena Gupta claimed she had been murdered by her husband. It turned out that in another part of

New Delhi, just a few years earlier, a woman named Gurdeep Kaur had been murdered by her husband under circumstances uncannily similar to the ones Reena described."

"She was murdered and reborn in the same city?"

"Murder victims, it seems, are often reborn shortly after their deaths, and in the same locality. I guess you might call it divine justice."

"Their lives are cut short, so they go to the head of the line."

"That's one way of looking at it." Bolton handed the book to Jordan. "This is probably Hemendra Banerjee's most famous and, for that matter, most verifiable case."

"Who's Hemendra Banerjee?"

"He founded the Indian Institute of Parapsychology. He even worked for a time with Ian Stevenson until they had a falling out."

"Who's Ian Stevenson?" Jordan asked, beginning to feel like he was back in sixth grade.

"Stevenson was a professor of psychiatry, later, head of the department, at the University of Virginia. In the mid-fifties, he became intrigued by reports of children who had very specific recollections of earlier lives. Over the next twenty-five years, he studied over two thousand such cases. He confined his research to children, particularly very young ones, because he felt there was no way they could be coached to give detailed responses to his questions, nor could they have acquired information through reading or watching movies."

"The Oscan case."

"You know about that?"

"Elinor told me."

Bolton smiled. "Yes, Stevenson wanted to avoid those problems."

"But you don't limit your practice to children. Why—"

"Because I'm less concerned with proving the truth of reincarnation than with helping people deal with crises in their lives. So, yes, I treat adults." Bolton glanced at his watch.

"And what should I do with Robin?" Jordan asked. "Should I tell her what happened under hypnosis or is she better off not knowing?"

"I suspect you'll have to tell her. You said she mentioned the name of her killer."

"John—"

"And you said she did so after the session ended, without your prompting her."

"Correct."

"In that case, it would be my guess that more memories of the hypnosis session will start to come to her."

"Yes, I had that same thought myself."

"Then, you'll just have to see how she reacts. What's her personality like?"

"I don't know her well. As I explained, she didn't come to me as a patient but, from what I've seen, she's pretty grounded."

"You said she was an actress?"

Jordan nodded. Bolton hummed an acknowledgment.

"A grounded actress? Sounds like an interesting woman."

"Should I take her under again?"

"It may be helpful, it may not. Your instincts seem pretty good to me. Follow them. I can tell you one thing, however. If you do regress her again, don't bring her out so quickly. Stay with her longer."

Jordan wondered if Bolton was pulling his leg. "Of course I brought her out. She was dead."

"Beverly Casper's body was dead," he said with complete conviction. "But not her spirit."

"Meaning?"

A buzzer sounded in the office, but Bolton ignored it. "Meaning that if you take her back to the minutes after she died, there's a good chance her spirit will be there, looking at her own body. She might have some very interesting things to tell you."

Jordan shifted uneasily in his chair. *Was Elinor right? Had all this past-life work pushed Bolton over the edge?* Until just a few moments ago, so much of what he said had seemed so sensible. But this? He thought of the wall that Elinor could not walk through with Bolton. *Maybe Bolton didn't see a door, after all. Maybe he just kept running into walls, and the collisions had loosened some screws.*

The buzzer sounded a second time. Bolton wrote his private

number on a business card, and told Jordan to be in touch if he had further questions.

"Don't forget what I told you. Take her back to the period after she was murdered."

Jordan chose not to respond, but as he turned toward the door, the puckish doctor started singing—to the tune of the George M. Cohan song—"Don't give my regards to Elinor, if you know what's good for you."

Tuesday, 6:10 P.M.

Lemoski looked down his "granny glasses" at a crime scene photo of Rachel Gordon, the "Messenger's" second victim. The eighteen-year-old woman had been found in the trunk of an abandoned car at Edison International Field, the home of the Anaheim Angels baseball team. Her hands had been bound together with duct tape, her knees bent so that she could fit into the restricted space. If you lifted her out of the trunk and placed her on the ground, Lemoski observed, she'd be in a position of supplication, of prayer. Like Monica Johnson and Erica Braun, the first victim, angel wings were strapped on her back. And, again like Johnson and Braun, she had been stripped of all her jewelry, and any nail polish and makeup had also been removed.

As if the crimes themselves and the lack of useful evidence wasn't bad enough, the killer was depositing his victims all over the Los Angeles basin—north in Pasadena, south in Anaheim, and now west. Multiple jurisdictions meant multiple complications. Detectives from all over the city, each with their own way of doing things, were pouring into the office. All available space, including the lunchroom, was being cleared to accommodate them, and though Lemoski appreciated the additional manpower, he didn't relish the additional headaches. The longer the case dragged on, the less of an investigator and more of an administrator he'd become. How long would it be before somebody complained about lack of access to a computer, or the mess in the ladies bathroom? Sure, he could delegate these inevitable problems to others—he'd find some sergeant with good people-skills—but in the end, everything would work its way back to him. Still, he was determined to stay in the middle of the action for as long as he possibly could.

An older detective, with a barrel chest and accompanying beer gut, entered the room. He gestured to the phone on Lemoski's desk. "Your wife."

The lieutenant looked down at the blinking light and then up at the man who had delivered the message.

"The call got routed to me somehow. The Mrs. asked that I deliver the message to you personally. I guess she's been calling."

"Along with the rest of world." The chief had called four times already today, and three city councilmen had left word that they expected to hear from him. "Thanks, Fred."

Fred Swain and Lemoski went back more than a few years. When Lemoski came to the West Valley, Swain was already a fixture there. The senior man in the office—some of his younger colleagues called him "Gramps" even though he was still in his fifties—Swain had been stationed in the West Valley almost before there was a West Valley to police. Nearly a decade older than Lemoski, passed over a half-dozen times for promotion, he was a thirty-two-year veteran in a job where twenty years was a lifetime. All the guys that Swain had been with at the academy had either retired or moved on to greener pastures, but the twice-divorced detective, now single again, stayed put. The station was as close to a home as he had ever found.

"Everybody's waiting for you in the pit," Swain added.

"I'll be right in." Lemoski scooped up the phone. "What's up, honey?" He gestured for Swain to wait.

"Ben, talk to your daughter."

"Pen, later. I have a team of detectives waiting for me."

"Ben. *Now!*"

There was a beat of silence. "Hi, Daddy."

"What's going on, Kathy? This is a terrible time—"

"Mommy is being totally unreasonable. I just want to meet some friends later, and she won't let me."

"Why not?"

"Exactly! Why not? She wants to keep me under house arrest till you bring in this 'Messenger' guy."

Penelope Lemoski reclaimed the phone. "Ben, I've been watching the news. I just don't think it's a good idea."

"Let me talk to her, Pen." Lemoski waited; from the corner of his eye, he saw Swain leafing through a folder. "Kathy, where are you planning to go?"

"It's called Hamburger Heaven. Christy, Jenny and Judy and a couple of other kids are meeting there. It's no big deal, Daddy."

"Hamburger Heaven? Where's that?"

Swain looked up from his folder. "It's in Malibu. Been there forever." He started for the door.

Lemoski covered the phone with his hand. "Tell them I'll be right in."

"Kathy, darling, that place is in Malibu."

"I know where it is. So what?"

Lemoski looked at the photo of Rachel Gordon. The question of why these girls had gotten into a strange man's car had been bothering him all day.

"Kathy, if your car broke down and someone stopped and said he'd drive you home or to a phone booth, would you go with him?"

"Of course not."

"Even if it was late and cold and you were in the middle of nowhere?"

"Well, I guess it would depend on the guy."

"In other words, if he was clean-cut and nice-looking, you might get in the car with him?"

Kathy laughed. "Daddy, you realize you're making a tremendous argument for a cell phone, don't you?"

"Can I get a straight answer?"

"Only you, Daddy."

"Only me, what?"

"I wouldn't get in the car with anyone except you. So, can I go to Hamburger Heaven?"

"Absolutely not."

"Daddy!"

"Stay home and do your homework for a change. Now let me talk to your mother."

A second later. "Thank you, Ben."

"Listen, honey, this might work for a night or two, but we can't keep her locked up."

"Maybe you'll catch this animal by then."

"Sure, and we'll win the lottery, too, and pay off the mortgage." Swain had reappeared in the doorway, waiting. Lemoski had to go, but he wanted time to linger. Penelope always made him feel better, and just now he needed to be near her, even if only via copper wire.

"I guess you don't know when you'll be back tonight," Penelope said.

"No, but I'll try not to make it too late."

She laughed. "As if you have a choice…. I love you."

He felt like gesturing with his thumb for Swain to leave. But, of course, he didn't. "Me, too," he finally said.

They walked down the hall to "the pit," the West Valley situation room. Crowded with cops—two detectives answered phones that never stopped ringing, two more tacked the latest crime scene photos to a bulletin board, others milled about, chatting—Lemoski scanned the faces of the newest members of his team: Karen Romero, Greg Davis and Josh Bobley. This was their first serial case. They looked so eager, exuded so much confidence, that Lemoski almost had to laugh. He knew just what they were feeling; he had felt the same way many years earlier when he was assigned to the "Night Stalker" detail. But he knew it was not brilliant police work that finally brought Richard Ramirez to ground; it was blind luck. Some irate neighbors had collared the son-of-a-bitch after he botched a carjacking.

Serial killers lived in a world of their own. Most murderers are caught through the application of common sense. After all, the average person doesn't have many people who want to kill him or her. But that's exactly what made serial killers almost impossible to apprehend. They had no motives, at least no discernable motives, and no previous connections to the victims. So you could know every detail of a victim's life from the moment she was born, and it still wouldn't help. To find "the Messenger" they would need a break, a hell of a lucky break. The question was, how many more girls would have to die before that break came?

"Greg, what did the FBI say? When can we get one of their profilers out here?"

The massive black cop shook his head. Upward of two hundred and fifty pounds, a former All-Pac 10 linebacker for USC, he made a strong impression on suspects. With his M.A. in criminology, he had an intellect to match his size. "They said they'd get us help as soon as they could, but, right now, they're backed up. Truth is, I don't think we'll be hearing from them any time soon. Too many murderers and too few profilers, I guess."

"Maybe they've got a five murder minimum," Swain commented, only half in jest. "They'll never say it, but I heard that once."

"A five murder minimum?" Karen Romero said. "Sounds like a pancake order in a restaurant."

Bobley gave a short laugh. "Not to worry. I gotta feeling we'll be making their 'minimum' pretty soon."

"Where the hell is Lee?" Lemoski barked, irritated by Bobley's typically smart-ass remark. That it was also probably true just made it that much more grating. "We need everybody at these sessions. What one person says could spark ideas in someone else."

"He's taking a call," Davis answered. "Seemed to think—"

"Look at the timeline," Bobley cut in. He had picked up on the cold look on his boss' face and knew it was directed at him. No more wisecracks now. Just facts, facts to bring the discussion back his way. "There was a full month between the first and second murders, and not even two weeks between numbers two and three."

Lemoski curtly nodded his assent. "Karen," he said, turning to Romero, "You're the computer whiz. Check if you can find any

murders in California, or anywhere else in the country for that matter, whose M.O. resembles these. Maybe this guy just moved into the
neighborhood."

"How far do you want me to go back?" Romero asked.

"Two years, maybe three, no, make it five."

"And I want interviews with everybody who saw Monica Johnson Sunday night, and for two, three days before," Lemoski said. "The
killer must have been stalking her. Compare those with the people
who saw Rachel Gordon and Erica Braun in the last days before they
were killed. Maybe some pattern will emerge, maybe somebody will
remember something... Do we know yet how he disables the cars?"

"Sand in the gas tank. Clogs the jets in maybe fifteen minutes.
Simple and effective." Davis piped in.

"Who would know that?" Romero asked.

"If you're asking if you'd have to be a mechanic, the answer is
maybe, maybe not."

"Does anybody have any thoughts as to why these girls would
get into a car with a stranger?"

"Their cars broke down," Romero said. "They were scared."

"How scared?" Lemoski asked. "I asked my daughter Kathy if
she would ever get into a car with a strange man and she said she
wouldn't."

"Because her father is a cop," Romero said. "On something like
this, she's more savvy than most girls."

Jimmy Lee, the last member of the team, burst into the room,
all five-feet-six, 145 pounds of him. "I just talked to a guy who saw
Monica Johnson and a man on Eagle Canyon Road around 11 P.M.
Sunday night."

"Details, Jimmy," Lemoski urged.

"He says the guy was in his mid-twenties, with shoulder length
dark hair and...."

"What was he wearing?" Davis interjected.

"A white, fish-net sweater."

Romero laughed. "Fish-net sweater? You mean fisherman's
knit."

"You spent too much time in vice, Jimmy," Bobley chuckled.

"Fish-net? Fishermen's knit? Sue me!"

"Race?" Davis asked.

"Caucasian, but could be Native American or Hispanic, I guess. Definitely not black."

"And where is this witness?" Lemoski asked.

"He was calling from his house."

Lemoski rolled his eyes. "Did you get a name?"

Lee looked down at the notepad in front of him. "Avery Conniston," he said.

Tuesday, 8:45 P.M.

An hour after his consultation with Bolton, Jordan was back in his Brentwood apartment. A small one-bedroom with a fine view of the alley, its modest size and lack of modern conveniences like air-conditioning belied its upscale zip code. Still, he was lucky to have it. There wasn't much to choose from in his price range in this part of town. When Carrie was alive, he spent most of his time, when he wasn't at the hospital or in class, at her place in Westwood. Now that was no longer an option.

To appease his growling stomach, he went straight to the kitchen and pulled out a slab of cold Dominos double cheese pizza and a Coke. Opening the book Bolton had loaned him with one hand, and lifting the pizza into his mouth with the other, he started to read about the strange death and life of Reena Gupta. When she was two years old, barely after she first learned to talk, Reena announced to her startled grandmother that she had a husband. "I have a *qharwala*. My *qharwala* was a very bad man. He killed me."

Reena would stand on her parents' balcony and stare at the people walking by: "I'm looking for my husband and children," she would explain. She told her parents that she had four children, and constantly complained of how unhappy she was to be separated from them. A few years later, a family friend who knew about the girl's memories told the mother that he had heard of a Sikh family in another part of New Delhi whose experiences seemed to correspond to Reena's recollections. So, with the parents' cooperation, this man contacted the family of Gurdeep Kaur, a woman who had been murdered in 1961 by her husband, Surjeet Singh.

Kaur's parents came to visit the Guptar family. When they arrived, Reena was napping, but when she awoke and saw the man and woman, her face broke into a large smile. "These are my father and mother," she declared.

The next day, Kaur's parents brought the woman's younger sister to Reena, and the child immediately called her Sarno, the girl's nickname. Then, another strange thing happened. In certain social circles in India, it's customary that a person may accept money only from someone older than himself. So when Sarno offered Reena two rupees, the girl shocked everyone by saying, 'How can I take money from Sarno? She is younger than me.'" A short time later, she easily identified a photograph of Gurdeep Kaur.

Meanwhile, Surjeet Singh, the murderer, had been released from prison after ten years, and heard about the girl claiming to be Gurdeep. He expressed interest in meeting her. However, Reena had no desire to see him; she was afraid he would kill her again.

Eventually, in 1975, when Reena was nine, a meeting was arranged. Their strange rendezvous was captured in a disturbing photograph of a dusky skinned young girl perched on the armrest of a chair, looking very much like she was ready to flee; next to her, a turban-clad man with a feral face and a snake charmer's smile.

Had someone told Jordan this story a week ago, he would have dismissed it as a tale out of the Arabian Nights; now, he wasn't so sure. The book was filled with dozens of other stories of people recounting past lives, some of them verified by this Dr. Ian Stevenson of whom Bolton had spoken. *Either these researchers are all frauds, or they are all very gullible, or at least some of us, like Robin Norris, have lived more than one life.*

And with that simple and disconcerting thought he went to bed and almost instantly fell into a deep sleep.

Wednesday

Wednesday, 7:30 A.M.

U p at seven, he began his morning as he did nearly every Wednesday (Mondays and Fridays as well), with a mile swim in the UCLA pool. As he free-styled his way back and forth through the chilly water, he tried to make sense of the last couple of days.

With each new lap, it seemed as if his mind would change. Every time he was prepared to accept Fischer's words of caution, he thought of Bolton and of the book's compelling tales of reincarnation. Each time he was prepared to trust Bolton's conclusions, he thought of Fischer's warnings, and of the last bizarre piece of advice Bolton had offered him. Still, he couldn't deny or discount what he himself had seen and heard during his session with Robin. But he had to be cautious; he thought of the Oscan case. He didn't want to rush ahead and make a fool of himself. Or worse. He needed to do more research; he simply didn't have enough data.

Pat Haman greeted him as soon as he stepped into the Dittmyer Institute. "The apple lady called."

"Did she leave a number?"

"No. She said she'd call back. I told her to call ten minutes before the hour."

Jordan nodded and continued into his office. He wondered if Pat had picked up the eagerness in his voice.

He had patients at 9, 10, and 11: a forty-five-year-old sitcom writer battling panic attacks as his career slipped from his grasp; a twenty-four-year-old man obsessed with Japanese bondage pornography who often masturbated six to eight times a day; and a UCLA student with a hatred bordering on the pathological for her mother, a high-powered feminist divorce attorney.

Jordan had been seeing the first patient since he started his analyst training, the second for the last six months, and the third for only two weeks. In exchange for a greatly reduced fee, a fraction of what it would cost them to see an analyst in private practice, they had each agreed to be ministered to by Dr. Jordan Geller, analyst-in-training.

Jordan had compassion, even fondness, for all three of these people. The screenwriter had real talent. Jordan had seen some of his shows. Ten years ago he was pulling down an income in the high six figures. Today he was begging twenty-five-year-old show runners for a single episode so that he could hang on to his health insurance. Once a sought-after gag writer, paid handsomely just to "punch-up" scripts, he now felt lost. For one thing, the style of the shows had changed. No longer plot-driven, everything in sitcoms now was bitchy, one character trying to out-insult another. The "situation" had gone out of the comedy. In the prime of his life, the screenwriter felt like a dinosaur, a fossil from another era. Yet, if he couldn't find work in sitcoms, how would he survive? Jordan tried to gently push him into writing feature-length scripts, but the TV writer didn't have the patience for that. "Twenty-three minutes is what I do," he told Jordan. "Hundred-yard-dash runners don't do marathons."

Jordan tried to get him to mine his other interests; the man loved food and wine, and had always fantasized about starting his own wine label. But was it financially feasible? He had a wife, two kids, two SUV's and two mortgages, both hefty. Could he risk the capital, now that so little new capital was coming in? Worse, could he risk another failure? "Lightning doesn't strike twice," he would tell Jordan. "I had my run as a comedy writer. Somehow, I don't think I'm going to make it as the maven of the wine world."

Brick by emotional brick Jordan worked to build up his patient's confidence. Some days the edifice stood, on other days the writer's inherent cynicism blew it down. That cynicism had sharpened the edge of his comedy writing, but now it was chiseling away at his hopes for happiness.

The twenty-four-year-old porn lover had a face full of acne scars, a body that was painfully lean, and an overbite. His chances of attracting a woman were never, to put it charitably, high. He compensated by masturbating over images of dominant sex scenes, both as depicted in Japanese bondage books and in his mind. There, he was king, Mr. Irresistible. But the fascination with pornography and with his penis was also shutting him off from any opportunity to connect with the opposite sex. And if he ever managed to start a relationship would he able to control his masturbation addiction—sure to be a major turnoff if the relationship got serious? Jordan realized his porn lover had to get a grip on himself, no pun intended. What he needed more than anything else was self-esteem, something he lacked, utterly and completely, when he had first walked into Jordan's office. What he did have was a good brain. When he wasn't playing with himself, he was writing computer code. If he could make some money, even make a bit of a name for himself, maybe he could attract a woman—at least for a first date, at least to give himself a chance. At this point, money and some professional success were the keys. So, in addition to helping the young man deal with his parents, who had always treated him like the runt of the litter, Jordan was helping him to package himself in the most compelling, self-confident way possible. It wasn't easy. The porn lover needed constant reassurance. But, as Jordan knew, it's hard to believe in the love of others when you feel so little reason to love yourself.

The last of this morning's trio was the mother-hating grad student. Her depth of hatred, as it almost always is, was self-destructive. The grad student had seven body-piercings, each intended to be a stab at mommy's heart. Each one missed the mark. Mommy, at least from the young woman's descriptions, didn't have a heart to stab. She wanted a radical feminist daughter to follow in her footsteps, but what she had ended up with instead was a young woman who as a child wanted nothing more than to dress in lace and take ballet lessons and who, now in her early twenties, wanted precisely those bourgeois rewards—husband, children, a house with a pool in the suburbs—that her mother so thoroughly rejected. You wouldn't guess it by looking at her. The piercings and other Goth paraphernalia she sported were about as far away as you could get from mid-America, but she was much closer to those middle class values (which she'd probably picked up from her hapless and long-departed father) than she was to the counterculture image she presented to the world. Embracing those middle-class values was how she could get back at her mother and save herself at the same time. But communicating this prescription to his patient was a tricky business.

Each week, Jordan would review his cases with Elinor. Today, although he was doing his best to concentrate on their various obsessions, he found it difficult. Even the intricacies of Japanese bondage literature, which he usually found perversely fascinating, were sailing over his head; what he really wanted to do was to talk to Robin. *Why the hell didn't she leave her number?*

Finally, just before noon, she called back.

"How are you feeling?" he asked.

"Good."

"And your problem?"

"I had a three-course meal last night for the first time in weeks. I can't tell you how grateful I am."

In light of the talk with Bolton, he felt immense relief. "I'm glad things are working out."

"Something weird, pretty disturbing, though, happened last night. I thought I should tell you about it."

"Go ahead." He tried to keep his voice measured, but he didn't feel calm at all.

"No, not now. There's something I need to show you. Can I come to your office late this afternoon?"

Jordan had a sudden vision of Robin walking into the office and running into Elinor. "No," he said, "remember what I told you, this is all unofficial. It would be better to meet somewhere else."

"Where?"

"Can you meet me at the Starbucks at Westwood and Lind-brook at four?"

"Five would be better," she said.

"Then five it is."

He hung up the phone and mulled over her words, "weird, pretty disturbing." It had taken precisely thirty seconds for him to go from relief to dread.

Wednesday, 12:15 P.M.

This guy makes more each week from TV reruns than we make in a year," Romero said. "Turn here."

Lemoski wheeled left, guiding the car higher into the narrow hillside streets of this, the city's wealthiest enclave, the dream world of Bel Air. A manicured jungle of exotic flora tended by an army of immigrant gardeners, everything green flourished here, especially money.

The window down, Lemoski inhaled the sharp, yet sweet smell of eucalyptus trees.

"And what's worse," Romero went on, "the shows are so stupid. Pure T and A."

"An original insight," Lemoski said. "This must be it."

He pulled up in front of a black steel gate. "LAPD to see Avery Conniston," he said into a beige box.

Within seconds, the gate started to recede. Lemoski followed the steep driveway up to a freshly painted Spanish adobe mansion.

"They do say he's got an amazing art collection," Romero concluded as they reached the massive mahogany door. "And the only reason I get to see it is because we're investigating—"

Lemoski pivoted abruptly. "Let's get this straight. You and I are not Avery Conniston's guests. We're not here to see his art or get a tour of his house. We're here to find out if he saw something relevant to a homicide investigation."

Romero nodded without much conviction. She'd minored in Art History at Berkeley. How many chances was she going to have to get a close look at a collection like Conniston's?

Lemoski reached for the bell, but before he made a connection, the door swung open. The pair found themselves face to face with a man who looked to be somewhere in his mid-fifties, give or take three years in either direction. He wore a black T-shirt that hugged a tapered waist; at the end of his tweed jacket, powerful, thick wrists. His green eyes swung back and forth between the two visitors, but held longer on Romero.

"Mr. Conniston?" Lemoski asked.

Before the man could respond, a second man, about the same age, but shorter, slighter, and wearing tortoise-shell glasses, stepped into the doorframe.

"I'm the man you're looking for, lieutenant," Avery Conniston said good-naturedly, as if he were surrendering himself to a TV detective in one of his old shows. "This is Mike Fields." He swung an arm lightly around the man. "We're cousins. Can you see the family resemblance?"

Lemoski's gaze shifted between the two. *Any family resemblance is wishful thinking on Conniston's part.* "I'm sorry if I startled you," Lemoski said to Fields.

"No problem," Fields answered.

"Ben Lemoski, LAPD." The lieutenant extended his hand, first to Conniston and then to his cousin.

Fields looked back to Romero. "And you're way too pretty to be anonymous," he said. "What's your name?"

"This is Detective Romero," Lemoski said.

"Do you have a first name?" Fields asked her directly.

"Mike, this isn't a social call," Conniston chided, more amused than vexed.

"Karen," Romero answered.

Fields fixed his gaze directly on her brown eyes. "She might be good for that show, Ave. You know, that idea I've been telling you about."

The producer smiled, "Well—"

"Karen Romero," Fields repeated. "If I ever need to speak to a cop, now I know a name to go with a face. And you, lieutenant, you're the one on the Messenger case, right?" Lemoski nodded. "Saw you on TV. Must be quite a challenge. Any good leads?"

Conniston broke in. "I doubt these two officers came here to give us a personal briefing." He guided Fields toward the driveway, his hand on his cousin's back. "By the way, after you get that script, could you pick up a box of cigars at Havana Studios? They're already set aside."

"Sure, Ave." Fields looked at Lemoski, then back to Romero. "So long, folks. Good luck on catching this Messenger guy."

"He your bodyguard?" Lemoski asked, as they stepped into the house.

"Bodyguard? That's an interesting thought. No. Mike just likes to hit the weights. He moved out from Phoenix a few months ago, following a divorce. He's pretty broken up about it. He wants to get into the business here, and I'm trying to help him out." Conniston shook his head, his thoughts clearly elsewhere. "Growing up, he saved my rear end on the playground a few times, I can tell you that."

Several minutes later, they had all taken seats in the large sunken living room. Conniston leaned forward on the white leather sofa. "I often cut through Eagle Canyon on my way back from my ranch in Santa Barbara. It's a more direct route than the freeway and a hell of a lot more fun to drive."

"Must have been very dark?" Lemoski noted.

"Yes, but that's part of the challenge. I just bought a new Jaguar sports car, the XK8. Have you seen one?"

"Dozens of times." The producer's face registered surprise. "In car magazines."

"Oh, good line." Conniston gave a short laugh. "Anyway, I wanted to see what it could do, so I took it through some paces."

Romero, the Art History minor, was under direct orders from

Lemoski to take notes. The problem was, Conniston's household decorations were far more interesting and distracting than his car bragging; she found her eyes darting from one modern masterpiece to another. Around the corner, one room over, she could see what appeared to be a Claes Oldenberg, but to confirm her suspicion, she would have to reposition herself, and she knew Lemoski already had one eye on her. She stayed put.

"You told Detective Lee," Lemoski continued, "that you saw a man with long hair."

"Yes, I think it was tied in a ponytail."

"Do you remember the color?"

"I can't be sure, but it was more light than dark."

"And did you see what he was wearing?"

"As I told the detective over the phone, I believe it was an Irish knit sweater."

"What was the time?"

"Oh, I couldn't say…"

"Approximately?"

Conniston canted his face to the ceiling. "Sometime between 10:45–11:15, I would guess. Is it very important that I narrow it down more?"

"It might be. Anyway, this guy with the ponytail—what was he doing in relation to the woman you saw?"

"Well, I only saw him for a few seconds, but it looked like he was helping her."

"Why do you say that?"

"The hood of her car was up."

"So why do you assume he was helping her?" Romero asked. "Maybe they were just together."

"Another car was parked in back of the first, and its headlights were on. I guess I just assumed he was the boyfriend or some good Samaritan who had come to the rescue."

"Are you even sure this person with the long hair and ponytail was a man?" Romero cut in.

Conniston paused. "Hmmm, I just assumed it…. My gut feeling was that I saw a man—I'd guess forties and a younger woman."

"Can you describe the cars you saw?"

"The first car, the one with the open hood, was a dark four-door."

"Make?"

"Inexpensive, but I couldn't tell."

"Can you be more specific?"

"I'm sorry. No."

"And the second car?"

Conniston rolled his eyes up toward washed oak beams that ribbed the twenty-foot ceiling. "A pick-up, I think. That's what I remember."

"Model?"

The TV producer shook his head and gave a rueful laugh. "What can I tell you? If I knew it might have been involved in a murder, I'd have looked more carefully."

"Okay, so you saw them as your headlights swept past them?"

"Yes."

"And then you drove on?"

"Exactly."

"How fast would you say were going?"

"Not very. No more than 40 at the point. It's a canyon road."

"You saw a lot," Lemoski noted. "Considering."

"Well, I've driven the road many times. I almost know it by heart. Plus, moving images are, literally, my life. I see things others don't."

"You never thought to call the police or Triple A?" Romero asked.

"I did think about turning around and asking them if they needed help. But you know how it is, you see something, a few minutes pass, and you forget about it. Besides, I figured if it were serious trouble, they'd have tried to flag me down. But they didn't, the girl was just standing next to him."

"And how would you describe her?"

"Well, her back was to me. Long blond hair, that's what struck me."

"But you didn't see her face?"

"No. You know how it is, you see a blonde—not a brunette mind you, but a blonde—from the back and you always want to see the face. But I couldn't."

"Thanks," the decidedly dark-haired Romero said.

Conniston's face showed a tinge of red. "My cousin was right. You're very pretty."

Romero laughed. "You and your cousin like to compliment women, Mr. Conniston."

"I'm serious. You have beautiful eyes, very sensitive. Doesn't she have sensitive eyes, lieutenant? Eyes you'd want to confess to?"

Conniston's daughter walked into the room at just that moment. "Daddy, you're embarrassing our guests."

"April, I would like to introduce you to Lieutenant Lemoski and Detective Romero."

April Conniston, fashionably dressed in a sea foam green business suit with a skirt just above the knee, and holding a light brown leather briefcase, stepped down three stairs into the sunken living room. "Detectives?"

"You know that horrible murder two nights ago in Eagle Canyon. I might have seen the man who did it when I was driving past there, coming back from the ranch."

She dropped onto the sofa. "Oh, my God." She looked at her father. "Two nights ago? But you didn't say anything."

"There was nothing to say. All I saw was a man who seemed to be helping a woman with her car. But last night on TV, they asked if anyone had seen a stranded car on Eagle Canyon Sunday night. So I called Lieutenant Lemoski's office. He's in charge of the case."

"Maybe I should stay here with you during the questioning."

"My daughter's an attorney," Conniston explained. "Worse, a criminal defense lawyer, fresh out of Yale Law School." Then, to April, "I think you're too late anyway. I was just trying to help, darling. But I don't think I have."

"If you don't mind," Lemoski said. "I'd like one of my team to take you to the spot on Eagle Canyon where you saw this man and woman."

"I can't imagine how—"

"Sometimes just being back at the scene of an event brings back memories. Would tomorrow morning be okay?"

"I'll clear my schedule."

"We appreciate your coming forward."

Conniston walked them to the foyer. "I'm curious. Did anyone else see this poor girl and this man together?"

"I'm sorry. I can't tell you that."

They shook hands and Conniston showed them out.

"His shows might be crappy, but he has taste," Romero offered as she checked her face in a compact mirror.

Lemoski turned the ignition, and guided the car back up the long, steep driveway. "What do you think of him?"

"Smooth."

"I don't mean his personality. What he told us."

"Not much. I guess we might know now that our guy sports a ponytail and is probably middle-aged, which would help, that is, if Conniston's story is accurate. But then, like I said, it could have been a woman he saw."

"I doubt it. The way he sized you up, I'm pretty sure he can tell what sex he's looking at—from any angle."

"That comment he made to me. It was bizarre, you know about my having eyes you want to confess to."

"I'm sure this guy has plenty of sins he could tell you about," Lemoski conceded. "But I don't think he's our man. When was the last time you heard of a successful TV producer and big-time art collector moonlighting as a serial killer?"

Romero nodded her head slowly. "So should I take him out to Eagle Canyon tomorrow?"

"No, you'd be a distraction. Davis can do it. Somehow I don't see Conniston flirting with him."

Winding his way out of Bel Air, windows down, Lemoski allowed himself a final whiff of eucalyptus. *I wonder what it's like never to have to worry about money... Avery Conniston? What kind of name is that? He plays the good citizen, feels righteous about himself and I waste a morning.* Then again, he had gotten out of the office, gone for a pleasant ride and breathed the aromatic air of wealth and privilege. When investigating a murder, Lemoski had learned to savor even the smallest of pleasures.

Wednesday, 5 P.M.

The welcoming aroma of ground coffee greeted Jordan as he entered the Starbucks on the corner of Westwood and Lindbrook. That smell, the scent of Mother Earth, tropical sunshine, soil and rain compacted into a bean, then roasted and released—that's what pulled people into these cafes. Who could resist that smell? Not many. There were over four hundred Starbucks in Los Angeles alone and more being added every month.

Robin was already at a table, beverage in hand. She motioned to Jordan as he came in, but he had already spotted her red hair from the window.

As he reached the table, she stood up. Catching her hand in his, he was conscious yet again of the softness of her skin.

"I'm not late, am I?"

"I'm early," she answered. "It's been so hectic today, you know, with only ten days to the opening. I was just so desperate for coffee, I couldn't wait."

He sat down opposite her.

"Aren't you getting something?" she asked.

"Maybe later." He studied Robin's face for a moment. "Your message concerned me. Are you okay?"

"Definitely." She lifted a half-finished croissant from the plate in front of her. "I'm eating, and I'm singing up a storm. For a change, even Walter isn't complaining."

He felt a jab of jealousy. "So what is it?"

Robin's red eyebrows knit together. "The truth is, the more I think about it, this might not even have anything to do with the hypnosis. Maybe it was stupid of me to call you."

"Of course not. We agreed that we were going to be in touch. But you sounded so mysterious on the phone. Just tell me about it."

"Okay, okay," she nodded, "there's not a lot to tell. I woke up this morning feeling normal. Fine. But then I saw an envelope on my night table with writing on it, and when I read it, it scared the hell out of me."

"You had no recollection of writing it?"

"Not at all. The only thing I can imagine is that I dreamed something and woke up in the middle of the night and wrote it down."

"Okay, that makes sense."

"Listen, Jordan, it's not that I wrote something down in the middle of the night that's bothering me. It's what I wrote."

Robin was already fishing inside her oversized black purse. She quickly pulled out a long envelope and handed it to him. *He's going to kill me* was written in an uneven, hurried scrawl; then under it: *I must stop him. How can I?*

Jordan's mouth went dry; immediately his mind catapulted back to the scene with Robin in his office. There it had been words pouring out of her. But now, seeing these words on paper made everything seem more ominous.

"You know, actors are pretty suggestible," Robin broke into his reverie. "When I was doing *Dial M for Murder* I got scared to use a scissors, and even dreamed once about a guy strangling me."

A guy strangling me, Jordan thought. He wished he could make a note on a piece of paper.

"But this," she leaned over to Jordan's side of the table and raised the envelope, "has nothing to do with *Carousel*."

"No, it doesn't," he conceded. "And I suppose you're wondering if it has anything to do with the hypnosis."

She looked at him closely. "It does, doesn't it?"

He nodded. "Robin, what I am going to tell you now will sound strange. I can't explain a whole lot about it, because I really don't know what it means. For all I know, it could even have something to do with that dream you just told me about, in which a guy tried to strangle you."

He then told her everything that had come out at his office. When he finished she laughed a shrill nervous laugh, one he had not heard from her before. "And you told me I wasn't crazy."

He stared straight into her vulnerable green eyes. "You're not, and you know that very well."

She lifted her arms and gestured to the patrons. When she spoke her voice was low. "So tell me, doctor, just how many of our coffee-drinking compatriots here have sick fantasies about—"

Jordan stopped her with his deliberate tone of voice. "Robin, your story has a second act." He filled her in on what he had found in the Bugliosi book and at the UCLA microfiche room. As he spoke, she made small but audible gasping sounds.

"Then all this really *happened*?" she asked when he finished.

He reached inside the inner pocket of his jacket and drew out several pages. "These are photocopies of the articles that came out in the *Times*. Do you—"

Robin grabbed the pages out of his hands even before he finished his question. He watched as she put them down on the table and started reading. A few times, her hands shook. A full five minutes passed before she looked up. Her face was pale. "When you told me about this, you didn't say anything about this call to Beverly Casper's parents."

"I was just giving you highlights," Jordan said. "I didn't mention everything."

"Like what else?"

He described how John, just as he was about to strangle her, had asked if she wanted to leave a message for her parents.

Robin looked up at him, her eyes wide. "This is not some sort of a sick joke. Promise me. I'm serious, Jordan. I met you doing party tricks. But there's nothing funny about this."

"I assure you this is not a joke."

Robin stared into her coffee. It was several moments before she looked up. "Aren't you thinking what I'm thinking... about that killing a few days ago?"

"What killing?"

"In Eagle Canyon. It was all over the TV and the papers."

"I never watch TV and half the time I don't even look at the paper." Jordan answered. "Certainly not the crime stuff."

"This girl left some restaurant in the Valley, and wasn't seen again until they discovered her body."

"That's horrible, Robin, but I would guess that there's probably been dozens of murders—"

"And in this case too," she continued, her voice overriding his, "the girl's parents got a call a few hours later with some sick message."

Jordan retreated into silence, absorbing the last comment. "You're sure?" he finally asked.

"It was everywhere. My mother's been calling me, telling me not to get into cars with strange men." Jordan's eyes narrowed. "You just have to know my mother."

"And it's all because of this crime?"

"The police are now saying it was the third such murder in the last two months. One in Pasadena, another I don't remember, but also around here."

Jordan looked up at the ceiling, considering, reflecting. "Tell me," he asked. "This last murder, when did it happen?"

"No more than a few days ago. Wait... it was Monday. Yes, that's when they found her. I saw it on TV with Walter. It was just before I went to see you."

If the body had been discovered on Monday, then it should be in yesterday's paper.

"How much time do you have?" he asked Robin.

She looked at her watch. "Not much."

"Enough to come back with me to my apartment to check the newspapers? It's just a few minutes from here. I want to read more about this murder."

"I would, too," she said, impulsively taking his hand in hers. "But I have to go. If I'm late again for a rehearsal, Walter will throw a fit."

She started to put on a sweater, but stopped and looked him square in the face. "Jordan, I owe you an apology."

"For what?"

"Look at what you're doing for me. I'm eating again, I'm singing. And how do I respond? With that little blowout, accusing you of making up some sort of stupid joke. I'm really sorry. I'm just so overwhelmed. I walk in here thinking that I just had some sort of weird nightmare, and next thing I know you're telling me I lived a previous life and was murdered."

"Robin, I'm not telling you that you lived before. For all we know this might all turn out to have an innocent explanation."

"Sure. Like what?"

"Maybe you heard about this murder somehow, and—"

"You don't believe that, do you?"

He gnawed at his lower lip, thinking of Fischer's critique, of the man who wrote in Oscan, and of Reena Gupta. "I don't know, I just don't know," he finally answered.

She looked down at her watch. "I gotta run."

"I'll let you know if I find out any more."

"So you really have turned out to be the mystery man."

We both have our mysteries, he thought as he watched her go.

Wednesday, 5:53 P.M.

Ten minutes later Jordan was home. It was a matter of seconds to work his way through the papers. There it was, in Wednesday's paper, not Tuesday's, big as death across the front page. An eighteen-year-old girl named Monica Johnson (under the headline, the paper had run an incongruously happy photo of the dead girl, flowing blonde hair and a dimpled smile) had left a Denny's restaurant in Agoura Hills on Sunday evening, and was not seen again. A few hours after the disappearance, her parents received a call from a man who claimed he had a message for them from Monica. They immediately alerted the police, who quickly discovered Monica's car parked on a dirt shoulder of Eagle Canyon Drive. A few hours later, a man hiking with his dog at dawn in a wooded area not more than a couple miles from the location of the car came across the body. Next to the article about Monica's murder was another story. A Lieutenant Ben Lemoski of the LAPD homicide division had reported that there appeared to be a new serial killer operating in the L.A. area. He claimed that police had identified similarities between Johnson's murder and the killings of Erica Braun in Pasadena six weeks earlier and Rachel Gordon in Anaheim a month after that.

Jordan's mind was racing. All three girls were between seventeen and nineteen; Beverly Casper had been seventeen. Two of them were seniors in high school, one a college freshman. Beverly had been going into her senior year in high school. Each had disappeared shortly after leaving a restaurant, and each had been alone in a car that had broken down. Again, just like Beverly. And now this: In all four cases, right after the disappearance, a call had been placed to the victim's family.

It was in Bolton's office that Jordan had first started wondering about John. If he was a real person, what had happened to him? Now, he started wondering something else.

Was John still out there?

Was John still killing?

When's your dad going to catch this Messenger guy?" Deena
Tulipan asked between sips of her cherry coke. "The way things are
going, I'd have a better curfew in a nunnery."

"Tell me about it," Kathy Lemoski nodded. "I told my mother
we had a late cheerleading practice, and she started wagging her finger
at me, 'And don't go out afterward with your friends.' I'm grounded
and I haven't done anything wrong."

Four high school seniors—Deena Tulipan, Kathy Lemoski,
Judy Cinch and Grace Ashworth—occupied the booth in the far
corner of the restaurant. In a tradition that was passed seamlessly
from one graduating class to the next, the girls had taken the trip
over the Santa Monica Mountains from the West Valley, where they
lived, to Malibu, where they dreamed of living. Like a lighthouse,
Hamburger Heaven sat on the north side of Pacific Coast Highway,
flush against a hillside. Over the years, mudslides and fires had wiped
out the buildings on either side of it, but somehow the restaurant had
survived. Except for a few vinyl seat replacements, it had remained
largely unchanged for forty years.

"This is like not funny," Judy Cinch said. "I was on the same road as that third girl who was murdered like two days—"

Grace Ashworth tapped lightly on Cinch's head. "Hello, Judy, you're using 'like' again like in every sentence."

"I used it once."

"Twice. And you told me to point—"

"I didn't tell you to be obnoxious about it."

"Fine," Grace continued. "Go on. Sound like some *Saturday Night Live* skit. See what I care." She reached for a French fry on the edge of Kathy Lemoski's plate.

"How does my skin look? Really, be honest," Deena asked the group.

"It looks way better than last week," Kathy assured her.

"God, was it really that bad last week?"

"Dig yourself out of this one, Lemoski," Grace snorted.

"Come on, you know what I mean, Deena," Kathy said. "Anyway, I'd rather have zits than freckles any day. Zits go away. Freckles are forever."

It was true. Kathy Lemoski's face was full of them.

"They look really cute on you," Judy ventured.

"Oh, yeah, sure. You want to trade skin?"

When Kathy Lemoski was eight, her father used to tell her that each freckle was painted specially by God. Even then she realized he was saying that to make her feel better, which of course only made her feel worse. But over this last year, during the long moments she spent staring at herself in the mirror, even she had to admit that she was pretty. After being convinced for years that her features were conspiring against her, now the freckles, the shiny strawberry blonde hair, the clear brown eyes all seemed to be working in concert.

And the proof was that the boys had begun to notice her. Now, unlike her freshman and sophomore years, they looked her in the eye when they said "Hi" in the hallway. When it first began to happen she couldn't understand it; now that it was common, she thought it was "cute."

"Chip Estes agrees with Judy," Grace said casually.

"How do you know?" Kathy asked, her voice wary.

"People talk to me. Tell me deep things. I don't know why but they do. Maybe I'll be a shrink when I grow up."

"Yeah," said Judy. "Just take out an ad, 'Obnoxious shrink open for business..'"

"Shut up, Judy," Kathy cut her off. "What exactly did Chip Estes say?"

"He told me he thinks you're hot."

"How hot?" Deena asked.

"*Tres* hot."

Kathy Lemoski savored this new intelligence. She had liked Chip Estes since he moved to the Valley, sophomore year. They had an easy rapport—going to movies and basketball games as part of a group on weekends—but she had always kept a safe distance. Now she knew her feelings were reciprocated, juicy gossip made all the sweeter because she was getting it "live," sitting with her friends, rather than over the phone. Such priceless info was worth a thousand lies to her mother about cheerleading practice running late.

"Look me in the eye, Grace," Kathy said.

Grace Ashland's blue eyes bore down on Kathy with exaggerated intensity.

"If you're putting me on about Chip, you'll have nothing to worry about from the Messenger. I'll come after you myself."

"Whew, baby! I seem to have touched a nerve."

"I'm serious."

"Well, I'm perfectly serious too. He told me. Does that mean that now I'm safe from you and the Messenger?!"

"Couldn't they come up with a better name than the Messenger?" Deena said. "Isn't that kinda lame?"

"He phones the parents after he kills," Grace said.

"Ugh! That is so gross."

"If this guy phoned my parents, they'd say, 'Judy who?'"

"Melodrama!" Deena, Kathy and Grace called out in unison, their standard retort when anyone in the group started bewailing their fate.

"Live with my parents for a few weeks and say that," Judy protested. "I'm the only teenager in America home more than her parents."

The girls knew this was an exaggeration, but only a slight one. Judy's father was a well-known cardiologist and her mother headed a venture capital firm. They both traveled extensively. When Judy was younger she had a nanny to look after her when her parents were away. Too old for a nanny now, her only chaperon was a live-in El Salvadoran housekeeper. Not surprisingly, her house was the meeting place of choice for the girls. In fact, if not for the Messenger-imposed curfew, they would have reconvened there after leaving Hamburger Heaven. Judy had a great CD collection, and the refrigerator, courtesy of the housekeeper, was always stocked.

Kathy turned toward Grace. "So Chip really said that?"

"That's what he said. Who knows, maybe when you get home, there'll be a message from him."

"Home? Shit, what time is it?"

"Yeah, we'd better get going. We don't want to trigger a panic," Deena said.

Kathy slid out first. She straightened her crimson cheerleader mini-skirt, then made way for Grace to slide out.

The girls were in too much of a hurry to notice the man hunched in the booth in front of theirs, his back to them. He was smiling in a funny way, covering his mouth with his hand. As they advanced toward the cashier, he pulled his hand away and took a quick sip from his coffee cup. *So that's what the lieutenant's daughter looks like. Sweet. Untouched by life. Pure.* He followed the girls' progress out of the restaurant, watching them as they waved good-by in the parking lot, watching to see which ones went into which cars. He felt excited and sentimental.

He withdrew a small notebook from an inside coat pocket, took out a pen and wrote down two words in small letters, all caps: CHIP ESTES.

Wednesday, 11:30 P.M.

Jordan did the math. Beverly Casper was murdered thirty-two years ago by a man she'd estimated to be twenty-five. He'd be in his mid-fifties now, give or take a few years. Still in his prime.

But was it plausible? Had John stopped killing for three decades and suddenly started again? Or had he been doing it all along, undetected? *Or have I been so taken in that I can't think straight anymore?*

He imagined the absurdity of going to the police and telling them, "I might know who this killer is."

And they'd ask him, "Who?"

"A middle-aged guy who calls himself John."

"What's John's last name?"

"I don't know. And I'm not sure that John's his real first name either."

"Oh, and what is his real first name?"

"I don't know. But he murdered a girl thirty-two years ago in the same way."

"How do you know?"

"Some woman I hypnotized told me."

"And how does she know?"

"She was the murdered girl in a previous life."

After they'd stop laughing, he might well find himself in a straight jacket, begging Elinor to convince the police he was not mad.

If he were ever going to be able to do anything with this information, he'd have to know a lot more about Beverly, about the night of the murder, and John. Most of all, John.

He went back to the notes he'd taken after Robin had left his office. On the one hand, it seemed as if she had told him a lot: Beverly Casper's name and age, the date, the place where her car had broken down, and, overshadowing everything else, the graphic, haunting and chilling description of Beverly Casper's final hour on earth. But now, as he reviewed his notes, concerned this one time not with Beverly's horrible pain, but with ferreting out clues to John's identity, he was far more conscious of all that he didn't know than of what he did.

What did he really know about John? Other than telling him that he looked twenty-five and claimed to have been in the Marines, Beverly had not told him almost anything else. Except for that strange line about his name, "They call me John." Logic dictated that he must have appeared relatively normal, no obvious tattoos, or anything that would have cautioned Beverly against entering the car with him. So he probably looked pretty clean-cut.

But what about those sounds Beverly heard him making—some sort of snapping, clicking noise, she said—wouldn't that have warned her away? No, not if they were only triggered after he had her under his domination. That's doubtless—when he would get excited and lose control.

Anything else? He seemed to know a lot about cars. Jordan certainly couldn't have done what John had—take a quick look under a car's hood and immediately detect what was wrong and the part needed to repair it. Then he laughed, ruefully. Just who was the source of the information that John was an authority on cars? John. Big deal. That proved nothing. If he had no intention of repairing her car, then of course he could diagnose what was wrong with it. Who was going to correct him?

He grabbed a yellow legal pad and decided to review his notes with fresh eyes, as if he had never seen them. Now, details he had glossed over before suddenly acquired a new significance.

Take Beverly's comment when she first described seeing John: "I don't know why, he looked familiar."

Jordan had asked from where and Beverly had said nothing, just shook her head.

"Familiar." At the time, Jordan had ignored this comment. For some reason, throughout and even after the session, he had automatically assumed that Beverly had been the victim of random, horrible luck, a classic case of being in the wrong place at the wrong time: her car had broken down, and a psychopath had come by, abused, and then murdered her. But now, this explanation started to seem less and less likely. The more he thought, the more this crime reeked of planning.

The fact that Beverly did not know from where John looked familiar did not necessarily mean much. Perhaps John had been following her for a few days. Discreetly. Possibly, she had noticed him, in the way that we sometimes notice people without really noticing them; maybe, once while walking, she had turned around and seen him behind her, or something like that. If true, this would reinforce his earlier assumption that John seemed normal enough. At least in his appearance and how he behaved. If there had been something very different about him—a scar, an obvious tattoo, or if he was very ugly or very handsome for that matter—Beverly wouldn't have spoken of him as looking familiar; she would have remembered him.

Now, as he considered the possibility of John having stalked Beverly, he rethought other things as well: For example, how just moments ago, he had rejected out-of-hand John's automotive abilities. Maybe he had been too quick with his dismissal. "He used technical language," Beverly had said, "like he was a mechanic or something."

Combine that statement with the comment that John looked familiar, and a very different scenario could be played out. What if John had been following Beverly? If so, was it mere coincidence that her car had broken down and he *happened* to come along? Wild scenarios started running through his head. Beverly had spent the evening at Hamburger Heaven, as the *L.A. Times* had said. Perhaps John had been there too. Followed her there, or maybe he had just been there and saw her come in. Maybe that was even the first time he had seen her, and it was from there that he looked familiar to her.

He imagined John sitting at a table by a window, listlessly drinking a coffee or a coke, with nothing to do, just aimlessly looking out. Suddenly, a teenage girl drives up. John sees her step out of her car and likes what he sees. Maybe, while Beverly is relaxing with her friends and chatting, he steps outside and finds a way to quickly and partially disable her car—cause a leak or something—knowing that it will go for only a short distance before it runs down. He could then follow behind, be Johnny-on-the-spot, the obliging Boy Scout.

Okay, so let's say he disabled her car, then followed her and picked her up. And let's say I'm hallucinating. No, the police will never buy this. They'll say I've dreamed up an elaborate theory that is absolutely unfounded.

But then, maybe there is a basis. What alternative explanations could be constructed? That the killer came upon a car that just happened to have broken down and that happened to have one occupant, a seventeen-year-old girl? And that everything then happened spontaneously? On the spur of the moment, he took Beverly in his car to some hidden spot in Topanga, forced her to have oral sex, then strangled her?

"Precisely," as Elinor would say in her clipped Argentinean accent. "Just because a theory is complicated doesn't mean it is true, and just because a theory is simple doesn't mean it is false."

Except for one detail that no simple theory could account for: the pit. John had prepared a pit. He remembered Beverly's words: "It looks like someone dug it."

So John knew he was going to be murdering someone.

And now another detail on the paper meshed in his mind. Nothing definite, but definitely suggestive: that call to the police hotline.

The day after Beverly Casper disappeared, the hotline had received a call informing them that Beverly had headed straight from Hamburger Heaven to her boyfriend's house. But Larry Keeton—the boy implicated in the call—was not Beverly's boyfriend; all he had done was ask her out on a date. And very few people knew that. Melissa Wine knew it, and the other girls at the restaurant that evening knew it, because Beverly had just confided this information to them. And maybe Keeton had told a friend or two.

So then who called the hotline? Was it one of these friends, someone who wanted to cause Keeton trouble? Doubtful. Implicating someone in a serious criminal investigation went way beyond any definition of a high school prank.

But what if John had been at the restaurant, what if he had been at a nearby table, listening? Listening to the group of high school girls giggling and gossiping and talking loudly, as girls of that age do. Listening in as Beverly Casper excitedly told her friends that Larry Keeton had asked her out.

She had gone from Hamburger Heaven to Keeton's house, the hotline caller had said. Just the sort of damning detail that would intrigue the police. And just the way he could imagine John's mind working. A few minutes in the car with Beverly and he was expecting her to acknowledge him as her boyfriend. To such a mind, just one call for a date would certainly qualify Beverly as Keeton's girlfriend. What evil pleasure he must have had when he learned the trouble his call had brought down on his "rival."

Indeed, the more he considered it, the more this theory was making sense. Beverly had said that John had looked familiar. She must have seen him earlier, and he must have seen her earlier that night, and done something to her car. Then come to her rescue like a knight on a white horse.

Now, as he reviewed his notes yet again, he began to realize that he knew more about John than he had earlier thought. Police, he knew, thrive on details, verifiable facts; thus, even on the extremely remote chance that they accepted the validity of the hypnosis, they would still tell him that, from their perspective, what had come out was of limited value. Because what could these notes tell them for sure? Two things. That John was in his mid-twenties—not a small detail—that would make him more or less in his mid-fifties. And that he claimed to have been in the Marines. This was important. There might be some records. And what else?

Superficially, that would seem to be it. But Beverly's testimony, he now realized, revealed a lot more.

John hated women and liked to humiliate them. Even when John had forced Beverly to follow his most humiliating commands, he still remained furious with her. Most of all, it was his hatred for women that stuck out. No matter what Beverly did, it was not enough. She had obeyed his every command, and yet he had still strangled her.

"So what else is new?" he imagined a seasoned detective responding. "Of course serial perps hate women. That's why they kill them."

And he'd be right.

Fair enough. But there was more inside these notes, certainly enough to yield details that might help police narrow the search.

He remembered what John had yelled at Beverly: "You fucking cunt! You've always been a cunt!" Jordan assumed that these odious words were directed at Beverly. But how could that be? He had just met her. He must have been speaking to another woman, confusing, in his schizophrenic state, Beverly with her. But who was *she*? A girlfriend? His wife? His mother? Who knows?

Great! Every time he seemed to be getting near the goal line, the posts moved back another ten yards.

He forced himself to look at his notes one final time. The name Robin seemed to have disappeared from his yellow pad. No more Robin or Robin/Beverly, just Beverly. Did that mean he believed all this had happened, just as Beverly had described it? Ask that question of his head, and he'd tell you he still didn't know. But his heart, Jordan knew, had already decided. Beverly Casper had been murdered, and some part of her—if only her final memories—had been reborn in Robin Norris.

That's when he realized he had broken out in a cold sweat.

He stepped to the sink, scooped some cold water into his hands, and splashed himself. It helped, but only for a few seconds. Soon he felt ill again, and sat down on a kitchen chair, fighting nausea. Was he out of his mind? He couldn't go to the police with these flimsy speculations, these thin threads suggesting some sort of connection between

Beverly Casper's disappearance and the current murders. As much as his heart or his gut might be telling him that there was a connection, his rational mind was screaming something else. It was this rational mind that he'd been training for the past seven years, the last three especially. Elinor, his guide to all things true and reasonable, was as close to a strict Freudian and as far away from alternative "New Age" therapies as you could get. That's why he had chosen to study under her, wasn't it? He liked the way her mind coolly, even unemotionally, assessed patients' neuroses. Isn't that the sort of psychiatrist he was intending to become? So, what was he agonizing about now? There was no decision to be made. There was nothing to be done—except to wait and watch and maybe, *maybe* collect more data. He felt like he had been standing at the edge of the abyss and had just stopped himself from leaping over.

Then, a minute later, he was back at the edge. There was a killer out there—a killer whose evil even an Elinor Fischer couldn't explain—who was torturing, then murdering, innocent young women. And it was he, Jordan Geller, who, through some bizarre coincidence or freak luck, might have information that could stop him. In the time to come, he might be able, after decades of work as a psychiatrist, to coach back to mental health any number of people, but how many chances would he be given to actually save a human life, maybe more than one?

In his indecision, Jordan thought of Carrie, something he often did in the early morning hours. Two years before that drunk driver split them up forever, he had wanted to leave her. He even had arranged to do his psychiatric residency at Sloan-Kettering. This was the easy way or, as he once put it to Elinor, the coward's way out of the relationship. If he could put a country between them, maybe he could find a way to tell her he had ceased to love her. But Carrie was a woman of fierce determination and unbending will. You didn't get to be the news director at the Los Angeles affiliate of NBC by being a mouse. She was quietly determined to find a way to keep her job and her boyfriend in the same city. Jordan admired Carrie's ambition and tenacity, even loved it, but ultimately had come to doubt that these were qualities he most wanted in a life partner. The paradox in her character was that, despite all her outward strength, the higher Carrie climbed the network news ladder, the more afraid of heights she became. She needed constant reassurance, exactly what Jordan had been doling out to patients all day and not what he wanted to spend his evenings doing.

Gradually, his love had worn itself out. A million times he thought of telling her, but he just didn't have the fortitude. If he had, she'd still be alive. His indecisiveness had cost Carrie her life. How ironic that it was Carrie who arranged his meeting with Elinor. She was doing a TV story on Dittmyer and came home all excited. She had found the mentor he'd been looking for. There was no longer any need to go to New York. Everything he needed was right here in Los Angeles. And it was true. Elinor dazzled him during his first interview with her. Until two nights ago, his protégé status with the renowned psychiatrist, and through her, his connection to Dittmyer, was one of the few things in his life that he felt sure about. But now even that was up in the air.

Beverly Casper... John... Robin... Carrie... Indecision... Death. One association leading to another... Now a new and unexpected one pushed its way into the silence: Kitty Genovese. In 1964, in Queens, New York, this poor woman was stabbed and beaten to death under the watchful eyes of dozens of her neighbors. Nobody confronted Kitty's attacker. Nobody even lifted a phone to call the police. The nation was embarrassed and outraged. How could this have happened? Jordan had studied this case in an early psychology class and had always been intrigued by it. After revisiting the investigation, psychologists determined that the reason the neighbors hadn't helped Kitty Genovese was not because they were afraid of getting involved, but because everyone assumed that since so many people were watching, that *someone else* must have already called the police. Had only one or two people witnessed Kitty Genovese in distress, they probably would have done something to help her. Was he making the same mistake with the Messenger? He was assuming that the police would track down their man. That was their job, not his. It wasn't necessary for him to get involved. But what if they had no good leads as to who the Messenger was? What if they were totally in the dark? Was it then incumbent upon him to act?

Sixty years ago, his father had made a fateful decision to stay where he was, and both of his siblings, all that was left of his immediate family, had died as a result. As Jordan knew only too well, his father had never made another important decision again. Maybe that's why he, Jordan, was attracted to women like Carrie and Elinor, strong, decisive women. Maybe that's why he wanted to become a shrink in the first place, because a shrink helps people make decisions, but doesn't have to make them himself.

He contemplated the weird circumstances that brought him to this point—Stanton forcing him to perform hypnosis, then Robin asking him to help her with her problem the following day, and finally her startling revelation. Was it all a coincidence or some cosmic message? And if so, a cosmic message from whom? From God?

How did God get into this? He had always hung onto his religious beliefs, even though he no longer practiced the rituals of his faith. Yet at one point, Jordan had even considered becoming a rabbi. His father shrugged when he tried to talk to him about God. Elinor made cracks about his biblical references. She tolerated his superstitions, he knew, because she didn't consider them a threat. More likely, she assumed her influence over him was greater than God's. Maybe this was a test, a test designed by a supernatural power. Now who was he going to follow? Elinor or the Creator of the Universe? Or maybe it was simpler. God was offended by the murders and had sent his own messenger to Jordan with some clues to help the police bring the murderer to justice.

Jordan fell back on the couch, a cool washcloth draped over his face. There had to be a way out of this—a sensible way that would allow him to help the police, if he really had any help to offer, and save his reputation, his position, and perhaps his sanity.

He prayed for an answer. An answer came a few hours later in a book that had been providing answers to people long before anyone heard of Sigmund Freud.

Thursday

Thursday, 9:07 A.M.

He rummaged through a pile of small pieces of paper that had accumulated in his shirt pocket till he found the one he wanted. He picked up the receiver and punched in Robin's number.

"It's Jordan," he announced, even before she could say hello. And then he plunged forward; he didn't want to run out of courage. "I need to ask for your permission."

"You really are Dr. Mysterious," Robin laughed. "What could you possibly need my permission for?"

"Those murders, Monica Johnson's, and the other two as well, you were right. They're all similar, frighteningly similar to what you described in hypnosis." He could hear Robin's sharp intake of breath. "I think I've got to speak to this Lieutenant Lemoski."

"Who?"

"The policeman in charge of the Messenger investigation."

"What exactly are you planning to tell him?"

"About the hypnosis."

"There's panic out there, Jordan; the city's spooked. The moment this story comes out, I can just see the headlines: 'Whacky Actress

Claims Murdered by Messenger Thirty-Two Years Ago.' After that, the only A List I'll ever make is of Hollywood kooks."

"No one will even know your name."

"Of course they will. You just said you're going to tell them about me."

"About you and what you told me, but not who you are. A doctor is not allowed to reveal a patient's name."

"But I'm not even your—"

"Better. The way I'm going to present this to them, they're not even going to be thinking this whole thing has anything to do with these Messenger killings. All I'm going to tell them is that I'm treating a patient who has an obsession about this old case, the disappearance of a young woman named Beverly Casper some thirty years ago. That's all the information I'll give them."

"What good's that going to do?"

"Then I'll tell them that in order to treat the patient, I need to find out as much about Beverly Casper as possible. I'll tell them that I want to see the police file on it."

"But even if they give you the file," Robin snapped, "so what? You'll know about the similarities; they won't."

"Once I look at the file, I may even be able to draw some more conclusions about John. But more important, when I return the files to the police, I'll tell them about some of those 'similarities' between Beverly Casper's disappearance and the spate of current murders. Just like all this occurred to me when I saw the files. The police themselves will see the connection, realize that the killer—."

"This is sounding pretty far—"

"Could be the same guy," Jordan continued, his voice overriding hers. "Then I'll back out of the case, and leave it up to them to find John. Your name will never be mentioned, even Elinor will never find out."

"There's one thing missing in your great plan."

"What's that?"

"Once the cops notice these similarities, aren't they going to be more interested than ever in finding this patient of yours?"

Jordan tapped his pen against his desk. "Appoint me your physician right now, just as a technicality, and I'll claim doctor-patient confidentiality."

"But whatever you say, Jordan, my name's going to come out. It has to."

"Appoint me your physician now."

"Okay. Poof. You're my doctor. Now what?"

Jordan hesitated. He had pushed her very hard, very fast.

"Listen, I don't want you to do anything you don't want to do. Maybe you should consult with your boyfriend about this. Ask him what he thinks."

"What are you talking about? I don't have a boyfriend."

"That guy at the party."

"Walter?"

"Yeah. With the long hair."

"He's my director. He's a good friend, but in case you didn't notice, he's also about thirty years older than me. Besides, I'm the wrong gender. Anyway, I can't talk to Walter about this. He thinks this hypnosis stuff is crazy."

"Even after seeing how it helped you with the singing?"

"He doesn't know you hypnotized me again. I told him it was his inspiration that made me better."

"Oh."

"Also, if I tell him this is your idea, that'll make it even worse.... He thinks you're a wanker."

"A what?"

"Let's just say it's the British version of jerk-off. Walter uses it for anyone he doesn't like. But don't feel bad, he doesn't like almost anyone."

"And what do you think?"

A brief eternity passed until she spoke. "I actually like you."

"Really?"

An easy silence ensued.

"Jordan, it's just that I've been working so hard to get my career started. I don't want to be labeled a nut."

"Any more than I want to be labeled a wanker."

Robin laughed.

"I'm serious," Jordan went on. "Worst case scenario—this thing about the reincarnation becomes known. It won't, but even if it does, so what? Look at Shirley MacLaine. Her roles didn't dry up. A psychiatrist, though, that's a different matter. Many patients' biggest fear is that their shrink is crazier than they are."

"So then why go in? What can you accomplish?"

"I just don't see an alternative. I'll tell you something, Robin; this is about as intimate a confession as you'll hear from a psychiatrist.... I believe in God."

"That's your confession?"

"I realize that must sound strange, but in the world in which I work holding that belief makes me part of a very small minority. I don't always practice my religion, at least I haven't for a long time, but I do believe there's something higher than us."

"What is your religion?"

"I'll give you three guesses: My name is Geller and I'm a psychiatrist."

"Okay, I guess I could have guessed. And, not that you asked, but my mother's a Jew, my father was a Catholic, and I was raised with no religion at all. But I believe there's a God."

"I hope you're now ready for my second confession. Sometimes I go to the Bible for guidance."

Robin laughed. "That's hardly the worst thing a guy has ever told me."

"There's a verse in Leviticus, chapter nineteen. I read it again last night. 'Don't stand by while your neighbor's blood is shed.' Those words keep coming back at me. How am I going to feel, how are you going to feel, if a week from now, another murder occurs, and we realize we might have been the ones who could have prevented it?"

Robin was quiet.

"If you tell me not to go, I won't."

Jordan heard no answer. Then: "Do what you think you must.... I just hope you're not a wanker."

Friday

Friday, 10:45 A.M.

Jordan, the recently confessed Bible reader, was now sitting in the Woodland Hills police station with one thought: *I'm no prophet.*

Ever since he had walked into the West Valley police station an hour earlier, nothing had gone as he had planned. He told the female officer at the front desk that he needed to speak to someone about a disappearance and possible murder that had occurred in August, 1970.

The cop did a double take, "Did you say 1970?" and then told Jordan she would schedule an appointment for him with the detective in charge of the Cold Case Squad, the unit that handles "non-active homicide investigations."

"I need something very soon. This is urgent."

The woman shrugged her shoulders; the detective with whom Jordan needed to speak was tied up in a current investigation.

"Officer, I'm a psychiatrist, and I'm treating a patient whose emotional disorders I have reason to believe are rooted in a trauma from her youth, the vanishing of a West Valley high school classmate." This last piece of information was more specific than he intended, but hitting this first wall, he felt it necessary. "I need to find out if my patient's recollections are accurate or fantasy."

"Doctor, do you have dates, a name, a city?"

"Yes."

"Then give me the information, and we'll see what we can do. But I'm telling you not to expect miracles; it could take a couple of weeks, maybe more."

Jordan groaned. Two weeks from now the Messenger could have claimed another victim, maybe two. "The patient I'm treating is in crisis. I need some answers now."

"I'll see what I can do." She turned away from Jordan and lifted a receiver. He edged closer to hear her end of the conversation, but she turned around, glared, and pointed to a chair.

Twenty minutes later, a harried detective, Fred Swain, entered, his manner abrupt: "You the psychiatrist?"

"Yes." Jordan said, rising.

Swain gave him the once over, taking in the smooth face and the youthful swimmer's physique. Jordan withdrew a card from his wallet.

Swain inspected the card. "What's Dittmyer?" he asked.

"A psychoanalytic institute."

The response quenched Swain's interest. "You picked a bad day, doctor. We're under a lot of pressure here. So, let me take the information from you quickly. Okay?"

Jordan dived into his cover story. Swain listened impatiently, his eyes following anyone who walked in or out of the open office area. But the detective's irked manner changed abruptly the moment Jordan mentioned the name, "Beverly Casper."

The cop repeated the name, his voice excited.

Jordan's first thought was that the police already had made the connection between the current murders and the Casper case. "You know who she is?"

Swain's voice grew wistful. "I joined the force in '69, straight out of the Marines. Beverly Casper was the first murder case—truth is, we weren't even sure it was a homicide—I had anything to do with. They pulled me in to do some grunt work." His demeanor darkened and his eyes bore into Jordan's. "Tell me more about this patient of yours. How old is she?"

"I'm sorry. I can't tell you that. You know the issue, doctor-patient confidentiality."

"I'm just asking her age."

"I didn't say anything about the patient's gender."

Swain looked at some hastily scribbled notes on a sheet. "You told Officer Campbell that this was about a trauma that stemmed from *her*, that is, your patient's youth. Is that correct?"

"Detective, please don't ask me more questions about my patient's identity."

Swain looked at the sheet again. "You also said something about the disappearance of a high school classmate. So what's the big secret about the woman's age?"

"I gave my patient my absolute assurance that if I spoke to the police, I would say nothing that could point to her identity."

Swain sighed. "What was the nature of your patient's relationship with Beverly Casper?"

Jordan felt like a fool. He had walked into this station with one selfless thought: use Robin's "revelation" to help the police connect Beverly Casper's murderer and the Messenger. But in his enthusiasm, he had failed to prepare himself for even the most obvious questions.

Swain pushed back on his swivel chair and reasoned aloud. "I know this woman can't be a sister, because Beverly Casper didn't have one. She had a brother. There were those girls with Beverly that night. One of them, what was her name, Twine, Brine—"

"Wine," Jordan blurted out.

"That's right. Wine, Melissa Wine. You treating her?"

Jordan shook his head.

"So then this patient of yours told you about Wine. She must be one of the other girls."

Jordan sat there in agony. He was uncomfortable telling lies to anyone, let alone the police. Yet what if he told the truth—*My informant, detective, is a twenty-five year old actress born seven years after Beverly Casper's disappearance*—how would Swain react?

"Well, did your patient tell you about Melissa Wine?"

"After my patient started speaking about Beverly Casper, I checked out the case in the *L.A. Times*. I just wanted to make sure it wasn't all fantasy. Melissa Wine's name appeared in the article." This was all true and Jordan said it with conviction.

"Yeah, there was quite a lot of coverage," Swain said, more conversational than confrontational this time. "Girl walks out of a restaurant and is never seen again. I interviewed the father. I'll never forget his face. He looked like he was a 100 years old."

Jordan felt a new surge of confidence. He had regained the initiative. "The case was never solved. Is that right?"

Swain shook his head.

"I came across another name in my research. Franklin Jonathan Cole."

Swain looked at him blankly. "Who the hell is that?"

"He murdered his girlfriend around the time of the Casper disappearance and dumped her body in—"

"Malibu Canyon. Yeah, yeah. That's right; it was some sort of wild sex game between them, if I remember. We questioned him once or twice. I was there. It's more than three decades now, so I don't remember all the details, but other than hiding a girl's body in a canyon, there was no connection. If I recall correctly, he had an alibi for Beverly Casper."

Jordan wanted to tell Swain about Robin's line, "They call me John." But how would he explain that?

"Anyway," Swain went on, "Cole's not your man. I remember hearing that he was killed years later in a prison fight."

"Are you sure?"

Swain marked down the name on a piece of paper. "I'll double check it." He looked up at Jordan. "Let's get back to your story. Did this woman, this patient of yours, know Beverly Casper?"

"In a manner of speaking."

Swain turned up his palms. "I'm a cop, not a dentist. I don't pull teeth. And even if I wanted to, the Supreme Court wouldn't let me. You're not giving me anything, so what did you come here for?"

"I want to see the Beverly Casper file."

"We don't show files of criminal investigations except to other law enforcement personnel. If civilians started reading police files, word would get out. Perps would end up learning who our witnesses were; they'd construct alibis. A million things."

"All of which don't apply in this case. Beverly Casper's killer got away with it," Jordan said in one breath. "By now, he's sure he's never going to be caught, and I suspect he's not planning on constructing an alibi. Anyway, who has an alibi all these years—"

"Doctor, you almost talk as if you know him. I wonder. Are you perhaps treating a patient who confided to you that he had kidnapped and killed Beverly Casper?"

"Absolutely not!"

"But you wouldn't tell me even if you were, would you?"

"I might, without revealing identification."

Swain laughed, an angry laugh. "For example, you might try to make me think it was a woman you were treating, not a man. No, doctor, you wouldn't tell me anything, even to help catch a murderer. Five minutes ago, you wouldn't even tell me the age of this supposed woman who's been obsessing about this case."

"It *is* a woman," Jordan said, frustrated all over again.

Swain answered with a condescending nod and then rephrased his initial question. "Come on, doc, tell me the real reason you came in here today?"

"How many times do I have to repeat this? I want to take a look at those files to find out information that can help me in the treatment of my patient's obsession with Beverly Casper."

"You're going to read the file and suddenly offer this patient a different type of drug? Frankly, that sounds like bullshit to me. If you've got something to tell me about the Casper case, tell me. Otherwise, I just don't have the time."

Jordan sat there, his mind racing through alternatives. Maybe Robin had been right, he should have kept his mouth shut and his theories at home. But now it was too late. If he stood up and walked out, all he would leave behind was a frustrated cop who might conclude he was treating Beverly Casper's killer. He imagined unmarked police cars following patients out of the Dittmyer office. So, should he open up and tell Swain what he really wanted to know? That verse from Leviticus, "Do not stand by while your neighbor's blood is shed," flashed in his mind again. The Messenger was out there killing; Jordan couldn't just walk away.

"I do have a patient who has discussed the Casper case with me. And I can assure you, under oath if necessary, that she is *definitely, definitely* not the killer."

"What makes you so sure of that?"

"She was born in 1977."

Swain laughed, this time a drop more pleasantly. "Okay. If true, that's an unexpected answer. Then again, maybe she's the killer's daughter."

"It's more complicated that that."

Swain looked down at his watch. "I'm going to give you two minutes to convince me why I should show any files to you."

Jordan was about to burst out of his skin. He thought that he might be able to convince this cop to give him the files. But so what? It would take a few days, at least, to get them, then, who knows how long before the cops made the right connections. He couldn't wait that long. He needed to press his point. Now.

"I'm not just here about the Beverly Casper case," he announced. "This also has to do with the Messenger killings"

Swain sat upright. "You want to run that by me again."

"There are similarities between the Casper case and the Messenger killings."

"Like what?"

"All the girls murdered were in their late teens. All of them were last seen leaving a restaurant, and all of them left an abandoned car on a canyon or a deserted road."

"A dozen murders a year happen on canyon roads. There are hundred of miles of them in the basin."

"True. But what else did Beverly Casper's presumed killer do the night she was abducted? I know it's over thirty years, but you investigated the case. Tell me."

Jordan could see the light go on in Swain's eyes. "The phone call to the parents."

"And how many times a year does that happen?"

"It can't be." Swain shook his head from side to side. "People don't stop killing and start again like that."

"From a psychological perspective, I can tell you it's quite possible," Jordan answered, with a lot more authority than he actually felt.

"Or maybe the guy never stopped killing." There was an edge of excitement in Swain's voice now. "Maybe he's just never been caught."

"I guess that's possible, too."

"Wait here a moment. There are some other cops who need to hear this story."

"But you don't need me to be the one to tell them, do you?"

"Don't go anywhere. I'll be right back."

Jordan was sorely tempted to slip out. He glanced at his watch. 11:20. He didn't relish running another gauntlet of questions; he didn't want anything to come out about Robin. But what was his choice? Leave? He was hardly anonymous. This cop had his card. Ten minutes later, Swain returned, alone.

"Follow me please, sir."

He led Jordan down a narrow hallway, then opened a door and pointed ahead into a windowless room. Four people studied him as he entered: two were sitting alongside a plain wooden table, the other two, one of them a woman, were standing.

The taller and older of the two men at the table stood up, extended a hand and introduced himself. "Lieutenant Ben Lemoski. These are Detectives Davis, Romero and Bobley." Each one nodded to Jordan in turn. "Detective Swain you already know. Excuse the elegant surroundings. We used to have a conference room, but we had to turn it into an office. Budget cuts. Please don't be intimidated. "

The bureaucratic green of the cinder block walls and the airless atmosphere certainly didn't relax Jordan. Nor did the ten eyes that focused on him.

Lemoski began. "Detective Swain tells me you have some idea that the Messenger killings might be related to an unsolved thirty-two-year-old disappearance?"

"*Might* be," Jordan emphasized.

"I understand there are issues of doctor-patient confidentiality, but please tell us everything you can."

Telling the story for the second time came more easily. Lemoski posed all the questions, often repeating them with a slightly different twist.

The other cops simply listened. Davis stood in one corner with his arms crossed like an upright Buddha; Romero rhythmically nodded her head. Only Bobley seemed disinterested, glancing up at the ceiling as if he were more fascinated by the Rorschach water stains than Jordan's narrative.

Under Lemoski's steady coaxing, Jordan found himself adding details—nothing major, he thought, but enough to establish the credibility of his source and help convince the detectives of the link between the crimes. He told them that Beverly Casper had been abducted after leaving Hamburger Heaven—the other cops looked over to Swain, who nodded; he shared with them what Robin had said about the necklace of little angel figures that the killer had placed around Beverly's neck; he even told them that his patient had heard something about the murder weapon being a man's belt.

When he finished, he looked around the room. No one's expression had changed. Finally, Lemoski spoke.

"So, based on what this patient told you, you're suggesting, Dr. Geller, that we should be looking for a man in his fifties with an obsession with angels?"

"I don't know if the angel obsession would still be valid. It might manifest itself in another way."

"And how might that be?"

"I really couldn't say."

"Do you think he might pose them as angels?" Romero asked.

Jordan caught Lemoski's glare at the woman.

"It's possible," he answered, then turned back to Lemoski. "Is that what he's doing?"

Lemoski didn't have to answer. Jordan could read it in his face. After a moment's pause, the lieutenant nodded. "That information doesn't go out of this office. Understood?"

Jordan mentally pumped his fist. His suspicions had been borne out. He'd accomplished his mission.

"Doctor, what you're telling us has monumental implications. Is there any chance we could meet with your patient?"

"That would be out of the question."

"With you present, of course," Lemoski added.

"Absolutely not," Jordan said. "I want to help you as much as I can. But the only reason my patient permitted me to come here was because I guaranteed her anonymity. Besides, I've already told you everything that could help you."

"We might be better judges of that."

"I'm sorry, lieutenant."

Lemoski surveyed the room. "Does anyone, in addition to Detective Romero, have any questions for Dr. Geller?"

The room was quiet.

"In that case, doctor, thank you. What you've told us is very helpful."

Lemoski rose to his feet.

"You think there's really a connection between the killings then?" Jordan asked.

"You've made a compelling case. We're going to look into it, I assure you, very, very carefully. If this patient tells you anything more that you think might be useful to us, please call me." He took a card out of his breast pocket, and wrote some numbers on it. "You can reach me twenty-four hours a day."

Jordan followed Lemoski to the door. "I've really helped you?"

"More than you realize."

Friday, 12:50 P.M.

Even before he started his car, he phoned Robin on his cell.

"It's Jordan," he announced when she picked up. "I'm in Woodland Hills. I've just left the police."

He pulled his decennial BMW 325 out onto Topanga Boulevard.

"And?"

"It worked," he said, his voice exultant. "They made the connection between Beverly Casper and these other girls. And your name wasn't mentioned."

Robin let out an audible sigh. "They really think the cases are connected?"

"Compelling. That's what Lemoski, the lieutenant in charge of the investigation, told me, 'You've made a compelling case.'"

"And how did you tell them you got all this information?"

"Just what we'd worked out: that I had a patient who was obsessing about Beverly Casper. They're assuming my patient is in her fifties."

Suddenly, there was a crackle on the line and the connection went dead. "Damn it," Jordan cursed.

He redialed the number. "Sorry," he said when she picked up. "I'm in my car."

"Jordan, I'm really glad you did this."

"I felt like you were there with me. I wouldn't have done it without your permission."

"And you're sure they've made the connection?"

"They made it. I had to point them to it, but they made it. And if they haven't, there's nothing more we can do. We're out of it."

"Thank God it's over."

"Actually, not fully."

"Oh!" Robin said, her voice suddenly anxious.

"There is one more thing we can do."

"What's that?"

"We can have dinner tonight."

Robin laughed. "Next time, ask without giving me a heart attack."

Next time. Jordan liked that.

"But unfortunately," she went on, "I'm rushing off to rehearsal, and it's going to run late."

"Well, how about a late dinner, then?"

"Late dinner? Sounds tempting."

"When should I pick you up? Ten?"

"Ten is great. But let's have dinner at my place."

"How are you going to have time to fix dinner?"

Robin gave a short laugh. "You're not the only one with mysterious talents." She gave him her address, then said, "See you tonight. I gotta run."

"Bye."

Jordan pressed the end button and dropped the phone on the passenger seat. Confined to a car, his body electric with energy, he started drumming his fingers on the steering wheel.

Suddenly, a thought occurred to him. He couldn't be more than a few miles from Eagle Canyon, the site of Monica Johnson's murder. He imagined the police had roped off the area, so it'd be easy to spot. He didn't know what to expect, but he wanted to see it, he wanted to make a statement to the victim. *Somebody cares, Monica. That bastard isn't going to get away with it because I, Jordan Geller, just guided the police to him. I took action.*

Who would hear this declaration? No one, of course, except the phantoms in Jordan's own sleep-deprived, adrenalin-charged brain. Yes, it was a crazy notion, but he was full of those lately. This was his week for crazy notions.

He pushed up on his turn signal, waited for a few cars to pass, then swung into a U-turn. A moment later, he dropped a disc of Peter Gabriel's greatest hits into his car's CD player, cranked up the volume and glided onto the Ventura Freeway.

Friday, 1:05 P.M.

Lemoski walked back to the interrogation room, fighting a smile. You never know when your luck might change. Radically change. Till now he had very little on which to build his investigation—Avery Conniston's sighting and not much more, and that, as he had predicted, had produced zip in the way of new leads. Davis had taken the TV producer to the place where he had seen the ponytailed man and a girl who likely had been Monica Johnson, but Conniston couldn't add anything to the thin gruel he had offered Lemoski and Romero on Wednesday. But that was this morning, ancient history. Now he had something he could work with, really sink his teeth into. Excited as he was, he'd learned, unlike his young disciples, to stifle his optimism; seventeen years of promising leads going up in smoke had taught him that. Then again, he'd never had a lead quite like this one.

"There would seem to be only three possibilities," Lemoski announced as he sat down.

Davis, spoke first. "Geller's the killer, one of his patients is the killer, or he's just another loony shrink."

Lemoski smiled, but held up his forefinger: "Evidence for possibility number one?"

"Only we and the Messenger know about the angel stuff." Romero said.

"He knows they were strangled by a belt," Davis added.

"All he said was that Beverly Casper was," Lemoski said.

"Fred," Bobley called over to Swain. "Didn't you say that Beverly Casper's body was never found?"

"Yeah."

"Then, even if his bullshit story about a patient was true, how would he know that the killer gave her a necklace?"

"More," Davis broke in, "how would he know she was strangled with a belt?"

"Good, good," Lemoski said. "But let's just put Beverly Casper aside for a minute. Could the angel thing have been leaked somehow?"

"Hasn't turned up in any press reports I've seen," Davis said.

"He's a doctor," Romero spoke up. "Maybe he knows the M.E. and, over a drink or something, the M.E. lets it slip that the killer is nuts for angels."

"Stretch, Romero," Bobley said.

"But we've got to check into everything," Lemoski answered. "So Geller knows things only the Messenger and we know. Which leads us to possibility number two—one of his patients is the killer."

"Why the elaborate cover story about Beverly Casper then?" Romero wondered.

"Loyalty to the patient." Swain said. "Maybe he's trying to figure out if his patient really is the Messenger. So he fishes for details—"

"Which Romero happily gave him," Bobley cut in.

"And maybe the story isn't so elaborate," Davis said. "Maybe the Messenger murdered Beverly Casper thirty-two years ago, and this guy's treating him."

"So, we need to find out if Geller's treating any 48- to 68-year-old patients. Good. And finally, possibility number three, he's chock full of nuts."

"Didn't seem like it to me, but who knows?" Davis said.

"Most important," Bobley said, "that wouldn't explain how he knows what he knows."

"Okay," Lemoski said. "Here's what we do. We put on a full court press. Twenty-four seven. Bumper tail, wire tap, surveillance—pictures and sound."

"Starting when?" Davis asked.

"I'm going straight from here to the DA to get a judge to approve a tap. Meanwhile, Jimmy's on him as we speak. Greg, you and Josh," Lemoski continued, gesturing to Davis and Bobley, "set up a stakeout outside his apartment. If he pops a blackhead, I want to know about it. Karen, check into his personal history, academic record, whatever you can come up with. Oh, and we'd better dig up the Beverly Casper file. Fred, can you take care of that?"

The phone rang. Lemoski scooped it up while it was still on the first ring.

He listened a moment. "That's excellent, really excellent. Just keep watching."

He put the phone down. "That was Lee," he announced. "It seems that when the good doctor left here, he drove two miles down on Ventura, then made a sudden U-turn and headed for Eagle Canyon."

Friday, 10 P.M.

T he house's one and only specialty," Robin announced to Jordan as she set down a portion of roasted chicken smothered in fried onions, and served over grilled parsnip and red peppers.

Jordan looked at her in amazement: "When did you prepare this? You were heading straight out for a rehearsal when I called."

"I always have some ready in the freezer." She sat down opposite him. "It's a legacy of my mother's. One of her few gifts to me that doesn't self-destruct." Anticipating his response, she spoke again. "If your psychiatrist's brain is thinking that I have real issues with my mother, your psychiatrist's brain is right."

The less said about his being a psychiatrist the better, Jordan figured. E might equal mc^2, but psychiatry plus mother-daughter tension doesn't equal romance. Instead, he cut off a piece of chicken, and took a bite. "This is really delicious."

"Don't go overboard."

"No, I mean it."

"I guess I should ask: What do you usually have?"

"Whatever's the daily special at Stan's Donut Shop and Grill."

"Donut Shop and Grill?"

"Their hamburgers are highly rated."

"Oh my God. We almost forgot the champagne." This had been Jordan's contribution to the celebration. Robin stood up and rushed to the fridge. She looked over the bottle.

"Nice label."

"I thought so, too. That's about as far as my expertise goes. I hope it's good."

He twisted off the metal retainer and dug his thumbs into the cork. After a few anxious moments—he definitely didn't want to appear puny—the cork started to loosen. Then it launched with that distinctive champagne bottle pop into the air, bouncing off the ceiling. As the aerosol of champagne grape wafted out of the bottleneck, Jordan poured. He thought of a few intimate toasts; then cautiously decided on something more neutral.

"To being able to breath easy."

Robin clinked her glass against his.

Jordan took a healthy sip and felt the pleasant chill of the wine on his throat. The burden that he had been carrying for the last two days had finally lifted. Just a few hours earlier, contemplating his trip to the police, he had been so fearful: he didn't want to involve Robin, and the truth is, he didn't want to involve himself. But he had succeeded. Everything had been kept secret: Robin, the hypnosis, and, most of all, the reincarnation.

"You know," Robin was saying. "Driving back home tonight, I was thinking about what happened in your office. And then I decided, I didn't want us to talk about it. At least not tonight."

"Why?"

"Because that's the way our relationship began; you, the hypnotist, then you the doctor. But it's not the way I want it to continue."

The champagne had warmed his throat; now her words.

"And how do you want our relationship to continue?" he asked.

"That, I don't know yet. I suppose, just to get to know each other, like we were meeting on a blind date. I mean you know everything about my prior life"—Robin laughed—"only very little about this one. And I don't know anything about you, this time around or any other."

"So what would you like to know?" Jordan asked.

"Honestly?"

"Nothing less."

"Are you involved with anyone?" she asked.

"No."

"Good. Now that's out of the way."

"And you?" Jordan asked.

She shook her head. "I had been seriously dating a guy back east. An investment banker with Saloman Smith Barney, Harvard M.B.A. The whole bit. My mother, of course, loves him."

"He sounds very loveable—from a mother's perspective."

"Come to think of it that probably was a strike against him."

Sounds like she's not going to let go of this one, Jordan thought. "If I ever meet your mother, I'll be sure to try and make a bad impression."

"That would probably be hard. Single doctors don't—"

"When I tell her how much psychiatrists make these days, that'll put her off."

Robin laughed. "I suppose she has a way of getting herself into my conversations, my mother does. I should probably work on that. You have some open slots in your schedule?"

Jordan smiled. "So, what happened to Mr. Harvard M.B.A.?"

"Lenny is very focused; he knows exactly how he wants his life to turn out. Anyway, when I told him I was going to L.A. to do *Carousel* he gave me an ultimatum. If I left, it was over. So I left."

"Do you miss him?"

She took a sip from her glass. "Had I married Lenny, my autobiography would have been written in advance. It wasn't for me." She smiled. "I like a bit of mystery."

Robin tilted her glass toward Jordan. "And you? Just before the hypnosis, some woman at the party told me you were one of L.A.'s top ten bachelors or something. How long has it been since you've been involved?"

"Over a year."

Robin waited for him to continue, but he didn't. "What happened?"

Jordan's eyes shifted a bit. He tried to look up. But he could only stare at a vague point to the left of her head. "She was killed by a hit-and-run driver."

"I'm so sorry."

A total, but not uncomfortable, silence engulfed them.

Jordan picked up his fork. "Thank you."

"So, are you still in mourning?" Robin's voice was delicate.

"My friend, Harry Stanton, you met him at the party—"

"The guy who introduced you."

Jordan nodded. "He saw me at a bookstore last week, and started hounding me about what a hermit I'd become. Then he stuck a note in my pocket with the address of the party."

"Then I say: Hurray for Harry!"

He lifted his champagne glass. "To Harry."

*

Later, Robin had insisted on escorting him to his car. He opened the front door, then turned to her. "You made me very happy this afternoon."

She frowned. "This afternoon?"

"On the phone. When I scared you and you said, 'Next time when you ask me out don't give me a heart attack first.' I like the way you said that, *next time*."

"My mother would say I was throwing myself at you."

"Your mother again."

"She thinks girls should play hard to get."

"I don't need you to do that."

"In that case…" She curled her hand behind his head and pulled him toward her. Their lips touched, as if greeting one another. It was a long moment until they drew apart.

"I had a suspicion you'd be a wonderful kisser," Robin said.

"I improve with practice."

He floated the rest of the way to his car. *Life is complex*, he thought, and here's a perfect example. A day that had begun in chaos had ended in perfect order.

Saturday

Saturday, 11:19 A.M.

The earliest joke Elinor Fischer could remember was one told to her parents after the family had resettled in Argentina. "It's three in the morning and a couple hear loud knocking on their door. The terrified husband goes out of the bedroom and calls out in a timid voice, 'Who is it?' A man answers. 'Don't worry; I'm not from the police. It's not even very serious. I just wanted to tell you that your house is on fire.'"

Thirty years in America—in a society where she sometimes wondered if the police had too little power—had done little to relieve her anxiety. She looked again at the solidly built man who had invaded her office five minutes ago, announcing himself as an LAPD lieutenant, and asking questions whose answers might have horrifying implications for the future of her institute.

"Does Dr. Jordan Geller work here?" Lemoski had begun.

"Yes, he's a resident."

"Which means what exactly?"

"Well, in Dr. Geller's case, it means that in a couple of months he'll be able to practice privately on his own, assuming he passes his oral examinations."

"Does Dr. Geller see patients now?"

"Yes, that's part of his residency. Lieutenant, before you ask me any more questions, I need to know what this is about. As I'm sure you're aware, there are very strict procedures regarding doctor-patient confidentiality."

"And is Dr. Geller your patient?"

"I'm not going to answer that. Please tell me why you're here."

Lemoski paused. When he spoke, his voice was measured and deliberate. "I'm investigating a murder, very likely a series of murders."

"And what do these murders have to do with Dr. Geller?"

"I will tell you very soon. I just need to clarify one thing. As the institute's director, you're Dr. Geller's boss. Correct?"

"His supervisor, yes."

"Dr. Geller informed us that he has a patient who witnessed or has some knowledge of a murder committed more than thirty years ago. Would you know anything about this patient?"

Studying her polished fingernails, Fischer repositioned herself in her chair. She gazed over her desk as if looking for something. *Had Jordan gone to the police with this reincarnation story? No, he couldn't have been that foolish. But how else would this police lieutenant know about it?*

"He has no such patient," she finally said, "and there is no such patient at Dittmyer."

Lemoski tilted his head to the side and rubbed his chin. "How many analysts practice at Dittmyer?"

"Six."

"And are you familiar with each doctor's caseload?"

"Dr. Geller is not yet fully certified. I know the history of each of his patients."

"But you said there's no such patient at Dittmyer?"

"There isn't."

"So I ask you again, are you familiar with each doctor's caseload?"

"Whenever something unusual comes up, and what you describe

sounds unusual, I'm consulted. So I can tell you with confidence, there is no such patient here."

"So no one, particularly Dr. Geller, has spoken to you about a patient who reported some connection to a disappearance or murder thirty-two years ago?"

"As I told you, there is no such patient here."

Lemoski gave a curt nod. "I assume that means, therefore, that if Dr. Geller told members of our department about the existence of such a patient, he was either mistaken or lying because, as you have told us, no such patient exists. Is that a fair conclusion?"

Fischer stared past the lieutenant. When she spoke, her voice was very firm: "The young woman to whom you are referring came to see Dr. Geller, but not as a patient."

"If not as a patient, then as what?"

"I've already told you too much."

"You haven't told me anything, Dr. Fischer. And if this woman was not a patient, then the laws of doctor-patient confidentiality don't apply. This woman came here, you just told me. People come to psychoanalytic clinics to see doctors as patients. If not, then who is she? A girlfriend, a— "

"Lieutenant, it's part of the training of any analyst to be in analysis himself. Dr. Geller told me of his relationship to this woman in the context of a private meeting between him and me. I can't reveal any more about our conversation. I'm sorry."

"Is Dr. Geller your patient?" Lemoski repeated.

"I can't speak to you any more about this matter." Elinor had decided that she needed to buy time, it was vital that she speak to Jordan. "You said you were investigating a series of murders...?"

"Are you familiar with the name, the Messenger?"

"The serial killer?" Fischer asked.

"Your trainee, Dr. Geller, seems to think there's a connection between these current murders and the disappearance of a woman thirty-two years ago."

Fischer's precisely penciled brows tightened into a deep frown. "That sounds absurd to me."

"We are investigating the possibility that such a connection exists."

"And how would you go about doing that?"

"I'm sorry. Police privilege," Lemoski answered, making no effort to hide his sarcasm. "Dr. Fischer, I would like to speak to your receptionist."

He walked out to the reception area, Fischer one step behind him. "This detective wants to ask you a couple of questions, Pat."

Lemoski pulled out a photo Jimmy Lee had taken of Jordan and Robin outside her house the previous night. He handed her the picture. "Do you recognize this woman?"

Haman looked over the lieutenant's shoulder at Fischer.

"Ms. Haman," Lemoski said. "Dr. Fischer has already informed me that this woman is not a patient here. Therefore, there is no issue of confidentiality. So, once more, have you ever seen this woman with Dr. Geller?"

"Dr. Fischer?" Haman said.

Fischer's lips were set in a tight line. "Answer the lieutenant's question, please, Pat."

"Yes, that woman came to this office one time."

"When?"

"Monday."

"Five days ago?"

"Yes."

"Do you know her name?"

"She told me a name, but I had the impression it was some sort of private joke between her and the doctor."

"What was the name she gave you?"

"Myra Apple."

"In other words," Lemoski said, "this woman, either at Dr. Geller's suggestion or on her own, gave you a false name. Do you have any idea why she would do that?"

Pat Haman shook her head.

"One more thing. Are any of Dr. Geller's patients males between the ages of forty-eight and sixty-eight?"

Haman looked over to Fischer. "If this will help you in your investigation," Fischer answered, "then I can assure you the answer is no. But that's also the last question of this sort I will answer."

"Thank you, Dr. Fischer. Thank you, Ms. Haman."

As soon as Lemoski left, Fischer barked an order: "Get me Jor—Get Dr. Geller on the phone, and tell him I want him down here immediately."

As the secretary lifted the phone, Fischer marched back and forth in front of the desk, her high heels clicking against the hard wood.

Panic time was over. Dr. Elinor Fischer was in a flat-out rage.

Saturday, 1:15 P.M.

H e doesn't have a criminal record." Romero said, taking the smallest of sips from her Miller Lite. As she once told a friend, "Lite beer is the worst beer, except for all the others." But what was she supposed to do when out with "the guys"—ask for Pelligrino?

"I would have been surprised if he did." Davis said. "This is not your typical purse snatcher or mugger; he's a doctor, for God's sakes."

"With an incredible academic record." Romero pressed. "He finished med school at twenty-four."

Bobley rolled his eyes. "If he's so smart, why didn't he become a brain surgeon?"

Davis laughed. "Maybe he became a shrink because he's screwed up and wanted to figure out why."

"Screwed up?" Bobley repeated. "That's a little mild. This guy has a terrible compulsion to kill."

"I'm just not buying it."

"Why, Romero? He's too cute? The name Ted Bundy mean anything to you?"

"Ted Bundy was a failure. This guy has succeeded at everything he's ever done."

"Including murdering three women. Maybe more."

Bobley raised his glass high and nodded to the waitress. "Another round."

"Not for me," Romero said.

"And a diet coke for the lady," he called out to the retreating waitress. "She hates beer."

"I don't hate beer."

"Every time you take your fiftieth of an ounce, you make a face." Bobley puckered his cheeks and crossed his eyes.

Romero cranked up her middle finger and held it up between Bobley's eyes.

"How about that witness who saw Mr. Ponytail standing with Monica Johnson?" Davis asked after he stopped laughing. "Geller has short hair."

"I'm sure Mr. Ponytail's going to turn out to be a red herring," Bobley broke in. "He stops to help Monica and she shoos him away. Then Boy Wonder comes along, flashes his MD and away they go—she to heaven and he, one day, to hell."

"And what about this old case?" Davis pressed on. "That Beverly Casper murder. Where does that come from?"

"Did you see Swain? He couldn't sit still. Like he was reliving the whole thing."

"A blast from Gramps' golden past," Bobley said. "Nothing a few stiff drinks won't wash away."

"All that detail about a murder that happened over thirty years ago. How could Geller know so much about it?" Romero asked. "He wasn't even born when it happened."

"Maybe he read about it in a magazine or on the Internet." Bobley answered. "More likely, he has a patient or had a patient who was obsessed with the case. You're the computer geek, Romero. Go surfing. I'll bet you'll find a ton of stuff about Beverly Casper."

Romero formed a circle out of her thumb and index finger. "Nada. I already checked. There are no Beverly Casper sites. No mention of her anywhere on the web. Her disappearance took place BC…

Before computers," she added, off her colleagues' puzzled expressions, "so maybe that has something to do with it. But as far as I can tell, she's been completely forgotten."

"All I know is that this guy's desperate for us to catch him, so desperate that he walks right in and tells us," Bobley insisted.

"Why?" Davis asked.

"Because he can't confess straight out. His conscious mind won't let him, so he ties himself into Beverly Casper, the Friendly Ghost, to give us an angle into his real self."

"So you're saying he's dropping bread crumbs? Follow Beverly Casper and you'll catch me?"

"Correct."

"And all this misdirection is really just a cry for help."

"Correct again."

"I don't buy it."

"Jesus!" Bobley exploded. "He goes to the scene of his last crime as soon as he leaves the police station. You don't find that a little odd? I mean, come on, this is textbook."

"What textbook is that?" Davis challenged.

At the front of bar, the door swung open and Lemoski entered. Even before he reached the table, he signaled a waitress. "Next round's on me."

Romero slid closer to the wall to make a space.

"Two items. I just got a call from the station. The guy Avery Conniston thought he saw—

"Mr. Ponytail," Bobley chimed in anxiously.

"He exists."

The three detectives, unconsciously, but almost in perfect unison, leaned forward on their elbows.

"Turns out he has a ponytail, tattoos up and down his arm, and drives a pick-up with those sexy-girl mud flaps. Unfortunately, it looks like he has one other thing—an air-tight alibi."

"How did you find this out?" Romero asked.

"He just turned himself in. He's waiting to talk to us now."

"Why did he—"

"Just what you'd figure. He wanted to keep his name out of the papers. Probably has a record. Who knows? Apparently, his girlfriend gave him so much grief he finally came forth. From what I gather, he did stop, did try to help Monica Johnson, and when he couldn't, offered to give her a lift. But she refused him, so he left."

"She was probably scared off by the tattoos and the long hair." Davis commented.

"How ironic. She turns down the biker and gets into a car with the nice-looking guy. Only the biker is a nice guy and the nice-looking guy is a psycho."

"We'll check him out, but it very much looks like we're going to have to take him out of the frame."

Nobody missed Bobley's smug "I-told-you-so-smile." As grating and obnoxious as the young detective could be, no one could dismiss his instincts. Right now, it looked like he had hit the bulls-eye.

"You said you had two items. What's the second one?" Davis asked.

"I just came from seeing Geller's boss, Dr. Elinor Fischer," Lemoski announced as he sat down. "Guess what? It turns out she's Geller's analyst as well as his supervisor."

"Which means, I assume, she wasn't talking." Davis concluded.

"Did she know anything about this patient who's obsessed with Beverly Casper?" Romero asked.

Lemoski leaned back in his booth, and looked straight into Romero's earnest brown eyes. "There is no such patient."

That got everyone's attention.

"She told you that flat out?" Romero said.

From the corner of her eye, she could see Bobley, an unconcealed grin adorning his face.

"There is a woman. Someone Geller is seeing. As a matter of fact, he told Fischer that all this stuff about Beverly Casper had come out under hypnosis."

"He never mentioned anything about hypnosis."

"Who cares?" Bobley said. "Either way it damns him."

"How so?" Lemoski asked.

"If it's a lie, that's just more proof that everything he's telling us is a scam. And if it's true, then it means he's been hypnotizing this lady, and putting who-knows-what crazy ideas in her head."

"Did you get the woman's name?" Romero asked.

"Apparently a phony one. Myra Apple. She's—"

"A phony one," Bobley snorted. "Perfect."

"I played a hunch," Lemoski resumed, "and showed the receptionist the photo Jimmy took last night." He withdrew the picture from an envelope and set it down in front of Romero.

"We got an ID yet?" Bobley asked.

Lemoski nodded. "Robin Norris. She's an actress."

Give this whole thing up!" Fischer demanded, her harsh stare cutting into her protégé. "The hypnosis, the reincarnation, this woman."

"That's not so easy." Jordan responded, his voice firm.

"I started Dittmyer from nothing—a two-room office and a part-time secretary." She rose from her chair, her anger surging with each passing moment. "There was no Avery Conniston then offering quarter-of-a-million dollar gifts. What I've built in twenty years, your youthful arrogance can destroy in twenty minutes."

"I would never do anything to harm you or this institute. You know that."

"Then why did you go to police with nonsense notions, and possibly expose the patients here to police questioning and investigations, and the institute's name to ridicule?"

"Because there are lives at stake."

She dismissed him with a stiff wave of her hand. "Until further notice, I'm suspending you from Dittmyer."

"I've got eight patients I'm dealing—"

"I don't think you're competent to deal with anything right now but your own problems."

"Let me at least call them. Explain."

"Absolutely not. I will speak to each of them myself. Who knows what strange ideas you might put in their heads?"

"Don't cut me off like this, Elinor."

"I thought we had worked through your issues together in analysis, but I can see now that my diagnosis was overly optimistic. That's my fault, ultimately, and I accept responsibility for it.

"This has nothing to do with my issues."

"Jordan, please. This New Age nonsense has softened your brain."

"Stop patronizing me. I really don't appreciate your condescending tone."

"Then stop acting like a fool." She was almost shouting now. "You're a month away from completing your residency and joining the faculty. Instead of embracing this wonderful opportunity, you're sabotaging it. You've created this elaborate fantasy to avoid committing yourself to the responsibilities that becoming an analyst here places on you." She turned to the window, throttling back her anger. "I made things worse, I realize now, by even suggesting that someday the burden of leadership might fall on your shoulders."

"You're the one is who speculating now. Not me. I have facts. You only have blind prejudice."

"Reincarnation is now a fact? Have you fallen so far so fast?" she bellowed, each sentence striking him like a whip. "Nothing you have done in the last week has made any sense except in the context of your pathological fear of making a commitment to a career, to marriage, to virtually anything of substance. I strongly suspect your infatuation with this actress is probably as meaningless and transitory as are her ravings about her past life."

Jordan wanted to lash back, but the words stuck in his throat.

"Your weakness will destroy you just as it destroyed your father," she pressed. "That Bible of yours is fond of saying the sins of the fathers are visited upon the sons. This time it may be right."

"Elinor, please—" Even as he spoke, he knew how pitiful he sounded.

"If you have a pathological need to commit professional suicide, I can't stop you, but I can stop you from destroying my institute." She turned back to the window, focusing her eyes on some distant object on the horizon. "Leave everything in your office. Leave your beeper with Pat."

Jordan unhooked the receiving device from his belt.

"Go now, Jordan. It hurts me too much to look at you."

Saturday, 3:30 P.M.

When Gary Bart, the stage manager, told Robin Norris that two police officers wanted to speak to her, she was seized with panic. Her mother must have been in some terrible accident. But, upon a moment's reflection, this didn't make sense. Adrian was meditating somewhere on a mountain outside of Aspen. Even had something befallen her, Robin wouldn't find out from the LAPD. That's when she realized that it must be about Jordan's trip to the police the previous day. Why else would they want to see her? Still, as she walked to the stage, she said a silent prayer that it was something else, an unpaid parking ticket, anything.

Her face glistened with sweat—Walter had just put the cast through two run-throughs of the picnic scene. She watched warily as the big cop showed her his badge. "Detectives Greg Davis and Karen Romero of the LAPD," he said. "And you are Robin Norris?"

"Yes."

"Have you ever used the name Myra Apple?"

Robin felt her stomach cramping like stage fright, only it was ten times worse. She resolved to tell the truth, wherever it led.

"Yes, once. A few days ago."

233

"In connection with a Dr. Jordan Geller?"

"Yes."

"Can you please tell us how you met Dr. Geller?"

Walter hurried to Robin's side. "What the hell's going on... Robin? We're one week from opening. Every minute counts. Did you invite people to come down here today?"

"They're police detectives, Walter."

"Police?" Walter said, then looked directly at Romero and Davis.

"Who are you, sir?" Romero asked.

"Walter Amicke. I'm directing this production."

"Walter, please just let me deal with this."

He looked at his watch. "What's this about, Robin?"

She sighed deeply. "Jordan Geller."

Walter turned to the cops. "She met him at a party Sunday night. That's all she knows."

Now it was truth time. Not only in front of the cops, but Walter, too.

"I saw him again on Monday. To get help for my voice."

"I told you to stay away from him," Walter said, his voice raw with irritation.

"Well, I didn't."

"You know Dr. Geller?" Romero asked the director.

"Know him? I know he's a wanker who does party tricks."

"He hypnotized me at a party Sunday night," Robin added, continuing her confession. "Walter was not exactly thrilled with the result."

"Then you saw him again on Monday?"

"Yes, I've been having problems with my throat—swallowing, even breathing. At the party, he hypnotized me and made me forget my name."

"And gave you a new one." Romero offered. "Myra Apple."

"Yes. Anyway, that night, after the party, I thought, since I responded so strongly to the hypnosis, that he could use it to help me get past this throat thing. It's affected my voice and with the show opening in a week, I was getting desperate for some relief. I'd already tried conventional therapies, but nothing worked."

"I hope this is sufficient, officers," Walter broke in, reaching for Robin's arm. "As Miss Norris has just told you, we have a play to do and very little time left for rehearsal."

"I'm sorry, sir," Davis said, chest to chest with the director. "We need to speak to Ms. Norris alone. Could you please step away?"

"What's he done now? Hypnotized some geezers and scammed them out of their Social Security checks?"

"Walter, please."

The director skulked off. He'd want to speak to her later, she knew, and she did not relish the prospect. But she dreaded the next few minutes even more.

"Dr. Geller came to our office yesterday," Romero began. "Are you aware of that?"

"Yes."

"Did he tell you in advance that he was coming?"

"Yes."

"Ms. Norris, are you in therapy with Dr. Geller?"

She hesitated a moment. "No, I am not."

"Then you are not his patient. Correct?"

"I did appoint him my physician."

Romero and Davis exchanged a glance. "Do you know the name Beverly Casper?" Romero asked.

Robin nodded.

"Are you the patient whom Dr. Geller told us was obsessing about the Casper case?"

Robin gave an uneasy laugh. "I don't know if I'd say obsessing. To tell you the truth, I really don't want to think about the Casper case."

"How old are you, Ms. Norris?" Davis asked.

"Twenty-five."

"Which means you were born years after Beverly Casper disappeared?"

Robin nodded.

"Then how do you know about her?"

"I don't. At least not consciously." She quickly told them what Jordan had told her had occurred under hypnosis, and how she had then immediately thought of the Messenger murders. When Jordan asked her permission to go the police, she had said okay, as long as he kept her name out of it. Both Romero and Davis tried to remain poker-faced as she told her story, but Robin's acting experience had made her expert at reading faces. She could see the subtle shifts of expression that betrayed, in both detectives, their skepticism at what she was relating. As she heard it in her own voice, telling this story for the first time, she had to admit it sounded more than a little hard to believe.

"Why did you want to keep yourself anonymous?" Romero asked.

"I'm trying to establish myself as a serious actress. I don't want to get the reputation of being a flake."

"You said that Dr. Geller told you that this is what happened under hypnosis?"

"Yes."

"Does that mean you have no recollection of it on your own?"

"I don't. That's correct."

"I've been to hypnosis shows," Davis said. "When people come out, they seem to remember what happened."

"Jordan... Dr. Geller told me that he instructed me to forget."

"Had he instructed you to forget when he hypnotized you at the party?"

"No."

"Only after this hypnosis about Beverly Casper?"

"Yes."

"Don't you find that a little odd?" Davis said.

"Why?'

"Is there a tape of this hypnosis?" he asked.

"I don't think so."

"So you only have Geller's word that you were hypnotized?"

A moment earlier, she had finally begun to cool down; only now, she suddenly felt very hot again.

"You don't know, then," Davis continued, "if you actually had these recollections. Dr. Geller could have told you anything."

"What do you mean, told me anything?"

"You only have his word that you had these past-life memories."

"Yes."

"Did you believe him?"

"Of course."

"Why?"

"Why would he make something like that up?"

"Do you believe in reincarnation, Ms. Norris?"

"I never thought about it until this happened."

"Have you spoken to Dr. Geller since he came to us?"

"Yes, we have spoken."

"And have you seen him?"

"I've had no sessions with him."

"Have you seen him?"

"I don't understand. Why do you need to know that?"

"Did he have dinner at your home last night?"

"Are you following him?" Robin asked, her green eyes wide.

"What did you talk about?" Davis asked.

"Nothing. It was personal."

"Just social?" Romero asked.

"Yeah, just social," she answered coldly.

"I thought you told us he was treating you as a physician," Davis said.

"He is."

"And yet you and he meet socially as well? That sounds a little inappropriate for a doctor, particularly a psychiatrist, don't you think?" Romero said.

"Are you aware that there are laws that restrict how a doctor and patient can interact socially?" Davis pursued.

"Yes, Dr. Geller told me that."

Davis raised an eyebrow at this response. "Did he tell you he could lose his license to practice medicine?"

"He wasn't that specific, no."

"Yet he asked you to dinner, a date, really."

"My being a patient of his was really just a ruse, " Robin admitted.

"A ruse?"

"So he wouldn't have to mention my name when he went to see the police." Robin stared into Davis' dark eyes. "Are you telling me that the L.A. police are putting doctors who meet with patients outside their office under surveillance?"

"Ms. Norris, did Dr. Geller talk about the Messenger murders on this date of yours?"

"Only that we were both happy that he had gone to the police with the information about Beverly Casper."

"Did he talk at all about Erica Braun, Rachel Gordon or Monica Johnson?"

"The murdered girls? No, not specifically."

"Are you planning on seeing Dr. Geller again either professionally or socially?"

"Is it a police matter now, whether I do or don't?"

Romero spoke. "Please, Ms. Norris. Listen to us very carefully. If you see Dr. Geller, and he says anything to you that you think might be important for the police to know, particularly in relation to the Messenger murders, please call us immediately."

"What does that mean 'important for the police to know'?"

"I'll leave that to your judgment. But if he says anything about these murders that you think we should know about, let us know as soon as you can. One of us can be reached at this number twenty-four hours a day."

Davis handed her his card. Robin took it and stared at it for a moment.

"Thank you for your time," Davis said. "By the way, *Carousel* is one of my favorite shows."

After the detectives left, Robin dropped onto the first chair she could find, a battered old kitchen chair used by the stagehands.

"So what did this Geller do?" Walter broke into her thoughts. Then, he saw her face. "Jesus, Robin, you're as a pale as a ghost."

Saturday, 4 P.M.

Jordan couldn't remember exactly what he did or where he went after Elinor threw him out of her office, out of the institute, out of what had been for the last year both literally and figuratively, his home. After Carrie's death he had spent more than a few nights there. He'd fall asleep on his office couch, usually reading, and just not bother to go back to his apartment. In the early morning, he'd make his way to the UCLA campus, do his laps, and shower. He kept a clean shirt and a spare tie at the office. Elinor might make the occasional crack about his using Dittmyer as a dormitory, but she never raised any objections. During the months following the tragedy, she cut him a lot of slack and he felt deeply grateful for her kindness.

But, now as he wandered aimlessly through Westwood, not caring where he was or where he was going, he wasn't thinking kind thoughts about Elinor. He was replaying the catastrophe in her office over and over in his head, self-righteous indignation, self-pity, and self-loathing mixing together in a mind stew that grew thicker with each stride. It irked him that she cut him off before he had a chance to speak, to explain. He realized, of course, on further reflection, that anything he would have told her about his encounter with the late

Beverly Casper would have been dismissed as dangerous nonsense. He could have walked into Elinor's office with Beverly Casper in the flesh and it wouldn't have made any difference. Elinor wasn't going to believe him no matter what proof he offered, because she wasn't interested in proofs. If she were, she would have asked him to rehypnotize Robin. That would have been the scientific thing to do, wouldn't it? He had made a claim. Elinor should have challenged him to prove it. But Elinor didn't do that. So, what was she afraid of? That there might be a reality beyond reason? That perhaps another dimension exists beyond this material world? Yes, of course, she was afraid. Elinor, who like her intellectual father, Sigmund Freud, scoffed at religion, followed a secular system of thought as orthodox as the most fundamentalist Christian, Jew or Muslim. "If it defies my reason, I can't accept it." That was Elinor's orthodoxy. If that certitude cracked, so would she.

And, then, there was her obsession with her precious institute. *Dittmeyer uber alles.* Nothing could threaten *her* institute. She would protect it at all costs: friendship, truth, scientific inquiry, loyalty, these values had to line up behind job one. How long had it taken to cast her protégé, her friend, her colleague over the side? A few minutes. That's how much or how little he meant to her. This hurt him deeply. She had been so understanding when Carrie died. More than a few times, he had broken down in her office. She listened. She understood. She brought to bear all her psychoanalytic training, asking the right questions, eliciting all that Jordan was willing to tell her. Did he think she would understand this crisis as she had the first one? Was that what he had been counting on? But the institute wasn't involved in Carrie's death. That was a personal crisis. This was a public one. The police, the press, the public all had a stake in the Messenger murders. It was easy to be generous after Carrie had been killed by a drunken driver. This was a truer test and, as far he was concerned, she failed it.

So, maybe this was all for the best. Maybe this is what had to happen. He didn't need Elinor, he didn't need the institute; what he needed was his honor and integrity. And that's what he had held on to, what he had refused to compromise. He had drawn a line in the sand. And he had done it, not for selfish reasons, but for the noblest one: *Pekuakh Nefesh*, the Jewish law that trumped all other laws—to save a life.

But just whose life have you saved, Mr. Righteous? He had no assurance that the information he had given the police would help them catch the Messenger. If anything, he had good reason to believe that they were misusing the information, bungling it. They had charged right to the institute looking for his "mystery patient." But why hadn't they searched the Beverly Casper file, as he had suggested? He had given them a gift and they had trashed it. Hadn't he been clear enough? They themselves said he had given them valuable information. "What you've told us is very helpful." Those were Lieutenant Lemoski's exact words.

A thought stopped him in his tracks. How clearly was he thinking? He couldn't tell. He felt dizzy. He leaned up against a tree to steady himself. *What have I done? What should I do?* Should I go back to the police and confess the whole story? Or should I go back to Elinor and offer a full and unconditional apology? *Maybe she's right and this whole psychic adventure is just leading me into a wilderness that I'll never get out of.* He wondered if he was having a nervous breakdown. What was that, after all, if not an inability to control one's thoughts?

He had made a bold decision—go to the police and draw them a road map to Beverly Casper and the Messenger. It was a gallant gesture, but where had it landed him? Right now, as he battled dizziness, his nausea, and his own confused thoughts the answer to that question was: it had got him exactly nowhere.

And nowhere was where he was going, until he found himself standing in front of Robin Norris' rented house.

Saturday, 6:30 P.M.

Whether the hell do you want?"

Walter stood framed in Robin's doorway. Even though Jordan had seen Walter at the party—it seemed like a year ago, not less than a week—he hadn't noticed until now how big he was. Jordan stood six feet. Walter was at least three inches taller. Although his steel-toed cowboy boots accounted for part of the height advantage, his hands were large, the fingers long and thick. To Jordan, it looked as if he spent every hour he was not working, working out.

"I want to see Robin. Is she home?"

"I warned her to stay away from you," Walter growled. "I told her you were bad news, but she wouldn't listen. She's listening now, though, now that the police are involved. She doesn't want to talk to you."

"The police?"

"The cops talked to her at the theater today. They seem to know all about you."

Jordan blinked. "What are you talking about?"

The director laughed derisively. "Why you don't ask the cops. I'm sure they'd be happy to spell it out for you."

His world was imploding. He had to talk to Robin to find out what the police had told her and, then, if she would listen, explain himself.

"I knew you were trouble. Why don't you just buzz off."

"Walter, listen. You can chaperone if you want. I need to talk to her and explain some things."

"For someone who went through medical school, you're not too fast on the uptake, are you? Let me spell it out. Robin said she doesn't want to see you."

Jordan wondered if he should push past him; with his twenty-year age advantage, and the muscles of a swimmer, he probably could. But then what? Bullying past Walter would hardly calm Robin's fury. And she had a right to be furious. He had promised her anonymity. Now the police knew who she was. How long would it be before others would know?

Jordan took in Walter's glaring blue eyes. "Tell her I'll call."

"She won't be answering."

Sunday

Sunday, 2:33 A.M.

Sleep, as desperately as he craved it, did not come. Even just sitting still was a trial. All he could do was pace, a prisoner in a cell, back and forth over the fading oriental rug he and Carrie had brought back from Turkey three years before.

The mental inventory of the past few days was not pretty: the relationship with Elinor shattered, perhaps irreparably; the relationship with a woman with whom he might have been falling in love, probably finished; his future as a psychiatrist likely deader than a med school cadaver. And all this for what? The possibility that the same person who murdered a young woman thirty plus years ago was back to murdering young women again?

He went to his bookshelf and pulled down the oversized Hebrew Bible, his grandfather's *bar mitzvah* gift to him. Strange, he thought, that in this crisis he would find comfort in a book that had become largely irrelevant to him, though so important to his childhood and adolescence. Had anyone asked him when he was fifteen what he wanted to be when he grew up, he would have said, "a rabbi." While most boys conjured any excuse they could think of to get out of Hebrew school, he had embraced it. There was a period of time when he spent more time with his rabbi than with his father. Rabbi Rosenthal was full of life, passionate, embracing—the very things his father was not. Jordan used to drift into the rabbi's office after school. Rosenthal, a slender scrap of a man, no more than 5 feet, 3 inches tall with a head that belonged on a body twice that size, would light up like a roman candle. "Fifteen minutes of Talmud!" he would shout and they'd study for almost an hour. Four years at Berkeley in pre-med and philosophy, four years of chemistry, biology, Hume, Kant and Freud, weakened his resolve enough to move him from religion to medicine. Still, whenever, he was really struggling, really down, he'd pick up his holy book.

He quickly turned to Samuel I, and his favorite passage there: "And David said to Saul: 'Let no man's courage fail him.'" That's what he needed now—courage, that most rare of human virtues.

Why had he gone to the police, he asked himself for the thousandth time, and for the thousandth time he came back with the same answer: to save a life. He could hear Rabbi Rosenthal as if he were across the room. "He who saves a single life, it's as if he saved an entire world. That's Talmud!" That's the standard Rosenthal would have employed. "Better that people think you're crazy but God knows that you've done right." So how could he have done nothing, have said nothing, as Elinor would have instructed him to do? The links between the murder of Beverly Casper and the three girls murdered in these last two months couldn't just be ignored. That these links had come through the bizarre medium of a past-life regression made things more complicated, but facts were facts, wherever they came from—whatever Elinor might think.

His attempts to finesse the police were over. He had been foolish to think he could manipulate them. He knew that now. He would have to tell them everything. But he couldn't go in alone. This was America in the 21st century. He needed a lawyer, and one whose clock wouldn't be ticking at $300 an hour, otherwise he'd be bankrupt in a few days. There was only one person he could ask to help him under these terms. If she couldn't, maybe she would know someone who could. He looked at the note she had slipped into his coat pocket a few days earlier and picked up the phone.

*

"Hello," April Conniston's sleepy voice answered on the other end.

"It's Jordan," he said.

"Jordan? What time is it?"

"I'm not sure. It's late."

"Oh, my God, it's 2:30."

"It is?" He looked at the kitchen clock. How did that happen? It was eleven, five minutes ago.

"Jordan, are you there?"

"I'm here. April, I'm sorry. I didn't realize—"

"What's wrong? Have you been in an accident?"

"No, I'm fine—physically anyway. I need some legal advice."

"Well, why don't you call me in the morning?"

"Sure."

"Wait. Hang on." There's was a rustling noise like she was sitting up. "What the hell is going on? You don't sound good."

"I got myself into a mess. Something very serious."

"I find that hard to believe."

"It's true."

He heard a light switch click on.

"Okay, I'm up—in a manner of speaking." Her voice was still groggy. "So, tell me."

"I need to talk to you in person. Can you meet me at Winchells in Westwood, say, in half an hour?"

April gave a rueful laugh.

"What's so funny?"

"That I've been trying to get you to ask me out for two years. Now you finally do. For donuts at 3 A.M."

"I'm sorry."

"Don't be sorry. But not Winchells. It's too bright. I'll come over."

"I've moved. Let me give you the address."

"Elinor told me."

"Elinor told you?"

"I asked her and she told me. At the party. I'll be there as soon as I can."

Sunday, 3:20 A.M.

If Jordan Geller wanted to sleep but couldn't, Robin Norris' situation was worse. She was afraid to sleep, afraid to lose consciousness, afraid she'd wake up and write another note like the one she had shown Jordan four days ago—*he's going to kill me.*

Who was *he*? The Messenger? Some horrible man named John? For two days, rehearsals had kept her too busy and too exhausted to think about her "past life," to wrestle with the possibility that it was true, that she could have lived before, and even been murdered. It was something that had happened to her, this past-life regression, but it was not her. But now, at three in the morning, as she sat in front of the TV watching an infomercial, she had to consider another possibility; that she had no past life, that Jordan had duped her, that somehow he was involved in these appalling crimes, and that he might even be the killer himself.

No, no, no, she repeated to herself. It's not possible. Jordan Geller is not a killer. Despite Walter, despite what those detectives had implied, she was sure of that. She felt awful that she hadn't come to the door when Jordan came over earlier. *He probably thinks I'm a heartless bitch.* She sat up and reached for the phone. On the third ring, Jordan's machine answered. *Why would he be out in the middle of the night?* She hesitated, and then hung up.

Sunday, 3:35 A.M.

The jeans-clad April was shaking her head from side to side. "This is just so weird," she kept saying.

"I know, I know," Jordan insisted. "But all these things came out in the hypnosis."

"No, it's not only that. This Lieutenant Lemoski you spoke to, I met him."

"When?"

"Two days ago." She quickly filled Jordan in on what her father had seen at Eagle Canyon and Lemoski and Romero's visit to their house.

"That my father should have had this connection to the Messenger killings, and now you. Don't you find that creepy?"

Jordan pulled a pen from his pocket and made a note.

"What are you writing?"

"You're right. I want to ask Bolton about it."

"Bolton?"

"A psychiatrist here in town who writes about reincarnation."

The phone started to ring.

"Do you always get calls at three in the morning?"

Jordan made a move to grab it.

"Don't answer. Let it pick up."

"Why?"

"I'm your lawyer. You're supposed to do what I say."

The ringing stopped. No message left. April shrugged and took a jolt from the cup of instant black coffee Jordan had "brewed" for her.

"Is this all you've got?" she asked with a grimace.

"Sorry."

"Let's get back to your story. Do I understand that everything you told me just now you also told the police?"

"I left out Robin's name, and everything about the hypnosis and the past life."

April looked straight at him. "I also take it you didn't tell them how hard you fell for this actress."

Jordan scratched the back of his scalp and turned away from her. "I don't think my feelings for Robin Norris, whatever they are, are relevant."

"I'll bet Elinor wouldn't agree with you."

He said nothing.

"Okay. You told the police what you told them. Nothing we can do about that. Then what happened?"

"The police have already been to see Elinor and Robin. I guess to check me out. I didn't figure on that. I was stupid."

"Oh, my God," April laughed. It was not a happy laugh. "Elinor must have been royally pissed. Right in the middle of Dittmyer's fundraising drive. And how did they find out about the actress?"

"I'm assuming that Pat Haman, the receptionist, must have identified her." Jordan threw his hands up in the air. "But that doesn't make sense. Pat didn't know her name. I don't know how they know these things. They find them out."

"What kind of questions did they ask your Robin? Did she tell you?"

"She left a message on my answering machine that she told them about the past-life regression. She wouldn't talk to me directly."

"Did she sound angry?'

"More distant. Disillusioned. I had promised her I would keep her name out of it."

April pushed her polished front teeth down on her lower lip and nodded her head as if she were talking to herself.

"Wait a second," she turned to Jordan. "If Robin came to Dittmyer, why wouldn't Pat Haman know her name?"

"She gave a phony name—it came out of the party hypnosis. Myra Apple."

"And still the police found her so quickly…. Jordan, let's go for a walk."

"It's almost four in the morning. What do I want to take a walk for?"

"The fresh air will do you some good. I know I need some. Come on."

*

April slid her arm though Jordan's as they strolled down the deserted street. The predawn fog diffused the light from the orange-colored street lamps.

"We're walking," Jordan said irritably. "Now what?"

"We had to get out of your apartment."

"Why?"

"Unless I'm guessing wrong, it's bugged."

"What!"

"You've probably been followed from the moment you left the police station. That's how they latched onto that actress so quickly. Your phone is almost certainly tapped. I wouldn't be surprised if somebody is watching us right now."

He turned around to see if any cars were moving. The street was quiet. "That's absurd."

"Jordan, you go to the cops with a crazy story in which you tell them things that probably only they and the killer know. That's suspicious enough. Then, they check out your story and it's full of lies and inconsistencies. What conclusion do you think they're going to draw?"

"Are you saying that the police think I'm a suspect?"

"Not a suspect, Jordan, *the* suspect."

*

By five in the morning, the Messenger task force had received fourteen calls from hysterical parents claiming that a caller had relayed to them a message from their daughters. Thirteen turned out to be pranks.

Sunday, 9 A.M.

Lemoski turned his face toward the video camera, then glanced down at his fifty-dollar digital watch. He announced the date and time.

"I am sitting here with Dr. Jordan Geller"—Bobley panned the camera toward Jordan—"and April Conniston, Dr. Geller's attorney. For the record, it should be noted that Avery Conniston, Ms. Conniston's father, recently met with members of the LAPD regarding a possible suspect Mr. Conniston had seen near the site of the Monica Johnson killing." Lemoski stopped for a moment to clear his throat: "Dr. Geller has come here today at his own request and of his own volition, and understands that anything he says this morning can be used against him."

Lemoski turned toward Jordan. "Is that correct, Dr. Geller?"

Jordan nodded.

"Please speak up so your response can be recorded."

"That is correct," Jordan now said. "I asked Lieutenant Lemoski to meet with Ms. Conniston and myself."

For the next twenty minutes, Lemoski allowed April to control the meeting's direction. She prompted Jordan, as he explained that his earlier meeting with the police had been motivated by his desire to procure the Beverly Casper file so that he could then alert them to the similarities between that case and the crimes of the Messenger.

"And I still want to see that file," he added.

Lemoski took a sip of coffee from a stained beige mug. He turned to Romero, "Please bring Dr. Geller the file."

Romero returned in under a minute, carrying a couple of overstuffed manila folders which she deposited in front of Jordan.

"You see, doctor," Lemoski said, "we're very willing to cooperate with you. Personally, I believe that when the Messenger is caught, and I suspect we're very near to doing so, he will bear no relationship to Beverly Casper's abductor. But since you expressed so strong a wish to see the file, we don't want you to feel that we're ignoring your request."

Lemoski turned to April. "And now that we've heard Dr. Geller's unusual account of why he came here on Friday, would it be alright if I asked him a few questions?"

"Certainly."

"Dr. Geller, you told us that an angel necklace was placed around Beverly Casper's throat. How do you know that?"

"She, that is Robin Norris, told me under hypnosis."

"Ms. Norris told us that she has no recollection of any such details."

"Of course not. Before bringing her out of hypnosis, I instructed her to forget everything that she had said or thought about during the session."

"Would you characterize Ms. Norris as a good hypnotic subject?"

"She is what is known as a deep trance subject. When hypnotized, she goes under very deeply."

"So that if you told her to forget something, she'd forget it."

"Yes."

"And if given details and told to remember them as happening to her, would she do so?"

Jordan paused; one did not have to be Einstein to see where Lemoski was heading. "Maybe, maybe not."

"You hypnotized Ms. Norris for the first time at a party last Sunday night. Correct?"

"Yes."

"Did you realize at that time that she was a deep trance subject?"

"When I hypnotized her, I did."

"In fact, you told her to come out of hypnosis believing that her name was Myra Apple. And she did. Correct?"

Jordan nodded.

"Please speak up so your voice can be heard."

"Yes," Jordan said.

"Okay, let's get back to Ms. Norris' visit to your office. According to your account, she had a regression to an earlier life, and revealed a great deal of information to you about Beverly Casper. Is that so?"

"She did—"

"Information which you then told her to forget. Is that standard procedure for hypnotists?"

"No, and for that matter, I'm not a hypnotist. I'm a psychiatrist who, on the rarest of occasions, has used hypnosis. What happened in this case was that Ms. Norris' memories were so traumatic, I thought it advisable to eliminate the recollections from her conscious mind, and to then consult with Dr. Fischer as to how to further treat her."

"Did you make a tape of this session?"

"No."

"I understand from Dr. Fischer that as an analyst-in-training you tape all sessions with patients. Is that correct?"

"Yes."

"Yet you didn't tape this one. Why not?"

"The whole thing occurred on the spur of the moment and, more important, I didn't regard Ms. Norris as a patient."

"You're telling me that she's not your patient?"

"No."

"When you came here two days ago, you told us she was your patient. Was that a lie?"

"In a manner—"

April cut in. "I'm instructing my client not to answer that question."

"Other than your word, doctor, a word that has not always been truthful—"

"I object," April cut in.

"This is not a courtroom, Ms. Conniston." Lemoski said to the young lawyer, who was rapidly reddening at her faux pas. "I'm just trying to be as open as possible here, and explain to both of you why I'm somewhat dubious about the story I'm getting from your client."

Jordan had the uneasy feeling that both he and April were out of their depth, and falling fast. Lemoski was in complete control. *What a picture he must have of us—the naïve shrink and the newly minted legal eagle, both graduates of snob schools, but both so unsophisticated in the ways of the real world. Easy prey for a wily fox like him.*

"Anyway, doctor, other than your word," Lemoski continued, "is it safe to conclude that you can offer no evidence to prove that Robin Norris had the recollections you have told us she had?"

Jordan breathed out slowly, his frustration building with each passing second. "Yes. I am the only witness to what she said."

"Then, a couple of days after this session with Ms. Norris, you come to this police station and tell us the details of a crime supposedly committed over thirty years ago, but which corresponds precisely to a series of crimes being committed right now."

"That is correct! So, why don't you read the damn file?" Jordan pounded his fist against the weathered manila folders beside him. "And make the connection for yourself!"

"I assure you we will look through the file."

"Well, please don't wait thirty years or more innocent girls will die."

"And how would you happen to know that?"

Jordan threw up his hands. "This is a waste of time."

"Is that what you think? That you're smarter than everyone else? Is that part of the fun, the thrill—toying with the cops? You come in and all but confess, but we still can't catch you? Is that your game?"

"I'm trying to help you. Is that impossible for you to understand?"

"What would you think if I told you that at this very moment a Crime Scene Unit is searching your apartment with a fine tooth comb."

Jordan stared at the lieutenant, but said nothing.

"This is outrageous!" April declared.

Lemoski pressed. "They're combing the rugs for fibers, blood stains, DNA, going through every square inch of every room. These people are very good at their jobs, very thorough. If there's anything to find, I assure you, they'll find it. Then, later this afternoon, we'll start sending out other cops to talk with your neighbors. So, my good doctor, if there is anything you would like to get off your chest, now is the time—"

April frantically waved a hand at him. "Jordan, you don't have to say a word."

"Did you murder Monica Johnson, Dr. Geller?"

"What? No, of course not." Jordan wanted the denial to come out quiet and firm; it didn't.

"Did you murder Rachel Gordon?"

"No."

"Did you murder Erica Braun."

"No."

"That's enough." April insisted. "This interview is over."

"Monica was strangled by a belt, right?" Lemoski said, ignoring her.

"Yes."

"How do you know?"

The question hung in the air. "What are you talking about," Jordan said with all the bluster he could manage. "The Messenger strangled Beverly Casper with his belt. That all came out in hypnosis. I've told you that already."

"I didn't ask you about Beverly Casper. I asked you how Monica Johnson was murdered. No one but the members of my team and the murderer knows the means."

"Come on. That was just a slip of the tongue. You know that's not what I meant."

"Freud makes a lot out of those sorts of slips, doesn't he? I'm not a psychiatrist but I know that."

April grabbed her client's arm. "I'm counseling you not to say anything more."

Jordan studied the random pattern of scratches on the battered wooden desk. Hard to believe that just six nights earlier, Elinor had introduced him at the Dittmyer party as the Institute's best hope for the new century.

"I *know* you didn't murder Beverly Casper." Lemoski concluded, his voice thick with sarcasm. "You're in the clear there."

There was hard rap on the door.

"Not now," Lemoski roared.

A second later, Jimmy Lee pushed his way into the room.

"Lieutenant, I'm sorry, but—"

"Not now, Jimmy." Lemoski gestured with thumb. "Go out, and close that goddamn door behind you."

Lee didn't move. "I have to speak to you, sir. Now."

A glowering Lemoski stood up and followed Lee outside into the hallway. Jordan turned to April.

"Don't worry," she said. Even in his state of despair, Jordan could see that April was straining to keep her voice steady. He wondered what impact Lemoski's words were having on her; after Robin spoke to the police, she wanted nothing further to do with him. What was April thinking now?

"He's just trying to intimidate you. This is his ballpark. Don't try to play his game. That's what he wants you to do."

"I can't believe how he tricked me." Then, peering into April's eyes. "How bad have I screwed myself?"

"I don't know. But I don't think you should say anything more. And certainly not now," she urged. "This pulling Lemoski out of here like that might be another trick. I'm sure they're listening to everything we're saying."

Jordan dropped his head into his hands.

She squeezed his shoulder. "Jordan, you need a more experienced attorney. I've done my best, but—"

"*April, I haven't done anything wrong!*"

She nodded. "It'll be alright."

But it didn't feel like it. He felt about as far away from all right as he could be.

Lemoski returned.

"I want you to come with me," he said to Jordan, his voice low.

"Are you arresting my client?" April asked.

Lemoski ignored her. "I want you to come with me," he repeated.

"Then I'm coming, too," April said.

Lemoski turned toward her and shook his head.

"Answer my question, lieutenant. Are you arresting my client?"

"No."

"Then why do you want him to come with you?"

"I need his help."

Sunday, 9:30 A.M.

Y ou know her better than anyone," Deb White said. She lifted
her coffee to her lips, holding her cup with both hands. "But she
really has been acting strange, don't you think?"

"She'll be fine," Walter Amicke answered curtly as he cut into
his vegetable omelet, making use, in the English style, of both his
knife and fork. "And if she's not," he continued, looking up, "you'll
be fine."

"Oh, I didn't mean anything like that. I love Robin, and I only
want the best for her."

"Of course. I don't doubt that for a second," Walter said.

"I'm just saying, if you need me, I'm ready. I've been working on
the songs every night, practicing all the things you've taught me."

"Deb, darling, you don't have a toothpick with you, do you?"

"No, but I think I saw some at the counter. Should I get you
one?"

"That would be lovely."

Left alone, he rubbed his tongue across the broccoli fragment
that had gotten wedged between his back molars. His mind, as it
had been all morning, was luxuriating on last night's triumph, more

specifically on the pliant young body from which he had taken so much pleasure. He didn't especially like Los Angeles, it was too bright and sunny for a man of so many dark moods, but it had its compensations, especially after sunset.

"Walter, is that you?"

The director looked up into the chubby face of a woman in her mid-fifties. With her dyed auburn hair swept up over her forehead, she looked a little like a Red Delicious apple.

"It was, the last time I checked my passport."

Deb returned from her mission. "I got two," she said, handing him the toothpicks. Walter took one and, oblivious to the woman standing in front of him, immediately set to work on the offending broccoli fragment.

"You don't recognize me?" she said, disappointed. "I haven't changed that much, have I? Peggy Kennedy." The woman turned to Deb. "We did *Hair* together right here in L.A.... at the Shrine. I played Sheila. We lived in the same house for that summer, the summer and fall of 1970." The woman laughed at the memory. "Boris, me, you, Della.... The place had exposed insulation for wallpaper. On Wilcox. How could you forget that?"

Convicted by the details, Walter rose half way up from his chair and tried to sound pleased. "Of course! How wonderful to see you, dear Peggy. It's been so long. My God! Please, sit down."

"No, I can't stay. I just couldn't resist saying hello."

"Wow, you directed *Hair*, Walter?" Deb said. "That's so cool. I love that show."

"No. Walter played Claude. He was very talented. We all thought he was going to be a star."

Walter forced a smile.

"No, I mean... of course you are. I saw in the paper that you're directing a production of *Carousel* at the Wadsworth."

"Yes. We open in a week. Deb is the understudy."

"How wonderful! My daughter wants to be an actress. She's sitting over there." She pointed to a golden-haired teenager across the restaurant.

"Very pretty, Peggy," Walter said. "Just like you at her age."

"She always gets the lead in her high school plays. She has a wonderful voice."

"Like an angel, I have no doubt," Walter filled in. He turned in the direction of the girl, and gave her a long look. "Yes," he said, finally working out the broccoli from between his teeth. "I can see from here that she has possibilities."

"Do you really think so?"

"How would she like to see the show?" Walter asked.

"She'd love it," Peggy said.

His eyes returned to the golden girl. "You'll both have to come as my guests."

After trading phone numbers and promises to meet backstage, the woman left.

"You played Claude?" Deb said. "Here in L.A.? How cool."

"Part of my misspent youth." Walter slapped a tip down on the table, all his phony geniality gone in an instant. "The less said about it, the better."

Sunday, 10 A.M.

Lemoski reached the metal door at the end of the hallway, pushed it open and stepped outside in one long stride. Jordan, a good three inches taller than the lieutenant, struggled to keep up.

"What's going on?" he asked, following Lemoski into the station's underground parking lot.

Lemoski opened the driver's side door of a late model Ford Taurus. "Get in," he called to Jordan over the top of the car.

"Where are you taking me?"

"Just get in."

Before he had a chance to fasten his seatbelt, Lemoski yanked the car out of its parking space. With a screech of the tires, the Taurus barreled up the ramp to the street.

"There's been another murder. And the kicker is," Lemoski continued, "you've got the best alibi in L.A. County. If we arrest you now, your lawyer could subpoena a dozen cops to testify for your defense."

Oh my God! April was right. They were watching me.

"By all rights, you should be leading the 5 o'clock news tonight."

"You really were going to arrest me?"

"Seemed like the thing to do."

"Shit," Jordan said, as much to himself as to Lemoski. Ironically, the surveillance had saved his hide. Who knows what would have happened had he been identified as a suspect? He thought of Larry Keeton, and his hellish descent from suspect to victim.

"Shit is right. Would have made my life a hell of a lot easier. I might have even made it home for dinner. That's not going to happen now."

"Sorry to disappoint you."

Lemoski wheeled the car onto Ventura Boulevard, without, it appeared to Jordan, checking to see if any traffic was coming from the right or left.

"I can only imagine what my apartment is going to look like," Jordan mused.

"Probably the way it looked when you left this morning."

"Somehow I don't imagine the Crime Scene Unit as being fastidious."

"Oh, that. I was only kidding."

"That's your idea of a joke?"

"You were stonewalling," Lemoski said without the slightest hint of remorse. "I wanted to make you a little less comfortable."

"A *little* less comfortable? My apartment is being ransacked. My name is going to be dragged through the neighborhood and probably the press." Jordan shook his head in disbelief. "And that trick of getting me to confuse Monica Johnson and Beverly Casper. That was a joke, too?"

"You fell right into that, didn't you?"

"I haven't had a lot experience with interrogations."

"It was a very damning mistake."

"So, then, why are you so convinced I'm not the killer."

" 'Cause you're not Houdini. Your apartment was cased by some of my best people. Your movements have been tracked from minute to minute. "

"Then you know I haven't slept for twenty-four hours."

"You're a doctor. You're used to it, right?"

"I'm used to spending all night at a hospital treating sick people, not worrying about whether I'm going to be arrested for murder. There's a big difference."

Lemoski shrugged. "I can see that."

"Would you mind telling me where we're going?"

Lemoski ignored the question. "This actress, Robin Norris, you really think she was Beverly Casper in a past life? Jesus, I can't believe I'm even saying this."

"There seems to be evidence to suggest that she might have been. Look, lieutenant, you don't know me, so you might not believe this, but I'm as rational as the next guy. All my training tells me that reincarnation is nonsense, but I can't ignore data, if data turns out to be true."

"Well, I'm in a bind. I know you can't be the killer, but you know things only the killer could know."

Lemoski swung into the left-turn lane, furiously passing cars on his right, his siren goosing any cars not moving fast enough.

"You said you wanted my help. What can I do?"

Fifteen minutes later Jordan was staring at a corpse—not a medical school cadaver, but a teenage girl. He had seen young people die in the hospital during his internship, but from diseases: AIDS, leukemia, Hodgkin's and a dozen other types of cancer. Their bodies had been ravaged. But not this girl. It looked like a good jolt of electricity could restore her to life.

The shop in which the body had been found was a mess, almost barren, half-wrecked and full of dust. Jordan and Lemoski had entered through the back door which had been pried open. Clearly, this was a not a going concern. It had been vacant for some time and had yet to be cleaned out by the owners of the property. A street person who made this place one of his several residences had come upon the unexpected "guest" and called the police.

The dead girl was seated in a torn beautician's chair, staring at her own reflection in a dusty, cracked mirror. The thought that the killer had made her witness her own death flickered through Jordan's mind. It both angered and sickened him. A blonde wig with big flip curls had been pulled over her naturally dark hair, make up wiped from her face, polish from her nails. Except for a cheap silver necklace of angel figures clasped around her neck, she had nothing on, and her entire body was doused in baby powder. Here was Beverly Casper's horrific end before Jordan's eyes. The details were different; the result the same.

But there was more: stuck between her fingers was a folded piece of lined paper which looked like it had been torn out of a school notebook.

"Jesus Christ. I know this girl," Jordan heard the lieutenant's voice cry out..

"What did you say?" Jordan asked.

"She's a friend of my daughter's. Her name is Judy…" His voice trailed off in silence.

"What's she holding between her fingers?" Bobley asked, entering the shop, Romero at his shoulder.

"Lieutenant, are you okay?" Romero asked Lemoski. "You look—"

"This girl is my daughter's friend," Lemoski repeated.

A tech from the Medical Examiner's office, his fingers encased in plastic gloves, gingerly extracted the note from the dead girl's hand.

The man gave Lemoski a pair of gloves. He waited for the lieutenant to put them on, then handed him the note. Lemoski quickly scanned it; then in a sudden movement, crushed the note into his fist.

"What are you doing?" Romero shouted. "That's evidence, important evidence."

Lemoski threw the paper down and stormed out through the front door, which had just been opened by a local locksmith.

Romero put on gloves and reached down for the paper.

"Read it aloud," Bobley ordered.

She unraveled the sheet.

"This could have been your own little cherub," Romero read in a monotone, *"but I took pity on you. You've got enough problems with your so-called investigation. Just remember when you go to sleep tonight*

that you owe your baby's life to me. By the way, we've met. I look forward to meeting you again. Your friend, The Messenger."

Romero looked at Bobley, her eyes wide with shock.

"What the hell does that mean, 'by the way, we've met'?" Bobley said.

Swain came in and walked over to Jordan: "The lieutenant wants to see you."

Outside, Lemoski leaned against a squad car smoking a cigarette he had bummed off one of the beat cops. Police vehicles had already filled the mini-mall's parking lot and on-lookers had begun to gather behind the yellow tape.

"I want to get something straight up front," Lemoski barked to Jordan. "I have no use for wackos, psychics, or shrinks—shrinks most of all. If I had a dime for every psycho who got an early parole or a cream puff sentence because of some stupid-ass psych evaluation, I'd be able to pay for my daughter's college tuition. So right off, I've got a big problem with you."

Jordan said nothing. He had some diatribes of his own about know-it-all police lieutenants, only now was not the time to deliver them.

"But I want to get this Messenger bastard and I want to get him now, so if I have to sit in on a séance to do it, I will."

"I don't do séances, lieutenant."

"I want you to turn Robin Norris into Beverly Casper again and I want to be there when you do it."

Lemoski turned and went back into the shop, leaving Jordan standing in front of an unlit neon sign: *Angel Hair,* it read. Underneath the sign, stacked helter-skelter, was a window display collection of beige plastic mannequin heads. *These mannequins had witnessed a murder, but they could no more speak about it than that dead girl inside.*

Then again, a dead girl had spoke once before—in his office. Maybe she would again. Maybe the odds would finally start to even out. Maybe somebody other than the Messenger could also deliver a message.

Sunday, 2 P.M.

As soon as she heard his voice on the phone, she let out a shriek. "I've been going crazy," April said. "From the way Lemoski spoke, it sounds like you're off the hook."

"It's true." The image of the dead girl was still running in a loop through his mind.

"Unbelievable," April said. "It was horrible in there. He was circling for the kill. So what happened?"

He filled her in quickly about the latest murder. April gasped audibly when she heard the details.

"He told me he hates shrinks." Jordan laughed nervously. "Only it turns out that I seem to be the only one with any relevant information."

"I've started in on the Casper files." April responded. "They're massive, and they also give me the creeps."

"In what way?"

"Just that Robin could have known all these things. It makes no sense."

"No conventional sense."

"No conventional sense," April repeated. "It's—"

"Damn," Jordan cursed. The line had gone dead, an infuriatingly common occurrence in Los Angeles. Cell phones had become ubiquitous in this the trendiest of cities. Cell phone technology, however, was still in the Dark Ages. Not a great combination. To have a conversation last more than five minutes without a disconnect was a minor miracle.

He turned off the 405 at the Wilshire exit. At the red light, he redialed April's number.

She picked up, her voice amused: "As I was saying before I was so rudely—"

"I owe you," Jordan interrupted. "Big time."

"And I was just thinking that maybe you and I have been together before, in some previous life."

Jordan laughed. "I like that thought. Just remember not to share it with Elinor."

"What about this life, Dr. Jordan Geller? Are our stars going to merge this time around?"

He considered her words. April had just done him an enormous favor, done it selflessly. She had listened to the story of Beverly Casper and accepted it on his say so. And she was attractive, very attractive. So why did he keep avoiding her? It wasn't fair. When the police bore down on Robin, she ran from him as if from a fire. But April had come through. Oh, she might have had a moment of doubt. But even of that he wasn't sure; one day he would ask her.

"So what about it, Jordan? There's a bottle of Dom Perignon chilling in daddy's fridge. He won't miss it."

He was turning onto Montana, his street. "You mean right now?"

"You got something better to do?"

She had a point. But just as he was about to agree to her plan, his words caught in his throat. Up ahead, in his driveway, he could see her. She was sitting on the trunk of her car, those haunting green eyes, the lush red hair, waiting for him. *What is she doing here?*

"Jordan," April said. "Dom and I could be there in twenty minutes."

Robin had spotted his car now. She lifted her right arm in a wave and smiled, a smile that was like a sunbeam between dark clouds.

"Jordan, are you there?"

"April," he said. "Not today. I'll call you, I promise."

"But soon," she said. "I don't think I have the patience to wait for you until my next lifetime."

Even before he could get out of the car, Robin approached him. He acknowledged the act with the slightest nod of his head.

"This is a surprise, Robin," he said soberly as he stepped out of the car.

"Do you hate me?"

"Of course I don't—"

"I'm so sorry," Robin cut in. "Really sorry."

"Why should you be sorry about anything?"

"I doubted you."

"Hardly surprising. You've known me for what—six days?"

"And all you've ever done for me is kindness. It's only because of you I'm eating and singing again. The police tried to make me think that you did the hypnosis at the party just to find a deep trance subject, someone into whose head you could put all sorts of strange thoughts. But there's no way you could have plotted this; at your office you did everything you could *not* to hypnotize me. I should have told the police that, right away. You kept resisting. Why did you do it, anyway?"

"The hypnosis?"

Robin nodded.

"Because you were going to leave if I didn't and I didn't want you to leave."

Her eyes lit up.

"And now I gather you heard what happened?" The news must have leaked out about the latest killing.

"Don't you understand what I'm trying to tell you, Jordan," she insisted. "I don't care what happened. And if those idiots Romero and Davis and know-it-all Walter want to think crazy things about you, then to hell with them."

"Wait a second," Jordan said. "You don't know what happened?"

"Of course I know. The police are investigating you in these killings. They made it pretty obvious."

"The police were following me—"

"I know, I know. Somebody saw you come to my house for dinner."

"But now I'm no longer a suspect."

"What!"

"Another girl's dead."

"What are you talking about?"

"Early this morning. The Messenger again. You didn't hear?'

"No. Another murder? Oh, God, that's horrible."

"This poor girl was killed within the last twenty-four hours. During the time they were watching me."

"Which means the police know you're innocent?"

"At what price? She was sixteen."

"What could you have done? Even if they'd taken the stuff about Beverly Casper seriously, they still couldn't have caught him in time."

"They're taking it seriously now," Jordan said. "What we told them about Beverly seems to be the only helpful information they have." Jordan's eyes shifted to Robin. "Just how guilty toward me are you feeling?"

"Awful. I feel like a total bitch."

"Then this is a good time for me to ask you for a favor. I want to put you under again."

"Hypnosis? As Beverly Casper?"

"Yes. I want to take you back to that event. To see if you can remember any more details."

Robin shuddered. "Anything, Jordan, but I don't know if I want to go back there."

"This man, John, the Messenger, whoever he is, has never been caught. Why? Because for all these years, he has managed to kill every potential witness against him. But now heaven, as it were, has sent a witness. You."

She mulled the thought in her mind.

"The police want to be there."

"Okay."

"What about your fears that people will find out?"

"This is too important. I'll take the risk."

His eyes scanned hers. "So you really didn't know about this newest murder?"

She shook her head.

"When you came here now to see me, you still thought I was a suspect?"

"I never really believed that."

"You didn't know," he repeated. "You really didn't know."

Sunday, 10 P.M.

P enelope Lemoski lifted a dinner plate out of the microwave oven and carried it to her husband. She had lived through many late nights with Ben, nights where she watched him eat the reheated dinner his family had finished hours earlier. But although the routine was the same this night, everything else was different.

She had been her husband's first call after he stormed out of the wig shop. The moment she picked up the phone, she knew something was terribly wrong. Normally, when he spoke to her from a crime scene his voice was calm, devoid of passion; under the worst circumstances, if the homicide was especially horrific, his voice might be tight, words emerging in grudging clusters. That's how he had sounded last week when he called from Eagle Canyon, the site of the Monica Johnson murder. He had needed to talk to her then, to reconnect for a few moments to the world where life was still being lived. But this time, after she answered, he barely spoke. At first, she thought it was a bad connection. The sounds she was hearing were guttural; then, she realized it was Ben, choking back tears. He wasn't speaking because he couldn't. That scared her. A minute later, after he had gathered himself and told her what he had seen, she trembled with horror. She had married a homicide detective, but murder had never come so close.

But he hadn't told her the worst part. He hadn't told her about the note.

After the call to his wife, Lemoski's next call had been to the station. He ordered a squad car to his house. He wanted a car there 24/7, not because he merited any special treatment, but because his daughter had been mentioned in the note. This made her a "threatened" witness. It was standard procedure to keep such witnesses under police protection.

The rest of the day, he kept in constant touch with Penelope, calling every hour, even if they could talk only for a minute. He also talked to Kathy twice, but only a few words were spoken. All she could do was cry. Just yesterday she had been with Judy at cheerleading practice, she told him in one of their short conversations. "We were laughing so hard together when she couldn't get her shimmy right. We couldn't stop laughing."

Tomorrow one of his team would have to question Kathy thoroughly; she had been one of the last people to see Judy Cinch alive.

Lemoski had told Penelope that officers had been dispatched to notify the Cinch family, but all they found was a housekeeper. Both parents were away on business trips. The police needed an official ID on the girl, but they both agreed Kathy couldn't do it; it would just have to wait till the parents returned.

"Ben," she was now saying to him, her arms folded, her back pressed against the kitchen counter, "this psychiatrist you were telling—"

Lemoski shook his head. "He was under surveillance when Judy was murdered."

"One of his patients?"

"Very unlikely."

"So you're back to square one."

"I don't know what square I'm on. Penny, I want you to take the kids and go to your mom."

She sat down next to him. "Ben, you know we can't do that." The Lemoskis had long made it family policy to keep nothing from each other. Most detectives did not bring their work home with them; Lemoski was an exception. It wasn't that he told Penelope every detail; just that he didn't hold anything back. Whatever questions she asked, he answered. Often, he volunteered information, always anxious to get her opinion. She had a medical background—she had been an emergency room nurse before choosing to be a stay-at-home mom—so she could handle the gory stuff. He liked that he could tell her anything. One reason, Lemoski knew, that he had never strayed outside of his marriage was that he didn't want to give up the pleasure of telling Penny whatever was on his mind. If he had an affair, he knew he would want to tell her about it, even get her opinion of the woman. But of course he wouldn't be able to do that; he would have to lie, hide the truth from her. That, in addition to the fact that he was still very attracted to his wife, was enough of an incentive to resist temptation. But today he broke the rules. Of the note in Judy Cinch's hand, he said nothing, and wasn't going to say anything about it. Ever.

"Penny, don't give me a hard time on this. Please, just do what I say."

"You've already got a car watching the house. Isn't that enough?"

"I don't want to take any chances."

"The lead detective in the case thinks the Messenger is so dangerous, he evacuates his own family. How is that going to look?"

"I don't give a crap how it looks." He pushed his ham and mashed potatoes together. "He might be targeting Kathy."

Penelope studied him. He busied himself with his food.

"Are you suggesting that Judy's murder was not a coincidence?" Until this moment, she had never considered the possibility. Now that she considered it, the answer was frighteningly clear.

"I'm just playing the odds," Lemoski went on. "Maybe. Who knows, there could be a connection."

"He murdered this poor, dear girl to send you a message? Oh, my God." And with that, this strong woman broke down. Hot tears streamed down her cheeks as she tried unsuccessfully to check her sobs. In an instant, her husband was at her side.

"I didn't say he did. We just have to be prepared, that's all. Do you now see why I want you to leave?"

Wiping her eyes, Penelope regained her composure. Her fear quickly turned to anger; and anger narrowed into a deadly logic.

"This man's diabolical, Ben. If he knew about Judy, he'd find some way to know where we'd be going."

"I've been getting plenty of exposure," Lemoski said, "and it's pretty easy to find me. But I don't see how he'd find your mother in Bluff City, Kansas. Unless...."

"What?"

"Unless the killer knows me. Really knows me." He thought of that line in the note: *By the way, we've met.*

"You mean another cop?"

"It wouldn't be the first time." He shook his head. "I'm getting punchy. The guy saw me on TV. A few Internet searches and he could probably get our addresses. If... if Judy Cinch's murder is *not* a coincidence."

"We're staying, Ben. We have to."

"There'll be a cop here whenever I'm not. Even picking the kids up from school. I want everybody's movements accounted for at all times."

"I agree."

He breathed a sigh of relief. "Is there any more ham? I didn't eat much today."

Penelope moved to the refrigerator.

"Penny, I want to ask you something." He began, then paused.

"Yes?"

"I want you to give me your honest feelings."

She nodded.

"Your gut level response."

"Okay, okay," she now turned toward him.

"What do you think about reincarnation?"

Sunday, 10:45 P.M.

He owed April a call. The whole afternoon, then evening, he knew he should have placed it, but didn't because he didn't want to call her when he was with Robin. April would say things, flirtatious things, and it would be awkward to answer with Robin present.

But now, it was nearing eleven, and Robin had left.

He checked his messages. There were two calls from April. Ten minutes apart. Her voice sounded excited. He ran the tape again, listening more carefully. On second hearing, she sounded anxious, even nervous. He played the tape a third time. Maybe she had found something in the Beverly Casper file. He felt like a jerk. Last night, when it had suited his needs, he'd called April at 2:30 in the morning. And she had come running. She deserved better from him. He punched in her number; her voice mail picked up on the fourth ring. He left a brief message, then hung up, mostly disappointed, but partly relieved. Tomorrow, he promised himself, he'd call her again. First thing.

Monday

Monday, 6:15 A.M.

The ringing roused Jordan from the deepest sleep he'd had in days. The first groggy thought that went through his head was that it must be Simon Cox, the one patient who had his home phone number.

He was wrong.

"Hello, Jordan," the clipped Argentinean accent on the other end half whispered.

Immediately he was alert.

"There's terrible news," Fischer continued. Her voice broke and she stopped herself. Over the years he'd seen and heard Elinor Fischer in many modes—analytic, authoritative, angry, melancholy, passionate—but he'd never before heard her cry.

"It's April," she finally managed to push out.

"April! What?"

"I just heard from Avery. April's car crashed."

"When?"

"Late last night. She was driving out to Santa Barbara."

"I just spoke to her yesterday afternoon. She didn't say—"

"Jordan, her car went off the road at Eagle Canyon.... April's dead." Again, her voice broke. "April's dead."

Fischer spoke in a distracted voice, a voice thick with weariness. A few more details emerged, a heavy fog... a slick road... a sharp curve taken too fast. Finally, they hung up, agreeing to meet at Avery's later.

Jordan lay in bed perfectly still, staring at the ceiling. He felt a physical nausea in the pit of his stomach. Images of April spun around in his mind: her keen intelligence, her wit, her loyalty, how desperately she had struggled to overcome bulimia, only to die way before her time. And he thought of their talk yesterday afternoon; she'd wanted to see him, and he had said no. Had he said yes, then maybe she wouldn't have gone to Santa Barbara. Or gone later. Even a few minutes could have determined a different fate. Road conditions might have been better. She might still be alive. But he had said no. Just as he had said no to Carrie. Carrie was dead, now April. *Why, damn it, why?* That relentless word again, ricocheting through his brain. He was sick of always asking. It was answers he wanted, not more questions. But who would he get them from?

April's last words kept resounding in his head: "I don't think I have the patience to wait for you until my next lifetime." A lighthearted crack less than twenty-four hours ago. What was it now?

Monday, 10:20 A.M.

A butler in a black suit, his voice barely above a whisper, admitted Jordan to the Conniston home. Jordan recognized him from the party a few nights earlier. "I was a friend of April's," said Jordan, as he stepped into a flower-filled entrance hall.

"A terrible, terrible tragedy," the butler intoned mournfully. "And could I have your name, sir?"

A voice in back of the butler answered. "That's Dr. Jordan Geller, Charles. Let him in."

It was Mike Fields, Avery's cousin.

"I'm so sorry," Jordan said, extending a hand.

Fields' eyes looked red. "April was everything to Avery. It's awful. I loved her, too."

"Does her mom know?"

Fields made no effort to disguise his bitterness. "Janet is flying back from wherever, Monaco, the Riviera."

"When's the funeral?"

"We gotta wait for Janet. Probably the day after tomorrow."

There were a hundred more questions he could have asked Fields. The truth was, he didn't have the heart or the guts to see Avery.

Confronting grief wasn't easy for him. He remembered one time when he'd had to go visit a couple whose daughter had hanged herself in her parents' bedroom. That time, he had to walk around the block three times before he could summon the courage to go inside.

Only there was one piece of business still on his mind. Something he needed to know. And since Fields was here, why not ask. He certainly couldn't ask Avery.

"I was wondering, Mike. April had something of mine. A folder. Actually a couple of folders."

Fields' eyes narrowed. "What did they look like?"

"Manila folders. Thick ones. Tattered. I was thinking they might still be in her room. I feel very funny asking about them at a time like this, but do you think it would be okay for me to look for them?"

Fields hesitated.

"I'll just look for a couple of minutes. You can come with me when I do it."

"It's really important?" Fields asked.

Jordan nodded.

"I suppose it would be okay."

He followed Fields outside the house; then returned to the house through a back entrance. "Avery's in the living room," Fields explained. "The only other way to get to April's room would have been to walk by him. I didn't think that would seem right."

"Of course," Jordan said, grateful for Fields' presence of mind.

April's room was painted a pleasant peach. Several small post-Modernist paintings, her personal favorites from her father's collection, decorated the walls. Nothing seemed to have been touched from the night before— a blouse tossed carelessly on the bed, papers scattered over the desk. Jordan imagined she must have been sitting there yesterday when she spoke to him on the phone. On the night table next to her bed was another phone, the one she undoubtedly answered when he awakened her at 2:30 in the morning. His heart tightened.

"What are these folders about?" Fields asked. "Maybe I'd have some idea where she put them."

"Something had come up in the treatment of one of my patients. It had to do with an old crime. I'd asked April to look into it."

"So this was some research she was doing for you?"

"In a manner of speaking."

"Because before you said they were your folders."

"They were folders somebody gave to me. April was going to look through them."

"They'll probably be at her office then," Fields said. "In Century City."

"I don't think so. I just gave them to her yesterday. She probably didn't go into her office on Sunday."

"I suppose you should check her desk then," Fields said.

Jordan did. Nothing. No folders, no envelopes. "Okay if I open a drawer?"

Fields nodded.

Plenty of folders. But not the bulky ones he was looking for.

"Maybe she had the folders with her," Jordan wondered aloud.

"She did have papers with her last night," Fields said. "I don't remember exactly what they looked like."

"You saw her leave?"

"Uh huh."

"About what time?"

"9:20, maybe a little later."

"Did she seem upset?"

"Not at all," Fields answered, shaking his head. "She seemed normal. You know April, always a little high strung." Fields paused. Several seconds passed before he spoke again. "I just can't get used to the idea she's gone."

Jordan looked up from the drawer, trying to get a measure of the room, but he didn't get any clear signals. Despite the clothes and papers here and there, it had that clean, almost polished look that rooms have when they are cleaned every day by a maid. There wasn't any dust anywhere. The only thing that struck him at all was the small collection of plushies—a lamb, a battered teddy bear, a chubby, pink pig. He had never seen April as a stuffed animal type. But wasn't that what she had been trying to tell him these past few days—that she wasn't "a type," that there were aspects to her that might surprise Jordan? He had a glimpse of that softer side last night. He had been deeply impressed by her compassion for his situation, how she had so generously and without hesitation come to his aid. Maybe she wasn't the right woman for him, but she certainly would have been for somebody. He recoiled at the waste. She had so much to give.

On top of the desk, above some law school textbooks, was a plaque with a small picture on it: The Oxnard High School Debate Team Award for 1957. The recipient was Earl Smith.

"Who's Earl Smith?" Jordan asked.

"Does this have anything to do with the missing folders?"

"No. I was just curious."

"Look at the picture closely," Fields said.

Jordan raised it near to his eyes. The face was lean, the eyes prominent; unmistakably, it was a very young Avery Conniston.

"I didn't know Avery changed his name."

Fields gave a small laugh. "My cousin's always been ambitious. Earl Smith didn't sound like the name of a successful Hollywood producer. So, he gave himself a new one. 'Avery' came from some book, 'Conniston' came from a men's clothing store in town. That's Ave all over. He's always making up things. The funny thing is, he found a home in the one place in the world that would believe him—Hollyweird."

Jordan barely heard the end of this biography. For the last couple of minutes his mind was locked on an earlier comment Fields had made: *She did have papers with her last night....* Was it the Beverly Casper file? If so, why would she take them to her father's place in Santa Barbara? Presumably, she was going to spend the next day or two out there and read them at her leisure.

"Did April suffer?" he asked Fields.

"The police think maybe for a few seconds, a few horrible seconds, but not much longer. That's the one consolation. As far as the police can tell, the car exploded as it was falling down the canyon." Jordan imagined April's terror and winced.

"The fire consumed everything." Fields continued. He examined Jordan's face. "Why, was that the only copy of your files?"

"I wasn't thinking about that," Jordan answered, too ashamed to admit that he had indeed been thinking at that moment about a pile of papers. "We'd better go."

Coming down the steps leading into the living room, he could hear the familiar Argentinean accent. "Of course April will live on," Elinor was saying. "Her courage, her intelligence, they're all a part of you, of me and of everyone who interacted with her."

Avery's pain was terrible to behold; his complexion was blotchy, his eyes hollow. His gaze was directed at Elinor, but Jordan couldn't tell if her words had even registered.

"I'll never speak with her again," he said, half to Elinor, half to himself. "And it was me she was coming to see."

"Because she loved you, Avery," Elinor said. "She wanted to be with you."

"And now she'll never be with me."

Elinor shrugged her shoulders. "When a body dies, the person doesn't disappear. She's there in your memory. Her good works live on in you."

"What good does that do?" Avery cried out. "Damn it. I want to see her again." He swept his fingers over his head. "I want to hear her voice. I want her to hear mine."

"I'm sorry, Avery." Elinor said. "We can't get everything we want, sometimes not even the things we most deserve."

"And maybe she is hearing you," Jordan said in a low voice.

Avery turned toward him. No nod of recognition. "What do you mean?" he asked.

Jordan kept his head rigid, his eyes straight on Avery. He didn't wish to look to his side; he knew Elinor was glaring at him. Yet, after all he'd learned these last days, how could he remain silent and deny Avery hope?

"Death might just be a night between two mornings," he said, citing a line he remembered Bolton quoting in one his books. "Avery, human beings have a body and a soul."

To his left, he could hear Elinor whisper, "Jordan," her tone peremptory.

"The body is much more vulnerable than the soul," he continued. "It succumbs easily to illness and accidents. But the soul, the spirit of a person, the consciousness, has much more staying power. I think it's quite possible that April's spirit is still alive, that she's hearing every word we're saying." He couldn't quite believe these words were coming out of his mouth. Yet at the same time, they seemed like the most natural thing he had ever said.

"My God," Elinor exclaimed, unable to contain herself. "Where have you been these last seven years—in medical school or rabbinical school?"

If not for the poignancy of the moment, Jordan probably would have laughed. Both of them, he and Elinor, were Jewish. Both, in different ways, had been touched by the Holocaust: she the child of Jewish refugees from Hitler; he, the child of a survivor. Yet rarely had the subject of their Jewishness ever been raised between them. And the irony, he thought, *I didn't even come to these ideas through anything Jewish.* Or did he? Everything, all his previous assumptions, were up for grabs.

Fischer's eyes tightened as if she were looking right through him: "Or have you been speaking with Geoffrey Bolton?"

"Jordan," Avery interrupted. "All those things you just said about April still being here, do you really believe them, or are you just saying them to comfort me?"

He looked from Avery's pained blue eyes to Elinor's cold, hardened stare.

"Why don't you answer Avery's question?" Fischer demanded, unable, despite the surroundings, to keep the hardness out of her voice.

"Yes," Jordan said. "I believe it."

"Really believe it?" Avery's voice was eager. "Because I want to know. You're a brilliant young man, Jordan. I want to know. How sure are you that April's spirit still lives. Tell me!"

Absolute certainty, Jordan knew, was the hallmark of the fanatic, secular and religious both. "As sure as I can be of anything that has to do with faith," he answered.

For the first time since he'd entered the room, Avery smiled. "Thank you, Jordan. You have no idea how much that means to me."

The granite stare on Fischer's face remained. It hadn't softened. One look at that face and Jordan knew; he'd never work at Dittmyer again.

But right now, it didn't matter. He had another job on his mind.

He reached the number ten and gently tapped her forehead. "Is it daytime or nighttime?"

"Daytime."

Jordan stared at Robin's expressionless face, her eyes closed. *Daytime;* he wondered where she was.

"Are you alone or with someone?"

"Alone."

Behind him, he heard Lemoski shuffle his chair.

"Where are you?"

"I'm in the boarding house," she said, only it came out as "borden house."

"Where is this boarding house?"

"In Astoria."

"That's a neighborhood in Queens," the New York-born Romero whispered across the room. Alongside her stood Bobley, a frown on his face, working the video equipment, the camera pointed straight at Robin.

"Is that in Queens?" Jordan started to ask, but then stopped; everything would collapse if he started leading her. "Don't talk," he mouthed at Romero, then turned back to Robin: "Where is Astoria?"

"Oregon," she answered. "In the Clatsop Plains, near the Willamette River."

"Where is that?"

"In Oregon."

"How did you get there?"

"We came together, over the Oregon Trail."

Romero and Davis laughed out loud. Bobley snorted. Swain just shook his head. Only Jimmy Lee registered no reaction.

The lieutenant stepped over to Jordan, his voice a whisper, but not soft enough to cover the sarcasm. "I gather this is not Beverly Casper."

Jordan didn't respond, keeping his attention on Robin. "Just keep focusing on your breathing," he instructed her. That same rush of "stage fright" he had felt in the interrogation room at the police station had returned. Heavy sweat formed at his temples and at his hairline. He brushed it away way with his bare hand, hoping that this seemingly casual gesture would go unnoticed. But these people were detectives, trained observers. Knowing that just made him more uncomfortable.

"What the hell is happening?" Lemoski asked urgently.

"She's apparently gone into a different life."

"A different life? Jesus."

As unpromising as things were looking for himself at this moment, Jordan actually felt more sorry for Lemoski. The lieutenant had gone out on a limb and now it was being sawed off. He wished he could think of something to say, throw up some medical terminology, if only to give Lemoski some cover. Instead he sounded like some weirdo from the Psychic Hotline.

"But we heard you telling her to go back to her memories as Beverly Casper." Lemoski said, his voice a mixture of frustration and anger.

"The subconscious isn't stupid. She's already relived the horror of that night once before. I suspect her subconscious doesn't want to go back there again."

He looked at Robin, her breathing steady, her face relaxed. "I don't want to take her out very suddenly. This is obviously an easier memory for her mind to accommodate. Let's just stay here a few minutes. Don't worry, I'm not giving up."

Lemoski nodded at Jordan to continue.

He turned back to Robin. "What's your name?"

"Rebecca Ketchum." Her accent seemed to be a sort of midwestern drawl, utterly unlike both that of Robin and Beverly Casper. Rebecca Ketchum went on to relate how she had been born in Ithaca, New York, and had gone to Independence, Missouri, in "eighteen hundred and fifty-two." She was twenty-three now, and had just arrived in Astoria over the Oregon Trail. Under Jordan's prodding questions, she revealed that she was looking to settle in a place that was "pleasantly situated." When Jordan asked her if she was married, she said, "No, the men here are too refractory."

Against their will, Lemoski, Romero and Davis were drawn in, Romero's mouth half open.

"Refractory?" the female cop mouthed silently to Davis.

The accent was convincing, and the language that of the nineteenth century. Bobley, holding the video camera, made little effort to disguise his scowl; Swain, too, seemed annoyed.

Jordan needed to move Robin ahead a hundred years. Much more of Rebecca Ketchum and he risked losing not only Beverly Casper, but the police as well. But Robin didn't want to leave, so instead of changing time periods, he changed subjects. By focusing on something dark in Rebecca's past—he was making an educated guess that life on the Oregon Trail had its share of tragedy—he might provide a segue to Beverly Casper's dark past.

He asked "Rebecca" if she had seen any deaths on the trail.

"Oh my God," she said, "We stared death in the face many a time. Some people would break off a leg from a dead cow on the road, roast it and call it steak. That's how hungry we were."

"Did you see any people die?'

"The Harvey boy. He fell off the tongue of the wagon."

"How old was he?"

"Eight. I'm feeling tired now."

"Did his parents—"

"I'm very tired," Robin cut in. "Please, I want to go now."

Jordan raised her hand. "It's been nice visiting here," he said. "But we still have another trip to take. If I could first make you feel less tired, would that be okay, Rebecca?"

Robin nodded.

"As I drop your hand, you will feel very, very relaxed." He let go of Robin's hand, and it fell limply to her side. Then, slowly, with carefully phrased suggestions he drew her away from Astoria, Oregon and 1853, and back into the present.

Then, he instructed her to focus on the end of her life as Beverly Casper, assuring her that she would be very safe with him. He started to count and when he reached ten, he again tapped her forehead.

"Daytime or nighttime?"

Silence.

"Are you alone or with someone?"

Silence.

"What is your name?"

"I don't want to be here," she said. "It hurts too much."

Lemoski threw up his hands.

"I want to come out," Robin said.

Jordan looked over at the cops; they were making no effort to disguise their disappointment. He felt a sense of desperation; like a child who had bragged to disbelieving adults about a magic trick he could do, but couldn't get to work.

Robin wanted out; part of him felt he should respect her wishes, but part of him wanted one more try. *There are lives at stake*, he wanted to yell at her. But how could he gain entrance back into her terror and not damage her? And then he remembered what Bolton had once said.

He turned to the hypnotized woman.

"Tell me your name."

Silence.

"Just tell me your name. Nothing more."

"Beverly Casper." Her voice was low, scared.

"Beverly, you are totally safe here. There are three policemen in this room with us. They guarantee me that they are not going to let you suffer any more pain. Isn't that true, officers?"

He turned to the cops. "Isn't that true, lieutenant?" he said, staring at Lemoski, his voice imploring. Lemoski shifted uncomfortably and said nothing. "Isn't that true, lieutenant?" Jordan repeated, louder this time.

"Yes," Lemoski answered. Jordan's right hand motioned the lieutenant for more. "I'm a lieutenant with the Los Angeles Police Department, and this man who hurt you, he's not going to hurt you ever again. I promise."

"Just focus on your breathing for a few minutes," he told Robin; then, turned to the cops again, his voice low. "I'm going to try something unconventional now. So no matter what you hear, please be quiet and don't say anything."

"If it gets any more unconventional than this," Lemoski said softly, "I'll be an ex-lieutenant."

Jordan turned back to Robin. "We're going backward in time, but to a very special point, to the moments *after* you died, the moments *after* you were murdered.

He waited a moment. "Are you there yet?"

"Yes," she answered.

"You're calm now, Beverly, you know that John can no longer hurt you. You know that, right?"

She nodded her head.

"Tell me where you are, what you see."

"My body's lying there," she said, her voice expressionless, the terror gone. From the corner of his eye, Jordan could see the cops straining forward. "He's taken out a big flashlight, and he's walking over now to see if I'm really dead."

"Who is he?"

"John."

"What is he doing?"

"He's raising my hand, feeling for my pulse. He holds it a second, then, lets the arm drop...." Her voice took on a little excitement. "He's talking to me."

"What's he saying?"

For a second she was quiet, as if listening to a faraway conversation. "You understand now, don't you? Up in heaven. I saved you just like I saved Loni. She'll be your friend. She'll tell you how good I am. I make angels. I'm the angel maker."

"Who's Loni?" Jordan asked.

Robin moved her head from side to side, but said nothing.

Lemoski scribbled some words and passed them to Jordan. He looked at the note, then turned to Beverly. "Can you see John, Beverly?"

"A little. It's very dark."

"Can you describe his face?'

"He has dark hair."

"What color?'

"Brown, dark brown."

Lemoski mouthed at him, "race."

"What color is John's skin?"

"He's white. He's forcing open one of my eyes and shining the flashlight on his own face. 'Tell Loni you saw me,' he's saying."

"Does he have any scars?" Jordan asked.

"No, but his eyes. I can see his eyes now. It's odd, they're not the same."

"How do you mean? Does one look larger than the other?"

"No, no, the color. One is brown, one green."

"Are you sure?" Lemoski blurted.

Jordan raised a restraining finger over his mouth.

"Who is that?" Beverly called out.

"It's a friend," Jordan answered. "One of those police who is here to help you. He wants to find out what he can about John, so that he can stop John from ever hurting anyone again. Do you understand?"

She nodded.

"Beverly, a moment ago, you said one eye is brown, the other green. Can you still see John?"

"It's getting very dark again."

"Are you sure about the different colored eyes?"

"Yes." She hesitated. "Yes, I'm sure."

Joseph Telushkin and Allen Estrin

"What's he doing now?"

"He's picking up my body. He's putting it into a big hole."

"Is he dragging your body?"

"Yes, but he's talking. Gently. 'Bye-bye, my angel.' He's making some sort of strange noise. Like snapping or... I don't know. He puts my body in the hole. He's covering it with earth."

Lemoski passed Jordan a note. "Can you see his car?"

"It's very dark. I want to leave here now."

"Can you tell me anything about John's car? Can you see a license number?"

"Please." For the first time, the tone of terror started to return to her voice. "I want to leave right now. Please. You promised you were going to help me."

Jordan turned to the officers and shrugged.

"A license number. Ask her—"

He cut Lemoski off. "I have to bring her out."

Suddenly, Beverly spoke again. "My mother is there."

"Your mother is there? Are you sure?"

"Standing next to my grave. She's all alone. No, there are other people there, but I can't make them out. Only my mom." Tears filled Robin's eyes, overflowing onto her cheeks.

"And a song. I can hear a song. It sounds so familiar." She was straining to hear it.

Jordan was lost. So was everybody else in the room. How did Beverly's mother get there? What was the song she was hearing? Who was singing it? Jordan had to regain control and regain it now. He had pushed Robin too hard.

"Beverly, I'm going to bring you out now. Listen very closely to my voice."

He started a slow procedure, bringing Beverly out one step at a time. He wanted to be sure that by the time she emerged, the terror had been buried with her body. It took a full six minutes, but he could finally see her starting to relax. "At the next number you will open your eyes and you will feel calm, confident, relaxed and fully aware. Five... let your eyes open."

Robin's eyes opened slowly, and she surveyed the room. She

had met all the police before the hypnosis, but it seemed to take her a minute to place them.

"How do you feel?" Jordan asked.

"I just want to be alone."

"Do you want all of us to leave?"

"Just them," she said, indicating the police with her hand.

The cops thanked Robin, and quickly gathered their equipment. "You might make a believer out of me yet," were Lemoski's parting words to Jordan. What about the others, Jordan wondered as they filed through the door. He glanced at the black cop and the woman, Romero. If he had to guess, he would have said they were impressed, especially the woman. The smirk on the third cop's face, Bobley, made him an easy read; the whole thing was a bad joke. The fourth one, the Asian, was the poker player in the group. His expression was blank. Swain, the older cop, just looked confused.

Then, he and Robin were alone.

She stood by the door, trembling. He reached for her.

"Are you alright?"

"You didn't tell me to forget everything before you brought me out," Robin said.

He was holding her closely now, but she wasn't shaking any less.

"I know. That was intentional" He stroked her hair, trying to calm her. "When I asked you in my office to go back in time to the source of your gagging fear, I expected you to go back to some early childhood trauma. But this Beverly Casper stuff is what you went back to. I was concerned that if I tried to eliminate these memories from your conscious mind, they would start expressing themselves symptomatically."

She forced a laugh. "You want to try that again in English?"

"I was afraid that if I pushed the memories back down into your subconscious mind, you would start expressing the symptoms again, that is, you would start gagging again." Jordan could not help but notice that Robin was extremely pale, almost white. "Should I have told you to forget?"

Her head curled inside his chest. She squeezed him harder and tighter. "Don't leave me, Jordan," she pleaded. "I'm afraid of him. He seemed very close to me. He seemed too close to me!"

"Who?"

"John. He was right here."

"In a sense, he was. Even though your body was dead, you were looking into his face."

"And that's not all of it. I'm also feeling terribly sad. I don't know why. And I still feel he's close, really near.... Jordan, I have a question."

"Ask anything."

"Just don't think I'm crazy."

"Robin, I actually think you're one of the sanest people I know."

"You know something about reincarnation, right?"

"A little. Very little. I need to know a lot more."

"There's something I'd really like to find out. Like right now."

"What's that?"

"Can a killer murder the same person twice?"

Monday, 3:45 P.M.

Okay, okay, I admit it, it's an unconventional approach," Romero said.

"Unconventional?" Bobley barked. "Is that what they'd call it at the U-ni-ver-sity of Southern California School of Cri-mi-no-lo-gy? On the street, they'd call it bullshit."

"So I gather you weren't the least bit impressed?"

"No." Bobley made a zero with his thumb and second finger. "Nada. Is that clear enough for you?"

"What about you, Jimmy, what do you think?"

Jimmy Lee tilted his head to the side as if he were literally ducking the question. "One minute she's riding the Oregon Trail and the next minute she's a dead spirit looking down on her corpse. Pretty freaking weird—"

"It's worse than weird," Bobley cut in. He took a long sip from his third beer in the past half hour. "This mumbo jumbo is a waste of time, time we should spending doing real detective work."

"And what if this mumbo jumbo helps us catch the Messenger?"

Bobley surveyed the bar. Uniformed cops coming off the seven to three shift crowded the bar. When he turned back to Romero, his look was scornful. "First of all, what did we learn?"

"That stuff about the two different colored eyes, for one thing."

"Perfect. I can just see us hauling in some poor creep with two different colored eyes and arresting him as the Messenger. When his shyster lawyer finds out how we got this brilliant lead, the jury will acquit so fast it'll make the O.J. jury look like a bunch of loafers."

"Who says any of it has to come out at the trial?

"It always comes out," Jimmy Lee answered.

"So, we say it was a tool, an aid. We didn't rely on it."

"The whole thing is a joke."

"Well, this joke is our best shot right now. I don't see how the Loo has any choice but to follow it."

Bobley looked down at his drink. "If Lemoski wants to make an ass of himself, that's his business. I just have no intention of being a part of it, that's all."

"No intention of being a part of it?" Jimmy Lee said, his voice incredulous. "Are you going to ask to be reassigned?"

"I don't know. I haven't decided yet."

Romero smirked. "But whatever you do, it'll be the best thing for Josh Bobley, that we can be sure of."

"Listen, sweetheart, some of us made it into homicide the old-fashioned way—"

"Right, by beating confessions out of innocent African-Americans and Hispanics."

"I *earned* my promotion." He leaned into Romero's face. "Unlike someone else I could mention."

"What's that supposed to mean?" Romero challenged.

"You've got the master's degree, you figure it out. But I'll give you a clue, and it don't come from no past life. Its initials are AA and straight white males don't qualify."

"Let me ask you something, Josh. Do you have any friends aside from a beer bottle?"

"Bite me."

"And come up with who knows what disease?"

"Affirmative Action," Bobley taunted.

"You know there is an AA that loves straight white males like you. Alcoholics Anonymous."

Fred Swain approached the table. "What's wrong with them?" he asked Jimmy Lee.

"Just their usual lovers quarrel."

"Swainy," Bobley said. "Detective Romero feels we had a deeply spiritual experience this afternoon. She, and our distinguished lieutenant, want to replace us all with Oiuja boards."

"You know what this is all about?" Romero cut in. "Your inability to admit that you were wrong about Geller."

"We'll see if I was wrong about Geller."

Romero stared straight at him, and gave an exaggerated roll of her dark brown eyes. "You still think he's 'our guy'?"

"What do you find more believable—that somehow Geller sneaked out of his apartment unseen and evaded police surveillance, or that a girl who's been dead for over thirty years has been reincarnated as an actress?"

"If there had been some point, Josh, when you were the only one watching Geller, I'd sure as hell assume that Geller might be the guy. As it is, I'm leaning toward the latter."

"Geller's fiancé was killed by a hit-and-run driver just over a year ago. I read that in his file."

"Yeah, so…"

"Now, his lawyer-girlfriend—"

"She wasn't his girlfriend."

"Well, she drives over a cliff. Whoever gets close to this guy ends up dead. You don't find that suspicious?"

"No, not really."

"I'm telling you this guy is a real Doctor Doom. All this hocus-pocus is a diversion. And when it comes out, we're all going to look like fools." He turned to Swain. "And what do you think about this afternoon's voodoo session, Gramps? Flat out fucking embarrassment or new tool in the detective's arsenal?"

"I'm not in charge of the investigation."

"We noticed, but that doesn't answer the question."

Swain stood up. "Want anything?" he asked Romero and Jimmy Lee.

They both shook their heads.

"Hey, what about me?" Bobley asked.

"You drink too much. You also talk too much."

Bobley raised his beer. "Enough with the lectures. Fess up. You thought it was a clown show. You would never have allowed something like that to happen. I was watching you there. You had that disgusted look; you know, the same one you get whenever they announce the bar is closing."

"Actually, Mr. Loud Mouth, it was the same disgusted look I got when I found out you were assigned to the Messenger force."

Romero made no effort to repress a derisive grin as Swain pivoted and walked away.

"How come he never made lieutenant?" Jimmy Lee asked. "He's got at least a few years seniority on—"

"I'm not gonna end up like that," Bobley said, tipping his beer glass toward his lips. "If I gotta go up against Lemoski, or anyone else for that matter, so be it."

Y ou know the way some couples fuse their last names, like Burke-Russell. Maybe I should just do it to myself, Robin Casper-Norris."

They were walking now. Even after the police had left, his apartment had still felt claustrophobic to Robin.

"No, I'm serious," she continued. "I don't know who I am anymore." After a few blocks, Robin repeated her words, and then added. "God, I sound like one giant adolescent cliché." She gave a joyless laugh. "But in my case, it's literally true!"

"Robin, anybody would admit that what's going on here is very strange. Don't make things more complex than they are. You're Robin Norris and that's it. Some part of you might have had a previous existence as Beverly Casper. But that's just something that might have happened to you, that's not who you are."

"Well, it seems pretty clear that what happened to Beverly Casper is still affecting me, so doesn't that mean that it also happened to me? She's strangled to death, and suddenly I start having trouble swallowing and singing." She paused a moment. "Jordan, I don't know if there's any separation between Beverly and me."

"You're not a direct victim of what happened to Beverly Casper anymore than someone who reads about a horrible rape and so identifies with the victim that she can't sleep at night is a direct—."

"I'm not reading some horror story about it," Robin broke in, her voice overriding his. "It happened to me. Oh, Jordan, there's a lot I didn't tell you."

"What do you mean?"

"Back there in your apartment, all I was doing was answering the questions you asked. But there are a lot of other things I saw that I didn't talk about because you never asked about them."

"Like what?"

"Beverly's mom. I kept thinking about her." Robin's eyes were suddenly brimming with tears. "I can't exactly describe it; I had an image of some sort of screaming match with my mother the night I was killed."

The green hue of Robin's eyes deepened a shade. "*The night I was killed*. I can't believe I said that. Anyway, this thought was there, in the back of my mind the whole time I was looking down at Beverly's dead body. 'I want to tell my mom how sorry I am.' Yet I had such contempt for her."

"Beverly's mom or yours?"

She was silent a moment, but when she spoke, her voice came out as an explosion. "Both." Robin paused. "Under hypnosis, everything became so clear—as Beverly, I was always fighting with her. Pudding Head or Pudding Face, I had some nasty nickname for her. And then, when I was—it's so weird to say this, 'dead,'—I just wanted to go back and hug her, to tell her that I knew how much she loved me, and I…"

Robin stopped speaking, hot tears choking her words. They sat down on a waist-high retaining wall in front of an apartment building. Jordan embraced her like a child, his palms gently massaging her back as he slowly rocked her back and forth. "It's awful, Jordan, I was dead! I finally understood how much I loved her! But it was too late!"

Jordan continued to rock Robin in his arms. "I understand," he finally said.

Robin pulled out a tissue from her jeans pocket, blew her

nose, and patted her eyes. "Can you tell me why I am having these memories?"

Jordan paused. "The one thing I'm sure of is that they have something to teach you."

"Teach me? If you hadn't noticed, it's a little late to learn any lessons. Beverly Casper is dead; she already failed the test. What could these memories, reincarnation, everything that's going on, what could they possibly teach me?"

He looked at the fear and confusion that clouded her eyes. "I don't know the answer, Robin, but I know someone who does."

Monday, 5 P.M.

*I*f it bleeds, it leads. That was their mantra. There he was again. Seven days running. Top of the hour. It would take a war to knock him off. Maybe even that wouldn't be enough.

He sipped his beer, then placed it neatly on the coaster. He liked this anchor. Really cute. A little old for him, too much plastic surgery and too thin—why were these women so thin?—but he was really growing quite fond of her. He liked the way she said the words "in the grip." "The city was in the grip of fear." She had the potential to go national. He could make it happen.

He liked Lemoski, too. They worked well together. They were a team. There's no ying without a yang. And visa versa. He made himself laugh.

The "Loo" knows who has the power. He didn't know before. But he does now. And he owes me. Big Time. I could have crushed him, but I didn't. He hasn't been the father he should have been. Letting his daughter out at all hours. Shameful. He's learned his lesson. Lots of fathers have. Lots of fathers haven't, though.

She was going on now about some pointless bank robbery. He muted the TV, then laughed again—he was cracking himself up—and started to hum. "*Oh what a beautiful morning. Oh what a beautiful day. I've got a wonderful feeling. Everything's going my way.*" But, even as he sang, a sudden cancerous fear punctured his revelry. *Nobody stays on top for long. He knew that. And once you're there, they always work to bring you down.*

But he had a mission. A sacred mission. *That's what drove him. That's what gave him his strength. Loni had charged him. She gave him the will.*

The will to kill.

Monday, 6 P.M.

J ordan pressed the buzzer and heard the ring inside. Seconds later, Geoffrey Bolton answered the door himself; inside, the office was empty.

"You're lucky I could see you on such short notice," Bolton said. "This is my one early day in the week." He turned to Robin. "And you, my friend," he said, taking her hand in a firm grip, "you must be the one Dr. Geller spoke to me about."

Robin nodded.

"I've been thinking about our meeting ever since," Bolton said, turning to Jordan. "It's extraordinary. By the way, did you tell Elinor?"

Jordan shook his head, and Bolton offered his puckish smile. "I didn't think you would."

"Anyway, I've left Dittmyer. Actually, Elinor suspended me."

Bolton's deep-set eyes froze.

"But that's not why we're here," Jordan continued. "Robin needs—we both need—we have to speak to you."

Bolton escorted them into his office and over to a soft brown sofa. He sat down in the armchair opposite.

It took Jordan more than twenty minutes to fill Bolton in on all that had happened in the five days since they'd met. "Extraordinary, extraordinary," Bolton kept interrupting, his forehead fully furrowed when he learned that Jordan had temporarily become a suspect in the Messenger killings.

"And the police videoed this session you did with Robin?" he asked.

"Yes."

"I'm not aware of the results of a reincarnation hypnosis having ever been used before in a police investigation. Either this Lieutenant Lemoski is very enlightened or very desperate." Bolton gave a short chuckle. "Just make sure the killer doesn't see that tape, that's all."

Robin's body visibly chilled. "What do you mean?"

"Imagine if he saw you describing a murder he'd committed, one he was sure had no witn—"

"The police have the only copy," Jordan broke in, never taking his eyes off Robin.

Bolton sighed. "Too bad." He focused his gaze on Jordan. "I'd really like to see it."

"I doubt that's possible. At least, until the Messenger is caught."

Bolton nodded. He turned to Robin. "After that first session, Dr. Geller told me that he had instructed you to forget everything. Do you—"

"I remember it all now."

"Good."

"We're not so sure it's good," Jordan said. He looked at Robin.

"I've been very upset," she said. "You see, everything came back to me, not just the murder, but this terrible tension with my mother."

Bolton leaned back in his chair. It was easy at that moment to see him as the mainstream analyst he once was, before he broke ranks. "Tell me about it," he said to Robin.

"There's not a lot to say. There was a lot of anger. Then, I died, and there was no peace with her."

"If you had to summarize, what was the issue, the major cause of tension between Beverly and her mother?"

"I want to say that her mother was afraid of everything."

Bolton made a rolling gesture with his hand. He wanted more.

"She treated Beverly like she was a little girl, not a young woman. It seemed like she was frightened of life. If Beverly wanted to be with friends, her mother would come up with reasons why she shouldn't go. I had this sensation, under hypnosis, it was vague but powerful, of her mother trying to keep her at home. And some sort of explosion between them."

Bolton stared down at his pen, rotating it between his fingers as was his habit. It was a few moments before he spoke.

"Given how intense your past-life recall has been, I think you should be prepared for…" He searched for the word. "Flashbacks from Beverly's life." He looked at Jordan. "You need to keep a close eye on her."

"What do you mean 'flashbacks?'" Robin asked.

"It's been my experience that in the special cases like yours, the ones where the past-life memories are so vivid, that subjects will suddenly and spontaneously—"

Robin interrupted. "Are you saying I'm going to have memories of my life as Beverly even when I'm not under hypnosis?"

"It's possible. Unfortunately, perhaps, very possible."

Robin slumped in her chair. "Great."

"How, may I ask, do you get along with your own mother?" Bolton asked, starting a new line of questions.

"Why does that matter?"

"As I understand reincarnation," Bolton answered, "we come into this world to correct past errors. I might be wrong, but I would be surprised if you, Robin Norris, had an easy relationship with your mother."

Robin sat forward as if she wanted to challenge him, but then thought better of it. "It's been hard."

"And your mom, Robin, do you think that she's also frightened of life?"

Robin laughed. "Adrian? She's off at some yoga retreat in Colorado right now."

"Do you always call your mother by her first name?"

"No, I've called her some other names though. She's the ultimate Jewish mother, so sure she knows what's best for me. Nothing I do is worthwhile. She even told me to drop out of my play because of the swallowing problem. Can you imagine that? I just hung up on her."

Bolton nodded, knowingly. Jordan watched transfixed. The parallels between Beverly and Robin seemed so obvious, but Robin wasn't seeing them. We all have our blind spots, he thought.

"When did this happen... your hanging up on her?" Bolton asked.

"Last week. Why?"

"That was the last time you spoke?"

"Yes. She left later that day on her trip, the same day I went to Jordan's office." Bolton regarded her with a long level stare.

"Say something," Robin said. "You're making me nervous."

When Bolton spoke, his words came out slowly, as if he was developing his thought and speaking at the same time. "Beverly Casper had some sort of explosion with her mother, probably stormed out of the house and never returned. Now, you hang up on your mom, then a few hours later, while doing a hypnotic regression, you go back into a life as Beverly Casper. I think, at the very least, that's rather interesting."

"But my mother's nothing like Beverly's mom."

"In some ways maybe not, but the dynamic between the two of you has some similarities."

"I'm sorry, but that's absurd."

"Is it? You want to be able to be a grown-up Robin Norris, and to have a loving relationship with your mom. And you wonder if you can. Beverly wanted to have friends and to have her parents, particularly her mother, accept that she was becoming an adult. But she felt her mother wouldn't grant her that. Her mother forbids her to go out. She disobeys, goes to a diner, and ends up being kidnapped and murdered. That must have been among her last thoughts—*if only I'd listened to my mom*. And look what happens to you? Your mother starts harping on your swallowing problem; something that in any case justifiably frightens you. She tells you to quit the play, just the sort of advice that would enrage a Beverly Casper and also enrages you. So you cut off the call, cutting her out of your life—"

"I wasn't cutting her out of my life."

"At that moment you were. Then, shortly thereafter, at some subconscious level, your mind reverts back to the experience of Beverly Casper."

"But this makes no sense," Robin protested. "I've had fights, much worse fights, with my mom my whole life. Why did I go back to Beverly Casper now?"

"Because you're worried that this swallowing problem could endanger your life. But you disregard your mother's advice. And then your subconscious recalls that when Beverly disregarded her mother's advice she died." Bolton spread his palms. "I don't know. I can't say for sure. I'm just speculating."

"Dr. Bolton," Jordan interrupted. "That's another thing. There are too many coincidences."

"I don't believe in coincidences," Bolton interrupted him. "People who believe in coincidences believe that things happen randomly. For no reason. I do not share in that belief."

"Then there are plenty of," Jordan groped for the right word, "mysteries here. The way I now have this connection with Robin, that this connection should lead to some connection with the Messenger killings, that Avery Conniston should then have been a possible witness to something also connected to the Messenger, that his daughter April should be my lawyer—"

"And then get killed? Yes." Bolton drummed his fingers on the small table alongside his chair. "Much of this might be less of a mystery than you think. The one thing we've discovered is that people often come back with significant people in their lives. A woman I was treating told me how she was teaching checkers to her four-year-old son, and he told her, 'I know how to play.' 'How?' she asked him. 'Because I once taught this game to you. When I was big and you were little.' You see, reincarnation is not a crap shoot: this time you live in the U.S., next time China, then Egypt, all the time coming back with souls you've never previously known. No, it's not like that at all. There are people with whom we've had issues, and we'll meet them again, and again if necessary, until these issues are resolved."

"So if you really don't like someone, you'd better try and make peace because otherwise, you'll keep coming back with them," Robin said only half-seriously.

"Don't laugh. There's something to that. But we also come back with good people, people who've protected and nourished us." Bolton raised a bushy eyebrow to Jordan and Robin, seated near each other on his couch. "Who knows, you two might have been very good to each other in some previous life?"

"Does that mean," Jordan asked, "that all of us, Robin, me, the Connistons might have some sort of connection?"

"Quite possibly. As I told you, my young colleague, things don't just happen. There's a reason." Bolton paused, his eyes on Jordan. "Right now these so-called coincidences are making me nervous."

"What are you thinking of?"

Bolton hesitated. "Be cautious. And careful. Very careful. Both of you."

Monday, 8 P.M.

The more Robin insisted that it wasn't necessary for Jordan to accompany her into the theater, the more he insisted it was. With Beverly Casper's memories now residing in Robin's conscious mind, he didn't want to leave her alone.

"I'll be fine, really," she told him one last time as he pulled into the Wadsworth Theater parking lot. "The show must go on and all that."

"I'll only stay for a few minutes...just till I know you're okay."

Robin yielded; there were worse things in life than having another person, especially a doctor, especially one she felt so attracted to, so concerned with her welfare.

"Find a seat," she said as they stepped inside, gesturing to the empty theater.

"The star has honored us with her presence," Walter intoned as Robin moved up to the front. He bowed. "And I see you've brought Dr. X with you. How charming."

"If you need me, I'll be back here," Jordan called out, choosing to ignore Walter's sarcasm. Robin turned around and nodded her response, then started toward the dressing room, Walter right behind her.

"I thought that money changer you were dating in New York defined mediocrity, but this charlatan makes him look like the catch of the century. At least with Big Bucks you could go to sleep at night without worrying about waking up dead."

Robin stopped walking and pivoted. "I've got a news flash for you. That charlatan is now helping the police with their investigations—at their request."

"LAPD. Figures." Walter clapped his arms tightly around her shoulder. "I came by this morning—where were you?"

She ducked and spun herself under his arms, freeing herself from his grip. "You run this show, Walter. You don't run my life."

"You didn't mind until he showed up."

She marched into her dressing room and slammed the door, leaving Walter to stare at the stenciled letters that spelled out her name. "If he doesn't strangle you," he shouted through the wooden barrier that separated them, "I will."

*

Waiting for Robin to appear on stage, Jordan's thoughts quickly turned back to April; he still couldn't grasp that she was gone. It just didn't seem possible. Or right. How could April be one moment and, then, in another moment, not be. If there was a God and if God was good (if God was not good, then life was indeed a cruel joke), then didn't it make sense that we would get more than one chance at life? There was so little one could truly accomplish in a single lifetime. And April hadn't even had that. She was dead at twenty-five; a third of a life. Didn't it make sense that she would get another bite of the apple? After all, if it seemed terribly wrong to ordinary mortals that someone like April would be deprived of life at such a young age, how much more wrong must it seem to God?

Almost immediately, another, less reassuring, thought crept into his mind. Bolton had insisted that April's death was not an accident. But if not, then what? Road rage? That, he could imagine. He remembered one car ride with April about a year ago when she had zigzagged through highway traffic at 90 mph. Maybe some crazy, pissed-off driver whom she had cut off on the canyon drove her off the road? But how likely was that? He thought of Bolton's categorical dismissal of coincidence. How likely was it that on just the day on which April had defended Jordan from the charge of being the Messenger, an enraged driver wreaked destruction on her? No, even to Jordan, a believer in the possibility of coincidence, that made no sense. April must have been killed because of something related to the Messenger case. But killed by whom? The Messenger? How would he have learned about her, and why would he kill her? There was only one answer, an answer that chilled him. The police. They, and Elinor, were the only ones who knew of Jordan's connection to April and to the Messenger case.

This disturbing deduction was silenced by the sound of a voice, a voice so clean, so clear, that it seemed to bypass his brain and go straight to his heart. His body shivered purely out of instinct, as if vibrating to a celestial chord. On stage he saw Robin, dressed in black tights and a loose-fitting gray sweatshirt, singing to another actor:

> *If I loved you, time and again I would try to say*
> *All I'd want you to know.*
> *If I loved you, words wouldn't come in an easy way,*
> *Round in circles I'd go.*
> *Longing to tell you but afraid and shy,*
> *I'd let my golden chances pass me by.*
> *Soon you'd leave me*
> *Off you would go in the mists of day*
> *Never, never to know*
> *How I loved you, if I loved you.*

For a week now, he had known Robin qua Robin, and that was quite enough. But now, suddenly, he was watching and listening to Robin Norris, singer and actress. It was yet another revelation in a week of unending revelations. She glided across the stage with a natural grace, her voice filling every crevice in the theater. *Oh, my God, I had no idea how good she was.* He leaned forward, his chin on his palms, and closed his eyes. Though he couldn't see Robin's face, he knew as certainly as he had ever known anything that she was singing directly to him. Every note, every nuance, was only for him.

He slipped out of the theater a few minutes later without saying goodbye. He didn't want to break the rhythm of the rehearsal and, while he had no fear of Walter, he had no desire to provoke "a scene" either. He understood now why Walter was so irrationally possessive of Robin He wanted to protect Robin's gift. Now Jordan did, too. He wanted to protect every part of her.

He pulled out of the parking lot, his cell phone ringing. It was Lemoski. He wanted a psychological profile of the killer, and since Jordan was so familiar with the case, who better?

"Doesn't the FBI do this stuff?" Jordan asked.

"Their dance card is full. I guess it's been a busy year for psychopaths. Please, doctor, I need you. Now."

Monday, 9:17 P.M.

Detective Karen Romero," the caller requested.

"Who's calling?" the station operator asked.

"Mike Fields."

A moment later, Romero picked up. "Mr. Fields?"

"You remember me?"

"I met you when I came to Avery Conniston's house with Lieutenant Lemoski. You're his cousin, right?"

"Yes," Fields responded, his voice pleased.

"I heard about April Conniston's accident. How awful."

"Yes. We're all very shook up. Avery's devastated."

"I can only imagine." Romero thought of how April had looked that first time she'd seen her. Style. Money. And smart. Everything. A dream life. Gone. "Please tell Mr. Conniston how sorry I am."

"I will, Detective Romero."

"Are you calling me in relation to April's death?"

"Indirectly."

"I'm listening."

"Detective Romero, may I call you Karen?"

"Sure."

"Call me Mike, okay?"

"Okay. Now tell me about this indirect connection."

"April told me something the night she was killed."

"Told you what?"

"We need to meet. It's not something I want to say over the phone."

She remembered how Fields had eyed her that day at Conniston's house; she wondered if he was one of those guys who got turned on by a woman being a cop. "I'm sorry, Mr.... Mike. I'm so caught up here in the Messenger investigation, I don't think we can arrange a meeting anytime soon."

"But that's exactly the point. It has to do with the Messenger investigation."

"How?"

"Before she left that evening, April told me she had the whole thing figured out, including who the Messenger was."

Romero's gasp was audible. "But that's impossible." Still, Lemoski had given April the Beverly Casper file. Had she seen something in that? It seemed unlikely, but not, as she had just blurted to Fields, impossible.

"Maybe it is. All I know is what she told me, and I thought I should pass it on to you."

"Have you spoken about this with anyone else?"

"No. That psychiatrist was at Avery's today. You know the guy?"

"Jordan Geller?"

"Yeah, him. I didn't say anything to him. Should I have?"

"No, no, it's fine you didn't. Okay, maybe we should get together, Mike."

"Fine. How's tomorrow morning?"

"We could still squeeze it in tonight."

"Even better. Avery just had his chauffeur take him back to Santa Barbara. To the ranch. You could meet me at the house."

"Where we met on Wednesday?"

"Yes."

"Mike, this is strictly business, right? I don't have time to waste."

"Strictly business, Karen, I promise."

Romero glanced at her watch. "I'm on my way."

Monday, 9:45 P.M.

H e sat by himself in the same airless interrogation room where Lemoski had questioned him only a few days earlier. He didn't like the room then and he didn't like it now. Five dead girls were keeping him company—Beverly Casper, Erica Braun, Rachel Gordon, Monica Johnson, and Judy Cinch. Lemoski had provided him the files of the last four. He didn't yet have a copy of the Beverly Casper file—the only other copy having been lost in April Conniston's burning car—but Lemoski promised he'd get it to him soon.

*The bold lieutenant was apparently bending, if not breaking the rules, by letting him look at the unexpurgated files. Normally, they would be "didacted"—that was the exact term Lemoski used—*by someone in the department who would scan the files with a heavy marker blacking out all information deemed highly sensitive or confidential, like witnesses' names and addresses. This is typically what a DA would give to a defense attorney. But Lemoski had deputized Jordan, pinned a badge on him, as it were, so an exception was made. The presence of a single uniformed cop on the other side of the door to make sure that Jordan didn't run off with the documents was the only concession

Lemoski had made to standard procedure. Everything about this case, it seemed, was exceptional.

The lieutenant wanted Jordan to profile the killer, and Jordan had readily agreed. Too readily, he now thought. For one thing, he felt terribly inadequate; profiling killers required special training. For another, he wasn't emotionally prepared. It was one thing to confront very explicit, even demented, fantasies in the comfortable setting of Dittmyer's Brentwood office, quite another to personally witness Judy Cinch's corpse, posed in that grotesque, humiliating way. He hadn't been able to shake off the realization that the killer had, in all probability, made her witness her own death in the mirror. Flipping through these crime-scene photos, each one coldly capturing a different perspective, was only marginally easier than being at the crime scene itself. In fact, he found it impossible to examine the pictures with the sort of dispassionate concentration that he was sure the job required.

It was a full minute later that he realized he'd been crying. How could anybody look at these hideous pictures and not cry? Maybe cops had to force themselves to supress their emotions in the face of evil, but he wasn't a cop. He wasn't a profiler, either. If he'd ever had the slightest notion that he might want to be one, that notion had now been fully expunged. *What the hell was he doing here?* He leaned back his chair, blew out of a breath, then wiped his eyes. Too much had happened in the last few days. He'd been whipsawed between love and death. His senses, his soul, everything was in overload. It was ridiculous for him to be here. How could he be sure of anything he was thinking? Maybe with a week of sleep, he'd be able to help Lemoski, but right now he probably couldn't do a crossword, let alone dissect the mind of a murderer.

A talmudic quote, or at least a variation of one, filtered through his consciousness. "If not me, who?" He breathed out again, reached for the file on Erica Braun and went to work.

Monday, 10:35 P.M.

Mike Fields led Romero to the living room where Avery had been receiving condolence callers that morning. Chairs were still arranged in a semi-circle.

Before sitting down, Romero peeked around the corner into the adjacent room and caught a glimpse of the Claes Oldenberg she had seen last week. She wondered if she could ask Fields to give her a tour, but then thought better of it. The hour was late and the request, under the circumstances, was inappropriate.

Fields had moved to the bar the next room over. "Drink?" Fields asked, pouring himself a whiskey.

"No, thanks."

"So how does someone like you get to be a cop? I mean you obviously love fine art. I can see the way you look at Ave's pictures."

"Mike, I'm here to talk about what April told you."

"You could probably teach me a few things about these masterpieces. All I know is how much they cost and what they're worth now. Ave loves to talk about what a killing he's made... How 'bout a Diet Coke?"

"Sure."

He popped open a can. "I'd guess you're twenty-seven, twenty-eight. Am I right?" He handed her the glass.

Romero took it, but didn't answer.

"Have a boyfriend?"

"Several."

"You're quick. I noticed that about you the other day." He took a sip of his drink. "You know I was serious the other day about getting you into show business. They're always looking for consultants for these cop shows. Ave knows everybody. There's really good money in it."

"If this conversation doesn't change direction immediately, I'm leaving."

"Okay, okay. I just have one last question. Would you ever go out with a guy as old as me?"

"I'm gone. Thanks for the Coke."

She started for the door.

"What if the information I give you, you know what April told me, causes you to break the case open? What then?"

"What do you mean, what then?"

"If what I tell you makes Karen Romero the cop who brings in the Messenger, will you go out with me then? Just once. I'll settle for coffee. I know I'm making a fool of myself, but I just got divorced. I'm outta practice."

Romero couldn't help but smile. Sure, he was too old for her—she guessed he was in his mid-fifties—but she had to admit he was in great shape and, all things considered, probably harmless. Plus, he had that teddy bear quality strong guys sometimes do. No, he wasn't without appeal.

"A smile. Thank God, a smile."

"Mike, just tell me what you know."

"I saw April two nights ago, just before the accident. She was carrying around some big folders, said something to me about having gotten them from the police."

"She told you that?"

"Why? Was it a secret?"

"I'm just curious that she told you."

"This morning, that psychiatrist, Geller, was asking me about those folders, looking for them."

Romero nodded.

"Anyway, everybody assumes April was heading for her dad's ranch in Santa Barbara when she had the accident. I'm not sure that's right."

"Wasn't she killed on Eagle Canyon?" she answered.

"Yeah. Right near where Monica Johnson died."

"A coincidence. They do happen, you know. Maybe you've been watching too much TV, Mike."

"I don't think so," Fields said sipping his drink, but tracking her intently with his eyes.

"Anyway, Conniston told us that Eagle Canyon is the shortest route to his ranch." She met his gaze. "Unless she told you she *wasn't* going to see her father?"

"No, she didn't say that exactly."

"What did she say—exactly?"

"She pointed to those folders and said it was crazy, the police were trying to connect up these crimes to something that happened thirty years ago. But it has nothing to do with that. That's what she told me."

"Did she tell you why she reached that conclusion?"

"That's what I've been trying to tell you. She said the Messenger was a kid, a crazy high school kid."

"How did she find this out?"

"Some calls she made, I don't know. She was rushing around, super excited. I'd never seen her like that. Karen, I think she was going to see *him*. To meet him somewhere, under some nutty pretense, I don't know. That's really why she was on Eagle Canyon. She was on her way to rendezvous with this kid."

"Did she give you a name?" Romero's face was flush.

Fields nodded. "Some classmate of Judy Cinch."

"What was the name, Mike?" Romero asked.

"What if I got it wrong. What if April did? I don't want to get anybody in trouble."

"It's important that I check it out."

"Yeah, I can see that."

He pulled a piece of paper with writing from his shirt pocket, as if to make sure that he made no error. "I wrote it down." The letters were in caps. CHIP ESTES.

Tuesday

Tuesday, 1:35 A.M.

T he belt bit into Robin's neck. *Where had he come from? How did he get in?* With a terrible, manic desperation, she clawed at the sharp edged leather that was cutting into her throat, trying to loosen its death grip. Her nails cracked at the effort, blood trickling from the soft edges of her fingers. She sucked hideously for air, but none entered. With a final ounce of strength, she tried to force her head around, to confront her murderer, to see his face. But he kept pushing her head back... away... as the belt tightened, squeezing out her final supply of oxygen.... Suddenly, sharply, a darkness, deep and profound, engulfed her. She had no feeling, no sensation in her limbs, except a sense of falling... into the black... down a bottomless pit... falling.

Robin shot straight up from her pillow, threw off the covers and jumped up. She was on the bed now, squatting on the mattress like a cornered animal, eyes wide open, fingers massaging her neck. Her head darted left, then right, looking for her attacker.

But he wasn't there. No one was there.

She pulled in a shallow breath. She tried to take another, but it didn't feel like she got any air. A fresh panic overtook her. She sat down on the side of the bed and told herself to relax; that it had been a nightmare, nothing more. She tried to remember what Jordan kept telling her during the sessions: Just focus on your breathing. Still, she had no sensation that any air was getting through. *Oh, my God,* she thought. *I'm going to die.*

She rushed to the bathroom and ran some water into a glass. She poured the water into her mouth, then spit it out; it wouldn't go down her throat. She felt the ends of her toes and fingers tingling, like they were drifting quickly into permanent sleep. She tried to speak. The words came out as a hoarse whisper: "Testing, testing." If she could talk, she must be getting some oxygen. The feeling of relief lasted until she tried to suck in her next breath.

She reached for the phone, punched 911, and managed to gasp out her address and the word "choking." As soon as she hung up, she opened her door: *Who knows if I'll be conscious when they arrive?*

Eleven minutes later, a man and a woman in dark blue uniforms and heavy boots trooped in. They found her in the living room, on her knees, dizzy and extremely light-headed, saliva dripping from the sides of her mouth, still struggling for air. When they asked her what was the matter, she pointed to her throat. When the female paramedic asked her whether something was stuck there, she turned up her palms; she didn't know how to reply.

"I think she's hyperventilating."

Her partner rushed back to the ambulance and returned with a plain, brown paper bag. "Put this over your mouth and try to breathe," he told her.

She took the bag, and stuck it over her mouth. She tried one breath, then threw the bag down in panic; she was suffocating.

"Can you walk?" The woman asked her.

She nodded.

The two paramedics rushed her, each one holding an arm, into the ambulance.

Tuesday, 2:09 A.M.

She didn't recognize the portly physician when he approached her behind a curtain in the UCLA Medical Center Emergency Room, but he remembered her.

"Well, if it isn't Myra Apple," Harry Stanton cracked, as a nurse checked her blood pressure. "What brings you here?"

When he got no recognition or response from the patient, Stanton took a new tack. Glancing at the paramedics' brief summary of the case, he sat down in a chair next to her, the smile gone, and fired a series of questions.

"Have you had any recent illness?"

She shook her head; then grabbed the oxygen mask at her side and sucked in a breath.

"Have you ever experienced these symptoms before?"

"Not exactly," she mouthed.

"Did you swallow something?"

Again, a shake of the head and another hit of the pure air. Stanton noticed how hard she pulled on the mask. She wasn't getting much air or, at least, didn't think she was.

"Are you taking any new medication... any sleeping pills... recreational drugs?"

To each question, she shook her head, her breathing still labored. While it looked like she might indeed still be hyperventilating, he was getting mixed signals, signals that made him hold back from making a diagnosis. Based on her responses to his battery of questions, he even considered the possibility that she might be suffering from Guillain-Barre disease, something that he had studied but never actually seen. The disease can strike anybody of any age, has no known cause, though it's assumed to be viral, and has no gender preference. It starts with tingling in the lower extremities, then, advances to a near total paralysis of the limbs and the upper chest. In severe cases, and right now this looked like one, the paralysis becomes so encompassing that it can end in total respiratory failure: death. Its unusual symptoms and unpredictable appearance had fascinated him in med-school. One day he knew he'd have to confront the disease. Maybe today was the day. How odd, he thought, that it would be someone he knew, if only briefly. Rubbing his hands with unconscious excitement, he was just about to put her on a respirator when he checked himself. Her symptoms didn't quite match the profile. Guillain-Barre started with a paralysis of the feet and worked up toward the chest. But this woman was experiencing simultaneous numbness in both her feet and hands. He actually felt a let down. Better proceed more traditionally, he told himself. Ditching the respirator idea, he ordered up a plain old ice pack and placed it over her forehead. The first thing he needed to do was to calm her down. Nothing like an ice pack for that. Finally, and quietly, he ordered a shotgun work-up, starting with an EKG.

Then, ten minutes after she arrived, she suddenly caught a breath. A real one. Then, a second. In a few more minutes, she seemed fine; whatever it was that caused her problem was gone. For Robin, it felt like she had finally, and fully, awoken from the most horrifying nightmare of her life.

After asking her a few questions to assure himself that she was really all right, Stanton asked the standard one, the one asked of any emergency room patient who has emerged from what likely was an extreme anxiety attack.

"Do you want to see a psychiatrist?"

"Yes."

"Do you know of any doctor in particular you wish to see?"

"Dr. Jordan Geller. I have his phone number in my purse."

"And I have his phone number in my Palm Pilot." Stanton smiled. "You don't remember me, do you?"

"Yes, you do look somewhat familiar…"

"I called you Myra Apple when you came in. Does that give you a hint?"

Her eyes widened. "Did you actually say that?"

Stanton nodded.

She laughed. "I thought it was part of the nightmare I was having." She studied his large oval face for a beat. "You're Jordan's friend. The one who introduced him at the party."

Stanton extended his fleshy hand. "Harry Stanton."

"Thanks for helping me out tonight."

"Do you have any idea why this happened to you?"

Robin hesitated. "I'd rather not talk about it just now. Is that okay?"

"Of course. But you most probably do need to speak to somebody. In the meantime, I think it would be a good idea if you stayed here at least until the morning—just in case you get another attack."

She nodded.

"Were you serious about wanting me to call Jordan?"

"I need to talk to him."

"Is he your psychiatrist?"

"No."

"But you just said—" Stanton interrupted himself. "I think I just figured it out."

Robin's cheeks started to redden.

"You and Jordan are seeing each other…socially."

"It's complicated. You're Jordan's friend. He should probably be the one to explain it."

Stanton rocked his head back against his shoulder. "Explain what, exactly?" he asked.

347

"I really can't talk about it."

"Can't or won't?"

"Both. Not now… please."

Stanton feigned acceptance, but, in truth, the only thing he liked more than food was gossip, particularly about such a close friend. Robin had whetted his appetite. In fact, right now, he was salivating.

Robin slowly pulled a deep draught of air into her lungs. "I can't tell you how good that feels. I don't think I'm ever going to take a breath of fresh air for granted again."

"Sure you will; in about another fifteen minutes. Listen, this anxiety attack, or whatever it is you experienced, does it have anything to do with your relationship to Jordan?"

"No… well maybe… like I told you, it's complicated."

"It might help if you tell me."

"Really, I wouldn't know where to begin."

He couldn't imagine what she was hiding, but he wanted to, no, he *had to* find out. What could send a woman, specifically a woman in a relationship with his friend Jordan Geller, into hysterics? The answer came to him as soon as he asked himself the question.

"Did Jordan tell you about Carrie? Is that why you got so upset?"

"Who's Carrie?"

Tuesday, 2:42 A.M.

Jordan found Stanton by the candy machine, unwrapping a Milky Way. "Where is she?" he asked.

"Third floor recovery room. She's resting now."

"Recovery room?" he asked Stanton. "What? You *operated*?!"

"No. That was the only place available."

"But she's okay?" Jordan asked.

"She is now. She wasn't when she got here."

Jordan took his first easy breath since receiving Stanton's call.

"So what's going on with you and this girl?"

"Harry, it's very complicated."

"What do you and she have? Code words? That's just what she said."

"Well, she's right."

"Have you guys been having a torrid affair?"

"I wish."

"Well, whatever it is, pal, it must be pretty heavy, 'cause she went right over the edge tonight. For a moment there, I was afraid she might have Guillain-Barre."

"You think everybody has Guillain-Barre. It's your favorite disease."

"Well, you gotta admit as diseases go, it's very cool. And she really had symptoms—trouble breathing, paralysis of the extremities—just not in the right order."

"I want to see her."

"Tell me what's going on first."

"I can't, Harry."

"Jordan, my old roommate. Since when—"

"It's a police matter. How's that?"

"Police matter?" Stanton snorted. "Why don't you cut the crap?"

"When it's over, I'll tell you everything. I promise. Meanwhile I'm heading for Recovery."

"You don't tell anybody anything," Stanton called out to his friend's retreating back.

Jordan pivoted. "Sorry, Harry, but thanks for being here tonight."

"You might change your mind on that," Stanton called back. He took a big bite out of the Milky Way.

Jordan moved alongside his corpulent friend.

"I can give you the silent treatment, too."

"You want to tell me why I might change my mind about your being here tonight."

"I told her."

"Told her what?"

"Well, when I realized she didn't have Guillain, I assumed she was having an anxiety attack. Extreme anxiety. I wanted to calm her down. So I spoke to her about Carrie."

"You what?" Jordan yelled, his words bouncing off the polished linoleum floor.

"Don't blame me, she asked."

"Yeah? And who brought her up first? You or Robin?"

"Alright, I did."

Jordan glared at his friend.

"I figured that finding out about your relationship with Carrie was the cause of her anxiety attack."

"Are you out of your friggin' mind?"

"Come on. It adds up. You and her are going hot and heavy and then you tell her about Carrie and she flips out."

"Right. A guy tells a woman about his ex-girlfriend and suddenly she can't breathe. Common diagnosis. You're a great ER physician, Harry, but you'd make a very bad psychiatrist. This has nothing to do with Carrie." A look of dread spread over Jordan's face. "So, what did you tell her?"

"Just the basics. That you'd been with this girl forever, you were engaged, that there was a terrible accident"

"I already told her about the accident," Jordan said.

"Then there's no big deal. I didn't tell her anything she didn't already know."

Jordan stared him down. There had to be more.

"Don't look at me like that, Jordan. She just kept asking."

"What else, Harry?"

Stanton clenched his teeth. "I told her how you took it so hard, stuff like that."

"That's it?"

"Don't worry, buddy. I downplayed it."

"Sure you did. Just enough to paint some idealized picture of Carrie in Robin's mind."

"Well, she was pretty ideal, Jordan, wasn't she?"

Tuesday, 3:00 A.M.

When Jordan reached the room in which Stanton had parked Robin Norris, he found the patient asleep. She was lying on her back, head turned at a slight angle, the cascade of red hair spread across the white pillow case.

He moved closer and watched her breathe, her chest rising and falling in a steady, peaceful rhythm. Looking down at this woman whom he had known now for a total of eight days, he seriously considered Bolton's suggestion that this was not the first lifetime they had shared together. Two weeks ago, he would have dismissed such an idea as just the sort of thinking that mandated a consultation with a psychiatrist; now, he wasn't so sure. There was almost nothing he was certain about at this moment, except one thing: he had fallen hard for Robin Norris. When did he know it? The first time he saw her at that party? Perhaps. But usually those initial chemical attractions flare and burn out. Not this one, though. In fact, the flame was getting hotter, burning beneath the surface, fed by a very combustible mixture of love, danger and death.

Very lightly, he pushed the back of his hand across her hair. Her eyes opened, and she smiled groggily at him. "Hello."

"I'm sorry," he said.

"Now that's a romantic greeting."

"I should have stayed with you. It must have been terrible, what you went through tonight."

"I made it much worse than it was." She paused. "I dreamt that John got into my bedroom, but it wasn't my bedroom; it was Beverly's. I tried to get a look at him, but he wouldn't let me turn my head. He was strangling me with a belt. When I woke up, I couldn't breathe."

He sat down on the side of her bed and smoothed a few locks of hair off her forehead. "You don't hate me for dragging you into this?"

"I didn't exactly go kicking and screaming."

"But how could you have known where it would lead?"

"And you did? Don't blame yourself for anything. I certainly don't."

He remembered something Bolton had told him, how he had treated a woman who had become panicked and insomniac after a terrifying hypnotic regression. He took Robin's hand and held it in his. "I was thinking. I could give you some hypnotic suggestions that would make it much less likely that what happened tonight would happen again."

"You mean like at your office, to make me forget everything?"

"No, not forget, but manage better. I'll give you a suggestion that will help your conscious mind remember only what it can accommodate, so that the memories won't overwhelm you."

Robin shook her head.

"I don't want you to go through this trauma again," Jordan said.

"I'm just having bad dreams. What happened to Beverly and Judy Cinch and those other girls was real."

"But Robin—"

"Listen, I know what's at stake. Bolton warned me I might have more flashbacks. But if I do, and they can help catch this evil man, then I want to have them. What if I had seen his face in my dream? Maybe I would have picked up something that could help the police. No, I don't want to be 'managed' in any way."

He studied her, impressed. "Robin, if you get very upset, it's within your power to calm yourself. Just focus on your breathing, and you can relax everything. Remember at the party how I made your arm feel like steel? You can do that, you can do the opposite; the most important thing is, you *can* fight off the panic. Just breathe and relax. The average person can't do this, but you're a deep trance subject. You can." He monitored her impassive expression. "Okay?"

"Okay." She sat up. "You know, before you came in, I was lying in bed thinking, I don't even know what Beverly Casper looks like."

Jordan nodded. "Of course. You're seeing things from her perspective."

"I want to meet her."

"What are you talking about?"

"I want to go to Madison High, to the library, and look her up in a yearbook. Who knows? It might jog some new memories."

He looked at her, worried. Three hours earlier, it was memories and the effect of those memories that had rushed her to this hospital in an ambulance. "Are you sure you want to do that?"

She nodded.

"I wish I could come with you," Jordan said. "But Lemoski's drafted me into the case. It seems the FBI is overloaded at the moment; he wants me to do a psychological profile of the killer."

"Interesting," Robin mused "I'm in Beverly Casper's mind, now you'll be in John's. But Jordan, have you had any experience in dealing with people like John, psychopaths?"

He shook his head. "Only in textbooks."

"Because I've been lying here, wondering. Is there any other way Beverly could have played it so that John wouldn't have killed her?"

"Like what?"

"For example, if she had acted like she was impressed with his being in the Marines, or that she really wanted to be his girlfriend. Something like that."

"I don't know," Jordan said. "But if you know what makes a person tick, even a very sick person, you might be able to find a way to get through to them or, maybe, anger them in such a way that they become unbalanced and you can gain control."

Robin ran a light finger across the dark circles under his eyes. "Listen, my hero detective. You're exhausted. You should go home and get some sleep."

"Can I get you something to eat before I go?"

"It's after midnight, " she said with a bemused expression.

"Perfect time for some breakfast. I could bring you back some eggs."

She smiled and shook her head.

"All right, then." He kissed her forehead.

"Call me later?"

"Of course. Harry's sure they'll release you in the morning, good as new. Do you have a rehearsal tomorrow?"

"Fortunately, Walter isn't doing anything with me till the afternoon."

"When do you think you'll finish?"

"Shouldn't be too late. He's said he'd have everybody out of there by six."

"How about an early dinner, like six-thirty?"

"Great."

"Moustache Café?"

She nodded.

"Robin, I would have told you more about Carrie. Harry's a sweet guy, but he doesn't—"

Robin pressed her index finger to his lips. "I shouldn't have asked him. I was out of line. You don't owe me any explanations, Jordan. We barely know each other."

He thought of Bolton's words, but didn't say anything. *Maybe we've known each other for a long, long time.*

Tuesday, 7:30 A.M.

Is Chip Estes home?" Karen Romero asked the ruddy-faced blonde who answered the door.

"Who are you?"

Jimmy Lee stepped in front of Romero and flashed his badge. "We're from the LAPD, ma'am. Is Chip your son?"

"Yes."

"And is he here?"

"Is this about that poor Cinch girl?"

"Yes."

"Chip barely knew her. She was just a friend of a girl he knows."

A barrel-chested man with short reddish brown hair appeared behind the woman.

"Can I help you?" he asked Romero and Lee.

"They're with the police, Hal. They want to ask Chip questions about the Cinch girl."

"He doesn't know anything about that."

"Are you Mr. Estes?" Romero asked.

"Yes."

"There are some questions we need to ask your son. We figured it'd be better to do so here rather than at his school or at the police station. Wouldn't you agree?"

Hal Estes stepped aside, clearing the way for the police to enter.

Forty-five minutes later, Romero and Lee had still not completed their questioning. Each time Hal Estes inquired why they were asking such seemingly irrelevant questions, Romero or Lee would simply respond, "It's just routine."

Chip Estes, they discovered, was a varsity wrestler with an aptitude for math. Fair-skinned like his mother, burly in build like his dad, he fidgeted throughout the interview, rocking back and forth in his living room chair, twiddling his thumbs, occasionally biting his nails. Probing into his personal history, Romero and Lee learned that in his early teens, Chip had spent a couple of years in therapy; he had a problem with aggression, which, his father pointedly claimed, he now had a handle on. Wrestling was his outlet.

This father was giving Romero a pain. He was clearly a control freak. Whenever his wife opened her mouth, he cut her off. After a couple of such humiliations, she clammed up completely. Romero made another note to check into Hal Estes' background, too. She could feel the man's anger simmering just below his confident demeanor. Maybe some of his anger had rubbed off on his son. Maybe Chip didn't know how to contain it. Maybe wrestling wasn't working so well. Romero made a further note to talk to the kid's therapist.

The boy had a simple alibi for the last two "Messenger" murders. He was home asleep. Both parents expressed certainty about his presence in the house. The detectives asked to see his room. There was nothing unusual in it: two posters of rock stars, a USC flag, a Yield sign he had pinched from a street corner. The thing that most caught the female detective's eye was a framed military medal above his bed. She asked Chip about it, but it was the father who cut in and answered.

"It's a bronze star."

"You were in the military?" Romero asked, just to keep this conversation going.

"The Marines...Vietnam."

Romero nodded.

"Chip is thinking of joining after high school. Isn't that right, son?"

"Yeah, maybe," the boy answered sullenly.

Chip's room, Romero now realized, was on the other side of the spacious ranch house from his parents' room. It would have been nothing for this athletic young man to climb out the window and return without his parents knowing.

As soon as they left the house, an excited Romero asked Jimmy Lee what he thought of their "visit." Lee never got a chance to answer.

"Oh, shit," Romero groaned.

They found themselves staring at a KABC news van parked in front of the house.

"How the hell did they get here?" Lee hissed.

A perky black reporter hurried toward the two detectives, adjusting her earpiece and straightening her sports jacket at the same time. As her cameraman moved into position behind her, she shoved a microphone in Romero's face. "Is Chip Estes a suspect in the Messenger killings?"

"This is just routine questioning." Romero answered.

"Are you going to question him further?" the reporter pressed.

"I have nothing to add to what I've already said."

But blood was already in the water. Even as Romero issued another denial, three more news vans raced up the street toward the Estes home.

Tuesday, 10:30 A.M.

Students streamed past Robin Norris as she pushed through the glass doors of Woodland Hills' Madison High School. Styles might change, she thought, as she surveyed the high schoolers, but that smell, that musty mix of floor wax, hair spray, and cafeteria food, never does. The sounds, too, were timeless: metal lockers opening and slamming shut, students laughing, grunting and calling to each other across the wide halls. It occurred to her that these sounds and smells were the same ones Beverly Casper had heard and smelled when she walked these halls three decades ago. For maybe the fifth time in the last two minutes, she paused, waiting, hoping for a déjà vu. It never came. All she felt were her own memories of Fortham High in St. Louis.

She stopped a bottle blonde in a fuschia T-shirt that came to within an inch of her navel. "Can you tell me where the library is?"

The girl stared at Robin. "Excuse me?"

"I'm looking for the library."

A heavy-set girl standing alongside the first laughed. "She's never been there. So, how could she know?"

"I know where the library is," Bottle Blonde said. "It's on the second floor."

"North side or south?"

The thin girl looked perplexed. "South side," she guessed.

Her hefty companion laughed. "You are such a ditz."

The two girls continued down the hallway trading insults, leaving Robin to deduce that the library was on the second floor, north side. A few seconds later, the period bell rang, sending students scrambling to their classes. Robin followed the chaotic stream past the large trophy case to the stairwell.

Only two people were in the library, a forlorn-looking Chicano boy at a long oak desk flipping through a magazine, and a man seated behind the reference desk. A small placard identified him as Mr. Black, Assistant Librarian. In his early twenties, a pair of thick-framed glasses perched on his thin nose, he looked like a fugitive from a Star Trek convention. Robin pegged him for a library science student on work-study.

"I'm looking for the school yearbooks," she told him.

The man slid away from his computer screen, and pushed up his glasses to get a better look at her. "What's going on, some sort of scavenger hunt?"

"Scavenger hunt?" Robin repeated.

Tucking in his blue shirt, the man walked her to a tall shelf of books behind and to the right of the checkout desk.

"Well, someone came here to see the yearbooks earlier this morning. You just wouldn't figure that happening twice in one day. Nothing happens twice in one day in this place." He pointed to the Chicano boy. "Like even two people coming in to read."

"What did this person look like?"

"He wasn't nearly as cute as you."

Robin gave a very brief, polite smile. "How old was he, Mr. Black?"

"Call me David," he said, extending a hand. "And you are?"

For a second, she thought of making up a name, then, decided against it. "Robin Norris... This man who came in, you were going to tell me how old he was."

"Forties, maybe older. I'm not good with ages and, to tell you the truth, I didn't really pay attention." Black paused. "Maybe if we could go out for coffee, I'd remember better."

"It's tempting, David, but I really need to look at these books."

The librarian shrugged. "You can't blame a guy for trying. All the kids who come in here are jail bait." He cleared his throat. "So, what years are you looking for?"

"1968 through 1971."

The librarian hummed a few spooky bars from the *Twilight Zone* theme song. "You're freaking me out, lady."

"What are you talking about?"

"That guy who came in, he asked for '70 and '71."

"Did he say why?"

"Nah, just made some stupid joke."

"What?"

"It was stupid."

"What did he say?"

"A dumb line. Something like, 'There was a girl who went here back then who I heard is dying to meet me.' And then he laughed, like it was the funniest thing in the world."

Robin shivered. *Had John come in? Had John heard about her? It seemed impossible. Only now anything seemed possible.*

The man pulled out the four thin volumes and carried them over to the table.

"Are you a private detective?" he asked, as he set them down.

"No."

"Looking up one of your parents maybe?"

Robin forced a smile.

"You'd like to be left alone, right?"

"I would. Thank you."

"This guy who came in earlier, maybe he was a private detective or maybe even a cop. He had that look." He shrugged. "Not that I'd really know."

As the librarian walked away, Robin was relieved to be alone.

It was probably someone from Lemoski's office. Doing some background checking on Beverly Casper.

She looked at the books, stacked chronologically on top of each other. She knew she should go straight to 1970 or 1971, but she wasn't ready. She wanted to ease into it. Start with 1968, Beverly's freshman year.

She took a deep breath and opened the textured burgundy leather cover. A dark-haired cheerleader, clapping her hands while looking out toward a football field, greeted her on the first page—*1968 Patriots. Volume 9. Published and edited by the students of Madison High School, Woodland Hills, California.*

Randomly, she opened to the middle of the book. Two pages of smiling seniors looked up at her, a girl with horn-rimmed glasses and buckteeth, another with a beehive, bright eyes and pearl necklace, and under them a boy with a buzz cut, broad smile and high forehead. She lingered on their faces for a moment, trying to imagine for an instant how their lives had turned out, trying to imagine if these were faces Beverly used to pass in the hall during her freshman year. And if she had, should they now look familiar? She turned a few more pages, *Vocational Training Classes*.... Pictures of the faculty.... Mr. Curtis Brooks, English and composition.

She turned to the name index in the back. *Beverly Casper, Frosh, 122, 187.* The entry on page 122 gave her a jolt. Most of the page was taken up by a photograph of a Girls Glee Club. *So Beverly was a singer.* Robin leaned forward to get a good look of the group shot. In the middle row, wearing a white blouse under a light-colored sweater, between a girl named Barbara Proesel and one named Shelly King, stood Beverly Casper. Her eyes looked straight into the camera, her wide mouth caught in a broad, goofy smile. Beverly's hair was light, and curled into her neck. It was a black and white photo, of course, but it was not hard to guess that Beverly was a blonde. On page 187, there was a group shot of the Freshman Class. Her face was not much more than a large dot on the page, but the same goofy grin shined through the gray tones, a small star of white light.

Robin pushed the 1968 book aside and picked up 1969. This time, she turned immediately to the index. *Beverly Casper, Soph. 99,*

124, 202. Page 99 was Glee Club again. This time, Beverly stood in the back row. The goofy smile was gone, and replaced by a purposeful, tight-lipped stare. Robin imagined Beverly, upset by her freshman pictures, standing in front of her mirror practicing this more sophisticated pose. She was a pretty girl; it made Robin happy to see that. Page 124 saw her on stage in a Drama Club production of "The Playboy of the Western World." A singer first, an actress second. For the second time that morning, Robin shivered.

There were five Beverly entries in the 1970 yearbook. The first was a spontaneous shot of her walking up the school's front steps, pointing to something up ahead. Under the picture was a caption: "Take me to your leader." *She must have gotten a major hoot out of that*, Robin thought. No Glee Club this year; instead, there was Musical Theater. The group shot showed the two dozen or so members of the troupe with their arms outstretched, heads tilted toward the sky, mouths all wide open as if belting out a song. The caption read, *"Bye Bye Birdie*, September, 1969."

On page 94, Beverly finally had her own picture entry. While the junior photos did not equal the senior ones in size, they were big enough for Robin to study. Beverly's hair was parted down the middle and extended out of the frame. She had full eyebrows, a wide mouth, and a forceful chin that tucked into a curl below her thin lips. Robin couldn't tell the color of her eyes. Her smile, absent from the sophomore book, had returned; this time, a moderate grin that suggested emerging confidence. It was the sort of picture that a father would gladly pull out of his wallet to show his coworkers, a picture full of life and promise.

She reached for the last book, 1971, what should have been Beverly's senior year. *Would there be a special page and tribute about Beverly? There'd better be*, she mumbled glumly to herself.

She found the tribute, a picture, on the front page, and what she saw rocked her to her core.

The picture filled a full page. Beverly was on stage, dressed simply as a girl from a New England fishing village singing to a rakish-looking fellow.

Robin didn't need to look at the caption. Beverly's character was Julie, the female lead in *Carousel*, the very character whom Robin would be playing at the Wadsworth in just a few days. *Oh my God! Beverly must have been rehearsing this role that summer between her junior and senior year.*

Centered inside the page was a larger version of Beverly's junior year photo. In white letters was written: *Beverly Casper. 1953–1970? You'll Never Walk Alone. The students, faculty and staff of Madison High.*

The page blurred in front of her.

"But every single person who means anything to me is going to be there, and I'm going to be left out. How do you expect me to ever belong to any group, to ever keep any friends? Do anything. How?"

She could see her dad wavering. Maybe, just maybe, she thought. But then she saw him looking at her mother, catching her disapproving glance.

"Just come home," he finally said.

She wanted to scream.

"Pip, come on, now."

She nodded, her face taut.

"I'm just worried about your safety, honey," her mother said in a low voice.

Robin tasted salt water on her lips; she didn't even know she'd been crying. She closed the book, then, started sobbing, harsh, heaving sobs from deep in her chest. A thought suddenly overwhelmed her: *Why do I pretend that I hate my mother? I don't hate her! I love her! I love her! And she has to know. I have to tell her. I have to tell her.*

The forlorn Chicano boy looked up from his magazine and stared at Robin. He blinked several times, then, not knowing what to do, returned to his magazine. The librarian came running over, offering some tissues. "What's the matter? Are you okay?"

"No, I'll be fine, thank you, thank you so much…"

She grabbed the tissues that he was holding out to her, jumped up and hurried from the room. *She had to talk to her mother. This instant. She had to explain.* She rushed down the empty stairwell. By the front doors, she found a bank of phones. She put some change into the slot and automatically dialed the number.

"Hello," the female voice answered flatly at the other end. It wasn't a voice that Robin had ever heard.

"Mom?" And then she remembered; her mother was in the Rockies. What was she thinking? And who was this on the other end of line?

'You must have the wrong number," the voice said.

"Wait. Don't hang up. What number is this?"

"673-0928.'

It was not a number that Robin knew.

"Who is this?" the voice on the other end asked.

"My name is Robin Norris."

"Well, I don't know any Robin Norris. Good—"

"Please," Robin pleaded. "Who am I speaking to?"

"I'm not in the habit of giving my name to strangers."

"Please, it's very important."

There was a long pause.

"My name is Alice Casper, if it's any business of yours. Good-bye."

Tuesday, 11:05 A.M.

Without the requisite training, his best shot, Jordan reasoned, was to stay focused on the one case he felt he knew best, the killer's connection to Beverly Casper. If he could understand "John" as a young man, maybe he would be able to understand how he would act as a mature one. Mature. He almost laughed; how inappropriate a word. Mature implied some growth, some sense of moral responsibility. John had none. He was a monster cloaked in the body of a human. Whatever he was, mature wasn't it.

Rereading both his initial and later notes, he felt a bittersweet sense of pride; the conclusions he had drawn before first going to the police had been, to the extent they were knowable, accurate. The Messenger was well organized, stalked his victims—the Judy Cinch murder certainly confirmed that—and knew enough about cars to disable them in a manner that would leave them stranded on a lightly traveled road and susceptible to his timely "aid." He also took sadistic satisfaction in torturing the victim's parents, most likely because of a twisted love/hate relationship he had with his mother. Those post-murder references to the mysterious Loni during the second hypnosis, Jordan guessed, were probably references to dear old mom. Maybe she beat him with a leather strap; that would explain his choice of weapon—doing to his victims what he had wanted but couldn't do to his mother. It also seemed like a good possibility that his mother was a prostitute. "They call me John," that strange phrase the killer used to describe himself, suggested it. No wonder he wanted to be a "John." It was the Johns who got close to his mother, who only saw the sweet side, never the belt. That's what he wanted, to be close to his mother. So, he externalized the fantasy and renamed himself. Even his obsession with angels fit in with this construction. He murdered young girls because they represented his mother in her idealized, pre-prostitute state: pure, angel-like. Kill them now before they get corrupted like mom did. That's what he wanted his victims to understand—he was doing them a great service. But, of course, they didn't understand; hence, his rage, his frustration, his sense of betrayal.

Jordan felt a clammy sweat at the roots of his scalp. *What is it about this room that makes me so damn uncomfortable? Because this is where you made a fool of yourself.* This was the place where, inadvertently, he had almost succeeded in convincing the police that he was the Messenger. *Don't make a fool of yourself again. The only thing you really know about "John" is that he's very adept at murdering young women.*

He reexamined his notes for the fourth time.

Focus, he told himself. *Tunnel in on supportable conclusions.*

But there weren't any. Not one. He didn't even know the killer's first name. "John" could easily just be a name he had made up, the most common name there is. Then, again, maybe the name did mean something. John planned carefully. He not only "fixed" the cars to get the girls he wanted, he carefully staged the murders. And he was patient. If the girl's car broke down too near a busy area or if she got help from someone else, John probably looked for a new victim. He didn't take chances. If events went his way, fine. If they didn't, there was always tomorrow.

One thing clearly didn't synch up between the Beverly Casper murder and the others. Beverly had been murdered and immediately dispatched into the earth. The current victims had all been elaborately posed. If Jordan had to speculate—that's all he was doing anyway—he'd guess that the difference rested in John's own evolving self-image. When killing as a young man, he had his whole life in front of him. Yet even murderers have ambitions, dreams of glory. Who knows what he thought he'd become, what juvenile fantasy he entertained about himself in his mid-twenties? Maybe he saw himself becoming a millionaire businessman, a famous actor, a race car driver, a general or even a police chief? But when his dreams didn't pan out, he became frustrated, even more bitter than before. With his persecution complex, life's disappointments, tough on anyone, seemed part of a conspiracy designed to thwart him. Now, for whatever reason, perhaps, in part, because he couldn't handle the failures, he starts killing again. He sees murder as a new road to fame. The world will finally take notice. So, not only does he need to kill, he needs to kill in style.

Jordan looked at his notes on more time. *Okay, give me something, maybe not fully supportable, but, at least, likely.* Two things jumped out. 1) John had eyes of two different colors: one brown, one green. 2) He served in the Marines.

Well, maybe. Assuming he chose the name "John" because it meant something to him, he could have easily given himself a fictitious military career. Maybe he figured that an armed forces background would certify his manhood; he certainly wouldn't be the first to have such a thought. But why lie to Beverly about it? You lie to a girl you're trying to impress and whom you want to convince to go out with you again. Why lie to someone whom you're going to murder? Which means it probably was true. That would narrow the database a bit... a very little bit. These were the Vietnam War years. Thousands of young men joined the Marines between 1963 and 1970; the years when John would have been between 18 to 25.

What if he had joined the Marines and washed out? Even more likely, what if he got a dishonorable discharge? Paranoid schizophrenics aren't known for handling authority well. Jordan could easily imagine a run-in with the military police or a punch thrown at a sergeant.

How many Marines between 1963 and 1970 received dishonorable discharges? The number, he guessed, would be fairly small.

And there was something else he might reasonably conclude: John was from the Los Angeles area, probably the Valley. Most discharged servicemen return to civilian life in their hometowns. Besides, in the mid-to-late sixties, L.A. was still the place to be; people were arriving in droves.

Beverly's "post-death" claim that "John" had two different colored eyes would narrow the database considerably more if, and this was one more big "if" in a whole string of "ifs," it just wasn't a trick of the light.

Before he had a chance to totally shred his own fanciful theories, Lemoski marched in. He surveyed the papers strewn over the table. "Come up with anything?"

"Look for an ex-Marine, in his fifties, with different colored eyes, who signed up somewhere in the Valley or L.A. between 1963 to 1970, and was dishonorably discharged."

Lemoski raised an eyebrow. "You sound pretty confident."

"I'm not. It's just a guess."

"What years did you say he was in the Marines?"

"Somewhere between '63 and '70. Do the Marines even keep those records?"

"I'm sure they do. I'll have Romero check it out."

Jordan had the impression that he might as well have given the detective the weather report.

Lemoski took a seat opposite Jordan. "Let me ask you something. Are you really sold on this reincarnation angle?"

Jordan felt like he'd been punched. He had been operating on the assumption that Lemoski believed, like him, that the all the murders had been committed by the same killer; that he, the psychiatrist, and, Lemoski, the cop, had walked the plank together. But now, as he processed Lemoski's simple question, he recognized how narcissistic this view was. He had naively placed himself at the center of the investigation. But he wasn't. Think about it, he told himself. The station he had walked through to get to this room had become a fortress of policemen dedicated to one task—catching the Messenger. Yet, except for Lemoski's core team, no one even knew who Jordan was. "The reincarnation angle" was to Lemoski just that, one possible angle. And not one he was anxious to have anyone know about. If it panned out, swell; if it didn't, something else would.

"Yes, lieutenant," he finally said. "Until some new information comes along that forces me to challenge that belief, I'm sold on the reincarnation angle."

Lemoski nodded slowly. "Does the name Chip Estes mean anything to you?"

He shook his head.

"It did to your lawyer friend, April Conniston. She apparently had information implicating Chip Estes in the Messenger murders."

Jordan's entire face folded into a look of confusion. "That makes no sense."

"She told Mike Fields, her father's—"

"I know who he is."

"And Fields told Romero."

"When?"

"Last night."

"Let me get this straight. April told Mike Fields that she suspected that this Chip Estes was the murderer."

"According to Fields, yes."

"On what did she base her suspicion?"

"Fields doesn't know. She said that we were barking up the wrong tree with Beverly Casper. She had proof that the murders were not connected."

"I find this very hard to believe."

"Did she say anything to you?"

"No. And she definitely would have."

"According to Fields, April told him this a short time before she started out in her car and got killed. Did you speak to her that day?"

"Yes, but it was much earlier, around two o'clock."

"And you didn't speak to her again?"

"No."

Lemoski paused, considering the last. "Did Miss Conniston try to reach you?"

Jordan nodded. "Twice. There were two messages on my voice mail."

Damn! If only I had called her earlier. Who knows what she needed to tell me? Suddenly, he felt very, very tired. "So, lieutenant, who is Chip Estes?"

"A senior at Forrester High School in Northridge." Lemoski's eyes met Jordan's. "And the boy my daughter has a crush on."

Tuesday, 11:15 A.M.

She rang the doorbell. No answer. She didn't even hear a stirring inside. She rang again and started to count. That was the deal she'd made with herself; if she got to twenty and no one came, she'd leave.

At seventeen, the door opened.

The woman looked about seventy, an old seventy; wrinkled skin, a flat, broad face. The white hair, though, was arranged in a neat bun. "Yes," the old woman said. "What is it?"

For a moment, she said nothing. She had acted so impulsively; she had prepared no cover story.

"What is it?" the woman repeated, a trace of irritation in her voice. "Who are you?"

"Robin Norris."

The woman's brown eyes hardened. "Wait a minute, are you... are you the one who called before, the wrong number."

"Yes."

"So, if it was a wrong number, why'd you come here?"

"I needed to meet you, Mrs. Casper."

"What do you want?"

375

"I knew Beverly," she finally said, her voice barely above a whisper.

The woman took a step forward and squinted up into her face. "What are you talking about?"

"I knew Beverly," Robin repeated.

"You must be confused, young lady."

"Didn't you have a daughter Beverly?"

"I did. How old are you?"

"Twenty-five."

"Beverly died before you were born. You're mixing her up with another Beverly." The woman started to close the door.

"Pip," she said, this time her voice loud.

The door swung back open. "What did you say?"

"Your husband used to call her Pip, but you used to call her by her real name."

When the woman spoke, her words came out angry, like bullets. "That's right. The only one who called her Pip was her father, and the only one who knew that aside from me was her brother Peter. Did Peter tell you that?"

"I don't know Peter."

The woman scrunched up her face again

"You had a brown Pontiac. A Grand Am."

"That's the car—"

"Beverly hated the color. She wanted a sports car, but you thought a sports car would be impractical." It was a silly detail, but it was all she could think to say. "She wanted to meet her friends in Malibu, but you didn't want her to go." She was being swept away by her own recollections, not even sure herself where they were coming from. "The road, you thought, was too dangerous for a seventeen-year-old girl who had only had her license for—"

"What sort of scam are you pulling?"

"No scam. I promise."

"My daughter disappeared thirty-two years ago. My husband died a few years later of a broken heart. And I have a son who hasn't spoken to me in ten years. And now you come here. Why?"

Robin looked at her, filled with compassion. The woman's

pain was fresh, as if Beverly had died a week ago. "I'm sorry I came," she said. "Forgive me for bothering you. I give you my word; I don't want anything from you. I'll just go now."

She turned around. The woman's voice was addressed to her back. "I'm sorry, it's been hard all these years. Come inside."

She led Robin into a living room and over to a frayed red couch. Robin felt as if she had entered a scene from *Great Expectations*. Paint had peeled from the ceiling, forming ugly pockets that looked like open sores, and the white stuffing inside the sofa pillows was jutting out here and there. She wondered if anything had changed in this room since 1970. Over on a piano, she saw a large framed photograph of Beverly; she recognized it from the yearbook, Beverly's junior picture. Alongside it was a photograph of a man in his forties with kind, deep-set eyes. The wide mouth and high cheek bones resembled Beverly's. *That must be Beverly's father.* She hoped he would look familiar, but he didn't.

"Is that your husband?"

Alice Casper nodded.

"When did he die?"

"1973."

"Only three years after Beverly—"

"That's right. Not even three years... Now tell me, please, why did you come here?"

"Mrs. Casper, I swear I mean you no harm."

"You've said that already."

"Please, I have a story to tell you, and it's very important that I don't feel rushed."

The old lady sat down in a rocking chair opposite Robin.

Robin told her everything, the swallowing, the trouble singing, how she'd gone to a psychiatrist to be hypnotized. How the psychiatrist had regressed her to discover the source of her problems; and how suddenly she wasn't Robin Norris any more. She was a teenage girl named Beverly Casper whose car had broken down, who'd been assisted by a passerby who turned out to be an evil man who called himself John.

"John," Alice Casper repeated in a thin voice. "John."

Robin nodded.

"We never heard anything about a John."

"The police never found out anything, did they?"

Alice Casper shook her head. "For a while, they thought it was the Keeton boy."

"Larry?" Robin cut in.

"You know about him?"

"It was in the papers."

"But they never found anything. Bill"—her head tilted in the direction of the picture on the piano—"that was my husband, used to call Lieutenant Broder constantly. After a while, he just stopped returning our calls. We even went to psychics, three of them. The first one told us that Beverly had run off with some AWOL soldier and was on a ship somewhere in the Pacific." She gave a short, stale laugh. "That 'information' ran us $300. Then we went to a lady who told us that Beverly would call us on Christmas. For years, I wouldn't step out of the house on Christmas. If I went to the bathroom I left the door open so I could hear if it rang." She paused. "It's twenty-eight years since I saw that psychic, and you can be sure it has ruined every Christmas since. Bill tried to go back to work after the disappearance; he sold insurance. But he wasn't able to sell anymore. He was too distracted. Like me, always down, depressed. Finally, he just stopped. We'd sit at home together. And one night, we were in front of the TV set and he just keeled over. Heart attack. The doctor said he was probably dead before he hit the floor."

Robin waited. "What about Peter?"

Alice ignored the question. "You said it was a psychiatrist who hypnotized you?"

"Yes."

"Well, it was some psychologist who convinced Peter–he was seven years younger than Beverly—that I was ruining his life, sucking him into my tragedy. He had to break away from me."

Misery built upon tragedy. "You said there was a third psychic," Robin said, hoping to turn their conversation back to Beverly.

"After that first Christmas when Beverly didn't call, I wanted to see another psychic. Bill stopped me. We had an awful argument.

'She's dead,' he yelled at me. 'Just accept that.' It was just awful. I told him that if Beverly was dead, it was his fault."

"His fault?"

"I shouldn't have said it. I should never have blamed it on him. You see, he told me how Beverly had called home that night and told him that the rehearsal was running late. But she was lying. It was obvious to me that night, and he finally admitted to me that he knew she was lying too. 'If you had only ordered her to come home,' I accused him. Anyway, when Bill died, I went to another psychic; a man who'd been on some big TV show. You know, show him a picture and he'd know all about the person. He held Beverly's picture against his face, then told me she'd been killed the night she was kidnapped, and buried somewhere in a canyon."

Robin paused. "He was right."

Alice reached for the arm of the chair and leaned over. With her other palm, she covered her forehead. "My head's always known that. It's just that without a body, it's so hard to accept."

"Mrs. Casper," Robin said, "I know this sounds incredible, crazy to you—it sounds crazy to me—but somehow, and I don't know how it happened, Beverly's inside my head." The woman nodded slowly, her face seemingly stripped of all emotion. Robin had no idea how this woman regarded her.

"There was terrible tension between you and Beverly, wasn't there?"

"What teenage daughter doesn't have tension with her mother?"

"But that night, the night she disappeared, in particular, there was—"

Alice Casper pushed forward in her chair. "Don't blame me. I was just—"

"No, no," Robin cut in. "I just want to tell you that in those last minutes, once Beverly realized this man was going to murder her…" Her voice trailed into silence. It was hard for her to say these words, say them in a way that would really communicate Beverly's feelings. "She loved you. She knew you loved her. And she was sorry, so sorry that the last words she spoke to you were angry ones." The room filled up suddenly with quiet warmth as if an angel had just entered. "Her last thoughts, her last thoughts were..." She was speaking now in a voice that wasn't her own, a voice that Alice Casper never thought she'd hear again. "Please tell my mom and dad that I'm sorry for everything, that I love them, and I know that I'll see them someday in heaven."

Alice Casper sat back in her chair, her mouth agape. "I've heard those words in my head a million times; for years, it seemed as if every time I'd close my eyes, I'd hear them. But it was always in his voice, that mocking, cruel voice." She stood up and started toward the younger woman. "Now, I've heard them from Beverly."

Robin stood up to meet her. They clasped each other's arms and then the two women embraced. Although they stood together for only a minute or so, time lost all meaning. Robin's limbs felt light—an energy radiated through her as if she had been charged. And she had the strangest sensation that something in the universe had shifted; that perhaps even Heaven had been stirred.

Tuesday, noon

By noon, everybody at Forrester High School in Northridge had heard the "Chip Estes" rumor.

By 12:15 people that Chip Estes didn't even know were pointing at him, giving him threatening looks.

At 12:45 between classes, somebody in the hall whispered "hey, killer," as he passed.

By 1:15 P.M., someone had spray painted a skull and cross bones on Chip Estes' locker.

By 2 P.M. the principal thought it best that Chip leave school for the day; his mother picked him up.

By the end of the last period, a new rumor quickly spread among the departing students—Chip Estes had confessed to murdering Judy Cinch.

Tuesday, 3:30 P.M.

Robin arrived at the theater by a quarter of two, a full half-hour early, emotionally exhausted from her encounter with Alice Casper. Oddly, though, she felt ready and eager to work. She badly needed the distraction. After what she had just been through, singing and acting seemed like the easiest things in world. Her relief, however, was short-lived. Trying a few basic vocal exercises, she couldn't loosen up her voice. In fact, the more vocal exercises she did, the more strained she sounded. The tightness in her throat was back, just as bad as it was when she first went to see Jordan. She hoped that she'd improve once she got to the stage. But she didn't. The high notes, the low ones, even the notes in between sounded hoarse and cracked. After forty minutes, Walter broke in during the middle of a song. He told the cast he was calling a ten-minute break, and pulled her aside.

"I'm sorry, darling, but I'm going to give your part to Deb White."

Her immediate instinct was to defend herself: "Just give me twenty minutes and I'll be fine." But she said nothing. She knew what he knew: her voice was gone and she had no way of knowing when it would come back.

"I don't know what this is all about, Robin—your voice, this reincarnation thing, whatever you've got going with this shrink...." His tone was more sad than angry. "But whatever it is, my first obligation is to the show. I don't have the confidence that you can do the job anymore. One day you're Judy Garland, the next day you're croaking like a frog."

She had no answer.

"Look," he said, "I'll make up something. I'll tell everyone we had creative differences."

Young actors don't have creative differences with established directors. Word would get out; she'd be branded unreliable. For a young actor, a reputation like that could easily be death.

"Go back to New York, angel," he offered soothingly. "This town can do crazy things to people. After the show is over, I'll call you. We'll work together again."

She turned his words over in her head. *This town can do crazy things to people.* Like her and Jordan. In one week, each had trashed a career they'd worked years to build.

With muted dignity, Robin graciously thanked each member of the cast and crew. They wished her well, and seemed genuinely compassionate. But she could detect the meaning behind their funereal smiles: her career had just been buried.

Deb White's eyes welled with tears, as she pulled at Robin's wrists, begging her not to go. Robin thought she went a little over the top, but that might have been an uncharitable thought. If it hadn't hit Deb already, it would hit her soon enough that she was now going to have to carry the show. That sort of realization would be enough to buckle the knees of even the hardiest ingénue.

As Robin walked out of the theater, a gym bag full of clothes and other possessions thrown over her shoulder, she glanced at the large poster next to the box office: *Rodgers and Hammerstein's CAROUSEL starring Robin Norris and Tom Reibman.* She stopped and lingered before the sign. Strange, but it didn't seem to have anything to do with her. It was her name. And it was her show. But somehow, it belonged to a different era.

She wondered if she'd ever see her name on a marquee again.

Tuesday, 4:40 P.M.

Jordan headed back toward Brentwood, a copy of the Beverly Casper file, two inches thick, enclosed in a fresh manila folder and secured by a thick rubber band, on the seat beside him, exactly what April had taken home with her two days before. Lemoski had placed the folder in his hand just as he was leaving the station. But it was presented more as a gift or a token. The detective's interest in "the reincarnation angle" had definitely waned now that he had a new suspect to pursue.

Jordan didn't know what to believe any more. So much had happened so fast in the last week, it wasn't easy for him to keep his thoughts straight. Assuming that these new murders had nothing to do with Beverly Casper's, then why couldn't Chip Estes be a legitimate suspect? Because he was too young? That hardly disqualified him. Hadn't even God complained in Genesis that "man is evil from his youth"? How many future murderers cut their teeth torturing animals, or their peers? There was that infamous case in England in the early nineties where two 10-year-old boys in Liverpool murdered a two-year-old. The killers made their tiny victim walk two and a half miles outside of town before they beat him to a pulp. In Chicago around the same time, an eight-year-old boy pushed a six-year old girl off the top of a building. Mass murder in high schools in Kentucky, Oregon and Colorado—new young killers, each one's crime seemingly more horrific than the last, popped up in the news every other month. So, why couldn't Chip Estes be the Messenger? The logical answer was that he could be. What made no sense to Jordan, however, what was really bugging him, was why April thought Estes was the killer. The answer, if there was one, had to be in the file. The answer to everything—he just had a hunch—was there.

As he guided his car down the steep Sepulveda Pass that linked the city to the valley, he marveled at how every new lead seemed to trace its way back to the same cluster of people. A degree of separation between them barely existed. Chip Estes was the latest addition to the group; he had a connection first through Lemoski's daughter, but also through April who had given his name to Mike Fields, Avery Conniston's cousin. And Avery himself had possibly seen the Messenger, or at least the Messenger's victim, just a few nights earlier.

Who else was part of the cluster? Robin, Walter, Bolton, Lemoski, Swain, Bobley, Romero? He considered the names. Then, one jumped out at him as if it were suddenly a three-dimensional object. *Swain*. Detective Fred Swain. He was there at the beginning, a young detective investigating the case, and now, here he was at the end. How's that for a coincidence? But there was more. Hadn't Swain told him the first time they'd met that he had been in the Marines? And what if Bolton was right and April's death was no accident? Swain would have been one of the few people who knew she had the Beverly Casper file.

Jordan checked himself. *Damn, it doesn't hold up.* For starters, Swain couldn't have been dishonorably discharged; you can't get into the police force with a dishonorable discharge on your record. *Then again, so what? Maybe I was wrong about that. He has trouble with authority, so instead of fighting it, he becomes it. Also, Swain doesn't have two different colored eyes. But perhaps Beverly really didn't see two differently colored eyes like he'd thought earlier. It might have just been a trick of the light.*

Maybe he should call Lemoski and have him check closely into

Swain's alibi. No, he didn't feel ready to do that. If he was wrong, he'd be doing the same thing to Swain that Lemoski had almost done to him, except that Lemoski had a lot more reason to believe that Jordan might be the killer than Jordan had reason to believe that Swain was. He had work to do before he pronounced his suspicions about anybody to anyone. He'd have to be, if not sure, then pretty close to it. The answer would be in the Casper file. It had to be. He thought of canceling his dinner plans with Robin and getting right to work. He even picked up his cell phone to call her, but just as quickly he changed his mind. He needed to see her. Even more, he needed, after last night's debacle, to reassure himself that she was okay. A phone conversation wouldn't cut it. He needed to look her in the eyes. He glanced at the digital clock in the middle of his dashboard. He barely had time to get home and shower.

Tuesday, 5:05 P.M.

*H*e set the cold beer down on the coffee table, not even thinking to slide a coaster between the wet can and the lacquered wood. What was supposed to have been a routine check of the top stories, himself prominently featured, had turned into something completely unexpected. He sat transfixed, elbows on his knees, eyes epoxied to the thirty-one-inch TV screen and the pretty Latino newsreader who filled it. When she finished reading her story, they started to air the footage. He couldn't believe what he was seeing and hearing, but at the same time, it all made perfect sense. His first instinct was to run. Of course, she would remember everything. How could she forget him? If she'd talked, then they knew. They might be at the door at any second.

He bounced from wall to wall, rubbing his hands over his arms, pulling at his hair. He felt like his skin was molting. The more he thought about it, the more agitated he became, until he worked himself into a righteous rage.

He could only imagine what Loni was thinking. She'd be furious. No, there was no point in running. If they weren't here yet, he was still safe. He could take care of the problem, the same way he took care of all his problems.

One of his angels had escaped.
He had to find her and send her back—tonight.

I called the theater," Romero told her agitated boss. "They said she left more than an hour ago. The woman who answered the phone also said she was no longer associated with the play."

"What?"

"She must have been fired," Romero responded. "Or maybe she quit. The woman wouldn't say."

"Did you call her home?"

"I've left three messages."

"Let me know as soon as she calls in."

Romero turned to exit, but Lemoski's voice stopped her. "Don't leave."

"I thought you were—"

"Close the door."

She did, gripping the knob hard to steady herself, bracing for the storm she knew was coming.

"Who did this?" he called out, all calmness gone.

"Sir?"

"You know what I'm asking. Who gave that video to the media?"

"I have no idea."

"What about Bobley?" the lieutenant asked, his voice rising.

"It might—" She cut herself off. "I really wouldn't want to speculate."

Lemoski was in no mood for such prevarications.

"Sit down, Karen," he bellowed.

She did.

"Bobley was mouthing off at the bar yesterday. I want to know exactly what he said."

Still, Romero resisted. As much as she despised Bobley, she didn't want to be the person responsible for maybe deep sixing his career. "Look, he had a few drinks."

"Goddamnit! Tell me what he said!" he shouted, slapping his hand hard on the desk. He peered down at her like an angry thunder god.

She had never seen the lieutenant this mad. She'd never seen anybody this mad.

Tuesday, 6 P.M.

You actually dialed her number."

"The whole day was like that," Robin continued. They were seated now in a rosewood booth at the Moustache Café, Jordan looking out at twenty other tables, Robin at the giant TV monitor dominating the bar area. "There were things I just knew, like the telephone number, and other things, just as important, that were so unfamiliar—like Alice, Beverly's mom; she didn't look anything like what I'd expected. Somehow, in hypnosis, I had felt her but not seen her. But little things were just pouring out of me. At one point I had to go to the bathroom, and Alice started telling me the direction, 'Go up the stairs,' and I just cut her off, 'Yes, up the stairs, take a right, the first door on the left.'"

"How did she react?"

"To my knowing where the bathroom was?" she said with a pixie smile.

He loved that grin, that kidding quality. It confirmed his early impression that behind the charm there was substance, fortitude.

"To everything."

"I felt holy, Jordan. It sounds weird, but it was as if I was sent there. Alice lost everybody, my dad, I mean Beverly's dad, died, feeling guilty that he hadn't ordered Beverly to come home from a rehearsal that evening. Alice's son, Peter, just ran away. It became a house of grief. And Alice, she was convinced that Beverly hated her. She wanted to die, Jordan. For years, once her husband passed on, she wanted to die. But she couldn't kill herself; she used a funny expression, 'I'd be like a sentinel who deserted my post.' She had to stay and learn what happened to Beverly. And when I told her how Beverly had loved her, it just closed a wound."

Jordan listened as Robin filled in the details of her morning and afternoon, beginning with her adventure at Madison High.

"Some guy was there at the library looking through old yearbooks?" Jordan exclaimed.

"The same years."

Jordan let out a low whistle.

"I'm just counting on it being one of Lemoski's people," Robin continued.

"We can't be too sure about anything. I'll check that with him."

"And, then, when I saw the photograph of Beverly rehearsing *Carousel—*"

Jordan felt his skin crawl. "You're sure you're right about that?"

"She was in virtually the same outfit I've been wearing."

"That would explain why your move to L.A. to star in this play triggered the whole swallowing problem."

"Seeing that photo of Beverly triggered more. Just like Bolton said it might." She told him how, at the library, her mind had drifted into the fight Beverly had had with her parents, and how a minute later her face was wet, her body heaving under her sobs. "I think I scared that librarian out of his wits. But you see, Jordan, that's exactly why I didn't want you to hypnotize me to forget. Do you understand now?"

"Of course, of course." Jordan glanced around and signaled for a waitress. He turned back to Robin. "I can't believe you made it to your rehearsal after that."

"There was no rehearsal," Robin said. "I tried to sing. I couldn't."

"You still have a few days. I can do some relaxation techniques with you."

"It's over, Jordan. Walter fired me."

"When? Today? Just now?"

"He's right. I don't have the voice to do the show. My understudy, Deb White, is taking over."

"There isn't enough time for her to get ready, is there? Wouldn't it have been better to call off the whole show?"

"Walter is an excellent director. He'll work with her day and night. And you know what I think? Let her have the chance."

"You really feel all right with it?"

"I swear to you, *Carousel* is not what I need to do now."

Jordan stared at her. "I'm impressed, really impressed."

"With what? That I've now increased the number of unemployed actresses in L.A. from fifty thousand to fifty thousand and one?"

"No, I'm serious. You've got your priorities in order; you know what you need. And you're right; in the long term, *Carousel* isn't what counts. I'm the psychiatrist and I wish I knew myself half as well."

"What are you talking about?"

He took her right hand and held it between his. "I don't want to mess up our relationship. I've screwed up relationships, Robin. I really have."

"But not the one that counted. Harry told me everything about you and Carrie. You're the one I envy. I've never had a relationship like that; long-term, beautiful, loving."

He smiled grimly. "I can only guess what Harry told you about the Myth of Carrie and Jordan. The truth is, it wasn't always so beautiful, and it certainly wasn't always so loving. The night Carrie died, we had a terrible fight."

"As all couples do," Robin said. "It only seems so terrible because she died that night."

"I wish it were that simple. Carrie was trying to push me that night into setting a wedding date. We'd been together four years, so you can't exactly accuse her of being unreasonable. But I refused. I was scared."

"Of getting married?"

"No. Of getting married to her. I hadn't been happy for a while. But I didn't know how to tell her." He winced at the memory. "Anyway, I wouldn't set a date. She was furious. Carrie had always had a temper, but this time it really got ugly. She accused me of having an affair with a medical student who I knew from my intern days. I denied it. But she didn't believe me. She went over to my bookcase and took down this giant Bible my grandfather gave me; his bar mitzvah present. She put it in my hands, and told me to swear that I hadn't slept with this woman."

"Oh, my God!"

"I put the Bible down, and said that if that's the sort of relationship we were going to have, what was the point; she was just going to have to accept my word. Only it didn't work. She continued screaming at me."

"What else could you have done?"

"I could have told the truth, Robin. *She was right*. I had slept with this woman. A few times. I felt guilty about it. But I did it, I think, as much to provoke a break up as anything else. Somehow I think Carrie knew. Maybe she had followed me to this woman's apartment, I don't know. Finally, she screamed, 'You're a liar. You're a liar and a coward.' And then she ran out of the apartment and right into the path of an oncoming car."

"That's so awful."

"Turned out the driver was a couple of points above the legal drinking limit. I still don't know if he was totally at fault or if Carrie had just run into the street, oblivious to everything. But I was just as responsible as he was. Probably more."

"That's ridiculous."

"Why? If I had told her the truth, not then, but months before when I knew I didn't love her, she'd be alive. It was my weakness, my flaw that caused her death."

They sat together in silence for a few beats.

"Everyone had this idealized picture of us; you heard Harry's version. And in public, we really seemed like the perfect couple. That was very important to Carrie. She was obsessed that no one ever see any tension between us. She wanted perfection. She demanded it of herself and of me. But I'm not perfect. I don't want anybody to ever think that I am."

"That's a funny thing for a psychiatrist to say."

"Why?"

"I'll bet that's exactly what your patients do think of you. Certainly that's what I felt when I walked out of your office."

"Psychiatrists and actresses. Two professions with high rates of divorce. You know why? Because it's a lot easier to get strangers to love you than to do the hard work to keep the love you have."

Jordan picked up his menu again. "Well, this conversation has been a lot of laughs."

When he looked up, Robin was gazing straight into his eyes. "I'm not looking for perfection, Jordan."

He met her gaze and held it.

"Have you decided yet?" the waitress asked, breaking the spell.

They both chose the grilled salmon. Jordan added a house salad and a bottle of California chardonnay. When the waitress left, Jordan turned back to Robin.

But Robin wasn't there.

Another person had taken her place. Yes, it was Robin's body, but the face wasn't that of the self-possessed woman he had just been talking to. He was now looking into the eyes of a girl shaking with terror.

"What's the matter?"

"John… he's here," her voice trembled. It was the voice he had first heard ten days ago, that first time in his office.

Jordan steadied her hand. "I'm here with you. Everything's fine, Robin."

She didn't hear him. She seemed to have gone into some sort of auto-hypnotic trance.

Jordan repositioned himself on his chair, but never once let go of Robin's hand. "Beverly, can you hear me?"

Still no response. Finally, she spoke. *"He's here. He's at another table, listening, listening to everything we're saying."*

Jordan looked around, half-expecting to see a new ominous face among his fellow diners. But the people were the same people who'd been there for the last fifteen minutes. He realized that Robin was at a restaurant, but it wasn't the Moustache Café. He had an impulse to jump up from his chair and run home. To the Beverly Casper file. *John must have been at the Hamburger Heaven that night.* He had seen Beverly and heard her and her friends talking. That's how he knew about Larry Keeton. Jordan had had this thought days ago, but he didn't know where to go with it. Now he did. The police must have questioned other patrons at the restaurant that evening. Maybe one of the names on the list would turn out to be a young man about twenty-five.

He focused again on Robin. Transformation. She took his hand, and touched it against her face.

"Do you know what just happened?" Jordan said.

"I just drifted out. Did I say something?"

He repeated to her what she'd said. "And I had this thought. If I go back to that Beverly Casper file—"

Robin's eyes grew wide.

"I think—" Jordan continued.

But she wasn't listening. Had she regressed again? So quickly?

She lifted a hand with shaking fingers and pointed to the TV monitor over the bar. Jordan turned around. Large words dominated the screen: REINCARNATION ANGLE IN MESSENGER KILLINGS?

It took Jordan all of three seconds to reach the elegant cherry wood counter. "Turn it up," he ordered the bartender. "Please, it's very important."

The news anchor was already into the story: "In addition to police questioning today of high school senior Chip Estes in relation to the Messenger slayings, we have learned of another, and, some would say, much more bizarre, angle the police are pursuing—that the answer to the Messenger slayings may be found in an abduction and murder that happened in this area over thirty years ago." Then the anchor picked up a field reporter who stood outside the West Hills station. The reporter told the anchor how he had gone that morning to Beverly Casper's high school; as he spoke, a blown-up photograph of Beverly was displayed. A few seconds later, and after a brief introduction, footage of the video of Robin's regression with the police started to air. One could see Jordan only from the back, and a pattern of dots in the middle of the screen made Robin impossible to identify. The video went on for only twenty seconds or so. Robin/Beverly was talking about how she was looking down at her own corpse. As the video clicked off, the reporter added: "In an eerie irony, we have learned that the hypnotized woman, an actress living in Westwood, is due to open in five days in the starring role of the very same musical in which Beverly Casper was to star at the time she disappeared."

They looked at each other, horrified. Jordan hurried back to their booth; the waitress was standing there with their wine. He reached into his pocket and threw down three twenties.

"Is something wrong?" the waitress asked.

Jordan didn't bother to answer. He grabbed Robin's hand.

"Where are we going?"

He tugged at her with commanding force. "To the Wadsworth. Now."

Tuesday, 6:15 P.M.

Deb White was trying what little was left of her imperious director's scant supply of patience. He was going to take her out for a quick dinner and then bring her back to the theater for a couple more hours of one-on-one rehearsal. Even at dinner he intended to review stagecraft and character motivation issues with her. She was playing Julie like a high school girl cheerleader. Walter was looking for a sophisticated approach. Julie's character was full of notions of romantic love, true; but her life in the fishing village had also made her clear-eyed and practical. Robin had been able to give him that complexity. He didn't know yet if he could get it from Deb. She had the raw talent. Did she have the skill? If she didn't, he would need every second until the opening to shape her performance, to get it to a place that wouldn't be an embarrassment to him or her. So time, he fretted to himself as he paced across the empty stage, was at a premium, too precious to waste. Fifteen minutes earlier she had gone to her dressing room for, in her words, "a presto change-o" and had yet to return. What the hell was keeping her, he wondered? All she had to do was throw on a pair of jeans and a sweater.

"Bloody hell, Deb! What are you doing in there?" he called

out as he approached the dressing room. "Redecorating?" The room, built to accommodate both star and entourage, was much more spacious than the little cubicle she had had when she was a mere understudy.

As he reached his destination, he noted with annoyance Robin Norris' name still stenciled on the door. He'd take care of that tomorrow first thing. Right now, he was seriously ticked at his new leading lady. He didn't have time to play games. He pushed the door open without bothering to knock.

There was a man in the room standing over Deb, his back to Walter. His glove-covered hands seemed to be pulling something. "I have to make you an angel again," the man said, his gentle voice belying the violence of his actions. "You understand, don't you?"

"Who the fuck are you?" Walter demanded.

The man pivoted, Deb White rotating with him. Her spine was pinned against the back of the chair, a leather belt wrapped impossibly tight around her neck. Her head flopped against her left shoulder. Her lifeless eyeballs bulged out of their sockets. Walter blinked twice. In the half-second it took to complete that reflexive act, he understood everything. All the pieces—Robin's past life, the Messenger murders—all snapped into place.

He started to laugh, a high-pitched laugh, bordering on hysteria. "You stupid fucking idiot! Robin isn't even in the play anymore. You've killed the wrong fucking girl!"

The man stared down at Deb and then back up at Walter. He reached across his body with his right hand. Walter didn't wait to see what he was reaching for. He turned toward the door and tried to run. But his legs had no spring. On his third stride, he felt a piercing pain between his shoulder blades and then a much more severe pain in his lungs. His legs, like soft lead weights now, buckled. His chin cracked on the hall floor...and he felt nothing...ever again.

Her name was on the door! As clear as day! On the door, he thought, as he ransacked through Deb's dressing room table. It took a few minutes, but he finally found what he was searching for, a list with the names and addresses of everyone on the cast and crew. He'd been around this town long enough to know that every show had one. At the top of the list, next to the name "Julie," he found the name and address he wanted.

His fury doubled by this case of mistaken identity—it wasn't his fault— he ran out of the room, a hissing, snapping sound spitting out of him as if bugs were flying into his mouth and dying there in one fierce, infernal zap.

Tuesday, 7:15 P.M.

T here's no answer." Robin held the car phone in her hand.

He willed himself to sound calm. "They've probably left already."

"They were going to work all night." Her voice was rising.

"Would they hear the phone if they were on stage?"

She paused. "Probably not."

"So that's where they are," Jordan added, with a lot more assurance than he felt. "Besides, we don't even know if the Messenger saw the news reports."

"Please, Jordan, hurry."

A horn blared at them as Jordan ran the red light at Lindbrook.

"Plus, how would he even know what theater to go to?"

"It would be easy. There have been ads in the paper for the last week with my name and the theater's name."

A solid wall of cars cascaded down Wilshire. Jordan forced his way into the traffic. "Maybe you'd better call Lemoski."

Robin was already dialing.

"Lieutentant Lemoski, please. It's an emergency."

Jordan bobbed and weaved through the heavy traffic, trying to gain a few precious seconds of time, at once overcome with a feeling of dread and wondering if he was absurdly over-reacting.

"They can't reach him."

"Leave a message that we're going to the Wadsworth Theater. He should meet as us there. Tell them it's absolutely urgent."

As Robin repeated his words into the phone, the Wadsworth, a large, imposing edifice on the edge of the Veteran's Hospital complex north of Wilshire Boulevard, came into view.

"We're almost there," Jordan said.

Robin nodded nervously as she bit the skin off her thumb, an idiosyncrasy that Jordan had not noticed before. By the time they reached their destination, after ten more minutes of aggressive driving, she had drawn blood.

A black and white, its rooftop hazard light sending off blue pulses toward the horizon, was waiting for them when they sped into the lot. There was only one other car present, a white Volvo.

"That's Walter's," Robin muttered.

A uniformed Chicano cop with a thick black moustache greeted them. "Are you Dr. Geller?"

"Yes."

"I'm Officer Perez. Lieutenant Lemoski got your message. He said to tell you he's on his way."

Even as they were talking, three more black and whites raced into the empty lot.

"I'm sorry," Perez said to Jordan and Robin, as the other officers rushed out of their cars, "but we can't let you go in until we've checked things out and secured the area."

Jordan nodded. He watched the cops unbuckle their gun holsters and enter the building.

Robin waited with Jordan for the cops to return. She was wrapped inside his arm, but they didn't speak. Ten minutes later, Lemoski, Romero, Davis, Swain and Jimmy Lee arrived in two unmarked cars.

Lemoski gave them a quick greeting, then headed straight into the theater, his junior officers trailing.

Inside, he intercepted Perez.

"There are two bodies, lieutenant," Perez said. "A woman who appears to be in her early twenties, no ID, and a man; he's got a ponytail, mid-fifties."

Lemoski nodded. "Have you checked out the rest of the building?"

"Yes, sir. There's no one else here."

"Let's just be safe, " Lemoski went on. "Call for more backup."

A minute later, Lemoski stepped outside, told Robin and Jordan what the Westwood cops had found, expressed his sympathy and returned to the theater. After he left, Robin started to shake. Jordan tightened his arm around her shoulder, but nothing he could do or say could smother the chill she felt in her heart.

"God, if I had stayed with the show…" Her mouth felt dry.

"So, then you'd have been murdered instead of Deb." It sounded harsh as he said it, but he didn't know what else to say.

"But what did Deb do to deserve this? And Walter?" She started to cry.

"They didn't do anything. And you didn't, either."

Robin pressed her face into his shoulder. Her could feel her legs shaking. She needed to get away from here and he needed, just as desperately, to get home and get into that file.

"Will you be okay for just one minute?" he asked her. She nodded an okay. He ran toward the building, catching Lemoski just as he was coming back out. "Can you have someone take Robin home? She has to get away from here."

"No problem. And don't worry. She's not going to be alone till we catch this animal." He called out for Jimmy Lee.

Lee, standing in the distance, started toward them. "If this doesn't prove the Casper connection to the Messenger," Lemoski said, "then I don't know what does. Ironically, Robin's safe now; she's probably never been safer."

"How's that?"

"Because the Messenger's sure he's eliminated the only eyewitness."

"But he killed the wrong woman."

"We know that, but he doesn't. I saw Robin's name on the dressing room door. Which means he saw it, too."

"I'm sure he did. Only by tomorrow morning the papers will be printing Deb White's name, not Robin Norris'. So what we've got is a pretty small window of safety. How was she killed?"

"The usual method. All the earmarks of the Messenger, except the angel bracelet. Probably because he got interrupted."

"And Walter?"

"Knife in the back."

Jordan cringed. "Listen, lieutenant, I've got to get home myself. There's something I must check out in that Casper file."

Lemoski, Jordan and Lee formed a delegation and walked over to Robin. The lieutenant explained that Jimmy Lee would drive her home and stay with her. Jordan promised to call her in half an hour.

By now, her teeth were chattering. She was clearly in shock. Jordan didn't want to leave her, but knew that he had to. He needed time alone, time to concentrate without worrying about her; without the police coming and going and asking him questions. He knew it sounded callous, but she was with the cops now, finally, absolutely safe. And he knew, as he told Robin, that as soon as he had finished checking the file at his apartment, he would rush right over to her. He wasn't sure that she heard him. Again, he assured her that everything would be fine; that she would be safe. She nodded robotically. He helped her into the police car and instructed Lee to wrap her in blankets as soon as he got her home.

On his way out of the parking lot, he couldn't help but wonder how John must be feeling now. How many people get to kill the same person twice?

Tuesday, 7:45 P.M.

J osh Bobley hadn't been in the theater dressing room more than five seconds when Lemoski charged him, shoving him hard against a concrete wall. "Do you see what you did? An innocent girl is dead because of you."

Bobley tried to squirm away, but his boss' grip was too strong. The lieutenant forced the young man's chin toward Deb White's corpse. "Proud of yourself?"

No one in the room—Romero and Davis, who had arrived at the scene a few minutes earlier, the two uniformed cops or the police photographer—moved a muscle.

Bobley gasped. "I don't know what you're talking about."

"The video tape you gave to the local news station. *That's* what I'm talking about."

"What video tape?" The words came out forced.

"You son-of-a-bitch. You were telling everyone at the bar how I was embarrassing the department."

Bobley grimaced. It was an effort to speak. Romero took a few steps closer. "Lieutenant, I think you're breaking his ribs."

"I should break his head." Lemoski pushed harder.

"I didn't do anything."

"Tell me the truth, Bobley." Lemoski's intensity was frightening. "Because God Himself won't be able to help you if you lie to me."

Bobley glared at him and then spoke, slowly enunciating each word. "I didn't give any tape to anyone."

"Lieutenant, let him go," Romero urged. "Sir... Please."

Lemoski released him. Bobley bent over and tried to suck in a breath.

Jimmy Lee strolled into the room. He pointed to Bobley. "What's going—"

"What are *you* doing here?" Lemoski barked. "I told you to take the girl home."

"Swain insisted on doing it. He kept telling me he could do more good there than here. He was really insistent. I didn't see any reason not to let him."

Perez, the mustached cop, entered the room. "Lieutenant, I found this in the hallway. It was in the middle of the trail of blood near the male victim. I don't know if it means anything." He held out his palm, which he had taken the standard precaution of covering with a surgical glove: a single contact lens with a bright green tint rested upon it.

Tuesday, 7:52 P.M.

Slumped against the back seat, Robin stared out of the window of the unmarked police car. The night landscape—cars, buildings, trees—rushed by in a dark purple blur. More than anything, she wanted not to think. But she couldn't stop herself. Walter was dead. Deb was dead. How was it possible? A week ago she and Walter had watched a TV news report about the latest Messenger murder. She had asked him to turn it off; she didn't want to listen to depressing news. It was awful, tragic, but had nothing to do with her. Now that talented, infuriating Englishman would be on the same news show tomorrow morning. The same pretty newsreader, the same respectful tone, the same recitation of heartbreaking particulars, everything will be the same; only the victims will be different. And how will viewers react when they see Walter's face—she wondered where they'd get a photo of him and hoped, she couldn't help smiling to herself, that it would be a flattering one or Walter would be pissed—and hear of the circumstances of his death? They'll tell themselves what a terrible shame it was, but they would also feel that it really had nothing to do with them. They'll get on with their day just as Robin had done.

Only her life will never be the same. Not now. Not after what happened tonight.

Swain broke into her reverie, his voice a low moan. "I did it."

"What did you say?" Robin asked, looking over the driver's seat. She had heard what he said, only the words made no sense.

Swain spun his head back toward Robin. His face was red, bloated. "I did it. I'm the one responsible for everything."

The strong stench of liquor on his breath made her turn away.

"Watch the road!" she screamed.

The car had veered over the double yellow line dividing the opposite lanes of traffic. Oncoming cars blasted them with their horns. Swain swerved back into his lane.

"Jesus, Jesus," he muttered. He lifted a silver flask from his jacket, brought it to his lips and took a pull.

Robin fought to keep calm. The man was sufficiently out of his mind; she didn't want to agitate him further. But what the hell was he talking about? How could he be responsible for anything? For everything? Maybe the stress of the job had pushed him over the edge. Cops cracked all the time, didn't they? She lifted her eyes and offered a silent prayer; there were only a few more blocks to her house.

"Please, just put the flask away. And drive slowly and carefully."

"Didn't you hear what I said?" Swain insisted, turning around again, his tone full of anger. "I murdered those two people."

Tuesday, 8:23 P.M.

I just walked in," he explained, picking up the phone on the third ring.

"Thank God you're there."

"What is it?"

"You've got to get here as soon as possible."

He put the Beverly Casper file down on the kitchen table. "What's wrong?"

"Swain drove me home. Not Jimmy Lee."

"So?"

"He's drunk."

"What?"

"From guilt and booze. He's the one who gave the tape to the news. He thought Lemoski was embarrassing the department. He wanted to expose him or something. Or maybe he was envious. I don't know. In the car, he kept calling himself a murderer."

"Where is he now?"

"In the living room."

"And where are you?"

"Bedroom."

"Okay, as soon as we hang up, call Lemoski." He gave her the lieutenant's number again. "Tell him you want him to send someone else over."

"Funny thing is," Robin mused, "I'm probably safer with Swain than with anybody. He keeps telling me that he'll protect me with his life. He seems to think I'm some sort of saint now, somebody sent from the Great Beyond to get the bad guy."

"It's ironic. For a while, I thought Swain could have been the killer," Jordan said, pulling the thick rubber band off the top manila folder. "He matched the profile I've been working on better than anybody, but at the theater tonight I realized that the Messenger only killed Deb White because he thought she was you, and Swain knows who you are. If he was the Messenger, he'd never have killed her."

"You thought he might be the killer, and I was in the car with him?"

"I was certain that you got into the car with Jimmy Lee. Listen, Robin, I need to look for something in the Beverly Casper file." Even as he was talking, he was already flipping through pages. "If it's there, it won't take long to find. Either way, I'll be at your place in twenty minutes, twenty-five tops."

"Can't you make it any sooner?"

"Call Lemoski, right now."

"He'll think I'm a prima donna."

"That's the last thing he would ever think. Call him."

"Jordan?"

"What?"

"I want to go home."

"You are home."

"To my mother's."

"But isn't she in Colorado?"

"I want to get away from this place."

"I'll take you to your mother's house, my house, anywhere you want. I promise."

"Please, Jordan, hurry."

Jordan hung up the phone and immediately resumed work on the file, turning pages quickly, until he found one headed "Hamburger Heaven." A Detective Thomas Peters, officer Fred Swain assisting, had filed the report.

There was a list of names, thirteen patrons, in addition to Beverly Casper's three friends, whom the police had been able to trace and who had been at Hamburger Heaven during the time Beverly was there. Five were women. Jordan skipped over them. There was a man named Canter, 56; one named Kelley, 43; another named Fineman, 41, and, in small handwritten letters at the bottom of the page, easy to miss if you weren't looking carefully, one more: Franklin Jonathan Cole, 23. Jordan's heart stopped. That was not a name he could forget. He quickly rechecked his original notes, the ones he made at the UCLA microfilm library, just to be absolutely sure. When he had been researching Beverly Casper, he'd come across Cole's name in the *L.A. Times*. Cole had been charged and convicted of murdering his girlfriend, a coed named Norma Thompson. The fact that her decomposed body had been found in a canyon several months after Beverly's disappearance led to speculation that the body might be Beverly's, but, of course, that didn't pan out. Cole's middle name and the nature of his crime had been what had caught Jordan's attention. He had even mentioned Cole to Swain, but Swain had said he had an alibi, and that furthermore he'd died in prison. Swain had been going to check on that last assertion, but, probably distracted by the current investigation, never did.

He looked further into the file. Swain's superior, Detective Peters, had questioned Cole twice. Cole claimed that he had simply left the restaurant after finishing his meal and immediately gone home, where, he said, he spent the evening watching a movie on television with his cousin, Earl Smith. Peters had questioned the cousin who, indeed, vouched for Cole's story. That was the alibi Swain had mentioned.

Jordan leaned back in his chair and blew out a breath. The name Smith couldn't be more common, but you don't run across many Earl's anymore. Earl Smith. Where had he heard that name before? It had been recently. This week. He was sure of it. Come on, you can remember the names of obscure diseases like most guys remember baseball stats. Where have you heard this name? Then, it dropped into his brain. He sat up in shock. He stumbled into his bedroom, to his dresser. He rifled through some scraps of paper till he found the one he wanted. It was the note April had handed him just a week earlier, at the party—"Give me a call. I don't bite, unless you want me to"—and under the words she had written down her various phone numbers, including the ranch in Santa Barbara. Now, he looked at the paper and punched in the numbers.

"Avery. It's Jordan Geller."

"Ah, Jordan. How good of you to call."

It truly pained him to intrude on this man's grief, but he had no choice.

"Elinor called me earlier today," Avery continued. "She's been calling every day since…. the accident. I was very shocked; she told me she had suspended you from the Institute."

"Yes."

"This is awful. Can I be of any assistance? Speak to her, maybe set things—"

"You can help me, actually. I need to ask you some questions."

"Certainly, if I can help"

"Your cousin Mike—"

"What does he have to do with you and Elinor?"

"It's complicated. Is Mike there?"

"No."

"Do you know where he is?"

"No."

"Good. Avery, I need to know something. Is Mike Fields your cousin's born name?"

Avery fell silent.

"Please," Jordan said. "It's important. Did Mike Fields change his name?"

"Yes."

"What was it before?"

"Franklin Cole."

Had the tragedy he was about to inflict not been so immense, he would have leaped up and pounded his fist in joy.

"Avery, do you know who Beverly Casper is?"

"That girl, they mentioned her on the news today, the one who disappeared in 1970."

"That's the one. Is her name familiar to you?"

"Well, like I said, it's been on the news."

"Avery, in 1970, you were questioned by the police as to the whereabouts of Franklin Jonathan Cole on the night Beverly Casper disappeared. Did you give him an alibi?'

The voice on the other end turned sharp. "How do you know this?"

"Because I have the police file on the Casper case. A police report shows that on the night of August 4, 1970, Cole was at a diner called Hamburger Heaven, the last known place at which Beverly Casper was seen. When she disappeared, the police questioned everyone they could locate who had been there. And after they questioned your cousin, they questioned you. You were his alibi. Is that correct?"

For a moment, Avery said nothing. Finally, when he spoke, the voice was very low. "Yes, Franklin is my cousin."

"Was your alibi true?'

"Of course. What an impertinent question."

"You must tell me the truth, Avery. Were you really with him at the time?"

"What are you talking about?" Conniston's voice exploded. "Elinor told me that you had become unhinged. As always, I can see now that she was right. And why do you have the police file?"

"April had it, too."

"April?"

"Yes, and Mike Fields saw her with it. He even told me. April must have read what I read, that a man named Earl Smith had provided the alibi for his cousin, Franklin Jonathan Cole. She was going to see you, I suspect to ask you about this."

"That's when she had the accident." Avery said into the phone. But he wasn't talking to Jordan. He was talking to himself.

There was a long pause. Jordan could hear him breathing.

Then, he spoke again, but there was no life in his voice.

"Franklin protected me from bullies when I was a kid… more than once. Everybody knew he had a temper, but he never turned it on me. He did on my schoolyard enemies, though. And I worshipped him for it. He asked me if I'd tell the police we were watching a movie. He said they were out to get him, to set him up. I never questioned him. He needed my help. I was glad to give it. I thought I owed him that." His voice became plaintive now. "What would you have done?"

"I'm not judging, Avery. I just need to know more about him. When did he change his name?"

"He was in prison."

"I know that," Jordan said.

"After he got out, he changed his name."

"Avery, who is Loni?'

"Loni?" The voice sounded old now, dazed.

"Was Loni Franklin Cole's mother?"

"No."

"Was Loni—"

"Loni was Franklin's sister."

"Sister? Where is she? I need to speak to her."

"Loni is dead."

"When did she die?"

"She was fifteen. Our families used to vacation at a lake out by Ojai. It was a hot, humid night. Oppressive. Funny that I should remember that, don't you think? There was a terrible accident. She drowned."

"Drowned? Were you there?"

"I was at the cabin. Not in the water. I was never a good swimmer. Not like Loni. We were all shocked. It was night. She would go swimming anytime. She was like that… I suppose it was foolish."

"Was anybody with her?"

"What?"

"Who was with her, Avery?"

"Franklin was. They often went together… No, it couldn't be."

There was another long pause, then, desperately: "They were very close. He was very protective of her. No, he was completely devastated. I saw him afterward. No, I can't believe—"

"Avery, tell me. What did Loni look like?"

"She was a beautiful girl. Long, blonde hair, bright smile. She was just starting to blossom when…" his voice trailed off.

Everything was becoming clear now. It only remained to know one more piece of information. "Avery, I know this will sound odd, but does your cousin have two different colored eyes?"

"What?" the voice was distant, far away now.

"His eyes—"

"Yes, he was always sensitive about that. He wears a contact lens to match them. Why do you ask?"

"Forgive me, Avery, but I've got to get off the phone."

"Tell me, Jordan. You said that Franklin knew that April had the file. Are you sure of that?"

"I'm sorry to tell you this. But yes, he knew."

"No, no. It can't be."

"I'm sorry, but I have to go."

As he was hanging up the phone, a favorite line of an old history professor reverberated in his head, "The mills of the gods grind slowly, but they grind exceedingly small."

Later, he wished that he had called Elinor immediately and told her to be in touch with Avery. He should have thought to do it. Only he didn't have time. Robin was waiting.

She entered the living room. Swain was on the couch, a copy of *People* magazine incongruously opened on his knees. She told him that she had decided to move out for a few days. The press would know soon enough she was the woman in the video; she didn't want to be around for that. "I'm going to go to my mother's," she said. "And Jordan will be over soon to take me."

"How soon will he be here?" the policeman said.

"I don't know. Fifteen minutes maybe."

Swain nodded. The redness on his cheeks was fading and his eyes weren't quite so bloodshot; he seemed to have sobered up a bit. "If that's what you want. But I'm coming as the escort. Lemoski will have my hide if I let you go anywhere without protection."

"Fine," she said. "Just follow us in your car." At this point, she was ready to say anything to pacify him. Lemoski had promised he'd be there in half-an-hour; let him deal with Swain.

She pointed to the kitchen. "Get a soda or some juice from the fridge if you want. I'm just going to go pack a few things."

She returned to her bedroom, pulled down her overnight bag, and then headed for the bathroom to pack her toiletries. In just a few minutes Jordan would be here. And in a little more than a day, her mother would be home. How odd. Ten days ago, she didn't know Jordan at all, and all she could say about her mother's love was that it was suffocating. *Good God, she almost laughed, what will I be thinking about them ten days from now.*

A terrible crash shattered her reflection. At first she thought it was an earthquake, but there was no shaking. The sound had come from the living room. The image of the giant vase by the dining room leapt to her mind. It must have fallen somehow. Maybe Swain had bumped into it or stumbled over it. Was he getting drunk all over again? She was already on her way to the sound when she heard another one, much more disturbing: a piercing cry of pain cut suddenly short. She called out as she ran, "Detective! Are you alright?"

He wasn't. He was stretched out on the floor, a large gash oozing red where once his throat had been. His gun was still in his holster.

Suddenly, the living room lights went out. She squinted into the darkness, her heart pounding in her chest like a hammer. Her eyes couldn't adjust.

All she could hear was a stinging noise, like insects flying into a bug zapper. The sound was coming closer. She could see a man's form. And then she heard a familiar voice.

Tuesday, 8:45 P.M.

Homicide," a female voice picked up.

"It's Dr. Jordan Geller," he said. "It's an emergency. Give me Lieutenant Lemoski." Never had he wanted to talk to somebody more.

"Hang on, please."

"Hurry."

He cursed the passing seconds. The connection cracked and then went dead. "Shit," he called out.

A red light loomed ahead; he glanced right and left then blew through it. He punched in Lemoski's number again, one eye on the road, one eye on his cell. He couldn't get a signal.

He'd call from Robin's house; it wouldn't be more than a couple of minutes.

Tuesday, 8:48 P.M.

H ello, my angel."

The terrible hissing, snapping sounds were becoming more rapid now. Rapid and closer.

"How did you get away?"

She could almost make him out. Older, fleshier. But unmistakably him. Lips twitching. And that sound.

"I'm glad I found you." Zeet! "This stupid cop tried to stop me. I hate cops. They try to stop everything. Things they don't understand." Zap!

Suddenly, a bright flashlight beam burned her eyes. She raised her arms in front her face. She tried to scream, but no sound came out. Only a whimper, a faint whimper. Then, he was on her. She tried to break away, but he was too strong. "You don't look the same." He buried his face in her neck, wrapping his hand around her hair. "You even smell different. But you can't fool me. I know my girls. But you, Bev, you were special. We really had something together, didn't we? Is that why you came back? Because you missed me? I understand. Nothing's changed. I'm here for you. Like I said I'd always be."

When she spoke, her voice was barely audible; just forming the words was an effort. But she had to talk, to find a way to stall. Jordan would be here any moment and the man seemed to have no gun. Two of them against one. Maybe they'd have a chance. "Whatever you think, I am not Beverly Casper. And I'm not going quietly." Again, she tried to break free of his arms, but couldn't. Like a slip rope, the harder she struggled, the tighter he held her.

"I screwed up once, Bev," he whispered, his lips pressed into her ear. "I don't know what I did wrong, but this time I'll get it right, and you'll go straight to heaven, straight to Loni." She heard the sound of a belt sliding through loops. "I promise."

The doorbell rang.

"Robin," she heard Jordan yelling from outside. Again she opened her mouth to call back, but hard as she tried a guttural whimper was all that emerged. He yanked her hands behind her, and fastened the belt around them. Before she knew what happened, he had wrapped her ankles together with duct tape. Another piece of tape closed her mouth.

Outside, she heard Jordan pounding at the door. Finally, it flew open. She could see him, outlined in the dark.

Then a flashlight in his face. "Stop right there, doc."

*

Jordan raised his hand to block the blinding brightness. He could make out two forms behind the light. Fields had one hand wound tight into Robin's hair; the other held a large Bowie knife against her throat.

His first instinct was to rush him, but he could slash Robin's throat before he took two steps. Even a gun, if he had one, wouldn't necessarily help now. Still, he needed a weapon.

"Hello, John," he began, his voice deceptively mild.

"You're too late, doc." Fields answered, lacing his sarcasm with laughter. He pushed the knife into Robin's neck. "Or you're just in time, depending on how you look at it."

"I've been looking for you, John. For a while. I have a message for you."

Fields laughed again, a throaty, confidant chuckle. "From who?

428

Your cop pal here?" He gestured to Swain's inert body. "Or maybe good old Ave."

"It's from your sister, John."

Field's eyes narrowed. "Bullshit. My sister's dead."

"No. She's not. Loni's alive. I talk to her every day. She's come back just like Beverly."

For a second, the knife shifted from Robin's throat, and pointed to Jordan. "You're a fucking liar."

"You saw today on television how I brought Beverly back. I brought your sister back, too. Loni's one of my patients." He had to start making educated guesses now to establish credibility. He'd better guess right. "She told me how you used to come to her bed at night, and touch her. Even when she was only a little girl."

"My sister was an angel. Nothing like that ever happened."

"Who's lying now, John?" He had to goad Fields, shatter his defenses, do exactly the opposite of what he'd been trained to do—disturb and destroy, rather than heal. "You slept with her, John. You fucked your own sister. Not even an animal does that. Loni finally realized that you were less than an animal."

"I told you to shut the fuck—"

The man was sick; manipulate the sickness, turn it back on him.

"And then when Loni told you she didn't want you to come to her anymore, you yelled at her. She even told me what you said: 'You fucking cunt. You've always been a cunt.' And then you killed her. You held her head underwater until she couldn't breath."

"Lies! Lies!"

His eyes had adjusted enough now to see the raw terror etched in Robin's face. "Loni told me all about the picnic. How it was so hot, how there were lots of insects flying around. I can hear those flies and mosquitoes right now. They're in your mouth, John! Swarms of them. Buzzing around. Spreading germs. You hear them, don't you, John? Exploding and putrefying between your teeth."

"I saved her!" Fields spit out.

Jordan could feel his enemy's rage building. *Push harder. Enrage him more. Until he loses all control.*

"Save her from what, John? From other boys?"

"Yes. Yes. From ugly boys. Dirty boys. From everyone."

"No, John. You saved her from *you*. Don't you see that? You drowned her in that lake so she'd never have to be fucked by *you* again, *you, John!* Because you know you're human vomit, John. Food for flies and mosquitoes. That's what Loni believes. You know why? Because I tell her every day."

Fields shoved Robin to the floor, and rushed forward, his knife raised. Jordan braced himself. Fields was on him in an instant, the knife thrusting down toward his chest. As much on instinct as anything, Jordan grabbed for Fields' wrist, deflecting the path of the blade away from his heart. But the force of the thrust was too strong. The serrated edge cut across Jordan's shoulder. He felt a sharp pain and fell back, crashing into the china cabinet. Fields fell with him, his knife hand crashing through the glass, the shards tearing at his flesh. Still, he raised the knife again, driving it toward Jordan a second time.

This can't be happening! Hands cinched by the belt behind her back, legs duct-taped together, Robin watched helplessly as Jordan struggled against his attacker. The older man seemed so much stronger than Jordan. How much longer would it be before he was overcome? If only she could get her hands free, she could get to Swain's gun. She twisted her wrists, the belt loosened, but not enough. She had to relax, she told herself. Brute force wouldn't work. Jordan had given her breathing techniques. *Use them to relax yourself free!* She closed her eyes. *Deep breath in. Slow breath out.* She imagined her wrists going limp as if they were loose, boneless. But she couldn't do it. All she could feel was terror, rank terror in every pore of her body. *He's going to murder Jordan and then me!*

Fields, relentless, came at Jordan again. Kicking out his right foot, Jordan shot his heel into his aggressor's shin, buckling Fields' leg. As the older man staggered, Jordan seized the advantage and drove his knee into Fields' jaw, sending him crashing into the opposite wall. The knife fell from his hand. But Fields seemed unconcerned and unhurt, as if he relished the combat. Now he came back at Jordan with renewed fury. A decade of swimming had strengthened the younger man, but not enough. Fields wrapped his thick hands around Jordan's throat, forcing his thumbs into the soft fleshy part, squeezing the air out of his lungs. Reaching out with his right hand, Jordan tried to push Fields' chin back, but he couldn't get the leverage he needed. It was the final, futile gesture of a dying man. With the confidence of a practiced killer, Fields snapped Jordan's head forward and then back hard against the corner of the shattered china cabinet. The impact of flesh and mahogany splintered the air with a sharp cracking sound. Jordan slumped unconscious, propped up against the cabinet door, defenseless. In one fluid motion, Fields recovered his fallen knife, and raised it high over the psychiatrist's chest.

"Get away from him, or I'll shoot," Robin shouted.

Fields stopped and turned, his cheeks ruddy, his breathing fast.

"I'll do it."

He looked at her, amused. "You used to be such a nice girl, Bev."

She remembered it all now. Everything. Beverly's short life of unfulfilled promise; that pathetic hour of terror; the agonizing moments by the pit pleading for her life; Alice Casper's three decades of torment; Bill Casper's death from a broken heart, and now Jordan lying unconscious across the room.

"Drop the knife."

She held the gun in both hands, and pointed it straight at him.

"Drop it." She cocked the trigger. The knife fell to the floor.

"You don't think I'd hurt you, do you?" His voice was soft, beseeching. "I want to protect you. From men like him." Fields pointed to Jordan.

"Do you have any last messages you want me to deliver, John?"

He stared at her, mystified.

"Your favorite question. Last chance."

"It's useless, Bev. You can't kill me. You know that. I'll come back. Just like you did. Forever."

He held her with his eyes, mesmerizing her like a wolf might freeze a fawn. For a second, she lost herself in his darkness. Then, with a hellish growl, he rushed her. Her hands shaking, she squeezed the trigger. The first bullet penetrated his throat. He grabbed at his neck. Blood gurgled up from his mouth. He staggered forward. She fired again. Straight into his chest. All the bullets that Swain had in his .38 revolver, save one. He fell to his knees, his eyes opened wide in disbelief. She stood over him.

"You're not coming back, John. Ever." She held the gun six inches from his head, then pulled hard. An instant later, he fell forward, his head shattering the glass coffee table.

She hurried over to Jordan; he was still unconscious. Without letting him go, she grabbed the phone and summoned help. Then, she cradled him in her arms and, kissing his wounds, prayed with her whole being that he was still alive.

That was how Lemoski found her when he arrived ten minutes later.

Thursday

Thursday, 10:15 A.M.

We were really afraid we might lose you," Romero said with genuine relief. Lemoski stood alongside her; and there was a third visitor, a young woman of about fifteen.

Jordan was sitting up in his hospital bed, Robin alongside him. Nasty purple bruises mapped his right cheek. Heavy white bandages circled his forehead.

Lemoski examined the invalid. "I don't know, I've seen worse."

Jordan managed a smile.

"So what do the doctors tell you?" the lieutenant continued.

"There's no internal bleeding. Assuming there are no changes, I'll be out in a couple of days."

Lemoski nodded, then turned to the young woman. "My daughter Kathy. She heard me talking about you so much at home, she insisted on coming."

Jordan took the girl's extended hand and held it firmly in his. "I'm so sorry about your friend Judy," he said.

"Thank you," the young woman answered, blinking quickly. "How are you feeling?"

"My head hurts, but I'll be okay. Thanks."

Then Lemoski introduced her to Robin. "Our two civilian heroes," he added when he finished. "And in light of how it turned out, I suppose we should be thankful that we didn't get there sooner."

Romero rolled her eyes. She knew what was coming.

Her disapproval didn't escape her boss' notice. "Romero, here, has problems with the death penalty."

"No. I'm ambivalent. That's all. It's a complex question."

"If ever a guy deserved the death sentence it was Franklin Jonathan Cole, Mike Fields, whatever you want to call him." Lemoski countered. "If we take him alive, he gets a trial and twenty years on death row and cable TV before the state gets around to finishing him off. That's if we get a death penalty conviction and if some judge doesn't overturn it. He looked at Robin. "I don't know who else is going to tell you this, but thank you. Everybody in this damn state should thank you."

"What do you say when somebody thanks you for killing someone?"

"Try 'you're welcome,'" Lemoski said. "Don't get sappy about this. The world's a better place without that monster in it."

Robin, buoyed by the lieutenant's bracing moral clarity, gratefully nodded an acknowledgement.

"Lieutenant," Jordan asked, "did you find anything at Fields' house?"

"Anything? Everything. He kept a murder diary. Details of every crime he committed. Worse; there was also a collection of jewelry he'd taken from the girls he killed, his trophies. He kept them in little velvet bags." Robin and Kathy shuddered. "We also hit pay dirt. A hand-drawn map of a small section of Topanga Canyon. We went out there yesterday morning; we were able to find where he buried Beverly Casper."

"Oh my God!" Robin cried out.

Romero nodded. "I was with Alice Casper last night. She's going to bury Beverly in Forrest Lawn, next to her husband."

"When?" Jordan asked, his hand on Robin's.

Romero withdrew a small notebook from her pocket. "Sunday,

II A.M." She turned to Robin. "Mrs. Casper asked me if I was going to see you. When I said probably, she specifically told me to ask you to come to the funeral."

"Of course, I'll be there," Robin said, then gave a nervous laugh. "I mean how often do you get to go to your own funeral while you're still alive?"

"What about Fields?" Jordan asked Lemoski. "How many people did he murder altogether?"

"We're just not sure, I don't know if we ever will be. It turns out he murdered the girlfriend—"

"Norma Thompson. I read about her when I first did research into Beverly."

"Yeah. Well, it turns out he murdered her, according to his own diary, a few weeks before Beverly."

"Even though her body was found months after Beverly's disappearance," Jordan presumed.

"Exactly."

"Unfortunately, his defense lawyer succeeded in convincing the jury that it was a rough sex game between the two of them that accidentally went too far. And he walked in seven years."

Avery talked and Cole walked, Jordan thought with bitterness. Avery could have stopped all the murders, save those of Loni, Norma Thompson and Beverly Casper had he told the truth. By not doing so, he had unleashed a Greek tragedy of unforeseen consequences. Had he told the truth to Swain thirty years ago, not only would Swain have been alive today, but his own daughter April. Somehow, the wealthy TV producer would have to live with this dreadful knowledge. Jordan wondered how.

"Anyway," Lemoski was saying, "a few years after he got out of prison, he changed his name; some dumb judge allowed that, too. Then he took off for the Philippines; he had been stationed there before he got booted out of the Marines. You were right about that. So he went back to the Philippines, found a bride there, and eventually brought her back to the States. We tracked her down in Phoenix. She was with him twenty-one years. For the first eighteen or so, she was Miss Subservient, which suited Fields fine."

"Yeah, that fits." Jordan interjected. "As long he could dominate her as he had his sister, he had no urge to kill."

"But then America began to make an impact." Lemoski continued. "She didn't want to be his slave any more, so she took off."

"Amazing he didn't kill her," Robin said.

"He was probably afraid. With one manslaughter conviction already on the record, he didn't want to risk a murder rap. Nope, from now on he was only going to kill strangers. Anyway, the wife left him about a year ago and as far as we can figure, the Messenger killings started eight or nine months later."

"So there were at least nine victims," Romero said.

"You should probably add April Conniston to the list," Lemoski said. "Our men rechecked the site. We'll never be able to prove it, and there's no need to, but he forced her off the road."

Jordan groaned. Lemoski had been poised to arrest him the day he had come into the station with April. But because Judy Cinch's body was discovered at just that time, Jordan was let off the hook, and drafted by Lemoski into the case. That left April to take the Casper file home. If she hadn't, Fields would never have seen her with it, and she'd still be alive.

"There's one more," Jordan added, in a low, dull voice. "The first of all the murders. His sister, Loni."

"He told you that?" Lemoski asked.

"No, but he did it. From what I can surmise, he was sexually abusing Loni from the time she was a very young girl, preadolescent. How and why he became fixated on her would only be speculation. It seems he felt a compulsion to protect her from any other males beside himself. All other influences except his were corrupting. "

Lemoski just shook his head. He'd long ago realized that there was no limit to human evil.

Jordan continued: "At some point, as she got older and knew herself better, she probably wanted him to leave her alone. She might have threatened to tell their parents what he'd been doing. Maybe he saw her talking to another boy and flipped out. I don't know. As far as anybody knows, she died in a swimming accident on a family vacation when she was fifteen, but he drowned her. Of that, I'm sure."

"And those awful sounds he made like bugs flying into a zapper. Where did that come from?" Robin asked.

"I would guess that those were the sounds he associated with Loni's murder. They went for a swim at night, something apparently they did frequently, only this time, he ended her life. It was midsummer, hot, humid, plenty of insects buzzing around, flying into those bug zappers. Somehow he internalized those sounds. Maybe they personified his real self-image. Whenever he went into killing mode, they came back as if he were reliving that first murder."

"A hot, humid summer night?" Romero mused. "How do you know all this?"

"Some of it I got from Avery Conniston. Some of it I pieced together."

"How could the family not know what was going on between them?" Robin asked.

"Maybe they did know, but couldn't face it and swept it under the rug," Jordan answered. "Remember, we're talking about the mid-Sixties. You know what else Avery told me? Loni had long blonde hair and a big smile."

They all looked at him, absorbing the last. Robin remembered the first time she had seen the victim's photographs on television, thinking they could all be sisters.

"And what about Chip Estes?" Kathy Lemoski asked him.

Jordan looked at the girl, the earnest face, the eyes that he knew could dissolve in tears with one wrong word. "Your dad tells me Chip has a crush on you."

Kathy Lemoski blushed.

"Let me tell you a story about a victim, another victim of the Messenger, one he couldn't be indicted for even if he was still alive. Thirty-two years ago, when Franklin Cole murdered Beverly Casper, he made an anonymous call to the police, and told them that the killer was a high school classmate of Beverly's. The boy's name was Larry Keeton. Larry liked Beverly and had asked her out on a date. The lieutenant in charge of the case questioned Keeton, and the story got into the papers. Beverly's body was never found, and some of the other kids at their high school thought, because of what was reported in the papers, that Keeton was guilty. They made his life miserable. Six months later, Larry Keeton, whose only crime was that he had liked Beverly Casper, took his dad's gun and shot himself. And when they asked the police lieutenant if Keeton was a suspect, he wouldn't say yes or no, just that the Casper case remained open." Jordan looked at Lemoski. "May I suggest a kind act for you to do?"

"I gotta feeling I'm not gonna like this."

"Make a party with Kathy at your house, the purpose of which will be to honor Judy Cinch's memory and publicly apologize to Chip Estes."

"Whoa," Lemoski broke in. "Part of my job is following every plausible lead. We had good reason to ask the boy some questions."

"Let me ask you a question, lieutenant. If a man is driving a car at a normal speed, and a little child runs right in front of it, out of nowhere, is the driver held responsible?"

"If he exercised caution, probably not."

"He's not responsible, but if he's a decent person, he's sorry, right? Everybody knows you headed the Messenger investigation. If you two throw the party, it'll do a lot for Chip."

Kathy Lemoski ran over and impulsively hugged her father. Looking up at him, she pleaded, "Will you do it, daddy?"

The lieutenant peered over at Jordan for a brief second, then nodded his acquiescence. "We'd better get going, before this visit becomes too expensive."

Jordan called Lemoski to his side. "I just want to thank you, lieutenant, for taking me seriously. I can only imagine the doubts you must have had."

Lemoski threw Romero a sidelong glance. "Doubts? Detective, did we ever doubt this man, even for a minute?"

Romero laughed. "I think Bobley's still checking into his alibi."

Lemoski rested his hand on Jordan's shoulder.

"Doctor, knowing you has been an education for me. Don't be a stranger."

Thursday, 10:47 P.M.

Fifty-four years. He punched in the numbers on his desktop calculator, 54 × 365. 18,710. He had lived 18,710 days, thirteen more when you counted leap years. Based on his family history, his healthy lifestyle and modern medicine, he could probably figure on living another thirty years. That would be 10,957 more days. And every one of them would be torture, self-inflicted torture.

April was dead; nothing could change that. Franklin, as the papers were now calling him, was dead, too. Only it was too late, much too late.

He thought back, not at length or with much focus—his thoughts were all jumbling together now—to when Franklin had come to him all those years ago. An alibi; Franklin needed an alibi. Some girl had disappeared in a canyon, a girl who'd been at a restaurant where Franklin had been eating. Of course he had nothing to do with it, but how could he prove that? The cops would come down hard on him; he'd had his run-ins with the law, juvenile offenses—a car theft, a few fights. So, Avery had become his alibi. A movie on TV he'd watched alone became a movie he'd seen with Franklin.

The police hadn't even pushed him hard. Fifteen minutes of

questioning and they were gone. What he had feared would be a hard lie to tell had been an easy one. Or so it seemed then. Not now. The day he told that lie was the day he had sealed April's fate.

A person makes choices, he thought, based on the information in front of his eyes. He had made a choice to help his cousin. He owed him. Franklin had protected him from those bastards at school. But, as a consequence of that choice, the universe had shifted.

Without the alibi he'd provided, the police might have pressed Franklin harder, they might have exposed the evil he had done, and all these people, all those innocent young women, would have been saved, not just April, but all of them.

The newspaper coverage had been horrific. It had been ten years since his last hit show, but suddenly it was as if he was still king of the airwaves. He read again the opening sentence of the *L.A. Times* story: "Messenger Killer Mike Fields, a.k.a. Franklin Jonathan Cole, first cousin of TV megaproducer Avery Conniston…"

The one thing that astonished him was this girl they were all talking about, Robin Norris; how Jordan had taken her back into a previous life as Beverly Casper. He thought of how Jordan had said during the condolence call at his house that April was hearing what he was saying, that April's spirit was still alive, that they'd meet again. Elinor had ridiculed her protege, but it seemed to him now that it was she, not the young doctor, who was wrong.

So there must be something to it, that this life is not all there is to our existence. Only it was too late to save April.

He called out her name and, as people always do in such circumstances, he glanced upward. "I'm sorry, my baby. I'm so, so sorry." Could she hear him now?

He needed to know.

He couldn't wait 10,957 days.

He needed to know. Now.

Without hesitation, he lifted the gun in front of him and stuck the barrel in his mouth.

Saturday

Saturday, 2:30 P.M.

He was behind his desk going through files, organizing some, discarding others, when Elinor walked through the half-open door.

"Pat told me you were here," she said, and came over to look at the bandage still on his forehead. "I was concerned. Did they tell you at the hospital that I had called?"

"Yes," he answered. "Thank you."

"I was afraid to come visit. I didn't want in any way to upset you."

"I would have been happy to see you," Jordan said.

For the first time since walking into the room, she smiled. "Good. It's good to hear that. Jordan, may I sit down?"

"Of course."

She arranged herself on the chair. "I've been thinking a lot these past days. It's been horrible, truly horrible."

Jordan knew what she was feeling. On his desk lay the *L.A. Times*, the bottom half of the front page dominated by a large photo and headline: "Hollywood Titan Suicide: Avery Conniston, 54, Shoots Self."

"You won't believe it," Elinor continued. "Avery's lawyer called me this morning to tell me, as he put it, of a 'silver lining' in all this tragedy."

"Silver lining?" Jordan repeated, his voice incredulous.

"It seems Avery's left Dittmyer the overwhelming bulk of his fortune. Originally, the lawyer explained, his estate was to be divided between us and April. But there was a clause that if April predeceased him, her share reverted to Dittmyer. It's over 20 million dollars." Suddenly, Elinor's eyes filled with tears, and her body started to shake.

"I was thinking, Jordan, that some good could come of this," she said, dabbing her eyes with a handkerchief. "What if we established, here at Dittmyer, a center to study the psychology of evil and how to transform it? Maybe we could find a way to really understand what makes a man like Mike Fields act as he did. I want to start the center here, and name it for Avery and April, the victims of this evil man."

"Oh, Avery was a victim, but not a totally innocent one. April was."

Elinor shrugged off his comment. "Jordan, I want you to work with me on this project. Maybe you even could head it. I've suffered too many losses. I want you back here with me."

He looked down at her, surprised by the offer, surprised even more by the intensity of her emotions. Two weeks ago, he would have considered the opportunity to work in conjunction with Elinor on such a project the greatest professional opportunity he might ever have. Only now was not two weeks ago.

"Does your offer come with any strings?" he asked, his voice cautious.

"It has to be scientific, Jordan. That's all I'm asking. The study of the mind must be; it must remain a science."

"Which means what exactly?"

She looked up at him, her eyes narrowing. "You know what it means. I want the Jordan Geller I know—the clear-thinking professional who introduced me at the fundraiser. I don't want all of your recent baggage, and certainly not Geoffrey Bolton's baggage."

"That baggage, Elinor, just solved the Messenger case."

"If I believed that, Jordan, I would retire. Immediately. Today.

This afternoon. There's no basis for such a belief. Information and memories reside in a brain. How could a person die, and the information inside the person's brain suddenly reappear in the mind of someone born three or twenty or two hundred years later? It makes no sense. You must see that."

Despite all that happened in the past two weeks, he still had great affection for this woman. The debt he owed to her, both professionally and personally, could never fully be repaid. But more than anything, he owed her the truth about himself, especially now. "Let's just say I'm an empiricist, Elinor. What works, works. I'll worry about the theoretical justification later."

"What do you mean 'what works'? Let's say you're right and everybody is reincarnated."

"I never said that. I don't know what the rules are. I don't know who comes back or why or when."

"Fine. That's a start anyway. You still have retained some of your skepticism, I see. But let's say, for the sake of argument, that everybody is the reincarnation of a past existence. What does it matter, anyway? What good would it do?"

"That's a good question, Elinor. I've given it a lot of thought the last few days and I think I have an answer."

His mentor stared back at him, her expression dubious.

"Can you imagine if nineteenth-century white Southerners thought they'd be coming back next time as black slaves? It would have transformed how they'd treated their slaves. They might even have abolished slavery on their own, without a Civil War. Or if Nazis had thought they'd come back as Jews? There'd never have been a Holocaust."

"Jordan, you can't be serious. This is the concussion talking."

"Maybe, but I'm not prepared to give it up just yet. Not before I do a lot more investigating."

Fischer shook her head. "Then I guess I'll just have to remain a rationalist relic."

Jordan remembered what Bolton had said about her: *Elinor doesn't like deviations. We came up against a wall. I saw a door and walked through. Elinor remained outside.* Then again, he didn't want

Bolton as his mentor either. What was that line of Abraham Maslow's he had once read? "When the only tool you have is a hammer, every problem presents itself as a nail." Reincarnation, he felt, was a tool, maybe an important one, but nonetheless one tool among many, and not always the right one. There would be times when he would need Elinor's psychological insights just like he would need Freud's and Jung's. And there were times New Age might even teach him something. And there would be other times he would need the wisdom of the Bible.

"Elinor," he answered. "You must know that everything I said at the dinner is true. You've been my greatest teacher, but I need to find my own way now. I need to think for myself."

She squinted her eyes, as if to see him better. Her face reflected both pride and defeat. "That night at Avery's, that dinner party, everything seemed so perfect." She sighed, turned and walked out.

Saturday, 3:30 P.M.

Adrian Norris had not expected to see her daughter waiting for her at the airport arrival gate. She had not expected that Robin would run up to her, arms outstretched, mouth upturned in a welcoming smile, and embrace her with a fervor that she had not shown since she was small child. She had not expected that her daughter would cry when she closed arms around her. She had not expected to cry herself, but she did. They were warm, sweet tears and she was not ashamed of them. She didn't yet know why her daughter was so excited to see her. All she knew was that something had happened, something important and life changing. She knew this instinctually and she wasn't afraid. She just enjoyed the moment and the feeling of profound peace that was filling up her soul, the peace a mother feels when her child is safe in her arms after a prolonged absence. The yoga instructors often described inner peace as "a light within," but only now, in her daughter's embrace, did she get a partial glimpse of what they meant.

"I love you, mom," Robin finally said, holding her mother's face in both her hands, tears streaming down her cheeks.

Adrian Norris thought they were the most beautiful words she had ever heard.

Sunday

Sunday, 11:24 A.M.

I n the late fall of 1964, a salesman in a seersucker suit, representing Forest Lawn Cemetery, came to Bill Casper's door. Thanks to all the movie stars interred there, Forest Lawn had acquired a national reputation. "People like the neighbors and the neighborhood," the salesman said, the mordant line lightening an otherwise very heavy topic. Casper told the salesman that he was interested, but needed some time to think it over. A week later, he bought a family plot.

He certainly didn't buy it because he had any premonition of death. He was forty-three, Alice thirty-eight, and his two children not even teenagers. But Bill Casper was a man who liked to plan ahead. He knew that when you put things off, you pay for them later. Land values were rising all around him. Burial plots would rise, too.

Seven years later, a few weeks after his fiftieth birthday, Bill Casper took up his final residence at Forest Lawn. Ensconced six feet into the side of a sloping hill with a view of the Ventura Freeway, Warner Brothers Studio, and the smoggy silhouette of the San Gabriel Mountains, he died, according to his death certificate, of a massive heart attack. But everyone who knew him knew the real cause—grief, three years of unending and inconsolable grief. It literally killed

Bill Casper that his daughter, the light of his life, disappeared one night and never returned. He was, by nature, a forgiving man, not especially religious, but a believer in the teachings of Christ. There was one person, however, he could never forgive, the person he held, above all others, responsible for his daughter's death—himself. He knew about her little subterfuge, where she was really going that night after rehearsal. He had been a co-conspirator. He thought he was being kind, granting her one of those little favors that were a father's privilege, but, in his mind ever after, he had never been more cruel, or more irresponsible. He could have stopped her, made her come home, but he didn't. He failed as a parent, failed fatally. That her body could not be found haunted him. He had a place for her, but nothing to put in that place.

It was here, at the edge of the broken man's grave, that two dozen or so mourners gathered to bury the recently recovered remains of Bill Casper's daughter. Included in the group was Peter Casper, who hadn't spoken to his mother in ten years, but who now stood with his arm around her as they listened to the minister recite the Twenty-third Psalm. Also present was the team of detectives led by Lieutenant Lemoski—Romero, Davis, Bobley and Jimmy Lee. This was their second funeral in two days. Yesterday they had buried Fred Swain with full police honors.

After the minister finished, Robin released her hand from Jordan's. Then she took a step forward and began to sing the closing song from *Carousel*:

> *When you walk through a storm, hold your head up high*
> *And don't be afraid of the dark.*
> *At the end of the storm is a golden sky*
> *And the sweet silver song of a lark.*
> *Walk on through the wind*
> *Walk on through the rain*
> *Though your dreams be tossed and blown.*
> *Walk on, walk on with hope in your heart*
> *And you'll never walk alone, you'll never walk alone.*

To everyone in attendance but one, the poignancy of these lyrics was heartbreaking. To Alice Casper, they were heart healing. As she listened to Robin's voice, clear and strong as Jordan had heard it that day in the theater, she felt the dry ice that had encased her soul for so long melt away. In her mind's eye, she saw her husband and her daughter, side by side, watching her and Peter and smiling. Some of the other attendees looked at her with compassion from tearing eyes. But Alice Casper hardly noticed. She continued to smile. Smiling at her Beverly. *Welcome home, my darling, she whispered to herself. Welcome home.*

*

Jordan swallowed hard to choke back his tears. He didn't want to cry; if he started he wouldn't stop. April and Avery, Deb White, Walter Amicke, Fred Swain, people he knew, some well, all dead, and he was the common denominator between them. He had brought them all together into a circle of death. He never meant to, but it happened. Had it somehow been predestined? Was there a purpose? A grand design? Had he prevented more murders, as he so wanted to believe, more loss of innocent life? Would a high school junior singing in a school musical somewhere in Los Angeles now live because of what he had done? Or was all that occurred over the last two weeks just a wild collision of stellar dust, a brief, bizarre episode captured in a few newspaper headlines that would soon be buried in a university research library?

And if there was ever a person condemned to walk alone, wasn't it Beverly Casper? She had been murdered, ironically, because she was so full of life. Her blonde hair and bright smile had summoned her executioner. Then he remembered a fragment from Robin's second regression, the one she did for Lemoski. Didn't Beverly say she heard a voice singing as her soul left her body? She had strained to hear, but she couldn't make out the melody. Could she have been listening to this moment, to Robin singing at her long-delayed funeral? It was possible, wasn't it? After death there is no time. No past. No future. A chill of epiphany ran down his spine. Maybe the song is right. We do never walk alone. Maybe God is always there, through the wind, the storms, even death. Perhaps the end is not the end. Perhaps every end is also a beginning.

Two Years Later

Excerpts from a *Los Angeles Times* investigative report as it appeared in the Sunday *L.A. Times Magazine*:

Two years ago, this city was stunned by a TV *news report that the* LAPD *had used information provided by a so called "past-life regression" to pursue the notorious Messenger killer. More startling still was the contention from reliable police sources that this information may have actually been useful in narrowing the suspect list. Most surprising of all is that the killer died at the hands of the woman who had presumably lived and died more than three decades before as one of his early victims.*

Even for Los Angeles, a Mecca for alternative views of life and death, this case pushed the proverbial envelope. Many questions have been raised by it. But one question towers over all. Is there such a thing as reincarnation? Depending on who you talk to the answer is obvious. For the skeptics this case is just the latest New Age fad and likely another hoax; for the believers it's one more proof of what they've always believed—there is life after life.

To reexamine this case and confront the question of reincarnation with fresh eyes, the L.A. Times *dispatched a team of reporters to track the lives of the two principal players: one dead, Beverly Casper, one alive, Robin Norris...*

The most tantalizing examples of reincarnation, like the famous Bridey Murphy and Oscan cases in the '50s, have faltered when investigators uncovered a link between the subject and the person whose life they once claim to have led...

"See there is no mystery," skeptics contend. Science has the answer: the mind unconsciously retains information that the conscious mind has no recollection of until it's shocked, for whatever reason, back into consciousness. It may be remarkable that people can remember a page from a book glanced at years ago, but, for skeptics this makes far more sense than does reincarnation...

But is the Beverly Casper case something new, something the breakthrough enthusiasts have been waiting for? With no agenda, pro reincarnation or con, here's what we found...

In June of 1983, Robin Norris and her parents (her father is now deceased) visited her aunt and uncle in Los Angeles. The aunt, Corrine Richards, and her husband, Robert, were friends with a man named Fred Keeton. One evening, during the Norris' visit, the Richards invited their friend to dinner. At that dinner, Mr. Keeton talked about his son, Larry, who had tragically taken his own life almost a decade earlier. Larry Keeton had been depressed for months before his suicide. His schoolmates at Madison High in Woodland Hills had blamed him for the unsolved disappearance and presumed death of an effervescent, talented young woman, Beverly Casper. An anonymous phone call had thrown suspicion on Larry and he couldn't shake that suspicion. Students left sick jokes and threatening notes in his locker and made phone calls to the house. Unable to take the stress, perhaps blaming himself in some unknown way for Beverly's death, the teen took his father's shotgun out of a basement cabinet and blew his brains out.

Fred Keeton blamed the police for the death of his son. Based on the anonymous phone call, they had made his son their prime suspect. Though they never charged him, they also never did anything to clear his name. That's how police investigations work. The Beverly Casper case became an obsession with Mr. Keeton. According to Corrine Richards, he would talk about it often. It was no surprise that he talked about it the night the Richards had him over to their house for dinner. Mr. Keeton had a theory about every aspect of the murder. He shared his theories with the fascinated and horrified Norris couple—and their five-year-old daughter, Robin, who was at the table.

Adrian Norris remembers the visit, but didn't, at first, remember the dinner with Fred Keeton. Her memory seemed somewhat refreshed when she was reminded of some of the details of the conversation, details provided during our interview with her and her sister, Corrine Richards. Even if it did take place, Adrian Norris insisted, she would have never let Robin listen to such a conversation. Nevertheless, so vivid are Ms. Richards' memories that she recalls that little Robin experienced a terrible nightmare when she went to bed that night. She woke up screaming that a man was trying to strangle her with his belt....

Robin Norris claims to have no memory of this nightmare. She also claims to have virtually no memory of the visit to Los Angeles. As she points out, she was only five years old. This is why, she told us, she didn't make this information known to the psychiatrist, Jordan Geller, who hypnotized her and guided her through her past-life regressions. When asked if she still, in light of this information, believed her reincarnation was genuine, Ms. Norris would not give a direct answer. She did say she was happy that the Messenger would not be taking any more lives and that she wanted to get on with hers... Ms. Norris has resumed her career as an actress. She is currently starring in the dinner theater production of The Fantastiks *in La Mirada. Asked if she ever gets asked about her critical role in the Messenger case, Ms. Norris laughed lightly. "I certainly don't advertise it. Even if I did, I doubt anyone would care. This is Los Angeles. The paranormal is normal here..."*

We caught up to Dr. Jordan Geller, the man at the center of all these psychic connections, in his small office in Westwood. During a break between patients, he listened pensively as we told him of Corrine Rich-ards' revelation—Robin had visited Los Angeles as a child, heard about Beverly Casper from a man who had been directly affected by her disap-pearance, and had on at least one occasion, perhaps more, a nightmare about her death. A handsome thirty-year-old man with penetrating eyes that suit his profession, Dr. Geller pointedly refused to speculate on this new information. "God," he told us, quoting a Jewish source, "created doubt." When we asked if this meant that he now doubted the efficacy of reincarnation, he said that he had witnessed something "very compelling and powerful." Whether that meant that reincarnation was a probability or not, he wasn't prepared to say. "My parents told me that I was born asking questions. I'm still asking them. For instance, how did Robin Norris know about the man named 'John' and that the Messenger had two differently colored eyes? If Robin Norris' past-life regression was not genuine, how did she know these things?"

We contacted Lieutenant Ben Lemoski, the detective in charge of the case, and asked him the same questions. He had no answer.

*

"'God created doubt.' Wow, did He ever."

Jordan looked up from the magazine he'd been barely reading. What do you say to someone who you think you love, who you know you've loved, but haven't seen or talked to for two years? Two years!

Her rich red hair was shorter; he liked that. The eyes, those lucid green eyes, hinted at a bit more depth and maturity. The confident actress smile was still there. But underneath it, the nervousness. He could only imagine what his own smile now looked like.

They'd been through so much together, two of the most intense weeks any two people had ever lived through—and they'd just barely done that—and then it had to end. The great irony! They had to be apart if they were ever going to have a chance to be together. It wasn't a choice. It was the law, the reason why he'd twisted himself into a pretzel trying to avoid making her his patient when she first walked into his office and he agreed to hypnotize her. But, of course, he had botched that badly. He barely avoided a career-ending censure by the state Board of Medical Quality Assurance. After a rancorous meeting, the board took the unusual circumstances of his case into account. Elinor Fischer, unsolicited, wrote an impassioned letter in his defense. He had no doubt that her letter, written by a physician renowned for her propriety, had swayed the disciplinary panel. But they were emphatic in their ruling. No contact with Robin Norris for two years. No phone calls. No e-mails. A two-year sentence with no parole. One violation and he'd lose his license.

He stood up now. He wanted to embrace her, to kiss her—he

knew the warmth of her lips—but after two years apart, that seemed much too forward. "It's wonderful to see you," was all he said.

Robin put her purse down and took a seat. "You really mean that? I was afraid you'd be angry."

"Angry? About what?"

"That stuff that came out about how I'd heard about Beverly when I was five. I wanted to call you before the article was published. But," she lifted her palms, "I couldn't call. You know. Anyway, I loved your answer. The two-colored eyes."

"It's true."

She studied a pattern in the table. "I would have told you, Jordan. I just didn't remember."

"I know that. The irony is, if your mother had been in town, it might have come out." He knew he was sounding stiff, awkward.

"I don't think so. Even now she says that she only remembers it because Corrine—how did they even find her?—reminded her."

"You want some coffee?" They were back in the same West-wood Starbucks, the one where Jordan had first introduced her to Beverly.

"Give me a minute." She searched his face. "Has it been as long for you as it has been for me?"

Oh, he marveled, the directness, the honesty. The tension drained, just a little.

"I don't think there's been two minutes when I haven't thought about you."

She nodded. "Have we changed?"

"Me, totally. Stopped reading entirely. Watch Wrestlemania whenever I can. Go to bars every night. Drink. You know that sort of stuff." She looked at him askance, then laughed. "I like your new hairstyle," Jordan said.

She tipped her head back and took a deep breath. "It's like we have to start over. I hope we can, but I don't know if this can work. I can't make any promises."

Jordan smiled. "I can't either."

"I'll take that coffee now."

He stood up to get it.

About the Authors

Joseph Telushkin   *Allen Estrin*

JOSEPH TELUSHKIN, named by *Talk Magazine* as one of the fifty best speakers in the United States, is the author of the Rabbi Daniel Winter murder mystery series, including the volumes, *The Unorthodox Murder of Rabbi Wahl*, and *An Eye for An Eye*. He has also written *Jewish Literacy* and *The Book of Jewish Values*. He serves on the board of the Jewish Book Council, and lectures throughout the United States.

ALLEN ESTRIN has worked successfully in both television and film. His recent credits, with Joseph Telushkin, include multiple episodes of Emmy award-winning shows, *The Practice, Boston Public* and *Touched by an Angel*. He produces *The Dennis Prager Show*, a nationally syndicated radio talk show, and is a senior lecturer in screenwriting at the American Film Institute, Los Angeles.